# MAJOR TOM'S WAR

# MAJOR TOM'S WAR

## VEE WALKER

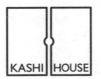

Almost all the people who appear in this novel are real.

Almost all the incidents described happened.

To find out more, explore the individual chapter notes at

www.majortomswar.com.

Published by KASHI HOUSE CIC 2018

© Vee Walker 2018

KASHI HOUSE CIC
27 Old Gloucester Street, London, WC1N 3AX
www.kashihouse.com

A CIP catalogue record for this book is available from the British Library
ISBN: 978 1 911271 14 7

Book design, layout and maps by Paul Smith (www.paulsmithdesign.com)
Cover artwork by Keerat Kaur (www.keerat-kaur.com)
Printed and bound by CPI Group (UK) Ltd, Croydon, CR0 4YY

*To my family past, present and future*

Then out spake brave Horatius,
The Captain of the Gate:
'To every man upon this earth
Death cometh soon or late.
And how can man die better
Than facing fearful odds,
For the ashes of his fathers,
And the temples of his Gods,'

...

'Hew down the bridge, Sir Consul,
With all the speed ye may;
I, with two more to help me,
Will hold the foe in play.
In yon strait path a thousand
May well be stopped by three.
Now who will stand on either hand,
And keep the bridge with me?'

Lord Thomas Babington McAulay, *Horatius*, 1842

# Contents

# Maps

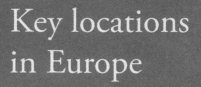

# Key locations
# in Europe

The Small Isles

Oban

Bewdley
Ribbesford

Fladbury

Burmington
Bridstow    Chastleton
Ross-on-Wye

Llanfairfechan

London

Berlin

Lawford

Amsterdam

Holzminden

Brussels
Waterloo
Cologne

Herbesthal

Thérouanne
Neuve-Chapelle

Amettes
Valenciennes
Vermelles

Saint-Waast-la-Vallée
Bavay

Frévent
Cambrai

Paris

Authuile

Hargicourt

Saint-Quentin

---- Western Front in June 1916

# Key locations
in India

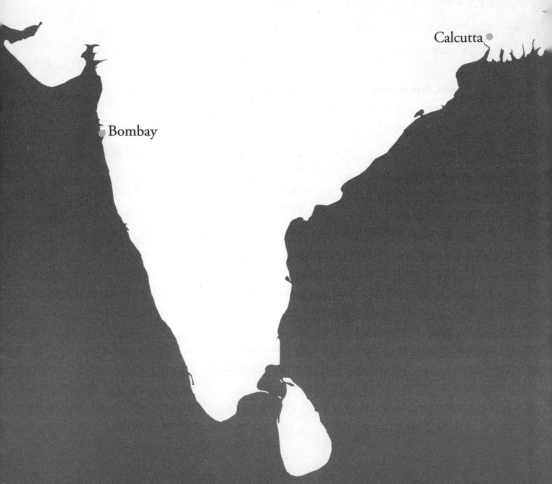

Amritsar

Simla

Delhi

Purnea

Calcutta

Bombay

# Dramatis Personae

## FROM INDIA

| | |
|---|---|
| AMAR SINGH, RISALDAR MAJOR | the leader and *granthi* to the cavalry Sikhs on the Western Front |
| ARCHIE PUGH, LIEUTENANT COLONEL | Tom's partner in the Calcutta legal firm Puanco |
| ARJAN SINGH, DAFADAR | Tom's young Sikh groom mid-war |
| HARNAM SINGH, RISALDAR | Tom's self-appointed protector, a Sikh cavalry officer in the Indian Army |
| HUTCHINSON, CAPTAIN | 'Hutch', another captain in Tom's regiment |
| THOMAS HORATIO WESTMACOTT, MAJOR | Tom, the author's grandfather, an Indian Army cavalry officer |
| YADRAM SINGH, SOWAR | a Hindu murderer whom Tom executes by firing-squad |

## FROM FRANCE

| | |
|---|---|
| ALPHONSE DEROME | Gaston's elder son |
| BOURGEAT, PÈRE | interpreter with Tom's Division and friend of Tom |
| FRANÇOIS DURIEZ, PÈRE | local priest, principal of the local school in Bavay |
| GASTON DEROME | mayor of Bavay throughout the First World War |
| JULES LEBRUN, ABBÉ | 'Maitre Corbeau', Gaston's second teacher, an enemy who becomes his friend |
| LÉON DEROME | Gaston's younger son |
| LÉONIE DEROME | Gaston's sister who helps him bring up his children |
| LUNEAU, PÈRE | interpreter with Tom's Division, friend of Tom |
| MARGUERITE BRASSEUR | 'la Doyenne', who is taken as a hostage to Holzminden |
| MARGUERITE DE MONTFORT | a nurse in charge of the hospital in Bavay |
| MARIE-FÉLICIE DEROME | Gaston's younger daughter and youngest child |
| THÉRÈSE DEROME | Gaston's elder daughter and oldest child |

## FROM GERMANY

| | |
|---|---|
| BARELMANN | a doctor who treats the first Allied casualties alongside his own |
| LARS HORSTBERG, KOMMANDANT | an officer in control of Bavay and the surrounding area, enemy of Gaston |
| KRAFT | an interpreter from Alsace |
| SCHLAGHECKE, KOMMANDANT | a commandant at the interrogation base at the château at St-Quentin |

## FROM SCOTLAND

| | |
|---|---|
| JAMES MACBANE OF LOCHDUBH, MAJOR | a Highland laird, enemy of Tom |
| MACKEDDIE, CORPORAL | Tom's groom at the end of the war, a Black Isler |
| MATHESON THE TRAP | Lochdubh's lifelong valet and groom |

## THE HORSES

| | |
|---|---|
| DAISY | Tom's second charger, a mare he purchases for his wife Mary |
| GOLDEN ROD | Tom's first charger, like Daisy, brought from India to France |
| PHOENIX | Reggie Durand's mare |
| SATAN | Lochdubh's big brute of a stallion |

# 1

# The Puanco Lift

The great grey-green trunk reached out gently to stroke his face. Then the stately elephant wound it around the waist of the small boy, raised him gently past it's gold-tipped tusks and broad shoulders and delicately placed him on its back. Parvati his *ayah* smiled at the curly-haired boy she loved as if he were her own, then glanced back at the house. No, all was quiet. The clouds massing above the roof threatened thunder, the air dry and oppressive on her lips.

'*Phir! Phir!*' the boy shouted, and again she smiled up at him, in her glittering pink sari that he so loved. She sparkled in the sun. For Tomulloo, Parvati was the sun.

The *mahout*, a young lad himself, threw his head back and laughed and patted his elephant on its brow. Then he tossed it a banana from a paper roll, which the beast caught with the very tip of its trunk, looping it neatly inwards, before popping it into its eager mouth. The little boy astride the warm, hard back clapped his hands and whooped with delight.

A rusty hinge creaked and his mother loomed through the doorway, her anger plain for all to see. Gripping the veranda rail to keep herself upright, she hauled herself towards them, one arm outstretched. Parvati shrank back towards the elephant.

He knew his mother, whom he too thought of as the *memsahib*, had been drinking again. Whenever she drank, she could not stand up very well. The stale stench lingered on her hands and clothes. When she kissed him good morning, the boy would break away as soon as he could.

Parvati on the other hand was soft and kind and smelled wonderful, of ginger and lilies and emerald moss.

Tomulloo had already devoured a thick slice of the sponge cake with five candles on it that morning, an exceptional treat. The timing was a little odd as the memsahib kept irregular mealtimes when she remembered to eat at all. This, meeting though, this was his secret, special present. The excitement was almost too much for him to bear alone. Parvati had whispered in his ear as she bathed him, *next week, Tomulloo, I will bring my brother and his elephant to meet you!*

The gentle Hindi nickname she had given him meant 'Tom the owl'. It was Parvati who had identified his poor vision, and Parvati who arranged with the memsahib to take him for his precious first pair of spectacles.

Tomulloo had been bursting with the sheer fabulous impossibility of an elephant in his very own garden for days; and now here it was. And it was so huge. Its great head was on a level with the awning over the veranda. It had peered at him with its tiny, wise eyes and flapped its square ears, then lifted its trunk to sniff his face politely. Tom sniffed it back, and both his ayah and the mahout had laughed again. Then it had touched his cheek.

Now the memsahib had spoiled it all.

They had thought his mother would remain asleep as usual. She invariably passed out in the afternoons, the half-empty bottle of gin beside her on the bed. And his father was not there, of course. Papa was almost never there.

The mahout, afraid, reached up for Tomulloo's skinny little leg and pulled him hurriedly from the elephant's back. The rough skin scratched his knee and the boy yelped and half-jumped, half-fell into his ayah's arms. The elephant, alarmed too, stamped its feet and put its ears forward uncertainly. Tomulloo shouted at his mother *Nahin maa, aap haathee ko dara rahe hain! Nahin!* Her contemptuous response: 'Speak English, Thomas Horatio! You are an English *sahib*, not some Indian savage!' Savage, thought the little boy in bewilderment, looking up into the dark, anxious eyes of his ayah. The elephant and mahout were already hurrying away, the mahout glancing back over his shoulder anxiously.

Tomulloo put his hand up to his cheek to try to hold the caress of the kindly elephant there. Parvati took his small hand in her own and led him back towards the bungalow. He fell upon his bed and cried himself hoarse, but it did no good. He knew what would happen. His dear ayah would be sent away without a reference for having somehow endangered him.

Perhaps he did look rather like an owl, he thought, as he washed his face as the memsahib had instructed. Owl eyes in round spectacles stared back from the cracked bathroom mirror. Lonely eyes, in a thin face so toasted by the sun that he could half-imagine he was a Hindu street urchin, like most of his friends.

Parvati had been his ayah for almost a year. They seldom stayed more than a few months. The pretty ones usually disappeared with Papa. And Mamma soon got rid of the kind ones.

When Thomas Horatio Westmacott, junior legal partner and dogsbody, stepped into the lift, the darkness of the shaft reached out to embrace him instead. There was no sense of falling. Only of crashing into the pile of dust and filthy debris accumulated over the years.

Neeraj Ram the Dalit always swept the contents of all the office floors into the lift shaft. Tom had seen him do it; remonstrated with him, told him it was a fire risk and a bad habit which simply would not do. Neeraj Ram had smiled and waggled his head in agreement and completely ignored him. Now Tom owed him his life.

His spectacles, where were they? Tom groped around, recoiling as he felt a sluggish city rat shift under his hand. He could not find their reassuring wire frames anywhere. Then he remembered. They were still safe on his desk, placed carefully across the striped back of the papier-maché tiger: a stiff-legged, pop-eyed beast, which reminded him of Archie Pugh. Pugh was not only his senior partner, but also the colonel of the reserve cavalry regiment of which Tom was now a major. The regiment often hunted tigers which had grown to fond of man-flesh. After all that had passed, Tom now saw himself as the unresisting gazelle in the tiger's maw.

There was an elephant too, which he liked much better. Mary had given them to him, the first two things she had braved the humidity, the flies and the din of the street-market to buy alone. He had not liked to tell her of his irrational dislike of the tiger when she had been so very proud of herself that day. Now they were the twin guardians of her memory.

He felt absurdly foolish. He so seldom took off his spectacles! A piece of grit had caught in his eye and he had removed them to try to wipe it out with his pocket handkerchief. One of Mary's, which he carried always. It still held the faintest trace of her lily-of-the-valley scent.

He had been dabbing at his eye when Pugh had barged into his office. He was in a filthy temper as always, demanding some obscure file from years ago on the Jabbar Lal case. He needed a deposition stored in the clerks' office on the ground floor (where the Jabbar Lal case now had a whole shelf all to itself, the earliest files covered in a fine layer of golden Calcutta dust). His own clerk was already out on an errand, so Tom would have to do.

Tom rose from his desk, knowing that nothing about the Jabbar Lal case could possibly be this urgent. It had already rumbled on for seven years or more, while the toad-like estate manager, Jabbar Lal, continued to profit from the inexperience and innate foolishness of the young Maharaja of Darmanga. Eton was no place to learn thrift and the young ruler had fallen into bad company. It also seemed to be in the young man's nature to absorb disreputable habits rather than good instruction. As a result, his kingdom was allegedly in decline, while Jabbar Lal distributed largesse to his numerous cronies, all the while living rent-free in the maharaja's palace.

Once the intricacies of petty feuds and double-dealing at the heart of the Calcutta *noblesse* had fascinated Tom. Now he navigated the twists and turns of Jabbar Lal's pervasive corruption and the maharaja's bafflingly bad choices with a hollow heart.

Tom had not thought his spectacles necessary for the simple trip down two flights. He usually walked, but these documents ran into many thousands of dull words and could be heavy. Another restless night had left him exhausted; weariness seldom seemed to leave him these days. For once, he had thought, why not take the lift both ways?

Now, never mind a speck of grit: his eyes, nose and throat were entirely choked with thick Calcutta dust. He struggled to catch his breath and started to move his limbs to see what, if anything, he had broken.

Then he heard the unmistakable rattle of the outer lattice doors closing above, the internal lattice shortly afterwards. The soft murmur of voices, as the small lift-boy Indroneel Bosu, whom he had appointed only the previous week, asked the passenger which floor. Perhaps it was Indroneel who had left the external lattice open on to the void; if so, Tom would not blame him, for he was very young.

The ancient lift shuddered and groaned and the cables and ropes underneath, barely visible in the blurred gloom, started to loop and shiver before they began to plunge.

Lying on his thick bier of Untouchable sweepings, he opened his dust-clogged mouth but no sound came out. Groping, he felt the remains of a flattened wooden crate on the shaft floor. A sharp edge pierced his thumb.

He watched the underside of the lift descend. Its uneasy grey coils transported him back to his fifth birthday in Purnea and a happy moment crushed. Parvati's face came to him through the decades, his nostrils filled with the scent of her, but her voice was that of Mary. *I am here, do not be afraid, Tomulloo. I have your hand in mine. Come with me. Come now.*

They told him later that he did make a sound then, that Indroneel Bosu's sharp little ears heard it, recognising the voice of the kind sahib who spoke to him every day in Hindi – the sahib who recalled the name of his mother and his little sister with the withered arm. And the boy stopped the lift just as the lowest coil grazed Tom's cheek, just before it put an end to him.

After that came the humiliating saga of getting him out. Voices argued somewhere overhead before wooden steps were finally set into the side of the lift shaft. Tom struggled to his feet and tried the bottom rung, but it crumbled away to dust. The anxious faces above disappeared. He heard a lengthy dispute, then footsteps. Eventually, a long metal ladder was found. Tom was hauled up on to the landing, filthy and bloodied. Devesh Bosu, the uncle of Indroneel, insisted on sponging Tom's grimy face and hands as his major-sahib lay gasping on the cool tiles like a landed carp.

Someone had fetched his senior partner, the belligerent Pugh who appeared, chalk-faced, and helped Tom back to his desk. Pugh, of course, called Tom a bally fool and muttered about lift maintenance and safety not being his responsibility. So whose would it be, Tom wondered, but did not say. Once he had ascertained that Tom was unscathed, besides the cut in his thumb, Pugh returned to his own office.

Old Devesh Bosu poured Tom cup after cup of hot sweet tea with shaking hands. As he gulped them down to try to clear the dust, Tom stared at the papier-maché tiger, which returned the look dispassionately.

Not yet, he thought. It would be soon, but not like this.

He took back his spectacles from the tiger and pushed them on to his nose.

An hour or so later, Devesh Bosu returned. It was clear that the old clerk was still badly rattled by the incident. How had Major Westmacott Sahib come to fall headlong into the lift shaft? Had his nephew failed in his duty? If so, he would be beaten and dismissed. Tom shook his head, wearily, and told Devesh Bosu a half-truth to keep the boy safe from the old man's wrath. Told him he had forgotten his spectacles and that he had opened the lattice himself, believing the lift to be present.

Devesh Bosu still stood at Tom's desk, trembling.

'What is it, Devesh Bosu? You have also had a nasty shock. Please sit.'

The old man refused, of course, but came closer still and spoke.

'You think of her, Tomulloo Sahib. You think of her all the time and it is too much.'

Devesh Bosu had not addressed him so personally since Tom's childhood, but it was already a day for extraordinary departures from normality. The old man continued: 'It was not your fault, Sahib. None of it. But to yearn for your lady so, when she is gone, it is unseemly.'

This really was beyond the pale, thought Tom, but he held his tongue. Devesh Bosu leaned forward to tap the *Calcutta Times* lying open on the desk. Tom could see the old man's teeth were stained yellow with betel.

'Read, Sahib. It is 1914. There is a war coming. Purify your soul as a great warrior would. Read!'

After the old man had left, Tom pulled the newspaper towards him and read the article. Things did sound bad in Europe. And he could not stay here much longer – it was clear enough that Pugh would not tolerate his inertia for ever. Tom took a blank sheet of paper from his desk, dipped his pen in his ink-well, and started to draft a telegram to his old father-in-law in England.

As he did so, he heard her sweet laugh peal from the void behind him, caught a glimpse of her glossy dark hair. He was used to such delusions now and continued to write. It was almost two years now since Mary's death and yet there she was, ever-present, beckoning to him from the corner of his eye.

He recalled their meeting in England as if it were yesterday. His Chastleton grandfather had known her old dry stick of a father, Fred Lawson; both were priests. The only thing for which Tom was at all grateful to his own father, Vesey, was the imaginative choice of the Indian Civil Service over a dull English parish.

Mary was a distant cousin, without a penny to her name, and with the same dark cloud of hair as the favourite ayah he had lost so many years before. Mary's smile made the corners of her eyes curve upwards. She did not seem to mind that he was a stuffy Calcutta lawyer who had never previously dreamt of marriage. He felt himself unfurl in the warmth of her unaccountable interest. It had been many years since any woman had been kind to him.

Tom had fallen in love instantly. She was the most beautiful living thing he had ever laid eyes on.

And then he had killed her.

# 2

# Losing Bessie

The rambling vicarage at Bewdley, never usually light or bright or cheerful, seemed especially dark that bitter winter day. The miasma of boiled cabbage roiled from the margins of the green baize door. Beyond this lay the kitchen and servants' quarters, or the 'Cook's Empire' as Mother liked to call it. Maudie had commented that the ground-floor rooms seemed to have smelled leguminous for days. *Leg-you-mean-us*. Evie had rolled the syllables around her mouth to fix them in her mind.

Evie disliked cabbage intensely, but dutifully soaked it in gravy and swallowed it because Mother said it was good for her. Teddy could eat any amount of the horrid stuff and she could not understand how.

The three of them were perched on the top step of the first flight of stairs. Mirrors were not encouraged in the Winnington-Ingram household to avoid falling prey to vanity. Evie had brushed her own mousy hair, which would keep tangling at the back, then Teddy's golden locks and Arthur's darker head.

None of the children appeared to look much like any of the others, and yet to anyone seeing all of them together, it was clear, in some mysterious way, that they were siblings. Evie considered herself plain in appearance compared with the others.

Sitting between her two brothers, she could see the wooden front door, studded with rivets and bolts; a relic of more volatile times long ago. When the family had lived at Ribbesford House a mile or two away, there would once have been a footman to open the door, but no longer. Something had happened to the family's fortunes. Although

Father never talked about it, Maudie had told them it was down to paying expensive school fees for the sons of previous generations. She showed Evie the old family recipe book dated 1810, created by their great-grandmother Jane Onslow when she became engaged into the Winnington-Ingram dynasty. This contained exquisitely handwritten recipes, all in different hands, for a selection of dishes both exotic and lavish. For the young children, it appeared that their portly forebear – her portrait hung on the dining-room wall – had squandered much of the family's wealth in paying for the sin of gluttony.

All of this meant that the vast family seat at Ribbesford had become too expensive to staff and run. Now it was let. Cold houses seemed to be their fate; the vicarage was especially cold this year and the water had already frozen twice in the bedroom ewers. Evie had made the boys put on their coats before sitting on the draughty stairs to wait. Quite what they were waiting for was unclear.

The three younger Winnington-Ingram siblings were playing that interminable family alphabet game, useful for occupying duller moments, called 'I Love My Love'. The mahogany grandfather clock outside Father's office, a reminder of more opulent times, ticked and tocked, but its chimes had been muffled with an old woollen stocking of Maudie's during the night. There was just the faintest murmur of female voices from the room upstairs. Father, thank goodness, had left the house on parish business.

Father never spoke, he pronounced. When he shouted, it was in capital letters, his words ringing decisively in their ears. Days when he was at home were punctuated by alarming bellows from his study about Noise and Disturbance! Evie had been very frightened of Father when she was as little as Arthur, who would soon be four. Now, at seven, she could see (through close observation of her two elder sisters) that Father was child-like in some ways and needed to be managed. Still, she did prefer it when he was out. They all did, except perhaps dear Maudie, who at twelve was the eldest of all five of them.

Father had been to see Mother in her room after breakfast. As the door to the room opened and closed, Evie had heard Mother wheezing and spluttering; her dry cough sounded so painful. She knew that there were special hospitals you could get sent to if you had a bad chest. One of the choirboys from Ribbesford Church had gone. Surely Mother should go there too?

When he had emerged from the bedroom, Father had paused, fumbling in his pocket. Evie wondered whether to ask him about the special hospital where Mother might get better. Then she had looked more closely at him and seen his reddened eyes, watched him blow his nose noisily on his pocket-handkerchief. She had thought it best to say nothing.

A pall of silence hung over the house, pierced only by the tick and tock of the great clock as it counted down the hours. Like Christmas Eve, she thought. She remembered the anticipation of the treasures in her stocking: an orange and a new handkerchief Mother had embroidered with the letter E, a little black jointed doll and a sugar mouse in the darned toe. They had excitedly opened them together in Mother's room. But this was a different waiting. This was unimaginable.

Evie had just reached the part of the game where she had to decide where she would take her love, whom Arthur had decided at length would be called Terence, to dine. 'I took him to the sign of the…to the sign of the…' she said, only half attending to the game.

'Um… the Tottering Towers?' asked Arthur, picking at a loose thread on the stair carpet.

'Tottering Towers sounds like poor old Ribbesford. Lucky Terence. Curlicues falling off the outside all the time, with buckets and drip-drip-dripping in every room,' said Teddy. 'Evie, I am rather bored with 'I Love My Love' now,' he added. 'Shall we have 'Happy Families' instead?'

Evie provided the automatic response, 'You can't be *bored*, Teddy, unless you live in a box with no windows,' before she pulled the dog-eared packet of paste cards out of her pinafore pocket. She started to deal them into three slow piles. Little Arthur, engrossed in the next move of the other game, ignored the cards. 'Terence could come from Town?' he suggested, 'Father goes to Town sometimes.' Teddy then began a long and dreary explanation about how 'town' could sometimes mean Hereford or Worcester, but also always meant London.

'And London is a city,' Teddy insisted, sounding just like Father, 'but you always call it Town and go up to it, not down.'

As she dealt the cards, Evie's mind wandered. She found herself looking down at the Happy Family cards, piled on the top step. She flipped over her hand, first one card, then another. Evie and Maudie had enjoyed a quiet rainy afternoon painting each one carefully with

Etty's best set of water-colours. Etty had been very cross when she found out and had protested to Mother. Mother as usual had been the peacemaker and told Evie and Maud to apologise for taking Etty's paints without asking her, but also told Etty to apologise to her sisters for being such a fuss-pot. They had all spent a joyful afternoon playing Happy Families with Mother, who had invented a different funny voice for each character in the pack.

Now Mrs Dip the Dyer's Wife glared at her, face like a skull, glowering at her red-stained hands. Something was very wrong today. Evie could no longer remember Mother's laughter as she played. The familiar cartoons' over-sized heads had become unsmiling, sharp-featured, malevolent. Evie swiftly gathered them up and put them away in the box, ignoring Teddy's protests.

What was happening up in Mother's room? Why had Maudie told her to stay with Teddy and Arthur? At seven, Evie was a little younger than Teddy but still felt as though she were looking after both her brothers. She longed to go and lose herself in some scales on the piano but to do so would disturb the heavy cloud of silence penetrating throughout the house.

There were no sounds from the estate carts or passers-by outside, which was unusual. Even little Kate, the runny-nosed scullery-maid, whose task it was to keep the fire in Father's study burning, seemed to do so almost silently today. Mother would surely say this was something of a miracle when Evie told her later.

There was a sound from the doorstep. Evie needed fresh air, even if only a gasp of it. She stood up, stretched her long back, walked to the front door and opened it, just a crack. The day was unexpectedly bright and she found the chilled sunlight a dazzling contrast to the murk of the house.

The road outside was covered with a thick blanket of straw, which was deadening the sounds from the wheels of the carts. They only did this if someone was very ill. Mother, she thought, uncertainly. The delivery boy hurrying away on his bicycle went to raise his cap but skidded on a patch of ice and almost collided with a tree. Evie lifted a hand, but he was already teetering off through the straw-matted snow into the distance, his basket laden with goods for others.

Looking down, she saw a tin on the doorstep. She lifted it – it was quite heavy – a fruit-cake perhaps, she wondered, her tummy gurgling with hunger. Father was naturally tall and lean and often forgot to eat. The children were frequently hungry but had learned not to complain. If they did, Father would sternly inform them that hunger was an appropriate Mortification of the Flesh.

There had been bacon at breakfast-time that day – Evie's mouth watered at the memory – and the breakfast-room would still be filled with its savoury aroma. Teddy sometimes said he could smell bacon a mile away. The crisp rashers were usually for Father alone, unless he were in a very decent mood and shared a little with them. If he appeared to be in good humour, one of them might ask, 'Shall there be any bacon for breakfast today, Father?' And Father would lift the silver dome over the chafing-dish and reply, 'None today.' That morning he had eaten rapidly in grim silence and gone straight back upstairs to see Mother. The children had not dared touch the bacon in its salver, only having one slice of cold toast and marmalade in silence: Arthur ate his usual little bowl of porridge and brown sugar too, which Mother said was to build up his legs.

Evie returned to the step between her brothers, carrying the heavy tin.

'Oh Evie, is it cake?' asked Teddy, eyeing it hungrily.

'I think so. It feels quite full.' Evie let Teddy hold it for a moment, Arthur next, then took it back on her lap. It was a pretty tin with a pale yellow background and decorated with embossed springtime flowers, primroses and daffodils and snowdrops.

'Could we just have one peep inside?' asked Teddy, one hand on the lid in anticipation.

'Oh Teddy, we can't. Gifts from the parish are for Father. You know that.'

'I know, Evie dear, but we would only be looking.'

'Please?' begged Arthur, although it came out as 'Pleeg?' Smiling with all his little pearly teeth, Evie could not resist him.

She sighed, and eased off the lid. A tiny card, addressed to Father, lay on top of the cake. The exotic aroma of currants and molasses, cinnamon and nutmeg, ginger and cardamom, perhaps even brandy, spiralled towards their nostrils. All three sniffed the greaseproof-paper-wrapped delight within.

'I think that's one of Lady de Vere's,' stated Teddy, who had an encyclopaedic memory for these parish food gifts. 'And it's not even

Christmas! Do you think we will be allowed a slice?'

'Who knows?' replied Evie as she reluctantly replaced the lid, feeling a final little puff of sweetness against her hand. She very much doubted it.

The Winnington-Ingram family often found small gifts of food from the parish on the doorstep – a jar of jam, or a gift of vegetables. Any glut among their neighbours encouraged a predictable excess of generosity, for which they always had to appear grateful. Cook, for instance, would make conserves and pies out of the basket-loads of apples or plums left at the entrance until even Father confessed he had eaten rather too many of them for one season. At present, the parish seemed to be dumping winter cabbage after unwanted winter cabbage at their door. The five children vastly preferred cake of course, but such delights were rare, unless it were Christmas or Easter.

Like Father's tirades, the parish always held a prominent place in the thoughts of the children. Evie saw it as a voracious, many-headed monster, constantly needing to be both caged and sustained by Father through his complex and little-understood ministrations. At the same time, the parish might leave them gifts, like pagans leaving votive offerings at a shrine, as Etty had said once to Father. That utterance had not gone down at all well – but in Evie's mind, the parish took far more than it gave.

The parish was entitled to knock on the door of the house at any hour of the day or night if some troubled soul needed succour. If Father were not present, then Mother would have to do. Maudie and Etty already went on parish rounds with Mother; Evie knew she would soon begin too. She dreaded this, the endless hours of sitting patiently at bedsides and at tea-tables, listening to the wheezing parishioners drone on about their ailments or the petty doings of the village. It would give her less time to practise.

Mother's sister Aunt Laura lived at Fladbury near Pershore with her husband Uncle Fred, who was a priest like Father. Laura, like her sister Bessie, was an accomplished pianist. She would often bring her daughters Mary, Grace and Ruth to stay, and Cousin Mary was Evie's best friend. Aunt Laura had recognised Evie's musical talent, for to Evie, music was not something she did, it was who and what she was. When Aunt Laura had inherited a better instrument from another member of the family, she had passed on to Evie her own good upright pianoforte, decorated with battered cherubs and two little candlesticks. Mother was very clear with Father that it was Evie's piano, so that it did not risk getting sold. She pointed out that it meant Evie would soon be able to accompany hymns on the organ in church. Evie knew it had taken Mother some time and effort to win Father over and loved her all the more for it.

The piano was placed in the library and all three girls played it, but Evie more than the others. Mother had taught her at first, but Evie quickly learned to read music and then practiced contentedly without supervision. The piano was kept in good order by a strange old man who could tune the piano without even using a tuning-fork. Evie did not see why this was such a feat. One day when he came to the house he had played a note or two and asked Evie what each was, and she guessed correctly, or rather simply knew. He later told Mother that Evie had perfect pitch, which had pleased both of them greatly. Evie did not consider herself to be talented in any other way.

She knew what the piano-tuner had said was true: when the instrument was in need of tuning, it set her teeth on edge and she could not practise until he had attended to it. Then she would sit and play her favourite tunes and scales over and over again, until Father shouted that he could Bear It No Longer!

Evie did not aspire to play the organ in church, with its musty atmosphere and familiar audience. She dreamed instead of glittering London concert halls and the applause of hundreds, but she had not yet mentioned these yearnings to anyone, even Mother.

Evie was the second youngest child of the five Winnington-Ingram children born to Bessie in quick succession between 1880 and 1888. She often felt a little like the central point of a pair of scales, keeping the balance between the boys and the girls. The first-born was Constance, known to all by her second name, Maud and by her youngest siblings as Maudie. Maudie was both strong of will and fair – not in the sense of beauty, which none of them had in abundance, but in justice. She most resembled Mother both in appearance and in behaviour, but she had Father's tenacity and resilience as well. As Mother became more and more poorly, Maudie protected them all from the worst of Father's temper and was increasingly helping him with his parish work. She appeared to enjoy this, which Evie could not understand at all.

Then there was Etty – Maudie had not been able to say Ethel early on and the childish nickname stuck – who had inherited Father's prodigious intellect but also his temper and moods, so naturally, at times, they clashed. Etty and Laura Evelyn – Evie – shared a bedroom, where Etty would pour out the daily injustices inflicted on her.

Then there were their two brothers. Even as a child, Evie knew that Father would perceive daughters as unfavourable, so his first two girls must have been a bit of a disappointment, if useful around the parish. Teddy (another Edward like Father) was the middle child, the charmer, with his fair hair, blue eyes and sense of humour. And little Arthur, not much more than a baby, who had bad legs but an always cheerful temperament. Father always referred to the 'Anstice ankles' as though it were Mother's fault in some way, and Evie knew that Bessie's own mother and now Aunt Laura both used a chair with wheels on it that had to be pushed about. Evie had once called him 'poor little Arthur'. Mother had gently rebuked her and said, 'Never let me hear you call your brother 'poor' again, as he is hardly impoverished in those who love him.' So Evie never did. Arthur went everywhere with his brother and sisters. His legs often pained him but he learned never to complain. When he could not walk, they carried him instead, even right up Snowdon, on their backs.

A doctor from London had come soon after Arthur was born and said that he might never be able to walk properly because his ankles were so badly malformed. Mother had said nonsense to that (but only once the doctor had left – Mother was never rude to anyone). She had helped Arthur learn to walk across the kitchen floor by pushing a little upturned stool in front of him on a soft cloth while she knelt behind him on the cold tiles, lest he should tumble backwards and injure himself.

When Arthur was about two, Mother had started to cough. She tried hard to continue with her parish work, but her condition had become gradually worse, and she had taken to her bed. Bronchial troubles brought on by an influenza, they had said at first. Pneumonia, they said now.

Sitting between her brothers, Evie heard a sound on the landing. She turned to look across at Maudie, who was coming quietly towards them. She seemed to have aged somehow, and held herself taller. Evie was conscious of her own back straightening. The sisters caught and held each other's eyes. Maud's were dry but full of grief. Evie could feel her own welling up, but she said not a word as her childhood fell away like a veil torn.

Maud bent down and gently lifted Arthur, popping him on to her hip. 'Evie, I think you and Teddy should go into Mother and Etty,' she said, her voice determinedly level. 'Come with me, now, Arthur; let's see if Cook has something good for lunch. There should be some cold beef for sandwiches. Oh, is that a cake in the pretty tin? We shall all have a nice big slice. Would you like that?' With that Maud pushed through the baize door with her little brother, who was thrilled with the promise of beef and cake.

Alone on the hall stairs, Evie gripped Teddy's now-clammy hand in hers. There could be only one possible reason why Maud would offer them cake intended for Father. They stood still for some minutes, not saying anything, trying to slow their breathing to match the muffled clock below. They heard it attempt to strike the hour and with its dulled sound Evie felt her entire world shift beneath her feet. She took a deep breath, squeezed Teddy's hand and then led him across the landing, softly opening the door of Mother's room.

There was a sickly sweetness in the air. It was not emanating from the vase of garden flowers on Mother's dressing table that Evie had picked for her after tea the previous day. Mother had been too exhausted to thank her, but she had smiled with her eyes and held her gaze for a moment.

Etty was sitting on one side of the bed with the nurse on the other. Mother was lying there. Although when Evie looked more closely she could see that she was not. There was a slight, grey husk of a person wrapped within the soft, white sheets. It had once contained Mother but no longer did. A linen cloth was tied around her head that made her dear round face look very small and distant. Her eyes, mercifully, were shut.

Etty's head was bowed but Evie did not think she could be praying.

'Etty, dear, it's me. And Teddy. Maud has taken Arthur down to Cook. I'm so sorry, Etty. Father should be here.' Evie's soft voice trembled.

Her sister looked up, eyes blazing in her blotched face. 'But Father's *not* here, is he? And where is he? Out on parish business. Always the parish first! Poor, poor Mummy!'

'Be quiet, Etty. Arthur might hear!' exclaimed Teddy, knowing he could not. The young nurse tactfully left the room, closing the door behind her.

'There, there, Etty. Hush now.' Evie stood behind her elder sister and started to stroke her hair. Etty gave a great sob. 'I shan't ever, *ever* marry,' she declared. Her voice crackled with emotion. '*None* of us should. Just look! Look at what happens! Five babies one after the other, not forgetting the two that didn't *live* to be babies. It's disgusting! And then a lifetime of *Father*!'

Teddy turned on his heel at that with a choking sound, and ran from the room.

Evie too was shocked by Etty's vehemence, but continued to stroke her sister's hair until her rage and grief subsided a little, both looking all the while at the little still form in the bed. Soon, they knew the old joiner from the village would come with a coffin on his cart and take her from them forever.

'Do you know what Mummy said as she died?' asked Etty. Evie could only shake her head, fearful. 'She kept repeating, "I'm so sorry, Edward." Over and over and over again, and he wasn't even here to hear it.'

They sat in silence for a long time after that.

Evie gradually realised something curious. She had always thought that a dead body would be a very frightening thing. This was the first she had seen; but she found she was wrong. Mother's body was an empty vessel, the life and love and warmth all gone.

'Oh Evie!' whispered Etty eventually. 'What *are* we going to do?' Her sister found her hand, and held it tightly, and put the other around her and squeezed her hard.

'We will be all right,' Evie assured her, willing herself to believe it. 'We will just have to carry on.'

# 3

# Maître Corbeau

The children of the senior class of the Notre-Dame-de-l'Assomption school in Bavay eyed their new *maître* with trepidation. As they watched, the Abbé Lebrun swept off his jet-black woollen cloak to hang it, precisely, on the single brass hook beside the classroom door.

Old *Père* Duriez had been a kind and gentle maître for so many years but now they were told by this stranger that he had gone away to live with his sister in Valenciennes. And although they did not yet know it, none of the boys would ever see Père Duriez again.

There was talk of little else in the playground. Some said the old priest had been taken ill, very ill, over the weekend. Others that parents had complained about his lack of discipline and unorthodox teaching methods.

At that moment, as the new, unsmiling maître came to stand behind Père Duriez's battered old desk, every boy in the class was sorry the old man was gone.

The small, slight, dark-haired boy in the back row nervously polished his round spectacles. Some of the older boys had mocked Père Duriez behind his back and called him nasty names but Gaston knew that they would have done that whether their teacher had been a martinet or a gentle soul. He thought Père Duriez had done well to have taught them as much as he did, considering some of the unruly boys he had had to contend with.

Many of the activities Père Duriez believed essential to learning were indeed unusual for the times. On a fine day, he liked to take them out of the classroom and into the countryside around the little town. He would wear his old *soutâne*, so faded it had become dove-grey and its hem darkened with Bavay dust. It was not uncommon for his pupils, ordered by height and age, to be seen skipping or strolling in pairs along the straight Roman streets that led out of the *cour* of the redbrick school at the heart of Bavay and into the lush, green fields and rolling hills. They often sang as they walked.

He had taken his pupils deep into the beechwoods of the ancient *Forêt de Mormal*, where he told them King Louis XIV himself had once hunted the teeming deer and wild boar. They had played long and elaborate games of hide and seek, the old man always starting the game with: 'Now, boys, hide! Hide as though your life depends upon it!' They clambered up trees, hid themselves behind fallen stumps on the ground and covered themselves in piles of dry leaves. From their places of concealment they loved to shoot out ecstatically, to alarm their teacher and friends.

Once they had let off steam, Père Duriez would teach them the names of wild plants and their properties; some were edible, others you could use for all kinds of medicine. He showed them which of the *champignons des bois* were good to eat. 'You never know when you might be hungry, and all this food costs nothing – nothing at all. It is the gift of *le bon Dieu*,' he would say to them as they filled their pockets.

Once, memorably, they had savoured a mountain of *girolles* cooked in butter flavoured with *marjolaine* and other foraged herbs. Each with his own spoon, they ladled them on to crisp *baguette* out of a battered copper pan that sat over the open fire Père Duriez had made. 'Look, *mes petits*,' he had said, pointing at the thin wisp of smoke drifting upwards through the trees. 'Dry wood gives off white smoke, less easy to see. Wet wood, grey or black. But if you wish to remain hidden from all, what kind of fire should you set?'

The other boys had leapt in with more and more outrageous suggestions of complex fire construction and different kinds of log, when thoughtful Gaston Derome had silenced them all by replying, 'You should light your fire only at night, *mon Père*.'

Gaston's favourite memory was of the day Père Duriez had led them down a narrow, winding track on the woodland edge where they made little baskets from the leaves of a sweet chestnut. These they filled with the tiny, fragrant *fraises des bois* which were growing in abundance along the sunny bank. Gaston had spent a long time looking at these before he picked any, stooping and scooping up a little soil between his fingers. Why did this kind of strawberry grow here and not elsewhere in the forest? Sunlight was a factor, certainly, but what about the soil? He sniffed at its earthy dryness and let it trickle through his fingers. It seemed to be very poor, sandy stuff to produce such a heavenly fruit. Not thick rich dark soil as in the *potager* at home. Curious. He must ask *Papa*.

Most of the boys had eaten their lush hoards of berries on the return walk, faces and lips sticky with the sweet juice. Gaston could always remember his mother's cry of pleasure when he had presented her with his proud little basket, still piled high.

But the most frequent destination of Père Duriez was a surprising one: Ancient Rome. Rome was hard to avoid in Bavay; it sat on the border between France and Belgium, at an intersection of six major roads, which led towards Maubeuge, Valenciennes, Houdain, Vermand, Mons, Avesnes and Quesnoy.

Using the town's magnificent Roman ruins as his classroom, the old man would often become quite animated, bringing to life tales of Hannibal crossing the Alps with his elephants, mad *Néron* playing his violin as Rome burned, or *Jules César* conquering Gaul. He encouraged the boys to act it all out. 'France was invaded once and will be again,' he liked to say, hobbling into the centre of the ancient ruined forum like a gladiator approaching the end of his career. 'Our next invaders may not bring as many benefits as did the Romans.'

Gaston once thought he saw the old man wipe away a tear from the corner of his eye, but he could not be sure or understand why, on such a day, with larks singing from a cloudless sky.

Gaston recalled the life-changing moment when Père Duriez had taken him to one side by the doorway after class had ended and asked whether Gaston could read the words on the blackboard from where he stood. The boy had replied with surprise that of course he could not, surely no-one could? Père Duriez had visited his home that very night.

On the morning after this unusual visit and the subsequent earnest conversation with *Maman*, Alphonse Derome had stared at his son long and hard over breakfast. The boy was oblivious to this scrutiny, enjoying hot chocolate and *pain à l'ancienne* smothered in Maman's *confitures maison*. Papa Derome had always assumed, if he was honest, that his son Gaston was a bit on the slow side. The only place he had appeared truly at home until now was in the abundant family *potager*, where roses bloomed alongside thickening leeks and carrots beneath the lacy pea-flowers of a wisteria, pruned to create an archway. There Gaston seemed interested in everything: tools, seeds, pests and even the steaming compost heap in its sunny corner, which their gardener Henri turned regularly with a wide-tined fork.

Once, aged about four, Gaston had rushed to find Henri, who was hoeing the peas, claiming he had seen a snake there; but when they had gone to look, the snake – probably a grass-snake, the gardener had explained – had slipped away. Henri had mentioned it to the boy's father, impressed with the observation. Alphonse was most relieved to find out that little Gaston might be brighter than he had thought.

And so Maman had taken her acutely myopic son to Valenciennes in the *poney-chaise* a few days later; there he had looked around him in silent wonder through a pair of test lenses, while the old Jewish optician sat back and nodded and Maman smiled and smiled. Then Gaston had asked a deluge of questions about how the miraculous device that had measured his eyes worked.

Of course *le petit* Gaston had been teased at first, and an occasional pair of spectacles got mysteriously broken or lost, but his relief at the world of clarity and order he now entered was so great, it outweighed any disadvantage.

And now, it seemed to Gaston this terrible morning that his childhood had ended with the departure of dear, gentle Père Duriez. Now they had this stern new and younger maître with a sombre face and a long nose and a soutâne as black as a raven's wing.

The first thing the man did was to pick up a glass jar from the desk. In this jar Père Duriez kept the little wrapped hard toffees named *chiques* as a special reward for effort. If you sucked them slowly they could last for almost an hour.

Père Duriez would often tell them the history of these sweeties: of how a soldier injured at the battle of Waterloo nearby was given shelter by a family of Bavay *paysans*, who remarked on his fine white teeth. The soldier explained that when he sucked a kind of hard minted caramel, the lead that remained in his mouth (when he bit off the cartridge tops) stuck to it. This, he said, prevented tooth loss and worse. In 1875, one Favier Fortin decided to mass-produce a mint, which would celebrate the famous tale.

Gaston thought the whole story a little dubious but enjoyed the regular ritual of its repetition (as well as an occasional chique reward). He also greatly admired Monsieur Fortin's vision in creating a local business from little more than a legend and some sugar-beet, just as Papa had himself had turned dung into gold to transform his own family fortunes.

Looking at them steadily, the new maître tipped the whole jar of chiques into the waste-paper-basket. There was an audible and involuntary gasp from all the boys; the atmosphere grew tense.

'Silence,' hissed the new maître, and silent they all fell.

The strange lesson that followed was about sugar and teeth and the necessity of brushing them to keep them clean. Cheese was healthier for the teeth than sugar, it seemed. The new maître announced he now never ate anything sweet other than fruit and that he had perfect teeth, which he then bared as evidence, causing every child to flinch, even the big boys.

Gaston tried to imagine never again eating Maman's confitures or a crisp *tarte aux croque-poux*, warm from the oven. What nonsense, he thought. He used a brush every day but for his hair, of course. His teeth he kept clean with a soft cloth and a little minted paste in a tin, as everyone did. He rashly let slip an audible chuckle at the thought of spreading some pungent and creamy *Maroilles* on his hairbrush and using it on his teeth.

His punishment was to copy out the most famous verse of La Fontaine's Fables, *Le Corbeau et le Renard*, not once, but ten times.

Gaston kept his nerve and pointed out, not unreasonably and very politely, that as it was a verse he knew off by heart already, what was the point of all the copying? He was immediately told to write it out a further ten times for insolence.

By the fifth copy, he hated the fox.

By the tenth copy, he really hated the stupid raven.

By the twentieth copy his hand ached so much he thought it would drop off. He now detested La Fontaine: why did the raven drop the cheese and sing to the fox in the first place? Were they not supposed to be the wisest of birds? And why did the mean old fox have to win?

By now of course, he also perfectly loathed his new master. The newcomer was henceforth known by Gaston, and soon by the entire neighbourhood, as Maître Corbeau. It seemed to suit his tall, dark, unsmiling person, slightly hunched as he walked, with his hooded cloak, long nose and beady, all-seeing eyes.

At nearly sixteen, Gaston was a practical boy, good at science and at mathematics. He took after his father, who was known about the town as a polite, decent sort and whose factory employed many local men. Maître Corbeau had high hopes of Gaston academically and had even begun to mention the *Grandes Ecoles* in Paris. Gaston himself knew he did not want to travel so far from home. He longed to be outside, doing something – anything – rather than sitting in school or the dark church, suffocating on incense. On Sundays he also had to invent convincing sins to confess to the odious man who taught him all week.

At school, as in the pulpit, Maître Corbeau appeared to dislike Gaston intensely. The unsmiling priest constantly pushed his clever pupil to do better and try harder by sniping at rather than encouraging him. Gaston's intelligence was thus slowly forged and tempered in the fires of Maître Corbeau's scorn. The worst thing for of all was the lack of escape from his dark shadow, for Maître Corbeau was not only to be found behind the master's desk all week, but often in the pulpit every Sunday.

Gaston's Papa was not a church-goer. In fact, he had not been seen in the church since he had married Maman. His excuse was that he was busy tending to his lands, which were extensive, and his varied livestock. Maman had always been to mass on Sunday. When Gaston had been very small, he used to love watching her get ready for church, wearing her pretty dress with a little black hat and veil. Then there had been a harmless old priest mumbling his way through the rite, for Père Duriez had never preached in church. Maître Corbeau now spread his great black wings over every corner of every hour of every day of Gaston's life, or so it felt to the boy.

Papa encouraged gritted teeth and tolerance. He had told him that Maman only attended mass because it made her feel close to *Mamie*, who had died when Gaston was just five. Gaston did not believe that Mamie, a cheerful old soul who had smelled of violets and loved her flower-drenched garden, could ever have wished to be remembered in this way; in darkness and with muttered words and sighs and stifled sobs. Earth to earth, the old priest had said at her funeral. What was more natural than that?

Once he heard Maman and Papa arguing about it. Maman said Papa would end up in hell because he never went to confession. At school, Gaston had overheard a vulgar boy in his class call an old lady who went into the church every day to clean the brasses a *grenouille de bénitier*. Gaston amused himself that night by drawing a friendly green frog with a bonnet like Maman's peeping over the top of the font. How Papa had laughed when he saw it! After that his parents appeared to agree to disagree about spiritual matters.

At school, matters came to a head when Gaston was sixteen. Maître Corbeau was teaching a long-winded lesson on the parable of the talents. Some boys were yawning and stretching, others were peering towards the daylight filtering down from the high, small windows. Gaston, unlike his peers, was listening. Some of the parables contained clear morality: be kind to others; or if you share things there will be enough for all, for example. With this one, he was baffled. He hardly felt his hand rise until it was there up in the air and his friends were looking at him with disbelief.

'*Oui?*' The maître had just finished his tale, where the master returns from a long absence to see how each of his servants has protected the money entrusted to him. The first and second have invested it wisely and increased its value, the third is punished because he just buried it. In fact, not merely punished, but flung into outer darkness.

'*Ce n'est pas logique, Maître*,' Gaston heard himself say. His classmates sat aghast: Gaston was clearly not just deranged, but suicidal to boot.

'Explain this interruption, Derome,' said the maître coldly. Gaston swallowed, and rose to his feet. 'It is not a logical parable, *Maître*,' he repeated. 'The master is surely a very bad master. He gives the servants different amounts of money according to their abilities. So obviously the third servant is not very clever. The master must know that. The third servant digs a hole and buries the money to keep it safe. That is not very imaginative perhaps, but he does not use it to buy wine or something, does he? And the other two servants basically gamble with the money. Supposing their plans had failed and they had lost the lot? Which one would have been the good and faithful servant then?'

There was a stunned silence from the class, and then a thunder of applause, and cheers, and stamping of feet, a terrific venting of pent-up frustration. The maître had to shout for nearly a minute to restore order. Gaston remained on his feet, for he knew this was not yet over.

'So,' said Maître Corbeau, quietly and dangerously, 'You presume to understand holy scripture better than I, do you, Derome?'

'*Mais non*, Maître!' protested Gaston, spreading out his hands in frustration. 'But surely it is at least acceptable to voice what I believe?'

'You, Gaston Derome, are still just a schoolboy. You have not yet earned the right to an opinion,' retorted Maître Corbeau. 'Your place is to be silent, to obey me, and to absorb the Holy Word of God.'

Gaston felt something inside him snap as a great weight lifted from his shoulders. He raised his wooden desk-lid and swiftly emptied its modest contents into his schoolbag. Then he turned and began to make for the classroom door. Every boy's mouth in the room was wide open in wonder at this rebellion.

'*Arrêtez-vous* Derome! What do you think you are doing? I forbid you to leave!' bellowed Maître Corbeau.

Gaston kept walking. His maître might not be weeping or wailing, he thought, remembering the perplexing parable, but he was certainly gnashing his big white teeth. One hand on the classroom door-handle, Gaston turned to look back at the man and found him strangely diminished.

'If you leave now, boy, be warned, you will never return!' spat his incensed teacher. 'You will amount to nothing! You will become just another paysan, earning his bread from shovelling shit in the fields!'

More shock. The maître had said shit! They had all heard him! *Formidable*!

'Maître, I would rather earn a living from shovelling honest shit than swallowing illogical cant such as the lesson I have just endured. I thank you for my education, which is now at an end.'

With that he was gone, leaving behind a frustrated and foolish young teacher who knew he had just lost his most able pupil, and a class in joyous uproar.

~

Dinner that night was interesting for its contrasts. Maman, weeping and wringing her hands. The shame of it! In front of every child from every family in Bavay. The whole community would now know of it.

To use such foul language in the classroom. How could Gaston do this to her?

Gaston wanted to point out that it was the maître who had used the bad language first, but wisely chose to hang his head and remain silent. He watched his father surreptitiously. Papa did not seem at all displeased. In fact, the corners of his mouth were twitching, now that Gaston looked closely.

His father rose, his blue eyes gleaming with suppressed laughter, and walked across to the great wooden cabinet in the corner. He brought out two cold bottles of Bavay beer, opened them both, then astonished and delighted Gaston by handing one to him. They chinked bottles and Papa held up his own, toasting his son with a proud smile and the words: 'from one shit-shoveller to another, *mon fils.*'

# 4

# Monarch of the Glen

For the briefest of instants as the Old Man fell, the boy had contemplated trying to prevent it.

Afterwards he wondered if he really could have done so. His father had been several paces ahead on the rocky path. The slate boulder had given way so abruptly, almost silently, until its shattering impact in the gully below.

Could he have run ahead, caught the Old Man's arm somehow? Or anticipated the angle at which he would fall, and plunged off down the slope to cushion his hideous landing? The boy told himself later that it was most unlikely and buried the flickering glimmer of doubt very deep indeed, until it seemed altogether snuffed out.

James Macbane of Lochdubh hated the end of term. He was surrounded by friends who seemed aglow with jollity at the thought of seeing their people again, chattering about all the japes they would get up to once at home. Sometimes, for shorter holidays, James would go to stay with his Aunt Gertrude near London, where she had married a wealthy politician. He got on well with his cousins and that was always fine fun. James regretted that his father, who never now went up to Town, had decided to let their own family house in Grosvenor Square.

Whenever the summer holidays loomed, he could not remember anything except this sense of impending doom. Eton was his sanctuary. Now he had to leave its bright positivity once more to return to his natal island.

James no longer had 'people' as such; he had only Father. The Old

Man. The *laird* himself – Alexander, Macbane of Lochdubh, and the mac-bane of his bally existence too. James grimaced as he folded up and packed away in his travelling trunk all the smart jackets and silk cravats and pressed trousers he knew he would never need this summer. Some of his friends were touring the ancient amphitheatres of Rhodes and Crete during the holidays. How he envied them their sun-kissed islands. He packed away his beloved volume of Shakespeare among his underclothes and brought down the lid.

Soon he found himself thinking of home as the heaving ferry butted through the west coast swell. Loch Dubh, the Black Loch, where he was born, was a deep, dark inlet on the coast of Meall Mòr. His family's island was the fifth of the Small Isles, a three-hour journey by ferry from Oban, about half the size again of Canna but smaller than Rhum; known as the Striped Isle from its abundance of quartz-veined slate. James would soon spy its oppressive bulk looming out of whatever gale or *haar* nature was inflicting on its beleaguered islanders that day. The people of Meall Mòr – James' people, although he could never avoid a shudder at the thought of such a birthright – became either quarriers, or worked on the land, or fished. Whatever their path through life, all were tenants of the Macbanes of Lochdubh at the Big House.

Once James had explained to all his chums at Eton that Meall Mòr meant the big bare breast in Scots Gaelic, which it actually did, and it had amused them no end.

The first few days at home always felt somewhat like being enfolded in a great hairy embrace by some brusque tweedy woman with an enormous bosom. Holidays never varied. Father would shout at him or ignore him or drag him off stalking. Cook would try to feed him with nursery puddings he had never really liked, as though he were still a baby in a high chair. And everyone, but everyone, would feel they had the right to approach him and ask him how he was doing and tell him he was looking well and he had grown and that he must be *awfy* glad to be home; all without waiting to hear an honest answer. There was no proper respect for his status as the son of the laird. That was it. It was not like school, where his best friend was the son of the Maharaja of Darmanga, for goodness' sake. It was not like dear old England.

No-one asked about Eton, of course, because it was alien to them.

Lochdubh did not meet his son at the ferry on this occasion, so that at least was something of a relief. Instead Matheson had come in the pony and trap. James always preferred Matheson's company to that of anyone else on the island, as he did not tend to chatter. There were many Mathesons on the island, all related. This one was known as Matheson the Trap or Trap for short, which also suited his economy with words.

The trim dappled pony in harness was new and gave them something to discuss. Young Lochdubh, as most knew James on the island, was a reasonable horseman. If he could have been left to his own devices to roam about the hills on the back of one of the *garrons*, James might have enjoyed his Meall Mòr holidays rather more. As it was, his father filled the boy's days with manly pursuits, most of which hinged on killing things: red deer on the hill, or the gentle black hares unique to Meall Mòr. These mountain hares were quite tame and sometimes stood up on their hind legs and gazed at you with meltingly deep eyes and a raised paw. Before, of course, your father instructed you to blow them to oblivion.

James' loathing of these huntin'-shootin'-fishin' activities was almost equal to his passion for an unexpected new-found talent: acting. He had spent his first few years at Eton resisting Shakespeare as utterly ludicrous and impenetrable. Now, thanks to an inspiring teacher and a natural flair for the dramatic, a turning-point had come while reading King Lear. James saw his father as Lear, naturally; he himself was the spurned and misunderstood Cordelia. He had taken on this leading role and sent his father an excited invitation in his exuberant curly script to come and see him perform it.

He had not come.

Lochdubh, standing in the great hall of the Big House, had taken the envelope from Matheson the Trap, who brought up all post from the ferry. Lochdubh had read the contents slowly, his mouth silently forming his only son's words. Then he shook his head and read it again, tight-lipped. Matheson had watched him crumple it into a ball then toss it into the embers of the fire, turn and leave the house, his old deerhound at his heels.

James knew nothing of this, for they had never discussed it afterwards. There had been other plays since. The Old Man had not come to those, either.

Alexander Macbane of Lochdubh, James' father, had not been sent to Eton. James' grandfather, the namesake who had anglicised the name from MacBean to Macbane after schooldays spent south of the border, drank the rents and could not then afford fancy schooling for his son. Young Alexander had had a tutor instead, who had also been a drunkard, but who had taught him all that he deemed necessary for the running of an island estate.

The laird's older sister Gertrude came back on a rare visit from London in 1889. She took one look at odd little James and his sickly mother and was convinced that it was quite essential the boy be sent away from Meall Mòr for his schooling. She told her brother she would arrange it, and then promptly and efficiently did so.

Lochdubh's delicate flower of a wife was a convenient heiress he had met in Edinburgh. She had propped up the fortunes of the sagging estate very nicely. At first she had begged the Old Man not to send her darling boy away. Initially Lochdubh had listened, as he was quite fond of the girl when she behaved herself. Then it became clear that her irritatingly persistent cough – she hacked away like a quarrier sometimes – was going to end in an early grave. Boarding had seemed the kinder course of action for the lad. Little James was soon despatched to a prep school in Perth.

These days Lochdubh was not so sure he had done the right thing by his son. This slight, fair young man with a fledgling moustache and expensive tastes seemed more of a stranger to him every time the ferry brought him home. More worrying still, young James appeared increasingly remote from the island he would one day inherit.

It had been in his headmaster's office that James, at the age of eight, had learned of his mother's demise. The man had been very kind. When James had wept a little, he clearly remembered the headmaster patting him on the shoulder. Then he had been given some tea and a slice of hot buttered toast to eat by the fire. Gazing into the watery blue flames, a fragment of memory flickered: a bruised cheek, the sound of his mother sobbing. His face? Hers? He could no longer tell.

That had been more than a decade ago and it all seemed very distant to him now. Eton had cut and polished him into someone who looked and behaved quite differently. And yet, whenever he took the ferry out of Oban over a choppy sea, he would feel the years peel away, revealing his puny, tender, younger self.

This time James had made a conscious decision. If he could not actually enjoy himself on Meall Mòr this summer, he would at least practice one of the skills he had learned to love. He would play the role of an enthusiastic country boy returning home for the holidays and see if it made any difference to his father's mood or to his own enjoyment.

The pony and trap jingled along the coastal track that wound from the harbour to the Big House. They passed the familiar piles of waste slate, blue and grey and purple and sparkling with pyrite, accumulated over the last century or two. Only a handful of the islanders were quarry workers now, and it was rare to hear the whistles that would signal a blast. Most of the slate came from the larger sites such as Easdale or Ballachulish, where the quantity was greater and the quality more consistent.

With Matheson, there was never any need for James to pretend. He asked eagerly after each of the horses, soaking up news of a new foal to one or a cast shoe of another. The horses who had been staunch companions in his younger years remained his allies now.

The Old Man had seen the trap coming and waited to greet him on the steps of the Big House, just as the sun was dipping behind the slate-veined mass of the crouching giant, the *Bodach*, Meall Mòr's only mountain. Lochdubh shook his son's hand awkwardly. 'Well then, there you are,' he said, without warmth. 'Does Trap have your trunk?'

'I left it at the harbour, sir – I have no immediate need of it. It can be sent up later.'

Sent up! Thought the Old Man, catching Matheson's eye. Who, precisely, did the young whelp think *would* be fetching it up to the Big House?

He said nothing, instead asking, 'Are ye well?' His father always looked for signs of the consumption that had carried off his mother, and James knew it. He tried to stand tall and project as hale and hearty an image as he could.

'Very well, thank you, sir. And yourself?'

The Old Man just snorted as usual and turned inside for the dining room.

'Where's Marchioness?' asked James, looking around for the old grey dog, the last of a deerhound dynasty named not after nobility, but sizes of slate tile. She stank; but did at least wag her tail when he entered a room.

'Dead,' responded the Old Man. 'Couldn't walk. Shot her myself.'

I'm sure you did, thought James.

They lapsed into silence to eat their dismal evening meal, a cold collation as Father termed it; Cook had not known precisely when he might arrive, the boats often being delayed by weather or tide. The hot nursery stodge would begin tomorrow.

At the end of the meal, Lochdubh wiped his mouth with a linen napkin, drained his glass of claret, turned to his son and said, as the boy knew he would, 'So. We'll take the Bodach left ridge, up past the West Quarry, tomorrow. There's a lame stag Trap has his eye on for you.'

'Ripping, father!' replied James promptly. To his satisfaction, the Old Man dropped his fork with a clatter. 'I shall look forward to that very much. When should we rise, just after dawn?'

Of course it would be just after dawn. No chance of being able to sleep a little longer on his first morning home. And it would be drizzling too. The midges, which never seemed to touch his father's leathery old hide, would descend in great black waves to eat him alive.

In the morning, it was a little brighter than expected and although it was painfully early, he felt a twinge of genuine anticipation as he saw Matheson lead out his favourite garron, Cailleach, who put her ears forward as she recognised him. She was named after one of the odder slate outcrop formations on the Bodach, which James had always imagined to be a witch.

He swung himself over the broad back of the beast who turned her head in acknowledgement, as if to say, 'well now, you're a bitty longer of limb than last time, young man.' The Old Man preferred to walk, as always. He held his hazel thumb-stick in one hand. It seemed to Trap that he leaned on it more than usual, but he knew better than to enquire after the old laird's health.

James, oblivious to any change in his father, was already kicking his pony into a trot up the uneven path.

They settled into a comfortable pace, James warming to his role, asking all kinds of appropriate and interested questions about the herd and even the weather, which he knew was almost always ghastly without being told. His father seemed notably more relaxed. Even Matheson was looking impressed, if a little sceptical. It really did seem as though today's activities might turn out rather better than usual, James thought with relief.

It took them three solid hours of uphill walking and scrambling to approach the herd. The deer browsed the thin mountain grass slightly below them on a sharp slate ridge. A few of them were more clearly visible against the sea in the far distance: none individually identifiable other than the great Grey Laird, the dominant stag with an abnormally light coat. In October during the rut, the grey gullies of the Bodach echoed with his hoarse bass bellow.

Matheson gestured to Lochdubh and his son to drop and they began crawling through the heather. James was aware of the nasty, itchy bits of moorland (and probably ticks to boot) getting stuck into his more awkward nooks and crannies. He prided himself on concealing his horror, turning a brilliant smile on his father whenever he saw him glance in his direction. Once he thought the Old Man almost smiled back.

All at once Matheson was beside him, helping him line up the gun-barrel, saying, 'There now, sir, see it? The one standing apart from the others, third from the left. Lame in the left hind leg. It'll no' last the winter. Ye'd be doing it a kindness.' Trap understood without ever having been told that James hated to slaughter these fine beasts.

'Take the shot,' hissed his Father, somewhere to his left.

James peered at the hillside slightly desperately and squeezed his trigger. The bruising report thudded into his shoulder. And with disbelief he saw the beast drop. 'Yes!' he said aloud, surprising himself by feeling something other than disgust in the kill, something chilling, and thrilling. 'Oh yes!'

Then his father groaned and shook his head. James saw Matheson's wretched face and looked back down to the ridge. The herd was dispersing rapidly at the gallop on the other side, including one young stag loping behind the others with a distinct limp. But he had seen it fall!

'Ye shot the Grey Laird,' said his father, coldly. 'Trap, away and fetch the beast back here.' Matheson stood, whistled to his dog and paced away over the moorland towards the ridge, leading his garron. Young Lochdubh could feel his grief and swallowed hard.

'I am so sorry, Father,' he stammered. And he was, if more for Matheson's sake. He knew Trap had spent years building up the stamina of the herd; and now, without the dominant male, the younger males would dissipate their energies on rivalry. Fewer youngsters would be born as a result and this in turn would reduce the income from the herd. Worse still, the Grey Laird was a stag his father had always viewed as a kind of family emblem.

Why did it always have to go so wrong?

He was surprised, then, when his father said nothing. The Old Man merely pulled himself to his feet, lit his pipe and puffed on it once or twice, causing a welcome break in the midges that surrounded them. Then, unexpectedly, he said, 'There's a war coming, boy. The old queen is not six months dead and her fool of a son is already spoiling for a scrap with his cousins.'

'Yes, Father.' James was grateful for the change of subject but also felt a chill of apprehension. There was always talk of war at school of course, but he had been so immersed in his acting that he had paid it little heed. 'Ye've a decent seat,' continued his father. 'They'd make a cavalry officer of you. Gertrude's man could find ye a commission, no doubt. And at least we know now ye're capable of killing *something*.' The last word was with a jerk of the head towards where Matheson and the lad from the stables were gralloching the stag. Steam rose from the entrails.

They both watched in silence as Matheson and his son lifted the emptied beast across the pony's saddlecloth and turned back towards them. 'When do you think the war will begin, Father?' he asked. The Old Man shrugged. 'Germany is always spoiling for a fight and so are those fools down in England, your uncle among them. Oh, ye'll have another few years of peace yet. But the signs are there for any fool to see. Make the most of your play-acting, laddie, because ye'll be hearing the trumpet's blast soon enough.' He blew another cloud of sweet-scented tobacco around them both and ended with a shake of the head. 'A fresh century. And that is how they plan to squander it.'

James could not recall ever hearing his father say so much, nor sound so human when he was doing it. He wondered, timidly, if his father now considered him more of a man by sharing such information.

Matheson and the boy approached and all at once the rare moment of intimacy was gone. Here was the grisly, lolling evidence of James' inept gun-handling. It was draped over the back of the blood-streaked little garron, which picked its way stoically through the heather, the dead beast's antlers so long they kept catching in the heather. Lochdubh stared at it without talking for some minutes, while James fidgeted and tried and failed to think of things to say.

His father's next words made it clear that his son's transgression had not been forgotten or forgiven.

'We'll spend the night on the hill.'

James thought about protesting but decided against it. There was little point.

'Ach no, Lochdubh,' replied Matheson in frustration, 'I've no brought what was needful. An' look yonder, there's rain coming in from the sea. An' no' even a moon to light the path. Ye'll have a miserable night.'

And that, thought James, was the whole point, surely. The Old Man wanted to give him yet another dreadful experience as a punishment for his stupidity. His father was always doing unkind things like this to try and toughen him up. He remembered being made to run round and round the turning-circle at the front of the Big House one winter in just his vest and pants 'until he came to his senses'. He could not recall the misdemeanour now, but he remembered the cold burning his chest as he breathed. James' mother had eventually rescued him from the kitchen entrance; his hands and feet had hurt so badly as they thawed out that it felt like being stabbed with hot needles.

His father continued to issue orders as though Matheson had not spoken. 'Go back now, Trap, and take both garrons and your own lad with you.'

Better and better. They were to walk back, then. James seethed at the injustice of it. He had not intended to bring down the wrong stag.

Matheson opened his mouth to speak, saw the laird's expression and closed it. Soon he and the pony and his son, whose simple life James sometimes envied, were just tiny dwindling dots on the path for home. Then they rounded a corner of the hill and were gone.

Lochdubh and his only son began to plod onwards and upwards. The Càrn Dubh bothy was another hour of steep uphill scrambling away. Sure enough, it began to spit with rain.

James tried to divert himself with memories of having once spent a night in the same bothy with both his parents when he was very small. His mother had ridden up side-saddle, laughing. He could just recall a very different and smiling father striding ahead, with James' pony on a leading-rein. Cook had made a game pie in crisp raised pastry. His mouth watered at the memory. Cook's catering had suffered in the years since she had lost her kind mistress.

There had been a crackling peat fire, and sweet-smelling mattresses of heather, sheets and rough blankets. 'There. Snug as a bug in a rug,' his mother had said, tucking him in for the night. He could not now remember her face, just her soft voice and a haze of golden hair, so like his own.

They were about twenty minutes away from the bothy when James, lagging behind to avoid conversation, saw that his father had stopped. Lochdubh, feeling his age, needed to catch his breath against a familiar projecting slate boulder, the pointed chin of the Cailleach. Once he would have paused there to rest his old Mons Meg telescope on it, but that was now propped up in a corner of his study, too heavy for him to carry. He would not entrust it to his maladroit son.

As Lochdubh paused to survey his island, he could not know that the weather had so eroded the base of the stone that it was now anchored by almost nothing. His added weight was all it took to tip the fragile balance between normality and catastrophe.

The fall itself, James would remember, was strangely silent. One moment his father was standing there, the next he was gone. The crunch, a cry cut off. James scrambled gingerly to the edge of the path and saw the Old Man lying spread-eagled below near a small burn, surrounded by jagged broken lumps of slate. 'Father!' he shouted and started to make his disbelieving way down the blue-grey scree of the gully. No response.

'Father?' James knelt breathlessly over him, struggling to take in what had just occurred. He looked at the Old Man's splayed-out limbs, the left leg lying at an impossible angle. The small child inside James wondered about starting to cry; the young man chose not to.

The Old Man's lips worked, wordlessly, but he did not open his eyes.

James felt sick, his world spinning. He knew he had to seek help, but where from? They were near the summit. This section of the mountain was entirely hidden from view of House by a succession of diminishing summits. Home was a good three hours walk away downhill. They were miles out of earshot. Darkness was falling and so was the rain. No moon to see the path by.

The Carn Dubh bothy was only about a mile distant uphill, tucked into a sheltered corner of the ridge not far from the summit. James looked down at the Old Man. Broader and more solid than he was, he knew he could not even carry his father back up to the path. No, his only hope was to hurry on to see if he could find something – anything – in the bothy with which to protect the Old Man from the elements overnight.

'Father, can you hear me?' he asked, leaning in close. He did not move or respond. James took off his rain cape and laid it over the old man's body.

'I'm going to get something more to cover you.' James then turned his back on the dreadful sight and slowly toiled between the sharp and unstable slate boulders up to the path, before setting off at a rapid pace.

As the rain began to soak through his tweeds, he stumbled upwards through the moonless gloom; feverishly, he told himself later. The cold began to seep into his bones and heart, just as it had done that terrible night he was punished as a child. He knew he ought to be brave. If he could only bring his father safely through this night, they would all look up to him then.

His feet slipped on the slick slate scree and he fell, bloodying his knees and hands.

Shaking, he scrambled up and plodded on. A sharp piece of slate had lodged itself in his left boot and was jagging him through his sock. His fingers were too numb to bend and untie the laces. He would have to *thole* it, as Matheson would say. When he thought of Matheson his lip trembled, but he mastered himself.

Onwards, upwards, in the gathering darkness. James could just see that the path now vanished into a black mist shrouding the top of the mountain. Looking back, it also disappeared a few yards below him. It was as though he had entered a strange limbo-land, where all certainty of landscape and even of the existence of humanity was lost.

It was here that a seductive thought crept out of a small, dark corner of his mind. Could he, or rather *should* he, allow nature to take its course? His father's leg was all smashed up. He had struck his head. He'd probably never be right again. Had the Old Man not often said that he wanted to end his days on the hill rather than in his bed?

The door was suddenly there. James staggered into the unlocked bothy trembling with cold and shock. The only cupboard contained a couple of worn blankets, a metal box with matches, some kindling and a few hard, dried biscuits. Nothing waterproof with which to cover a dying man.

James lit a small fire in the grate with the few dry logs stacked in a corner, stripped off his wet clothes and pulled one of the two rough woollen blankets around his shoulders. As Matheson had said, he had not really 'brought what was needful', but the basics were there. After only a moment's hesitation, his teeth chattering, James wrapped the second blanket around his own icy legs. It would not have done his father any good now anyway. Would it?

The dark thought spread as the flames licked across the kindling. Matheson was always putting injured animals out of their misery. Well, Father had been miserable towards him for almost as many years as James could remember. It would not be as though he had *done* anything, either, would it?

Hanging his soaked tweeds neatly on the back of the three-legged chair, James ate a biscuit, lay down on one of the truckle beds and looked at the underside of the snug heather thatch. He found himself contemplating the latest Shakespeare play in which he had performed at school. A minor role this time, but as a result he had found ample time to observe the two leading men. The most compelling had not been the tragic hero, Othello, played by a fatuous fellow with a face smeared with cocoa, but his persuasive, charming, deadly friend.

James Macbane of Lochdubh fell into an exhausted yet strangely untroubled sleep.

~

The skylarks and a sudden clatter of a grouse outside woke him. James peered at his pocket-watch. The Old Man had given it to him when he went to school: its heart ticked in his warm palm. Five o' clock!

The bothy door opened on to what his mother used to call a peerless day: blue sky, the air washed clean, a whisper of breeze carrying the sound of a thousand burns in spate.

The events of the previous night felt rather different in this bright morning light. His father was, after all, as strong and as *thrawn* as an ox. Perhaps James had been wrong about the Old Man's injuries? It had been getting dark. Perhaps he had recovered himself enough to hobble away down the path, vowing to disinherit the son who had abandoned him?

Appalled by the thought of being cut off without a shilling, James pulled on his still-damp clothes and ran back down to the gully path.

He almost missed the new chinless profile of the Cailleach in daylight. When he looked over its raw edge, he started and cried out. There was his rain cape, right enough, but discarded down near the little burn. The Old Man somehow lay turned face upward, gazing blankly at his son, only just below the path where James stood. He had somehow crawled back through the darkness, almost the whole way up. One torn hand reached above his head. His bloodied hazel thumb-stick lay nearby – he must have used it to drag himself upwards, inch by agonising inch.

His eyes were set and glassy. A spider moved slowly over his cheek.

James shook his head, not wanting to dwell on the implications of his father's last, desperate struggle for life. Then with a jolt: oh, dear God, it will be clear to them all that I left him.

The response came swiftly, surely from heaven, in the voice of his beloved drama teacher: just act a way through it, dear boy.

It was then that Iago came to his aid.

His teeth clenched, his mind numb, James half pushed, half rolled his father's battered body back down the slate scree again, using the Old Man's own thumb-stick to prod it into motion. His son slithered down behind as the corpse jolted sickeningly downhill and came to rest not far from where it had first fallen. There he bent to retrieve his rain cape and rinsed it under a waterfall nearby. Without looking at his father again, he climbed back up between the rocks, taking the path towards the bothy. Once through the door, he quickly but carefully arranged things inside to look as though two, not one, had spent the night inside.

Later, as he strode down towards to the Big House, he continued to act the part, just in case. He felt a strange elation and did not even glance into the dismal gully below the Cailleach. A few miles further on it dawned on him that he, James, was now the laird. *The* Macbane of Lochdubh.

All this bally awful drenched bogland was now his.

By the time he reached the Big House, he was whistling cheerfully, unthinkingly swishing his father's stained thumb-stick through the chilly morning air.

Matheson the Trap was standing in the stable yard, watching him come. 'Where is *Himself*?' he asked, already looking beyond the boy, scanning the slopes above.

This was the moment. James opened both eyes and mouth, wide and guileless. 'He's not here?' He knew he looked the epitome of shock. He could almost believe his own next words.

'You mean the Old Man's not down before me?'

Both Matheson and James were mounted within minutes. Accompanied on foot by every able-bodied male from the Big House staff, they set off back up the hill, calling and scanning the horizon with Mons Meg, which someone had thought to retrieve from the laird's study. James had told them that the Old Man had been up at first light, about four he thought. Although James had stirred and offered to rise and accompany him – a nice touch he thought – his father had left him to slumber on.

Just before they reached the steepest section James dismounted and stopped to tie a bootlace that was not untied. In this way he ensured that Matheson the Trap was well ahead of him. He heard Trap's cry, rode up to the edge of the path with an 'Oh no! Father!' worthy of Edmund Keane and was soon plunging into the ravine ahead of everyone.

He reached the Old Man first and knelt beside him, a picture of filial concern.

I don't care, he thought, numbly, holding the cold stiff fingers. I really don't care that you are dead, you horrid old man.

that you are dead, you horrid old man.

The body was lifted across the back of the garron and carried back to the Big House. Matheson led the procession, his head bared and bowed. The new laird, James Macbane of Lochdubh, rode behind his father. He felt strangely light-headed, almost giddy. There was a pattern to all this. How many great stags had the Old Man felled and transported down the hill across a garron's back? Game, they called it once the beast was shot. Now his beastly father was just another piece of meat. Dead game.

He felt nothing. He was free.

Most of the staff and tenants who had turned out to join in the search had already come forward to acknowledge him as the new laird. They had said how sorry they were, some of them wiping away tears. James acknowledged their grief with moist eyes and appropriate words. His eyes were only watering because he had got away with it. He felt a dangerous temptation to laugh, which he quelled.

Trap Matheson knew a thing or two about a carcass and had noted the way the old laird lay. He had crouched down and stared at the scarred hands, paying particularly close attention to their battered fingertips, then up at the scree where a few traces of blood remained in spite of the storm. There was the laird's thumb-stick, too, which the boy had carried with him down the hill.

Trap had thought deeply about all this as he brought his late master home for the last time. Whatever had happened up on the hill was known only to the boy. There were no witnesses either, other than the Bodach and the Cailleach, and that ancient pair kept their secrets well.

Ach, he had seen how they were together. There was cruelty in the way of life forced on the motherless lad. Who knew what he had become at that English school, so far away from his home? He could not understand this driving urge to send the sons of lairds south for their book-learning. Matheson knew his history. This system had been forced on the Jacobite clan chiefs in the aftermath of the last great Rising and the Battle of Culloden. Civil war, only a generation or two before. Almost forgotten, or so it seemed. Those who had been sent to school south of the border would now bankrupt their lands to cover school fees for their own sons.

Madness.

He thought of his own plump wife and their happy wee *bairns*, snug in their cosy estate house. For how long? A job and a home for life, he had believed, better than working in a quarry, as his father had done. Now his own future and that of the island people of Meall Mòr lay in the inexperienced hands of this boy.

Matheson the Trap resolved to say nothing of his doubts. At least for now.

# 5

# Quick March

LONDON, ENGLAND
FEBRUARY 1907

The stone caught Evie just below the eye. She yelped in pain and staggered, bringing both hands up to her cheek, clutching the tender spot where it had hit her. The last few women ahead of them were chattering with excitement and did not notice what had happened. They marched on.

The idea had taken shape with an exchange of letters between Mary and Evie more than two months before. It was Evie who had got wind of the march first, from a Miss Fox, who lived in Ross-on-Wye. Miss Fox was very plain but very clever, and Evie admired her. She was devoted to 'The Cause', the grand campaign for universal suffrage. After church one Sunday Miss Fox had confided in her that a grand march of suffragettes was planned through London in March. She hoped that hundreds or even thousands of women would attend.

Evie longed to go too but knew she could not; duty and responsibility to the parish had to come first. She said as much to Mary in a lengthy letter that otherwise bemoaned how long it was since they had seen each other and how dull she found her current activities, especially having to visit old Mr Lugg, who was as deaf as a post and had a rather nasty ulcerated leg. Harriett had taught her to make a healing poultice, which Evie now had to make up in his fetid kitchen and apply twice weekly.

Mary's reply came back so quickly that Evie knew her cousin must have written her response and posted it on the very same day. 'Oh

Evie! I will if you will,' it read. 'Bother Mr Lugg's bad leg just this once, go on, do please let's march!' The last word was underlined twice in very black ink and had smudged in her haste to fold the sheet and place it in the envelope.

Subterfuge had been required, if not actual deceit, but fate had also played into their hands. Harriett, Evie's rather nice stepmother and Father, who had mellowed under new management, had decided to go away for a few days on a diocesan visit to Salisbury. Maud, contentedly juggling a multitude of parish activities as usual, accepted their story without question.

Surely, Evie decided, it was simply meant to be.

The great day arrived, an unpromising and damp Thursday in February. They had agreed to meet in Town. Both trains had been late and so they arrived after the other marchers had begun to move off. They had to rush through Hyde Park to catch up and were right at the rear of the long line of protesting women as a result.

'Never mind!' said Mary, panting. 'We are *here*! We managed it. We are *really* here!' She gave Evie a brief, fierce hug, which almost dislodged both their hats. Then she dug into her handbag and pulled out two blue sashes, fastening one across Evie as they walked. Evie did the same for her.

Even from right at the back, it was quite a thrilling spectacle. Three thousand women armed with umbrellas had formed into triple ranks in the drizzle, some of them singing, just like soldiers going on manoeuvres. And now there they all were, sisters united by the common cause, marching to the Strand, where they were promised inspiring words from speakers the cousins had, until then, only read about.

It had always seemed ludicrous to Evie and her sisters, who knew themselves to be intellectually every bit the equal of their brothers, that women of their class and education were unable to vote for their Member of Parliament. Now both Evie and Mary felt sure that they were about to change their world for the better. For the first time in their lives they felt part of something even more significant than the mighty Church of England. Evie had never felt so proud and excited in all her days. They even got a friendly nod from Miss Fox, when she dropped back to speak to someone just in front.

It was when Mary stopped to fiddle with a snag in her sash and they fell behind the others that Evie noticed the men. Three of them had appeared from nowhere, quite a way off, standing under a plane tree dripping with rain on the trampled edge of the park. Two wore drenched tweed caps and raincoats splashed with mud. There was also a single, very wet policeman. As they came closer, the men began to jeer and point; the policeman, slightly set apart, just watched. No-one else appeared to have noticed.

Evie's world was a peaceful one and she could not imagine that these vulgar fellows could possibly do anything more than call them a nasty name or two. All the same, something stirred in the instinctive depths of her brain and she felt a twinge of alarm.

One of the men stooped to pick up something he had dropped, or so she thought. When he straightened up again he was tossing something between his two hands as Teddy might a cricket ball, testing its weight. Then the other man said something and laughed. The first man drew back his arm and aimed the small, sharp stone right at her face.

Mary caught Evie by the shoulder as she staggered back and pulled her quickly to one side. They were now closer still to the beastly men, but there was nowhere else to go. The sounds of tramping feet and singing and excited female chatter died away. There they all stood, Evie holding her face, while the policeman stared at them both. When later she thought back to what had happened, Evie could still feel the absurd shock of his reaction and tears would prick her eyes. Policemen were there to help. If you are lost, ask a policeman. Mother had always said so.

Mary stormed up to the three men. 'How dare you hurt my friend!' she had shouted into their faces, her hands balled in fury. Not just my cousin, thought Evie. My friend. That meant a lot, with hindsight. 'And as for you!' Mary turned on the policeman, 'You clearly saw what happened. Why don't you arrest them?' The constable's unyielding expression did not change and he remained silent.

All at once they found Miss Fox beside them. She must still have been near the rear of the procession and had noticed the incident. 'Pray, Miss Lawson, do not persist,' she hissed into Mary's ear, loud enough for Evie to hear her too. 'The other policemen have been very decent so far. This one is surely the exception, not the rule. And he could arrest you and Miss Winnington-Ingram instead of the real culprits, for causing an affray.'

Arrest *them*! Where was British justice?

The policeman glared at Miss Fox, as if he had been considering just this course of action, then turned and walked off, following the tail-end of the procession. One of the men, the one who had thrown the stone, wiped his muddy hand on his coat, spat the words 'bloody women!' then followed. The younger of the two did now look rather more sheepish, as though Mary's anger had broken the spell. All the same, he too then turned and hurried after the others.

'I... I want to go home,' Evie said, aware she sounded like a plaintive little girl. Miss Fox, who volunteered with the Red Cross, tilted her head to look at her injury more closely. She whistled under her breath. 'I don't think anything is broken, but there'll be no hiding that bruise for a week or two, I'm afraid. Yes, you will need to get back to Paddington before it comes out too badly or you will catch it from people on the train too. It is so very important that this march is seen to be a peaceful protest. You do understand that, ladies, don't you? Now, forgive me, I must catch up the others.' With that she was off, holding on to her hat and veil, running through the mud in the direction of the Strand.

Mary and Evie were abandoned.

Evie's face was already swelling from the impact, a livid red mark spreading across her cheekbone, and her best raincoat was filthy where both stone and mud had struck her. It was very unsettling to think that Miss Fox might want them gone; not just for their own sakes, but also for the convenience of The Cause to which, only minutes previously, both Mary and Evie had believed themselves so devoted.

Evie could see that Mary was bitterly disappointed, but her cousin knew where her duty lay. She also wanted as few people as possible to see Evie in such disarray. She sensibly removed their N.U.W.S.S. badges and sashes and bundled them back into her handbag. 'Come on, old thing,' she said, gently. 'You need a cup of tea. Let's go home.'

The journey back was something of an ordeal. Their railway carriage remained sparsely occupied for the first few stops. When an old lady got on, Evie pretended to doze. Mary mentioned an entirely fictional, but very nasty, fall in the mud. Their fellow-passenger had sympathetically tutted and had even offered Evie a sniff of her *sal volatile*, which Evie kindly declined. They disembarked together at Hereford but it was here, where they changed trains on to the local line, that their problems really began. 'Miss Winnington-Ingram!' sang out a voice Evie recognised. There, clasping his cap in his hands and beaming all over his genial round face was John Armitage, their post-boy. Evie knew he was rather sweet on her. As he approached, his expression crumpled with concern. 'Oh Miss Evie, what 'ave ee been about?'

Evie could feel herself blushing. Mary stepped in gallantly with the tale of the fall in the mud as John helped them up into the carriage. As he climbed aboard himself, then reached back to close the door, another passenger rushed up and hauled himself in beside them, puffing and blowing. Evie, with considerable dismay, recognised the features of one of Father's rat-like curates.

'Mr Snodgrass!' she pre-empted, aware of a faint sound from Mary beside her. He removed his hat and then noticed Evie's cheek. 'Goodness gracious me, Miss Winnington-Ingram,' he exclaimed in his nasal voice, 'What a very nasty bruise!'

Poor John Armitage fell silent, out-gunned by the curate's displeasing familiarity, but he still stared at Evie with concern all the way to Ross-on-Wye, sometimes opening his mouth, then shutting it again. Evie could feel words rising to the tip of his tongue then subsiding again, like a pan of milk being slid on and off the hotplate on the range.

By the end of tomorrow's postal round the whole of Ross-on-Wye would know of Miss Evie's nasty fall and soon most of the diocese of Hereford and Worcester would too. It was too bad.

Evie decided slightly more explanation of what had occurred was required for Mr Snodgrass. With her fingers tightly crossed inside her glove, she told him the story she and Mary had agreed. His face brightened. 'How wondrous, ladies. You heard Archbishop Davidson himself speak? You are indeed most fortunate. Pray, what was the topic of his homily?'

Mary now appeared to be trying to eat her pocket-handkerchief. Evie realised with a jolt that her cousin was trying to smother laughter. Did she not realise how serious this was? How could she find anything even slightly funny in their plight? Evie explained rather lamely that in fact her fall had occurred on her way to the meeting they had planned to attend. Mr Snodgrass expressed fulsome regret at their ill fortune. Mary made a strange choking sound and Evie had to pretend to pat her on the back. Then she fell back on pretending to doze again.

As if they had not suffered enough, Mary and Evie still got the most frightful lecture from an altogether unexpected quarter when they got back. Cook had taken a few days off to see her soldier son who was on leave from his Highland regiment. So they sat around the table in the draughty kitchen at Ross-on-Wye, drinking strong and comforting tea made by Maud instead. Evie was holding a block of ice to her throbbing cheekbone, feeling rather sick. Mary wolfed down some bread and jam and told the story, at first with high drama and extravagant gestures. Maud's face steadily darkened as she heard it. Evie could see the storm brewing from long experience but at first Mary remained oblivious. Dear Etty might have been more understanding but she was away teaching.

Mary, finally noticing her eldest cousin's thunderous taut expression, faltered to a close. No-one ever laughed when Maud got cross. She proceeded to give them an absolute roasting and made them both feel thoroughly ashamed of themselves. What had possessed them? Supposing there had been a photographer there from The Times? Had Evie and Mary not thought of poor Father? What it might do to him, to his career, to have one of his daughters caught up in this sort of thing, or even arrested? And dear Uncle Arthur as Bishop of London? Think of the impact the scandal might have had on him. Not to mention Etty and Maud's reputations as teachers. There was no escaping the family name and responsibilities. They were people of note and there it was.

'It is one thing to support universal suffrage, you know we all do.' Maud spoke with great conviction. 'It is quite another to go up to Town for a dangerous protest. Especially,' she continued grimly while Mary and Evie avoided eye contact, 'When your poor sister thinks you are attending a meeting of the Society for the Propagation of Christian Knowledge.'

Lesson learned. Fibbing to Maudie was never, ever a good idea.

# 6

# A Letter from India

The two sisters were slacking. This was a rare event.

Maud and Evie strolled, wicker baskets swinging, beside the Wye, its waters sparkling with fragments of ice; they clung to the brightness of its bank. It was market day and Ross-on-Wye had been busy with people, most of them former or actual parishioners. They had made pleasantly slow progress around the stalls. Afterwards they had stopped to visit the grave of their Aunt Annie. Dear Aunt Annie, who had never married, had saved the day shortly after Mother died by arriving on their doorstep clutching a portmanteau and a parrot named Puck in a wire cage. Their aunt had become a refuge for the children and later moved with them from Bewdley, leaving the draughty vicarage there with few regrets. She and a string of inexpensive governesses (most of them intellectually inferior to their charges) had seen to the girls' early education while the boys were away at school.

When in 1899 Edward had unexpectedly remarried Harriett Bernard, Aunt Annie had discreetly retired to a little house in Ross. Then they had been living in the busy town centre rectory nearby, but in 1910, Father had paid the grand architects, Nicholson & Hartree, to make more rooms for the family in the roof of the parish vicarage at Bridstow, just outside Ross. Although the rooms were a little smaller than at any of their former homes, it was easier to manage now the boys were at school. Evie loved her new bedroom under the eaves, where she could hear the swallows tweedling to each other in summer. Father's responsibilities changed regularly within the diocese, but there in Bridstow they settled and remained. The vicarage had a lovely orchard, a vegetable plot, a small walled rose garden and views across Ross to the distant blue hills beyond.

When visiting Aunt Annie in times past, each of the girls liked to feel she had returned to the nursery for a few moments. Aunt Annie would fuss around them, commenting on their clothes and hairstyles. Maud still cut all their thick dark hair, including her own, out of habit rather than economy.

Evie was wearing a new winter coat that day. Father seldom understood the need for new clothing but had finally agreed when he saw her long arms were protruding a good few inches beyond the sleeves of her old blue wool, worn until it was threadbare. Often in the past she had worn hand-me-downs as she was the smallest of the three sisters, but Maud and Etty were bigger-boned and their clothing so often swam on her. Evie relished her fine new black coat with its little silk collar and matching felt hat. She still somehow wanted to show it off, imagining Aunt Annie throwing up her hands and saying that Evie looked like a Russian princess as she had been wont to do. When she glanced in a mirror, which was seldom, Evie did sometimes fancy that her eyes and cheekbones looked somewhat Slavic.

The sisters' juvenile mood had lasted, prompted by the crisp glitter of the winter air. They had enjoyed a glass of warming ginger beer in the thin sunshine outside the White Lion, then played the pine-cone race under the bridge with two dry cones. Maud had found these at the bottom of the pocket in her own worn winter coat (she collected such natural bounty for Sunday School activities). The cones had left behind papery shed seeds that the sisters scattered together on the water, watching them flutter and land like little brown insects. The sisters wondered aloud if they were planting a new pine forest somewhere along the Wye's meandering banks. As it was so cold, they had accepted a lift with a carter they knew, up the road to Wilton. From there they continued on foot, swinging their baskets and singing a hymn or two to keep warm.

Visiting Aunt Annie's grave would fulfil their obligation to tell Father of a Good Work of some kind that night. They invariably found something to describe over dinner, because they had been brought up by Father and by Mother, Aunt Annie and now their kindly stepmother Harriett, to fill every waking moment with beneficial activity. The girls might be beginning to spread their wings beyond the Rectory, but this too needed to be in a direction towards which Edward Winnington-Ingram would approve.

Etty was more bookish than the others. Two years ago she had obtained a First Class Honours degree in English from the University of London, one of the first women in the country to do so. She was often away teaching. Maud and Evie accepted that the bulk of the household chores and parish duties would now fall to them. Maud with the lighter heart, as she seemed to thrive on the needs of others, whereas Evie felt differently; but she kept this to herself. If only Mary were there to talk to, but Mary was now a married woman, a thousand miles and more away in India.

Days like this, when they made up an excuse to go out and enjoy a walk from home, were an exception. Walking for pleasure was something they had undertaken with enthusiasm only on their annual family summer holiday in Wales. All six of them, plus Kate their parlour maid, would board a train and enjoy the changing landscape as it chugged towards Llanfairfechan, where they took a boarding-house. It was a wonderful place to holiday, with opportunities for sea bathing and exploring the hills around Snowdon. They were fit and lithe and loved to climb the great mountain, even Arthur, whom they took it in turns to carry or support when his legs failed him. *Mens sana in corpore sana*, Father would say, and he was right, for dear Arthur was growing stronger and they no longer feared for his health. He had left home last autumn to follow in father's footsteps and was now doing well at the school at Hereford Cathedral.

That morning Maud and Evie had no real need to idle into the town to fetch eggs for Cook, but each had felt the call of the frosty out-of-doors. 'Days like this smell of snow,' Evie had said as they left the house.

They had hatched their plot over breakfast. Father had left early for a long morning's meeting at the Cathedral. Harriett was out on her parish rounds. It did not take long for Evie to talk Maud out of the pile of Sunday School marking (too inviting outside!) and the turning of the compost heap (too smelly!) that should have been the morning's chores. To their delight, Father had left them a little of his bacon in the silver warmer, which they savoured. Etty was still asleep, having doubtless stayed awake again into the wee small hours writing some rant or other for one of her women's journals. Without discussion, her sisters decided that this time there was not quite enough bacon for three.

It really had been a blissful morning. Evie would remember that later, how perfect it had all been, as if it were a gift from God in advance of the sorrows to follow.

The girls approached home, relishing the winter sunshine on their faces, carrying their baskets: the eggs in Maud's and freshly-made winter marmalade from the market in Evie's. The postman passed them heading back for the town, pushing his bicycle. He doffed his cap, commented on the weather and pulled his muffler more tightly around his neck.

As Maud and Evie approached, the front door burst open and Etty ran out to the top step between the clipped yews, which she always referred to as the yew-topiary, waving something white in her hand. 'I say, Evie!' she called cheerfully. 'Letter from India! Oh, and by the way, sisters mine, you didn't leave me one scrap of Father's bacon. That really is the absolute limit, you know. I could even smell it.'

Evie, snug in her woollen coat, grinned with delight. On the day of Mary and Tom's wedding just over a year ago, it had been so very hot. She had been relieved to change out of her unwieldy hat and ridiculous, fussy dress back into her usual comfortable clothing; but so very sad to wave her dear Mary goodbye as the carriage and pair carried her away from the reception. She could still see her little hand gloved in white satin waving and waving until the carriage had turned the corner by the rectory at Fladbury. Two days later, Mary and Tom had set sail on the *Sicilia*, bound for Calcutta.

Mary's letters from India took several weeks to arrive. They were always funny and full of detail but never long enough for Evie. The last had told how Mary's husband Tom loved horses and that she was learning to ride. Mary described his patience and her own ineptitude with affection. Many men might have preferred a noisy and smelly new motor-car, which were now becoming fashionable everywhere, even in India, but not Tom. He also liked to eat oddly-spiced food with strange names and could speak several Indian languages, as well as a bit of French and even some German. Evie added these quirks to the list of reasons she had already decided upon for disliking him – he ate strange things and he had been born in India. Why, he was virtually a native!

Tom's linguistic abilities and exotic tastes in food had however impressed Father no end. For some time after they had received Mary's letter detailing such exotic fare, he had taken to asking Cook to prepare kedgeree for breakfast every Sunday morning. Cook was outraged, but compliant. The girls swallowed it because it was food, but preferred Father's bacon when they could get it.

Father had once told Evie that vivacious Mary reminded him a little of their mother, Bessie, when she had been young.

Evie's letters from Mary were always to be savoured alone at first, then shared. They offered a glimpse of a doubly exotic world, which all the sisters acknowledged they were never likely to experience: that of India, with its colours and heat and dust, and that of marriage, with all its unattractive duties. No-one ever came courting the three Winnington-Ingram girls. They were known to be clever but rather peculiar, and people knew that most of the family money was long gone. There was no likelihood of their being considered beauties, either. And, without beauty, few men would wish to marry a wife more intelligent than he was.

Maud and Etty cheerfully espoused the new term 'blue-stocking' and with it a more independent destiny. Evie was less certain of her own path. In secret she still hoped to become a concert pianist, although Father was unlikely to approve of such a flighty choice. Perhaps Harriett might talk him round one day.

Evie hung her new coat on the coat-stand, took the letter from Etty and looked down at the envelope. There was a moment of utter stillness that all three sisters felt as a kind of shiver between them, as though the temperature in the hall had plummeted even further. Then Evie was into the library, the door not quite slammed, but certainly shut firmly behind her. Maud and Etty sensed rather than heard the old key turn in its well-oiled lock.

'Etty,' said Maud, slowly. 'Did you notice if that letter was definitely from Mary? Could it have been from someone else?'

Etty shook her head. 'All I noticed was the pretty stamp for Arthur's collection. No, I am not completely certain it was addressed in Mary's hand.'

Inside the library, Evie had started to play. *Die Jagd.* Her noisiest Beethoven. She played it when distressed. Maud wondered how long she would play for. Father was due to return in about an hour and he could not bear that piece. She wondered what to do for the best. Door-banging and locking oneself in were more Etty's talents than Evie's: her younger sister had never behaved in this manner before.

She handed Etty both baskets and told her to take them down to Cook. Maud watched Etty go, poor thing, sniffing and rubbing her eyes with the back of her hand. The cleverest of them all, Maud reflected, and yet she often showed no common sense whatsoever. Etty was Cook's favourite, so Cook would reassure and comfort her. And perhaps there was no real cause for concern? There had been no black border to the letter that she had noticed. Perhaps Mary was simply indisposed, and Tom had written the address and posted it for her? Perhaps she could even be expecting their first child. Could that be it? Gently Maud tried the big oak handle of the drawing-room door. It was still locked from the inside.

Maud went back out of the front door. She was pleased to see that Kate had left one of the high library windows ajar to air the room: the smoke often drifted a little when the fire was first lit. Hitching up her skirts as though she were again climbing a tree, just as she had enjoyed in childhood, she scrambled over the clipped box under the windows, feeling a sharp twig rip through her petticoat and scratch her leg. She sighed. More mending for Kate later.

Evie's back was to the window and she saw nothing of her elder sister's arrival until Maud landed in a heap on the polished wooden floor. The playing stopped, but only for a moment, and then resumed. The noise was deafening, but had Beethoven not been going deaf when he composed the piece? No wonder Father hated it, even though he was now hard of hearing too. Maud got to her feet and picked some pieces of box from her skirt. She could see the letter from India placed alongside the music.

'Evie dear?'

No response and, again, the playing barely faltered. Maud approached, slid in beside Evie on the second piano-stool. Sometimes they would play silly Strauss duets like the *Tritsch-Tratsch Polka*, Evie's skilled fingers releasing the sparkling upper line, Maud thumping away doggedly at the bass chords. Not today.

Maud took the letter and examined it. 'Evie!' she said in frustration. 'For goodness' sake! You haven't even opened it.'

Evie, looking dead ahead, stopped playing, her hands held in the air above the keys. 'I can't.' she said. 'I simply can't, Maudie. I think something has happened to Mary. That's not her handwriting. So it must be from Tom.'

'Surely if something were wrong, Tom would have written to Father, not you?'

Evie shook her head. 'Mary's Tom didn't spend much time with Father at all. He had to leave the wedding party early, do you recall, because of some Parish business? I was Evie's bridesmaid. I am her closest friend. He knows that. But why write at all? I can only think of one reason.' Maud looked more closely. The writing was cramped and dense and very black. The envelope had the letters PUANCO embossed in the paper. Otherwise there was no clue as to its contents.

Maud shivered, but her common sense took over. 'Now, look here. We're both being ridiculous. Mary was quite well when she last wrote. She might easily have given Tom the letter to address and post from his office in Calcutta. Puanco, see? That's where he works, I am sure of it.'

'Will you open it instead? Open it for me, Maudie?'

Maud held the letter, looking down at it, frowning. Then she pulled out the heavy *chatelaine* she still wore around her waist whenever their stepmother was absent and opened the tiny mother-of-pearl paperknife to slit the envelope neatly. She eased out the single folded sheet within and began to read. Evie watched in silence.

Maud felt her throat constrict and her eyes fill. She raised her face to Evie's and shook her head, words failing her. Evie held her gaze for a moment then walked to the door and unlocked it in silence. Maud heard Evie's footsteps die away as she walked upstairs to her room.

Maud read the letter twice, not wanting to believe its wretched contents. Then she heard the front door and Father's familiar voice boom: 'Girls?' Maud remembered then that Harriett, their stepmother, was taking luncheon elsewhere. Harriett might have known what to say or do.

Maud went to take his coat. She would have to tell Father and was at a loss as to how to put what she had just read into words. In the end, she chose to tell him that they had received some very sad news from India and handed him the letter.

Father placed the letter to one side of his plate and ate his lunch, slowly, chewing each mouthful more times than was strictly necessary.

He and Maud were alone, Etty eating in the kitchen and Evie upstairs, staring at her bedroom wall as though it too could shatter into a million fragments in an instant.

Father dabbed his mouth with his napkin and told Maud all about his morning's trying meeting, how the rural dean was a fool, and the bishop little better. They could save a king's ransom in diocesan finances if they only followed everything he recommended, but would they? Maud made sympathetic noises and waited.

The letter, Father, she thought, as he started to cut his apple into neat, even segments. Please read the letter now! Once he had swallowed his last bite, Edward Winnington-Ingram did, at last, pick up the envelope. Like Maud, he read it twice. Then he cleared his throat. 'Dear me. Poor Tom,' he said.

Poor *Tom*? thought Maud.

'I shall write to him today to express our deepest sympathies.' He paused, shaking his head. 'Awful business. I shall add some words of comfort from scripture. Can… can you think of anything particularly suitable, Maud? Something from Lamentations, perhaps?' Maud knew he too was deeply upset. It was just that he had a limited capacity for showing it.

She considered her vast store of useful phrases during parish visits in the event of a bereavement. 'Song of Solomon 8:6?' she suggested. 'You could paraphrase the first part?'

Her father nodded sombrely. 'Yes, that will serve. Thank you, my dear, as always.'

Yes, thought Maud, for 8:6 continues with 'Jealousy is cruel as the grave: the coals thereof are coals of fire, which has a most vehement flame.' And perhaps that was appropriate too. Poor Evie.

She was about to clear their plates – Cook would have her work cut out with comforting Etty – when Father reached across the corner of the oak dining-table and caught her hand. 'Will you see to Evie, Maud? And Etty? They did both love little Mary so. I do wish your mother were here.' Father seldom mentioned his first wife since he had remarried. Touched by this rare and unusual gesture, Maud placed her other hand over his and squeezed it tight. 'Of course I shall, Father,' she promised, more resolutely than she felt. She watched him rise from the table and go into his study carrying the letter among the other papers, closing the door behind him. She thought he looked a little stooped, somehow aged by the news the letter had imparted.

Later, after dinner, she would gather both her sisters into her own bed and they would cuddle together like little wrens in winter, just as they had done soon after Mother had died: Evie would be red-eyed, silent and wretched, Etty dismal and vocal. Then and only then, when they could hold each other tightly and absorb the shock between them, would Maud reveal what little Tom Westmacott had told them of how he had come to kill their beloved cousin.

# 7

# Just Another Day at the Office

CALCUTTA, INDIA
JULY 1914

Tom Westmacott had been a partner in the respected Calcutta legal firm everyone knew as Puanco for almost 20 years. Pugh and Company worked within the Indian Civil Service and the Law Courts in Calcutta. Their other clients were generally drawn from the great and the good, as well as any of the bad willing to pay them handsomely for their services. Pugh seldom turned down any client with money.

Pugh's original partner had died of malaria some years previously and Pugh, lieutenant-colonel of the Calcutta Light Horse, had seen an ideal successor in the young, bright and ambitious Tom Westmacott. The fellow had good languages, a nice easy manner with his clients. Moreover, he was a superb horseman and would be an asset to his cavalry regiment. Westmacott had also attended Rugby, a decent school, so he arrived with some well-placed contacts. And he was cheap, which Pugh appreciated. You never had to pay these Indian-born Englishmen quite as much as you did those fresh off the boat, whose expectations were higher.

On his part, Tom had at first been elated with his Puanco partnership and had worked very hard. He had considered himself a confirmed bachelor, married to the law. The impact of meeting Mary unexpectedly in England, on a visit to see his ailing, feckless father just before he died, was all the more colossal. Tom and Mary had fallen hopelessly in love in record time.

What a happy day their wedding at Fladbury had been, even if the service had dragged on, to accommodate roles for the family's many priests. Mary's four bridesmaids had looked like giant meringues in their cream dresses and hats. Tom noticed that one of them, Mary's cousin, Evelyn Winnington-Ingram, appeared to sulk throughout beneath the brim of her hat. He had barely seen her face. Perhaps she did not like her attire. She certainly did not suit it. A strange, rather plain girl, who had hardly addressed a word to him at the reception, either.

His beloved bride had outshone all her bridesmaids, of course. Mary's billowing brown hair, which would seldom stay beribboned or pinned for long, was constantly threatening to escape from beneath her delicate veil. His heart contracted as she walked up the aisle, so slender on the arm of her stout old father; her smiling face fixed on Tom's, her brown eyes brimming with joy.

Archie Pugh's legendary temper had been much easier for Tom to endure when there was Mary to share it with later as a funny story.

Now Tom thought of Puanco as a hole in which he rotted.

It was not as though he could even remember actively choosing to become a solicitor. It had just happened. Tom had watched his Rugby peers veer off into different and more interesting professions. Many had family estates to run, of course. This was not the case with his own strange familial blend of church and the arts, as most of his forebears had been either priests or sculptors. Sometimes Tom had found himself watching Mary as she slept, wondering how he would render her soft curves in white clay or a block of marble. Mary had joked that there was more artistry in his soul than Tom would ever care to admit. Especially to the likes of Archie Pugh.

Some of his friends chose the traditional second-son route of the Church, but Tom knew himself too sceptical for that. He had grown up familiar with churches, *gurdwaras*, *mandirs* and *mosques* in equal measure and had a great deal more respect for other religions than would be seemly in a Christian priest. Many of his peers had joined the army but Tom's poor eyesight had ruled out a permanent military position.

Now Tom was just going through the motions of caring about the law: winning some cases, losing others, an average sort of lawyer, neither very good nor very bad. He was a disappointingly lacklustre partner for the fiery Welshman Pugh, who had had such high hopes of the young man before that dubious business with his wife.

Tom now relied on routine to get him through the week. Monday to Friday he rose at six and ate a breakfast of tea and kedgeree prepared by Mehitabel, his elderly servant. He then, reluctantly, boarded the electric tram for the Esplanade, where their practice was located on the first, second and third floors of an ugly modern block. Tom and Pugh's offices were on the marginally cooler third floor, with their senior Indian staff on the second and the clerks and servants at hotter, dustier street level.

Puanco was located close to the Whiteway Laidlaw department store in bustling central Calcutta. He had enjoyed taking Mary there once to buy a new gown for a Lady's Day event with the regiment. She had turned heads, he remembered with a grimace, bobbing through the crowd in her froth of pretty lace. Why had he not also accompanied her to Bourne & Shepherd for a decent likeness of them together? All he had of her now was their crowded wedding photograph and the papier-maché elephant and tiger. And Daisy.

Tom would walk for an hour at lunchtime to loosen his limbs after sitting at his desk for so long and buy a *puri* from one of the vendors along the Esplanade. Some of the more fashionable Europeans would look at him curiously as he ate his spicy lunch in neat bites and chatted with the stallholder in Hindi or Bengali. On darker days, he would take his food and consume it alone in the shade of the Shaheed Minar, looking up at its lofty balconies, while children played happily below them.

And would then return to his desk at the appointed hour. The afternoon was divided into two by tiffin; hot strong tea and something sweet to eat provided by Devesh Bosu. Then another grinding hour or two and home, sometime before seven. Mehitabel would have left him a chafing dish of curry and some fruit, which he would eat before reading a little (Kipling featured prominently in his library). Then he would retire to the small bed in the little spare guest-room. Too many memories haunted the larger room he had shared with Mary.

For some time, Tom had continued to ride Golden Rod, his hunter, down to the office from his home on the outskirts of Calcutta. On the day Rod was clipped by a careless truck it became clear that this increasingly modern city was no place for his horse. Vile trams, trucks and motor cars could now screech and grind around any street corner when you were least expecting it. The air blared with their horns and stank of fuel and rubber tyres.

Saturdays and Sundays were better than working days, as Tom could leave the grime of Calcutta behind him and take the train to greener

Midnapore where he now stabled his beloved horses, including his polo pony Champa. Mary had named Champa when Tom told her he liked to call his horses after flowers. The creamy-coloured magnolia, which bloomed against their house, suited the little pale mare, who could turn on sixpence for polo or tent-pegging. He soon bought a slightly smaller horse, a docile young chestnut mare on which Mary could learn to ride. She had called her Daisy and liked to stick a daisy or marigold into her bridle when she rode her.

Tom would often hunt wild boar with the regiment and occasionally a tiger. The Calcutta Light Horse would keep the peace (the regimental motto was 'defence not defiance'), drill the *sowars*, play polo, challenge for tent-pegging trophies. Some reservists would drink and often to excess, Pugh among them, but Tom seldom joined them. His friends knew he struggled with a demon of a different kind and generally kept conversation to small talk about horses.

His third-floor office window looked out towards the silken Hoogly, with its jostling and fragrant boats laden with fish or spices. Before, he had barely ever glanced out at this vibrant view, so intent had he been on his work. He had always been so proud to tell Mary how he had solved such-and-such a case with a brilliant observation or piece of research, eager for praise and further promotion from Pugh. And she would laugh that laugh and smile that smile and all would be well, however hard his day.

Now Tom found himself staring out of the window a good deal more. He was doing this, lost in thought, when Devesh Bosu's footsteps approached his door. The old fellow was shakier on his feet than he had been a few years ago. Tom could hear the whole tinkling one-man-band of his solemn person plus a tea tray negotiate the uneven landing. He knocked, then entered.

Tom was determined not to look up. Pugh had departed early to go to the club, setting Tom the task of preparing the latest overdue prosecution case against Jabbar Lal. Tom did not want to engage in another awkward chinwag with Devesh Bosu that night.

The tray contained Tom's usual white porcelain cup and saucer, a slightly battered tin teapot and a cracked sugar basin with silver tongs protruding. Few Indian-born Englishmen took milk in their tea, as it curdled so fast in the heat.

'Your *chai*, *sahib*?' Tom nodded and thanked the old man but remained head bowed, brow furrowed, pencilling notes into the margin of a document already criss-crossed with corrections. He gestured to Devesh Bosu to place the tray on the only corner of the desk not occupied by the tattered bundles of writs and testimonies, some of them yellowing with age. Tom could still feel Devesh Bosu's eyes on him. The old man was clearly not going to budge.

'Sahib, there is a telegram. From England.'

That got Tom's attention all right. 'When did it come?'

Devesh Bosu smiled. 'This afternoon, sahib.' The two men held each other's gaze for a moment. Each knew the other to be perfectly aware that the standing instruction at Puanco was that any telegram, incoming or outgoing, had to be personally sanctioned or read by Pugh. But Pugh had left the office.

Devesh Bosu cleared this throat for the lie. 'I am sorry, sahib. The boy brought it just after lunch. I was busy making tea for Colonel Pugh sahib. I placed the envelope to one side and forgot to take it to Colonel Pugh sahib in time.'

Tom smiled inwardly. 'Well, he will be downing a *chota peg* at the Royal Calcutta by now.'

'Indeed, sahib. And the telegram is addressed to you personally, is it not?'

There was the buff envelope in Devesh Bosu's outstretched hand. Tom wondered how much he knew about the contents and sighed. Probably everything. There was little confidentiality about the central telegraph office of Calcutta and Devesh Bosu had family in every dim corner of this vast city and far beyond. Just as Devesh Bosu would have known precisely what the outgoing telegram, sent without Pugh's knowledge, had asked of his father-in-law.

For a moment, they both listened to Pugh's garrulous grandfather clock on the landing chiming the hour. Tom then took the envelope, slit it open crisply with his ivory paper-knife, slid out and unfolded the telegram. He read:

Indian Telegraphs

WESTMACOTT PUANCO CALCUTTA

CAPTAINS COMMISSION OFFERED WORCESTERSHIRE YEOMANRY

LAWSON

Although he had asked for this, there was still a fleeting moment of shock. As a captain? When he was a major? That was strange. He read it twice more, digesting its implication. It was real. His escape route from Pugh, from Puanco, from India. From the shadow of Mary.

He looked up at Devesh Bosu.

'Yes, sahib?'

'If I wished to get to England as soon as possible, how would I best go about it?'

Devesh Bosu nodded, having come prepared. The tickets were already under the teapot. 'Yes, sahib. The mail train leaves Howrah Junction at ten past midnight tomorrow. It gets to the Ballard Pier Mole in Bombay on Friday morning. The next available mail steamer leaves on the first tide at nine o'clock. Peninsula & Orient, sahib. The *Arabia*. Your tickets are all here, ready, you see?'

Devesh Bosu stood patiently waiting as the younger man, whom he had known since he was a little boy playing in the streets of Purnea, stared back at him. Tom was reflecting on a very awkward conversation he had had only days before with Pugh about Page, one of the office juniors. Page had been bold and foolhardy enough to test the waters on how Pugh might feel about his staff volunteering for immediate military service in France. The response had been unenthusiastic, to put it mildly, as their departure would not be in the interests of one Colonel Archibald Pugh.

Pugh had confided in him afterwards that he thought Page might well abscond.

Devesh Bosu knew Tom was deciding whether or not to run for it. And it was high time, in his opinion, that Tom did so. It had been presumptuous of him to acquire the tickets, of course, but he knew the trains would be fully booked. One of his many regular Puanco duties involved the reservation of tickets, so he had been able to pull a few strings. Without the tickets, he thought, the man he knew both as Westmacott sahib and as the boy Tomulloo would never escape his past, or his present.

'I have just – goodness! – just a day, then?'

Ah, thought Devesh Bosu. There it was. A bright, alert expression in Tom's eyes that he had not seen for some years. He watched approvingly as his major-sahib stood up. Then looked down again. 'But this, Devesh. All this.' Tom gestured helplessly to the huge pile of papers that spilled over the edges of his desk. 'I have my responsibilities here.'

'Tomulloo.' Devesh Bosu had not been so familiar with him for years. 'Tomulloo sahib, listen to old Devesh Bosu who must now guide you as he would guide his own son. If you work with Colonel Pugh sahib for five minutes more, or five days, or five weeks, or five years, Jabbar Lal will still be cheating his fool of a Maharajah, and Colonel Pugh sahib will still be making money from it. You know in your heart that this is so. There is nothing left for you here.'

Tom removed his glasses, reddening, and polished the lenses with Mary's little handkerchief.

The old man persisted, 'If you delay, it will be too late. You may not get away. The time is right. India has taken enough from you. Go home to England. Find a new start. But first prepare yourself for the struggle ahead.'

Tom stood, and turned his back on the old man, gazing out across the Hoogly as if seeing it for the first time. He was not sure what exactly he could expect to find in England, but the Lawsons had always been kind. 'What will you tell Colonel Pugh if I go?'

Devesh Bosu stretched out his hands, palms down, fingers spread, and laughed. 'I will tell him that you went home early, looking flushed and feverish, which is the plain truth of it, sahib. He will imagine you are sick and curse you for a slacker, but then he will think nothing of your being absent from work tomorrow.'

'Devesh Bosu, you will get into trouble.' A statement they both knew to be all too true.

The old man shrugged, then shook his head. 'Major Westmacott sahib will be on the steamer crossing the *Kala Pani* by then, and that is the most important thing,' he said. 'And Colonel Pugh sahib understands how useful old Devesh Bosu is to him, here in Calcutta. Oh, yes, once he finds out, he will be furious, but I believe he needs me too much to send me away entirely. And even if he did, I am old now, sahib, perhaps it is time I stopped making so much tea, *né?*'

There was silence for a while, then, in barely a whisper: 'The horses.'

'Sahib, if you wish, I will look after your fine horses until your return.' Both men knew he might never do so. Devesh Bosu paused and said, 'Permit an old man to give you a word of advice?'

Tom turned from the window to look at him, forlorn.

'Sahib, I think you must take your horses. They will be a comfort to you where you are going. I already secured two transport chits, just in case.' And he had paid a ridiculous amount of money to bring about a mysterious double-booking for those two stalls. He would make sure the bill was well buried within the Puanco receipts. 'There were no more to be had. Many are leaving in haste for England. You must choose two out of your three horses.' Tom nodded. It was obvious. He would take Rod and Champa, leaving Daisy and the memories she carried behind in India.

Devesh Bosu continued, 'The war is coming. I think soon they will take cavalrymen from India too. They will not like their local officers leaving willy-nilly in this way. So, I give my advice to you as to my own son. Do not wear your officer's uniform, Tomulloo, and do not mention the regiment, or the war, as you travel to Bombay, and even beyond.'

Tom swallowed hard. He walked quickly around the desk, took Devesh Bosu's hand in both his own and shook it. 'Thank you, old friend,' he said in Hindi. 'You are right, as always. I might have travelled in my uniform and got turned back at the port, like a complete fool.'

'And now, sahib, you must go! You have only a day. There is much to do.' With that, Devesh Bosu slid the tickets and livestock chits from underneath the teapot and carefully placed them beneath the papier-mâché elephant on Tom's desk, so the ceiling fan would not blow them away. He then lifted his precious tea-tray, decorated with the face of the elderly Queen Victoria, and was gone.

Tom ran a hand through his hair, surveying his chaotic desk one last time. Then he turned and took his coat from the old mahogany coat-stand by the window, pulling his arms into its sleeves. Picking up the tickets and chits, he popped the little papier-mâché tiger and elephant, his ivory paper-knife and a few other personal items into his pockets and prepared to turn his back on 10, Old Post Office Street, Calcutta, possibly forever.

A day and a half later, word reached Archie Pugh that Tom was not in bed with a fever and had in fact boarded the night train for Bombay the previous day. To take off like this after the discussion they had just had about Page! It was beyond the pale. Pugh was livid and ranted at Devesh Bosu, as was predicted, for some time. Afterwards, the Welshman left the office in a hurry and went directly to the government buildings whereupon the Government of India no less (in the person of Pugh's crony Hazelmere) sent an urgent telegram to ensure that Major Thomas Westmacott should be stopped before he boarded the steamer for England.

Unfortunately, the little telegram boy had eaten no breakfast and enjoyed a *keema naan* paid for with some coins provided by a cousin of Devesh Bosu's. When the lad did finally turn up at the pier, he found that the steamer was just pulling away from the port.

Once it became clear that Tom was gone for good, Pugh, being Pugh, opted to make the best of it. Westmacott had been poor company in recent times in any case. He knew from their days in the regiment together that his younger partner had owned a few nice horses, but when he sent to Midnapore via Devesh Bosu, the old man informed him that two of the three had vanished, and no-one knew whither; he assumed that Tom had taken them. If that were the case, Pugh was mystified as to why Tom had left behind Champa. Tom's superb polo pony was the most valuable of all three. Once he was certain that Tom was gone for the duration, he sold her on to another polo champion for a very pretty sum. No-one dared question his authority to do so.

As Tom had not had much time to do anything other than lock the front door of his small house in the outskirts of Calcutta, Pugh also decided that he, as Tom's senior partner and *ipso facto* employer, would have to take matters in hand. Much to old Mehitabel's distress, as Tom had left her some money and a set of keys to keep an eye on the place, Pugh had one of his men break in and change the locks, 'as a security measure,' or so he claimed.

The house was profitably let within months.

If Pugh ever heard from that damned Westmacott again, he would give him short shrift.

# 8

# All Her Own

Seven years on from the infamous Mud March, Evie sat in the library at Bridstow vicarage, one hand on the keys, picking out the tune of the stirring suffragette hymn she had sung with Mary that day. Aunt Laura's piano had just about survived the move up from Ross. Three of the top keys remained obstinately sharp, in spite of the best efforts of nice Mr Turner, the piano-tuner. Rather than not play at all, Evie avoided these notes, lending her music an oddly staccato rhythm to those few who could hear her. The plangent piece was complete for Evie herself, as she could hear the gaps at the correct pitch in her head.

The suffrage movement, on which she had briefly pinned her hopes for a purposeful life, seemed to be getting on famously without her services. Evie now counted herself as a moderate and progressive suffragist rather than among the more extreme suffragettes. Miss Fox had remained true to 'The Cause' and had even daringly chained herself to the railings at the House of Commons. She was said to have narrowly escaped arrest. Inwardly, Evie still secretly thought it all rather thrilling.

Miss Fox had told Evie that there had been over 15,000 people, men as well as women, at the last march, five times as many as at the first. Would all that progress soon be swept away by the impending conflict?

Last Tuesday, the villagers had gathered in the church to hear Father read the declaration of war. People had been braced for the news for some months and as soon as the bell had started to toll, they obeyed its call. Father repeated Mr Asquith's stirring words from the pulpit and then led them all in heartfelt prayers for victory. Presumably the Germans were offering up prayers of their own, thought Evie, wondering whether Saint Bridget, to whom the little church was dedicated, would approve or disapprove. Etty had told Evie with relish that Saint Bridget was not a proper saint at all, but some kind of pagan fire goddess.

Father was now solemnly invoking Saint Bridget to come to their aid. Evie had long ceased to believe that prayer was quite as straightforward as people seemed to think, especially since losing Mary. Even if she were rejoicing in a blessed afterlife of some kind, as the scriptures taught, no amount of prayer to Saint Bridget or any other saint or deity would ever bring Mary back.

And now there was to be more death, it appeared, this time on a global scale.

Her mind wandered in shock, from the sickly perfume of the lilac by the altar to the sun slanting in through the stained glass, catching all the motes of dust and turning them to gold. That was how she felt, a tiny speck adrift in the fierce August heat of a rapidly changing world.

It felt incredible to Evie that after so much threat and strutting and posturing, the men who ruled were at last girding their loins for war. There had been the assassination of the heir to the Austro-Hungarian Empire, the Archduke Franz Ferdinand. Father had read it all aloud from *The Times*, shaking his head about the state of the Balkans. Maud and Evie had then tried and failed to locate Sarajevo on Father's old globe, with its comforting crimson swathes of a British Empire now much diminished. Etty pointed out the Balkans later when she got back from Cheltenham. Everyone seemed to be forgetting, she pointed out, that the archduke's young wife had been murdered too, and what harm could that unfortunate woman ever have done to anybody?

It all seemed a long way away and rather meaningless, and yet was being used as the excuse for bloodshed. So many men they knew talked of little else, their own brothers included.

Neither of the boys had grown into robust men, and Arthur still had difficulty walking, especially when the weather was damp and the wind was from the east. 'Teddy is just about silly and brave enough to join up anyway,' Maud had observed. 'I shall ask Father to have a word to remind him that his first duty must be to his parish.'

Standing on the threshold of war, Evie felt a sweeping sense of frustration about her life. She could not express it, even to her sisters. The past years had already been so unkind: she had been only seven when they had lost their mother; and Harriett Bernard, the sweet-natured stepmother she had grown to love, had died suddenly just two years ago. Episodes of rheumatic fever during Evie's childhood had left her with stiff joints and strange aches and pains. And she was plain.

Worst of all, Mary was gone, and that had been such a terrible and sudden shock. She was fond of Mary's sister Grace, of course, but she was 'a bit of a Holy Joe,' as Etty put it bluntly. The other one, Ruth, now a sister at the Anglican nunnery in Wantage, had taken the veil in her agony of loss. Evie loved her own sisters with all her heart too, of course, but neither had ever had quite the same sense of daring fun as Mary.

At the time of the Mud March in 1907, neither Mary nor Evie had ever dreamed of marrying anyone. Instead they had enjoyed many earnest conversations about the absurdity of women being denied the same liberties as men. 'Why shouldn't it be we who propose, Mary?' asked Evie in frustration one day when a friend in Ross, half as intelligent but twice as beautiful as either of the cousins, had announced her engagement to a local worthy. Neither Evie nor Mary had serious expectations of a proposal, but it was fun to discuss it.

'In any case, Evie,' Mary had giggled, 'whoever wanted permission would have to brave our fathers. Just picture it. The voice from the study booming 'enter'! Yours would terrify him, and mine would render him unconscious with a long reading from the Book of Job.'

Evie, encouraged by Maud and Etty, had followed them to Cheltenham Ladies' College, endured the institution for a few trying months and then come home again. It was Mary who had understood her sense of failure and who had comforted her. Evie had loved Mary – not in the same intense way that Etty loved some of her female companions, which both her sisters accepted – but as a true kindred spirit and confidante.

Then one day there had been two vivid red spots on Mary's cheeks and a sparkle in her eyes that Evie had never seen before. Her cousin blurted out that she was to marry Tom Westmacott. And live in India. It had all seemed quite out of the blue but as Mary stumbled through her explanation, Evie realised that her best friend had known about her impending engagement for some time and – the horror of it! – had clearly chosen not to tell Evie.

'Oh Mary, are you sure?' Evie had choked back tears. 'He's so old! Do you love him?' Mary had hugged her then. 'Yes, I think I really might. I do find myself thinking of him a good deal. My heart certainly beats faster when he enters the room. He is only nine years older than I am, you know. That's not so very much. And he is very kind to me. She leaned a little closer to Evie and continued in a lower, more urgent voice, 'I am no Charlotte Lucas, Evie. Please, just think. Twenty-six years of Father and the parish. Twenty-six years! I am practically an old maid. Darling girl, don't you think I deserve a little adventure? Oh, no, Evie, no. Please don't cry…'

Later that night, once she had calmed down, Evie tried to persuade herself that in marrying Tom Westmacott, Mary was being most courageous.

Losing her mother so early had made Evie very aware of the less pleasant side to married life. There had been all those half-overheard conversations about the impact on her own mother's health of so many pregnancies: eight children conceived in eight years, of which only five had survived. Etty still maintained that frail little Bessie Anstice had died of neglect. She blamed Father for their mother's death. Evie also thought that was probably why her sister had come to prefer the company of her own sex.

Father had mellowed after his unexpected remarriage. Harriett had proved a real asset to the household. Even Etty, who had sworn initially that she could never ever accept any stepmother, was won over by Harriett's unrelenting practicality and kindness. Under her gentle and loving eye, the girls had become a little more socially adept, learning to dress their hair, choose their clothes more carefully and even make small-talk at parties. Before this intervention, they would joke that Etty's conversation alone meant that no man would survive more than a minute with them without making an excuse to bolt. And now Harriett was gone too, and Father grew more frail and querulous every day.

It was Harriett, shortly before her sudden demise, who had stepped in to have a firm talk to Evie about her attitude towards Mary's engagement. And so of course Evie had sought out Mary and embraced her, then assured her that she thought it all quite marvellous, and that she would write almost every day. She made suitably bright comments about elephants and maharajas and servants. Both knew Evie was lying, but it was necessary.

Evie had then endured the wedding, a dry affair with five priests in the family present, including 'Uncle Arthur Bishop', who had come up from his residence at Fulham Palace to preside. Mary herself admitted she had slightly lost her head when it came to the attire of her bridesmaids. Evie was one of four, all wearing frightfully impractical cream lace and satin and matching vast hats, which the east wind had threatened to remove at any moment as they left the ancient churchyard. She had likened it to walking with a fully-laden tea tray on her head, which made Mary laugh.

Etty had sidled up to Evie at the reception, held in the sheltered and sunny garden of the Rectory in Fladbury, and asked what she thought of Tom. Evie looked over at him, as he chatted politely to some ancient guest or other, with Mary at his side, holding his arm and smiling. Tom was perfectly inoffensive but just so… well, so ordinary. Not dull, that would be too unkind, as he did seem capable of conversation, at least. Tom Westmacott was not particularly handsome, or intelligent, or even particularly tall. How could he – in fact how could any man – be worthy of Mary? And yet this very ordinary fellow had opened up an immense gulf of matrimony between Mary and Evie. It would never be the same now.

Evie could only look down at her feet, the lump in her throat too big to swallow. She did not like the dark and bitter green substance that was seeping into the cracks of her heart.

Etty soon got bored and wandered off again, in search of wedding-cake and another man to alarm.

Sitting at the piano, lost in a past she shared with Mary alone, Evie continued to play soft chords in the key of E-flat minor, which perfectly matched her mood. All the keys had different colours and textures to her; Evie could never understand why others did not feel these too. E-flat minor was an icy, brooding slate-grey.

Today Maud was in the kitchen plotting dinner with Cook, and

Etty had walked into the village to comfort some of the parishioners. She had joined them only last night to play her own part in parish work for as long as she was needed.

Evie preferred to droop over the keyboard and allow her melancholy to flow from her heart down her arms and out through her hands. She was so lost in the music that she did not hear the door open. She started as her sister put down a small wooden tray on top of the piano; it carried two porcelain cups and saucers, a sugar bowl, a milk jug and the old familiar silver teapot muffled in a cosy their own mother had knitted. Then Maud sat beside Evie companionably, letting her play on for a few minutes before placing a sisterly hand over hers.

'Lovely, but eat now, Evie dear,' she instructed, passing her a piece of shortbread sprinkled with sugar crystals, a speciality of Cook's that she knew her sister liked. Maud believed that the solution to any form of melancholia was some good food, a sympathetic ear and firm shoulder. Evie bit into it, feeling its sharp sweetness work its magic. 'I noticed you didn't take breakfast again,' continued Maud. 'You are losing weight. Evie and I can see you are miserable. We all are in this terrible situation. But if you just mope about like this, it makes it far worse for us all. We have to do our duty and keep struggling on.'

'That's all very well, Maudie,' said Evie, rising to look out of the open window. The peaceful scents of warm rosemary and sage drifted into the room. 'I just don't know what to struggle on *with*, precisely. I want to be use-ful, but I feel perfectly use-less.'

Her eldest sister came to stand beside her and passed Evie her cup and saucer. Evie sipped her tea gratefully and continued. 'It's just that I can see you and Etty are going to be marvellous around the parish for however long this beastly war lasts, supporting Father, and Teddy and Arthur too if need be. And you've both got your teaching and there are always new students, even in wartime. But you know I've never been much good at all that. Oh!' she turned to Maud, frowning, 'How I wish I could play the bagpipes! I could be leading Cook's brave boy and the other Seaforth Highlanders into battle!'

Maud smiled. 'I do see your point. No-one is going to be pushing a piano across the battlefield, are they? But there are other ways of helping the war effort. Perhaps you could give a little piano concert in the hall? Or up at Caradoc Court? I am sure Colonel Heywood would agree?'

Evie shook her head. 'That hall piano is agony. It really does sound like it has already taken part in the Charge of the Light Brigade. Even Mr Turner can't put it right – oh goodness, I suppose *he* will join up too, then what will I do? And I really don't want to perform at Caradoc Court either. In fact, I don't want to play the piano at all to raise funds. I am not even sure I agree with this wretched war.'

Maud was not shocked, as the sisters often discussed politics and society, but she quickly voiced her concerns. 'Now listen to me, Evie. Whatever your intellect may tell you, I must insist that you are cautious and do not go around the parish saying such things. Yesterday outside the Post Office there was already talk of tarring and feathering people who were not going to do their duty – Miss Bunce was spouting about it as we left church. Silly woman. I can just see her marching up and down the High Street rattling a tin and handing out white feathers, can't you? You must look supportive, dear, even if in your heart you may not be; for Father's sake, and Uncle Arthur's, as much as anything else. Promise me, Evie?'

Evie nodded, miserably. Duty first, she thought. Always duty.

'I do have one idea, though,' continued Maud. 'I had such an interesting conversation with that nice Miss Fox on Tuesday.' Evie looked guilty, even though it was some years since the notorious Mud March. Her sister pretended not to notice and carried on. 'Miss Fox seems to think this war will be a much more protracted affair than anyone believes.'

'But they're saying it's bound to be over and done with by Christmas?'

'Well, there are those who think otherwise,' sighed Maud. 'Miss Fox is a clever woman and explained her reasoning to me. Although I pray she is wrong, I very much fear she may be right. She foresees the need for many more Red Cross hospitals to cope with the wounded and has already been talking to the War Office about it. She even hopes to start one here. Old Colonel Heywood will probably let her have one of his estate houses, she says. It will be a convalescent home; men will go there to recover from wounds and so forth. Not too onerous I wouldn't think. Making cups of tea, rolling bandages, helping them to write letters and so on. Miss Fox asked if I thought you might consider assisting her. She seems still to hold you in high esteem, for some curious reason.' She was pleased to see a rare smile flit across her youngest sister's features. 'I do hope you will think about it, Evie. I believe that what you need is to find something that is all your own.

You must dare to be different from the rest of us.'

In her mind's eye, Evie was already dressed in a starched, white uniform, drifting between beds like Florence Nightingale as she comforted ailing soldiers. Yes. That was a role she could play. She was stronger than she looked, too. She could lift men, turn them if need be. Perhaps even sing or play to them to cheer them up.

Maud sat down again on the piano stool and tentatively struck up the first few bass chords of Mozart's *Rondo alla Turca* in A major, which they had often practised as a duet in happier times. To her relief, Evie slid in beside her to join in with the top line. As they approached the final brilliant chords, Evie spoke at last, eyes shining. 'It is kind of you to go to so much trouble for me, Maudie.' The last of the notes rippled out through her fingertips. 'I shall go and call on Miss Fox directly.'

Maud gave inward thanks to her Creator.

And with that, Evie brought down the piano lid. The melody continued to resonate long after the door of the library had closed behind them.

# 9

# Invasion

Gaston Derome looked down at the shattered remains of the young English boy in the hospital bed. Marguerite de Montfort had stopped nursing him and now sat quietly beside the lad, holding his limp hand. His lips, bluish and chapped, were moving. He was calling for someone, his mother perhaps. Marguerite bent low and murmured: 'I am here, my dear one. Always here beside you.'

Gaston had not known that she spoke English, and it was almost without an accent. Unlike his own. English had never come easily to him. He had never had good reason to learn. As a rule, unless Gaston Derome could conceive of a use for a skill, he tended not to waste time on it. His busy life was all practicality. His working days were spent in the service of his community and on commerce: from the substantial fertiliser factory that bore his name – *Engrais Derome* was the town's largest employer – to the large family he had created with his much-missed wife, Louise, who had died the previous year.

Now here was a boy almost of an age to be his own son, close to death in a little white bed. Could he imagine Alphonse holding the hand of a strange woman in a foreign land as he lay dying? No, he thought, sadly. It was better not to. At least his dear wife had not been forced to endure these terrible times alongside him. Gaston was certain that she too would have joined her friend Marguerite de Montfort to work at the hurriedly-improvised Red Cross hospital, which Marguerite had now established in the local *collège*.

Only months before, Gaston had felt so proud to welcome the great British General Sir John French into the *mairie*. The general had been such a solid, reliable-looking officer with a confident, firm manner and a handshake to match. His staff and interpreter, a jovial chef named Nougier, seemed to look up to the general greatly, which Derome took as a good sign.

English soldiers had packed the town square. They appeared relaxed, excited and supremely confident. Some soldiers who had brought a fiddle and a mouth organ had started to play little tunes and others were singing along. One danced a jig, the others laughing as they watched.

The little artist from Valenciennes, Lucien Jonas, he of the floppy hair and flamboyant neck-ties, had set up his easel beside the column and was doing a roaring trade in quick individual pastel sketches of the troops. They would make fine keepsakes for their families. Jonas was even producing whole albums of sketches, which could be ordered one day and collected by the client the next. The man must have been working around the clock; but Gaston could see he needed to mine this rich seam while it lasted. It made Bavay feel strangely cosmopolitan, like the Place du Tertre at Montmartre.

General French had told Gaston that morning through an interpreter that he was convinced the Kaiser's bold sally into France was a mere flash in the pan. He reassured Gaston as the Mayor of Bavay that the *Boche* would be rapidly beaten into submission by his own doughty (and yet much smaller, Gaston had observed even then) British Expeditionary Force. The war, such as it was or would ever be, would surely be over by Christmas.

Gaston fervently hoped that General French (surely his name alone made him the right man for the job) was correct. For somewhere in the mists of memory the voice of Père Duriez whispered to remind him that France had been invaded more than once and would be again. And his little town of Bavay was still a strategic junction between main routes close to the Belgian border and risked damage or even annihilation at the hands of any enemy.

The general had been received at the Town Hall with rousing cheers and huzzas. Marguerite de Montfort had presented Gaston with a silk Union Jack flag she had unearthed from somewhere and he had hung it with pride from the balcony. He had drunk a rapid *vin d'honneur* with the Englishmen and offered them some morsels of crisp bread with local Maroilles cheese. Together they had toasted the quick defeat of their mutual enemy.

Then the general had spread out a great map on the uneven surface of the old polished wooden table where so many young Bavay couples had officialised their weddings. The general's staff had gathered round the plan, mangling the names of towns and villages Gaston knew and loved and, as they debated their strategy, he had discreetly withdrawn, closing the door behind.

And now, only weeks later, he had watched the same trucks and troops and mounted cavalry stream back through his town in increasing disarray. The Germans were hard on their heels. The B.E.F. had been outnumbered by about ten units to three, they said. Those units in the rear of the retreat had done all they could to delay the enemy advance but were decimated as a result. Both the retreating and advancing armies had been split by the massive and ancient *Forêt de Mormal* in their path. The woodland fringes where he had so often played as a boy had become a bloodied battleground.

The retreat of *les Anglais* had begun in good order, but rapidly deteriorated into a long straggle of men on foot and on horseback and in any vehicle onto which they could lay their hand. Gaston had witnessed the extraordinary spectacle of a battered London omnibus lumbering through the narrow streets of his town, loaded with sombre-faced troops.

Gaston untied and retrieved the British flag from the balcony overlooking the square and quickly bundled the handful of silk into the back of his desk drawer. It was no time to be displaying that now. Where was the great General French today, he wondered? Already safe and sound somewhere out of harm's way, possibly even over the Channel? Not sweating his life away in a lonely bed in a foreign land, calling for his mother. Gazing out over the now-peaceful town square with its little flowerbeds, it seemed impossible that anything untoward could be happening in Bavay that day. And yet, just yesterday, it was here that Totman had fallen from a lorry, which had taken the corner too fast, only to be crushed by the wheels of another close behind. The lad had probably joined up dreaming of death or glory, but not this kind of end.

Gaston had earlier caught little Louis Delavigne, not yet out of short trousers, boasting about how he was going to bait the Germans when they marched into town by singing the *Marseillaise* with some new words of his own making concerning their parental origins. This was as the English retreat streamed past them. Gaston had picked the boy up by his shoulders and tried to shake sense into him, forbidding him from trying any such foolish trick. Germans were far from stupid in Gaston's experience and invaders were seldom tolerant men.

Gaston's job, as he saw it now, was to try to protect them all and make sure his little community survived what was to come: invasion, conquest, subjugation, deprivation. Even colonisation? Once they arrived, would *les Boches* ever leave?

The Scottish doctor had tried so long and hard to save the young soldier Totman. His other patient, the sapper Ezard, had died of his injuries only the previous day. This doctor had obstinately remained at the boy's side long after his comrades-in-arms had taken the road towards the sea and escape. Gaston and Marguerite de Montfort urged him to leave but the man refused. He spoke little French but led them to believe with words and gestures that as his work there was not yet over, he could not go.

The door of the room opened with a groan and there, impossibly somehow, stood a German officer in his forties in an impeccable grey greatcoat, buttons shining. He then pulled off a leather helmet and gloves, ran one hand through his sparse grey hair, smiled and bowed towards Marguerite and then Gaston. 'You, sir, are the Mayor of Bavay?' he asked Gaston in almost perfect French, pronouncing Bavay with the emphasis on the first a.

'I am he,' replied Gaston, standing up. What now?

Marguerite also rose to her feet and stared at the German officer who, in turn, was looking coolly at the tired Scotsman in his dusty uniform. Unperturbed, he continued to check his young patient's pulse, ignoring the new arrival. Gaston felt a monumental sense of frustration that this dedicated young doctor would now become the first prisoner-of-war taken in Bavay.

The German officer nodded briefly to Gaston and then walked over to the patient's bed. The doctor did not even look up and continued to check Totman's faltering pulse. The new arrival stood to attention and saluted him. 'Barelmann,' he said, by way of an introduction, and continued in passable English, 'My patient, now, I think, *Herr Doktor?*' Gaston and Marguerite exchanged looks of surprise.

The German continued, 'Please. I must explain quickly. They

have sent me here ahead of the others. I came on my... He hesitated for the first time, seeking the right word. '...my *motorrad*.' Seeing their bewildered expressions, he mimicked the revving throttle of a motorbike, then continued. 'Two of my men are downstairs, also. We have our own wounded. We will need fourteen beds. And I shall care for this Englishman as one of our own. I give you my word as a physician.'

The Scots doctor stood up and passed a hand across his eyes. He seemed to sag a little. The German put a firm hand between his shoulder-blades and turned him towards the door with a little push. 'You must move now, my friend. Go. My *kommandant* and his men are only fifteen, perhaps twenty minutes behind.'

Picking up his leather bag the young Scot half smiled, half shrugged at Gaston and Marguerite de Montfort. 'It's still no go, I am afraid,' he said to them all with a brave smile. 'I have no means of getting away. The others have all gone, the transport with them. So, sir,' he continued, turning to face the German, 'You will be taking me as your prisoner after all.'

His German counterpart looked appalled, took a step backwards and shook his head. 'Wait,' said Gaston thinking quickly. 'Can you ride a *vélo*?' Both doctors looked blank. '*Bicyclette*?' continued Gaston, urgently, miming someone pedalling, just as Marguerite uttered the correct English word. The young doctor's face lit up, as did the German's. 'You have a bicycle?' said the Scot. 'Aye, I think I can just about remember how to ride one o' them!'

Taking a piece of paper and a pencil from the desk at the end of the room, Gaston quickly scribbled a rough route for the coast, key village place-names in capitals, bypassing most of the main towns. With luck, the good doctor would get safely away on his son's new vélo. Gaston had borrowed it that morning to pedal up to the hospital. His elder boy Alphonse would not be best pleased, but *tant pis*, it had been rather too large for him anyway. Gaston feared that there would be far worse losses before this war was over.

Gaston saw the young Scot off on the right road. The pleasant enemy doctor did not appear to pose any risk to the virtue of the elderly Marguerite and so Gaston decided not to return upstairs. He wondered what to do next. In the end, he walked back through the town to the mairie to await the other Germans there. Mademoiselle

Brasseur of the brewery in Bavay rattled over the cobbles past him in her carriage. He raised a hand and she nodded at him, even more grim-faced than usual, and with good cause.

She at least had the good sense to return home. He had instructed the other *habitants* to remain indoors but many, he noted with frustration, had disobeyed. Some were loitering out of curiosity, one or two perhaps because they welcomed the turn of events. There was more than one family with German kin living in the area, after all.

As he approached the church, a familiar figure appeared from the opposite direction. Gaston sighed inwardly. Maître Corbeau was not someone he wished to engage with on such a day. The priest had finally relented all those years ago and recommended Gaston for admission to the Institut Industriel de Lille, where Gaston had excelled in both chemistry and engineering. In spite of this grudging capitulation, their relations had never recovered from that momentous day when Gaston had walked out of Maître Corbeau's classroom for ever.

Under normal circumstances, each would have feigned not to see the other. Today, the Abbé Lebrun chose to stop. *'Monsieur le Maire.'*

'Maître?' Gaston could never bear to call him the more formal 'mon Père'. I had only one father, he thought, and now he lies in the town cemetery. Maître Corbeau could never take his place.

He could now see that his former schoolmaster appeared to be trembling slightly. At first, Gaston thought him unwell. Then, as time rolled back thirty years, the Mayor of Bavay realised that his town's priest was in fact furious.

'You are telling people to keep to their houses!' he exclaimed.

Gaston nodded. 'Yes, Maître, until the Germans have taken control. Until we know what is to happen here, it is safer that way for all, especially for the children of the town.' Maître Corbeau was already shaking his head, gesticulating at the church door. 'There!' he said, passionately. 'Can you not understand? That is where all people should be in such a moment. Beseeching their God to have mercy on us all in our hour of need. The Germans will soon be upon us!'

Gaston was in no mood for a theological debate. 'They are here already,' he retorted, watching with some small satisfaction Maître Corbeau's shock at the news. 'A German doctor has just taken over the infirmary. If you are needed anywhere it is there, at the bedside of a dying boy. And have no doubt,' he continued, 'There will be plenty of

Germans in Berlin and Frankfurt and Dusseldorf also at this moment on their knees praying for a German victory. Your God takes sides in war, it would seem.'

Maître Corbeau opened his mouth to respond but Gaston was already striding away towards the mairie. Over his shoulder he shouted, 'I would never prevent anyone from entering your church, Maître. But nor would I encourage it, and especially not today.' Gaston did not see the half-broken look that crossed the priest's face as he turned towards the church door.

Old Madame Hauquier caught Gaston's sleeve as he trudged past the front door of her *estaminet-auberge* with a heavy heart. 'Eh! Monsieur le Maire,' she whispered. 'Come with me, *s'il vous plaît*.' He was slightly surprised and encouraged; if anyone would have been at the church begging the Almighty to save her skin, it would surely have been Madame Hauquier. Perhaps Maître Corbeau was alone in his incense-reeking domain after all, facing row upon row of empty pews. He did not have the heart to rebuff the good lady, and so followed her into the house. Her husband, monosyllabic unless he was drunk, was waiting inside the *bar-salon*. It was invariably Madame who did the talking. Gaston recalled the day when, as a youngster, he had slipped into her garden at the back, intent on stealing an apple or two. She had pounced and caught him; but then she had fed him on different varieties to compare the flavours, telling him the name and origin of each bite he enjoyed.

'See!' she said, pointing at the counter. On it stood a single, dusty, very ancient bottle of champagne. Madame Hauquier took it and wrapped it in an old newspaper. Cradling it like a baby, she got down on her hands and knees, poked her finger into a knothole and lifted a plank. There she gently laid the bottle to rest between a pair of silver candlesticks and beside the family Bible, then re-covered the treasures. As she gestured to her husband to help her up, she muttered, *'Eh! Mon pt'it Gaston*. If these *sales Boches* come to our house, we will die of thirst and hunger before we give up that bottle.' Her silent husband hawked and spat into the fireplace for emphasis.

Touched and heartened, Gaston replied with a certainty he did not feel that he was sure they would soon be drinking *la bonne bouteille* in celebration of liberty. At the mairie steps, he looked back and saw both Monsieur and Madame Hauquier hastening from the Auberge du Bellevue towards the church, where the ancient, defiant bells had begun to peal.

Looking out across the almost-deserted town square, he felt sickened. What would happen here at the great heart of his proud little town? Would they imprison him, or even execute him on the spot and replace him with a German mayor? Or a collaborator? He briefly considered fleeing, hiding in the woods, conducting a campaign of heroic harassment against the Germans. This notion was quickly dismissed. He would be abandoning not just his sister and four children in Rue des Juifs but his community, which looked to him for leadership and guidance too. It was impossible. He could do nothing except wait. A small part of Gaston Derome was curious to know what would happen next. Surely they could not kill everyone?

In the end, he climbed the stairs to the *salle d'honneur*, which he loved, and paced to and fro across its squeaking, uneven floorboards while he waited. He opened the windows on to the balcony, so that he would hear the arrival of the invaders of Bavay.

An hour later, the room was as full of German officers as it had been of Englishmen. Gaston stood in a corner and waited as they spoke at him in their guttural tongue. He understood a little German but did not wish to make it easy for them. Their leader was a good-looking young man with fair hair and blue eyes. A French-speaking interpreter, a man from Alsace named Kraft, translated his words. Kommandant Horstberg was delighted to meet Monsieur le Maire and was sure he could count on his full co-operation during these trying circumstances while his community adapted to benign German rule. Monsieur le Maire would see, as the weeks unfolded, just how enlightened the German army could be in its dealings with the civilian populace. Soon his community would be free to go about its business, just as it had done before their arrival.

Gaston remained impassive. 'Arrival' rather than invasion! The language made it sound as though these men were all here on a nice little holiday.

'I will do all I can do to ensure the safety and well-being of the community that has elected me its mayor,' he responded. It was a phrase he would often repeat in the coming months. Once this was translated, the leader of the Germans looked a little disappointed at its content or brevity or both and said something else, gesturing while staring at Gaston. Kraft looked at him for a moment, then translated it. 'My kommandant would particularly like you to know that he loves France. He has already spent many holidays in Paris. He greatly admires the fine forests and streams and pastures of Bavay.'

There was an expectant silence, which Gaston did not fill. What on earth did they expect, he wondered, as the kommandant shook his head and turned away to talk to his men; an enthusiastic discussion about the finer restaurants along the Champs-Elysées?

Horstberg swung back to Kraft and jabbered again. Gaston could hear the change of tone. The kommandant impatiently tapped a leather riding-crop against his leg as Kraft nodded and turned to Derome. 'We have another forty men who will require billets, places to sleep. You will help us.' It was clearly not a request.

Gaston had thought this possibility through in advance. 'There is a factory — my own factory — in the town. The main works area will easily accommodate forty men, and there is grazing for the horses nearby. There is a small *cantine* that can be used to prepare food.' Better to have them all in one place where they could be watched, he reasoned. Since so many men had been away fighting, production had virtually stopped in any case. They would not know about the smell until everything was agreed, and by then it would be too late. *Tant pis.* 'The officers can of course be billeted in the large houses around the town, my own included.' He had realised that leading the way would be the best means of getting his townsfolk to accept the situation peaceably.

Kraft brightened at the mention of 'large houses' as did Horstberg once Kraft had translated. He said something else. Kraft managed a smile this time. 'My kommandant asks if there is good hunting in the local forest?'

Here was a direct question that Gaston could not really avoid. And in spite of himself, he felt a pang of sympathy for the young fellow. This Horstberg man was trying very hard to be civil in difficult circumstances. And who knew how long they would have to work alongside each other?

Gaston nodded in turn and met the kommandant's gaze, but still did not smile in response. 'Yes, *mon commandant*, if you like to hunt, there is some wild boar and some roe deer. Birds, rabbits and such like. Yes, indeed, there is good hunting to be had in the Forêt de Mormal.'

The relief on the face of the kommandant was palpable. He said something to his comrades and there was laughter.

Gaston Derome waited to be dismissed.

As he trudged downstairs under the eye of a German private holding a gun, he tripped and almost fell headlong. It was the first time he had ever lost his footing there in all his years as mayor. He felt shameful tears well in his eyes, not because he had hurt himself, but because of the uncertainty he now felt pressing down on him. His beloved mairie was his no longer. And how would his little town, and decent people like Monsieur and Madame Hauquier, fare under the heel of the invader?

# 10

# Meeting Satan

Tom leaned on the lee rail and fixed his eye on the horizon line. This was not only due to the sea-sickness, which plagued all his sea voyages, but also the appeal of that infinity of sharp grey line where sea and sky met but did not merge. The ship was mid-channel now. England had disappeared into a grey mist, while France – Saint-Valéry-sur-Somme to be precise – had yet to come into view. A maritime limbo-land.

The air was redolent of sea-salt and slick piles of panicked horse-dung. One fretful whinny was invariably followed by many others. Poor brutes, thought Tom. Rod (his first charger) and Daisy had had the three-week ordeal out from Bombay in the old p&o rust-bucket, the *Arabia*, to become used to the horrors of embarkation and the pitch and toss of the ship. Nonetheless, he did as he had always done, whispering into Daisy's ear in Hindi, telling her she was a *maharani* among horses, a gem, and the wonder of all India.

He was still at a loss as to how Daisy quite came to be there at all. He had gone to Midnapore to take away Rod and Champa, knowing he could sell his champion polo pony for a small fortune in England and make more than enough to buy a decent second charger. But Daisy had seemed so pleased to see him. She had trotted up and nuzzled his pocket for a sugar-lump, just as she always did with Mary. And with that, poor Champa had been abandoned to an unknown fate.

To prepare his horses for boarding the ferry to France, Tom had gently wrapped a length of *pagri* cloth around their eyes and ears. He could then more easily lead them over the ramp on to the flat-bottomed apology for a vessel; it was an ancient dredger or some such, recently adapted. On the voyage from India, he had learned from an old *syce* that this was the best way to get them down the jetty and up over the planks and into the stalls in the bowels of the steamer.

Some of the wranglers onshore had watched him curiously; others could already see what he was about and would perhaps have the sense to copy him. Others, the more stupid and brutal ones, were still using oath and fist and stick to goad their creatures on board. Of course, most of these frightened horses and mules were destined to become beasts of burden, not riding-horses like his own. He pitied them their fate. Wrenched from their familiar farms and families, these bewildered hunters or cart-horses would be fortunate to find anyone in France to care for them at all, beyond what physical tasks they could perform.

Tom noticed a groom in uniform waiting to board in the long queue of impatient men and nervy horses, standing a little apart from them. The fellow held the reins of a big-boned black stallion with a crooked white blaze like lightning down its nose. It was aiming a determined bite with its long yellow teeth at anyone who came too near, but Tom noted approvingly that the man knew how to calm the horse. He also had a piece of sacking to hand as a blindfold when he needed to manoeuvre the beast on-board. A man used to transporting horses overseas.

Once his stallion was tethered fore and aft (it had aimed a sly kick at one of the sailors) Tom was touched to see the man turn and plod back down the ramp towards him. Taking the reins from Tom with an affable nod, he led Rod up the gangway. Tom followed behind them with Daisy, who scarcely needed her *pagri* blindfold. She had already impressed him greatly with her obedience during the voyage; she often seemed to Tom more dog than horse.

The ferry, open to the elements, had rudimentary stalls down both the port and starboard sides, with a small amount of hay and water available and a removable head-board in between each stall. The groom tethered Rod with one empty stall in between his own charge and Tom's and said, 'Aye, just in case auld Satan works out how tae kick roond the corner.'

'I wouldn't put it past him,' said Tom admiringly, stifling a chuckle as the horse turned and flared his nostrils at him balefully. 'He'll put the fear of God into the Hun.' No-one made use of the unoccupied stall: Satan turned as far as he could to roll his eyes and bare his teeth at all who approached, one hoof poised to lash out at the unsuspecting.

The Scots groom was looking concerned now, staring out into the crowds that thronged the jetty. He shrugged and then gestured in the direction of Daisy and Golden Rod. 'Beauties,' he said approvingly. 'Your own, are they, sir?'

Tom, who had followed the advice of Devesh Bosu and wore civilian clothing, nodded in turn. The man's recognition of his bearing rather than any uniform pleased him. 'The horses are both good sailors. Unlike myself. We came over from Calcutta just a week or so ago. Then a few days with my in-laws in England. The aftermath of a bereavement, in a way. And, well, here we all are.'

The man smiled back, introducing himself as a Private Matheson, signed on as a servant and groom. 'Wee black Satan there hates everyone except the laird. He just aboot tolerates me because I give him an occasional bucket of oats and brush the thistles oot o' his tail. A one-man horse, if ever there was one.' He patted Satan on the rump and the great black beast turned again and glowered. 'An' I think your master is about tae miss the ferry, which will put him into a fine bate.'

Sure enough, just as the crew had cast off, a slight, fair officer elbowed his way on to the jetty packed with crowds (mostly women, weeping and energetically waving pocket-handkerchiefs) and bellowed an order. The sailors stood and looked at him momentarily, in two minds as to whether to obey. Then they saw his irate countenance and rank insignia and hurriedly flung a rope back to a startled stevedore, who looped it around the capstan. They pushed out a single gangplank and the officer – a major, Tom now noted from his uniform – stormed on board carrying a large leather valise in one hand and a saddle over the other. He was soon in deep and disgusted conversation with the Scots groom. Poor fellow, Tom thought. He's catching it, for some reason, and I'll wager it is no fault of his.

Tom tethered Daisy and Rod together in the one stall as he had onboard the steamer – it was something of a tight fit but Tom knew they would settle better that way. There was one rope fastening to a bulkhead at the bridle and again at the saddle. If by any chance it got very rough during the crossing, the two horses could prop each other up and just roll with the heaving sea. He knew all this from experience. Rod, the younger of the two horses, had in fact eaten part of Daisy's mane while on the long voyage across the *Kala Pani*; not because he was lacking in fodder, but for comfort, just as a baby would suck its thumb. He was mumbling on a mouthful of it already.

It had been a strange voyage from India. All the talk at mealtimes was of the war. There was a kind of glee about it, a sickening urgency. There were many uniformed men on board strutting about and braying at each other. Tom had boarded at dawn with the servants and syces to avoid scrutiny. Later he overheard raised voices and risked a look over the side to witness several other would-be volunteers find themselves refused passage altogether. One of them was the youngster Page from Puanco, smartly turned out in his Calcutta Light Horse lieutenant's uniform, who did not see Tom. He felt for him. Pugh would make the boy's life a misery when he returned. Tom had no such qualms, as he did not expect to live to see Pugh again.

Conversation on-board had had to be restricted for the same cautious reasons but when pressed, he told others that he was returning to England due to a close family bereavement; partially true, of course. Tom had more than one reason to wish to remain unrecognised.

Tom had spent much of his time with the horses and the few syces caring for them, many of whom were also bound, like himself, for France. Conversing in Hindi and other familiar languages helped him with the disbelief he felt that his years in India could be over. It was like the closing of a great book, full of colourful pictures and tales of his life to date. All that was left now was the closed book, the cracked spine and a fading memory of what lay within.

At times he felt physically overwhelmed by the rapidity of the change and found that leaning his head against a horse's broad warm neck was greatly reassuring.

One acquaintance become increasingly unavoidable. Wherever Tom went on board, he would meet a friendly young puppy of a lieutenant in cavalry uniform, legitimately travelling to London. Tom dodged him once, just as the boy was coming out of his cabin. Tom noticed the name Durand on the door label. Tom himself was travelling several decks below, second class, sharing a small cabin with a mysterious commercial traveller from Port Saïd. It was all a far cry from his joyful honeymoon passage to India with Mary on board the elegant Sicilia.

Tom had instantly recognised the boy's surname, of course; the Durands were a great old Indian cavalry dynasty. The boy had looked at him with clear grey eyes and said 'Hello there!' in such a cheery, breezy manner that Tom thought for an anxious moment he might have been recognised. He chose to nod brusquely and walk on down the corridor, as the boy's curiosity prickled between his shoulder blades.

They had then met again one day of exceptionally heavy swell, when Tom was, as usual, grimly watching the horizon line from the lee rail. The young man had approached unseen – he had the gift of almost silent footfall – and paused at the rail beside Tom. Tom could hardly bolt for his cabin, so he stayed put, looking out to sea through narrowed eyes, willing the boy to leave and his breakfast to stay where it was. For a while they kept an almost-companionable silence. Then Durand had glanced to his left and muttered 'Fishing fleet ahoy, old man – look sharp!' Tom scanned the horizon in confusion before realising that the vessel in question was female and lurching in their direction across the heaving deck.

Inevitably, she accidentally-on-purpose toppled into them. 'Oh dear. What a dreadful sea today. I am so very sorry, gentlemen. Now, have we met?' Forty if she was a day, thought Tom, rather dismayed at this turn of events, and uncertain how to deal with it.

Durand had sensed an opportunity for some fun and decided to play along. 'No, and the loss is all our own,' he responded gallantly. 'The name is Durand. Norman conquests, all that. We pronounce it in the English fashion rather than the French. Reginald Heber Marion Durand, at your service.' He bent to kiss her hand. 'And you are, madam? Or should I say - miss?'

She laughed coquettishly, and Tom, although amused, felt a stab of panic. 'Elsie Smith,' she said, smiling at Durand.

The youngster beamed back at her. 'I have always wondered what Elsie is short for?' he asked, quite genuinely.

Elsie was plain Elsie Smith but inventive, as well as slightly desperate. 'Oh, I believe my grandmother was called Elsinore,' she announced. Elsie could barely recall her Irish barmaid mother, let alone an aristocratic grandmother: but she was close enough to see that neither man's hand bore a wedding ring nor even an engagement ring and she was an eternal optimist. 'And is this a friend of yours?'

Tom opened his mouth to speak but Durand got there first. 'Oh yes, an old friend,' he said firmly, placing an arm across Tom's shoulders. 'You should see him play polo!'

Tom stiffened. This wretched Durand boy really did appear to know something of him. How much, that was the question. Of course, Tom had met many Durands in India – they were a bristling, military family that was hard to avoid – but he did not remember this one. Why would he? It was Tom himself who was notorious.

Meanwhile Elsie had decided that of the two distinctly appealing men before her, Tom might be her best chance of avoiding the necessity of moving in with her widowed and God-fearing sister in Eastbourne. Much as she liked to dream, the other little charmer with his melting eyes and good teeth and pretty smile was too young for her. Shame, but she had to be practical.

This older fellow, now. He was nearer her own age, with a hint of melancholy, which could mean a convenient widower. Well, she could match him sorrow for sorrow with tales of her dearly departed Alfred (who had been a womaniser and drinker, but had had his moments before he left her penniless). Decent-looking, average height, trim, nice little moustache, round spectacles. So he might not notice the tiny lines around her eyes and mouth, which became more of a threat to her future each day.

'Does your quiet friend have a name?' Elsie had asked Durand, now determinedly simpering at Tom, who had turned his back to the sea and was scanning the boat deck for an escape route.

Durand replied, turning to Tom, 'I'm sure he does, but I am dashed if I can recall it?'

This confused Elsie and she looked momentarily wrong-footed. Enough, thought Tom. This is not fair on the woman or the boy. 'My name is Westmacott, madam,' he said. 'You will have heard my name in the papers, I am sure?'

The Durand boy looked troubled, then stricken as the penny dropped. He said 'My dear chap, I didn't mean... I only recalled seeing you play polo at Midnapore or Simla, I forget which. Years ago. You were a marvel. I didn't realise you were...' He fell silent.

The intrusive Elsie woman had gone pale and taken several steps back from them. That dreadful Westmacott business! It had been in all the papers. A scandal. She had followed it avidly. Nothing ever proved, of course, but so many unanswered questions. And this was him. In the flesh!

The vessel juddered. Tom suddenly gagged, swinging round from them to be copiously but neatly sick over the side. Elsie made a sound of disgust and he heard their footsteps die away cross the boat-deck.

Tom assumed with relief that he was alone again. He watched the bleak horizon and the foamy bow-wave for a long time. When he at last drew back from the rail and turned, there stood that light-footed joker Durand, looking chastened. He proffered a small glass dish of sugared ginger and a clean linen napkin in one hand and a miraculous glass of brandy in the other.

'I am so damnably sorry, Westmacott,' he had said. 'I am an absolute fool.'

Tom had parted from Reggie Durand in London, by which time he knew rather more about the boy's hopes and dreams than he wanted to. Reggie had told him how he hoped to become engaged to a wonderful girl, who was (of course) as beautiful as the day and a perfect angel. Her mother had said they could not marry or even announce an engagement until after the war for some reason, which Reggie regarded as unnecessarily petty for the sake of a few months apart; and Tom thought sound good sense.

Reggie's grandfather had arranged for him to get out of India quickly in case the war ended too soon for him to participate. Technically the boy was on leave. He did not know what he was to do or where he would be sent. He hoped it would be soon though. They said it would all be over by Christmas.

The boy was clearly anxious to live up to the family's reputation for courage in the battlefield. He had brought his collection of lead soldiers, he said, which had inspired him to a military career (along with your entire family since the day you were born, thought Tom). He had had to leave his own horses behind in India, due to a last-minute double-booking at Bombay. Tom wondered with a twinge of guilt if this might have been the work of Devesh Bosu but said nothing. Durand seemed happy enough. He knew his London uncle's horses well, it seemed, and had been offered the pick of his stable for France.

They had even accompanied each other up to the centre of town on the boat-train, Reggie proving a good hand with a horse. Tom was bound for an old-fashioned inn with stables near Paddington Station, which his father-in-law Fred Lawson had recommended – he would be able to leave Daisy and Golden Rod safely there for the few days before taking them on to France. Reggie was destined for a tearful reunion with his mother and adoring sisters at the family's London house in Beaufort Gardens. There would be no such homecoming for Tom, as his father Vesey was three years dead and little regretted, his estranged mother still somewhere in India.

It had been at Vesey's funeral that Tom had first met Mary. She had accompanied her father to the service at Chastleton. Tom had sat in the front pew beside Dick, his younger brother. They stood to sing the first hymn and looked at each other in wonder when a soaring descant pealed out on the penultimate verse. When greeting the guests in the great panelled hall of Chastleton House afterwards, it did not take Tom long to decide which of the mourners was the only possible candidate for such a heavenly voice.

Once Tom had boarded the train for Pershore, he felt the shade of Mary take the empty seat beside his own. The last time he had travelled on this train it had been speeding in the opposite direction, carrying the newlyweds to London and thence to the south coast and the steamer for India. 'Gosh, Tom,' Mary had said as they scrambled into the carriage at Pershore, laughing, 'This is it.'

'This is it,' he had agreed, gazing at her in wonder. Once the carriage had emptied, he had taken his new wife in his arms and kissed her, with all the madness of early love.

Now he would be returning to Fladbury without Mary for the first time since her death.

~

Dear, kind Grace. Mary's sister had been waiting for him in the rectory parlour. She looked up from her mending with nothing but joy in her face as he entered the room. He had hugged her and could not speak for some moments.

What a lot she had lost, he thought as they embraced. More than he had himself, really, for Ruth her elder sister was now a nun at Wantage, her mother an invalid and Mary... well, yes, Mary.

He soon found that plain, sweet, patient Grace, whose only role was now to care for her ailing mother and deaf old parson father, lived, ate and breathed scripture. Quoting it was a great comfort to Grace, but it had the opposite effect on Tom. Old Fred generously limited his censure of Tom to asking him, Bible shaking in arthritic hands, whether his daughter had had a Christian burial among the heathens. Laura, Mary's mother, was much reduced in health by her loss and was more often now confined to her wheelchair. She kept to her room for the most part. Tom was a walking reminder of her daughter's absence.

Grace alone did not seem to blame him in any way. In their short time together, Tom had been able to feast on her childhood stories of Mary, some of them quite strange. Grace told him that Mary had once had a vivid dream that she would be attacked by the village idiot as he sat on a stile. She had walked that way the following day and there the man was, sitting there, just as she had foreseen it. And Mary had walked up to him, bold as brass, smiled and asked him to help carry her basket down the village. He had done so, chattering all the way, and she had come to no harm.

Tom tried not to think of Mary too much, as he found it weakened his joints and slowed his heart, but childhood tales like these he found sufficiently distant to enjoy. Mary. Oh, Mary.

Tom abruptly found himself back on the rolling deck of the rickety cross-channel ferry. The young major had interrupted his reverie. The man was stroking Rod's velvet nose in a thoughtful manner. Daisy whickered at this uncertainly. The major threw his head back and laughed in a way designed to turn heads: 'Oh, so, jealous, are you, madam?

Tom felt uneasy. Before him was a slender young aristocrat with fair hair and brilliant blue eyes, which cast great light but no warmth at all, rather like the new electricity that was sweeping away all the old cosy oil lamps and candles of times past.

As Tom now held a captain's commission, this stranger was a superior officer, not an equal: but then again Tom was out of uniform. Uniformed or not, it was still dashed bad form to start petting another fellow's horse that way without so much as a by-your-leave.

As if sensing his discomfiture, the man turned to him and smiled. Although outwardly warm, Tom felt chilled by it. Conversation was now inevitable. 'You were cutting it a bit fine there, sir,' he said, testing the water as he courteously acknowledged the young major's rank.

'Not my bally fault, old boy.' The voice was a strange mixture of the worst toadies Tom had known at Rugby and the groom's Scots accent. The major extended an elegant hand. 'Macbane of Lochdubh.' Tom shook it but without waiting for him to respond, Lochdubh continued his rant. 'We had a devil of a job to find stabling at all at the docks and ended up in different sordid premises at opposite ends of the port, can you credit it? Matheson there came on ahead with Satan and left me to take my breakfast – and my hack. But my mare fell sick last night. They told me it was a fit of some kind so I have had to leave her. Dashed inconvenient. I swear that the innkeeper drugged her or fed her soap or something. Probably does a roaring trade in fine back-door horseflesh with all the requisitioning that's going on.'

'Och, ye've never sold the Demon?' his groom asked, ashen-faced, forgetting the 'sir' this time. The young major did not appear to notice this or care, suggesting a long acquaintance.

'No option, Trap. No good to me in that condition on the battlefield. 'Cannons to the left of 'em, cannons to the right of 'em' and all that.' He shrugged. 'Whereas…' he now slapped Daisy familiarly across the rump, making her start and Tom wince. 'Look at that!' he said, 'Lovely little creature. I'll wager she'd go like the wind if you spurred her hard enough. I'll take her instead.'

Tom, torn between outrage and amusement, shook his head once and said quietly, 'I am afraid that's quite out of the question. Sir.'

'Privately-owned horses, Lochdubh sir, not army requisition,' added the groom quickly, siding with Tom. The major stared at them both for a few moments, and then aimed another deliberate and icy smile at the civilian among them. 'In that case, what will you take for her, old fellow? As a cavalry major, I cannot arrive in France with only the one decent mount. You must surely see that? There is a war to be won! Now be a good man and name your price. You shall have your pick of all the others on board, or in France should you prefer it.'

Tom was speechless. Losing Daisy to this odious stranger was impossible, major (how could he be a major?) or not, but how to make this clear? In the end, he could only think of the one simple word.

'No.' There was silence for a moment. 'Daisy was my late wife's horse, you see. I can never sell her. Sir,' he added again, only as an afterthought.

'I see.' There was another awkward pause, during which the officer stared at him. In a quite different tone Lochdubh then sneered, 'Daisy. Why not 'Lily' or 'Tulip' while you were about it? A feeble choice of name for a war-horse.'

The words stung, but Tom said nothing. In truth he was unnerved by the man's accurate assumption that he too was heading for the war, in spite of his civilian rig. The young major flicked at the stubbly area of Daisy's mane, where Rod had nibbled it, with the tips of his elegant fingers. 'She's even a bit mangy, now I look more closely,' he said. Tom remained silent. He had met many of this kind in India.

With a grunt of exasperation, Lochdubh turned and shoved his way through the men who had gathered on the deck to spectate. The only covered area available on board was accessible through a doorway marked 'Officers Only'. The young major vanished within.

Matheson was brushing Satan's mane despondently. 'I cannae credit it, sir. I birthed that one as a foal,' he said bitterly. 'Nice wee roan. Good as gold, nothing of the devil about her. I dinnae name them. There was nothing wrong with my wee Demon when I left her.'

Tom expressed his sympathy but found himself irritated to be in partial agreement with the unpleasant younger man. A sick horse, if indeed she were sick, had no place on the battlefield. At least the mare would have a chance of recovery in England. In France, it was likely that a bullet would have awaited her in any case. He promised himself that if anything serious were to befall Rod or Daisy, he would shoot them himself.

Of course, the voice came back again then: oh yes, Tom, for you are so very good at killing the things you love. Cradled in his arms, Mary jolted awake from her fevered dream, her body slick with sweat, babbling a warning of something bright, something sinister, slipping towards them through the darkness.

# 11

# La Fôret de Mormal

BAVAY, FRANCE
SEPTEMBER 1914

They were just so correct, these dashed Boches, thought Gaston Derome despondently. He locked the door of the mairie with the great iron key, put it into his coat pocket and turned for home. Even their infernal posters (that were appearing daily on every tree, every street corner) were *politesse* itself. He was finding it increasingly hard to keep the professional distance and *froideur* required by the circumstances.

They had even been decent about taking over his own home. The interpreter, Kraft, an oily fellow, had translated every word. Monsieur le Maire must surely understand that Kommandant Horstberg, as the area's supervising officer, must now be suitably accommodated in Bavay. Kommandant Horstberg would look after Derome's fine house as he would his own. The kommandant would be based at Landrecies, sometimes at Aulnoye, but alas, he could not predict his movements. The Bavay house would therefore need to be at the kommandant's continuous disposal.

Gaston had anticipated this requisition. He had already asked his unmarried sister Léonie (who had kept house for him since Louise had died) to move their household, along with a wagonload or two of personal effects. The family was taking up residence in an inferior family house not far away, uninhabited since an old relative had died. It was inconvenient of course. He would especially begrudge the produce of his prized potager, which would now be feeding the Boches rather than his own family, but to pick everything would have seemed pusillanimous and that was not in his interest. In many communities he knew, the German soldiers' billets had to all be *chez les habitants*

95

rather than in a convenient local factory. This was causing all kinds of friction elsewhere in the area. He imagined a brawny Hun arriving on Monsieur and Madame Hauquier's doorstep, kitbag in hand, and shuddered. At least he had been able to prevent this kind of calamity in Bavay for the moment, but he did not doubt that more troops would follow the first.

Gaston had also shrewdly offered Horstberg the services of his able servant Marthe. He had judged correctly that her ready smile, guileless, wide-spaced eyes, dimples and blonde hair would dupe them into thinking her witless. Marthe was far from that. Her excellent cuisine would also help the German officers relax and talk in her presence, as they learned to rejoice in good French cooking: they had been living, it would appear, on treacly black bread, cold ham and pickles.

Marthe had agreed to the plan readily, and Léonie would manage to cook for Gaston and the children well enough. And so they settled into the smaller family house located at Place-Verte, near the cross-roads not far from the Hauquier's Auberge du Bellevue; the children a little tearfully, as they did not like leaving their beloved Marthe *chez les Boches*.

Horstberg had taken Gaston's offer of his servant's services (over and above the factory billet for Horstberg's men) as an act of generosity, if not actual complicity. His gratitude was almost touching. As a result, Derome gained the opportunity to learn a little more about the man who now governed Bavay and the surrounding area. Horstberg was a provincial engineer and a local politician of sorts, a reservist rather than a professional soldier. He had worked in a role not dissimilar from Gaston's own, but within an urban commune in the town of Bremen. Horstberg, eager with *bonhomie*, had tried to tell Derome some confusing folktale about a noisy cockerel, which stood on top of a cat on top of a dog on top of a donkey, all of whom apparently lived there. This flight of fancy pushed Kraft's translating skills to the limit. In the end, they gave up and spoke of other things.

One evening, Gaston had had the surreal experience of sitting again in his own *salon*, which his late wife had made so pretty and airy with white paint and *voiles* at the windows, as a guest of Horstberg. Gaston barely wetted his lips with a glass of his own red wine, which his host also sipped, although Gaston could tell he was longing to empty his glass in great Teutonic gulps with an appreciative smack of the lips, followed by a swift refill. And then Horstberg dismissed his unsmiling interpreter and began to speak halting French, startling Gaston by a demonstration of just how quickly the man was learning it. Kommandant Horstberg was certainly no fool.

During these stilted and one-sided evening chats, Horstberg would regale him with the innumerable benefits that France would be certain to enjoy as part of the great pan-European German empire, which would, he believed, lead to a peaceful and prosperous future for all. Derome would nod and say as little as possible, waiting for the moment when he could safely excuse himself and return to his anxious sister and the children. Gaston knew that many in the town would take it wrongly if he were to be seen in the same room as the kommandant. He also knew he had no choice in this fraternisation, and that this was clearly understood by the more moderate members of his community. He had to grit his teeth and work with this man to protect all their interests.

One fine night, as Gaston was walking back from the mairie towards the old house at the crossroads, the situation changed. He was hoping he would not be summoned again to the Rue des Juifs that evening as it had been a long enough day already. Old Monsieur Hauquier had got drunk on some terrible home-made apple brandy and started to berate a group of German soldiers who had stopped to water their horses at the fountain in the square. Gaston managed to intervene to save the old devil's skin just as the men's patience was starting to wear thin and their mood turn sour.

Gaston was crossing the road when he became aware of footsteps behind him, approaching rapidly. He slowed his pace and to his surprise a short, grizzled man he knew slightly by sight, one of the many *garde-chasses* of the forest, drew alongside him and politely removed his hat. 'Monsieur le Maire? It's about the firewood,' he said.

'Ah yes, the firewood,' replied Gaston, as they passed a nervy young German lieutenant trying and failing to impress a local girl. Gaston knew full well that he had ordered no logs - his wood-store was already prudently full. 'Is it to be the beech again this year? Or more ash?'

The gamekeeper, whose name was Taisne, he now recalled, responded unhappily, 'There is perhaps a fine glade of young English oak available, Monsieur.' This stopped Gaston in his tracks, fortunately on a section of lane where they could talk more freely. 'Des Anglais?' he whispered.

'Oui, Monsieur le Maire. I cannot tell you precisely where.'

'No, no. If I should be taken...'

'*Exacte.*' There was silence for a moment as they walked on. Then Taisne sighed, and Gaston realised how tired the man looked. He was not young, and doubtless he was out in the woods by night as well as by daylight if he were supporting hidden Englishmen. 'What happened?' Gaston asked. 'I had thought the Germans had killed or captured them all?' Taisne shook his head, and Gaston could now see, approvingly, that he was carefully working out how much to tell him. 'They climbed the trees,' he replied. 'Many are from places with forests. Scots, Irish, some English, all different units. It was just their instinct to survive, I think.'

Gaston nodded thoughtfully. It sounded very possible. The retreat of the English in the face of the German advance had happened so rapidly it had astonished everyone, not least the British themselves.

These Allied survivors would have understood that their friends were done for. They were men from those gallant units ordered to stay behind and fight, to give the likes of General French and his staff the chance to escape. Who could blame some for melting into the cover available? There were so many men on the ground for the Germans to shoot or grab that they would not have thought to look up in the branches above their heads. Forests always looked after their own.

Taisne rubbed his eyes wearily with the back of his hand, then glanced at a woman he did not know approaching them holding a small boy by the hand. He said loudly. 'I shall be felling that big holly soon, Monsieur le Maire. Holly burns like wax.' They continued discussing the relative merits of different timbers until the strangers were out of earshot.

'What can I do?' asked Gaston.

'There is a group in the north, not far. Seven men. They have a little house in the forest that I showed them. They are lying low, staying out of sight. Sensible men. Reading, playing cards. The villagers are managing to feed them, for now. But there is another group in the south. Bigger – twenty-three of them. More organised. They have a young lieutenant in charge. They have built a shelter and dug out a kind of bunker where they plan to spend the winter. It even has electricity and an alarm system.' He laughed, suddenly looking less careworn. 'Even my own house in the forest has no electricity!' Then he continued, serious once more. 'I came to warn you, Monsieur le Maire. There are sappers among this second group. And tomorrow they plan to blow up the railway line between Aulnoye and Landrecies.'

Derome experienced a wave of immense frustration. He could imagine of course how these young men felt, trapped in occupied France months after their compatriots had retreated. They must want to do something – anything! But did they not realise the possible repercussions on those innocents who had sheltered them?

'Can they be stopped?'

Taisne shook his head. 'Everyone who goes there with food has tried. But this English lieutenant is of an old school. You know the kind? He has that look in his eye. His men are impressed by his courage. In truth, they are bored, I believe. Young and naive, also. We even caught them marking the trees. So they could easily find their way back to their own camp from hunting trips. Can you credit it? Fools. Now you know! If you need to contact us, Madame Sohier is the one.' With that, Taisne turned and walked away, tossing back over his shoulder for the benefit of the young German private walking towards them, *'Hé*, Monsieur le Maire, I cannot help the prices, everything is more expensive, even firewood. There is a war!'

'Ah, *mais enfin!*' Gaston retorted. He felt in turmoil, bludgeoned by the man's words. Gaston had worked so very hard to create a rapport with the occupying Germans. Now he had to adapt to the news that he had thirty unwanted Englishmen hiding out in his forest.

For a few brief seconds, he considered informing on them to protect his own community. If he did so, the English would be captured, interned, but surely not shot? But then again, could he be so sure of that? Posters had gone up warning that concealed French or English soldiers should give themselves up or the communities sheltering them would face extreme penalties.

Then, of course, he dismissed the idea as entirely unthinkable. How could he live with himself after such an act? No, he would have to help protect these inconvenient guests as best he could, for the sake of young Totman, who now lay cold in the town graveyard.

The following day he made sure he was very visible about the town. It was just after midday when Horstberg came to seek him out and found him in the square. The man was pale and holding a telegram, Kraft at his side, never a good sign. Without waiting for the instruction,

Kraft barked, 'What do you know of this, Derome?'

'Of what, Monsieur?' Gaston asked, mildly.

'There has been an attempt to blow up the railway line this morning!'

'Goodness!' exclaimed Gaston as convincingly as he could. 'You surely cannot think that I had anything to do with it?'

'Well? Did you?' asked Horstberg in French. He looked as if he might weep, thought Gaston with a touch of sympathy. Poor fellow, he had thought it was all going so well. And so had Gaston himself, until now.

'Monsieur le Commandant, I think this is an incredible act of stupidity,' Gaston responded quite truthfully, 'France needs her railways just as much as Germany does.'

Horstberg spoke rapidly and angrily to Kraft, who translated and reported: 'This was a military act. Not a civilian one. Unsuccessful of course, with a pitifully small amount of explosive. The locomotive was only slightly damaged, the track not at all. The trains still run on time between Aulnoye and Landrecies.'

All for nothing! Gaston thought in disbelief. He understood now that this action would become more about the humiliation of the Germans than the escapade itself. The very same local communities that were offering the Germans hospitality had somehow, right under their noses, also secretly sustained sufficient Allied soldiers to carry out such an attack.

'I see,' he said. 'Well, here in Bavay we make fertiliser, *Messieurs*, as you know, and precious little of that since the war began, with your soldiers occupying my factory. I know no one in my community who could make or who would want to make a bomb. I am sorry, and I regret what has happened, but I know nothing of this matter.' A statement that was almost true, he thought, as he turned and walked away, feeling their hostility at his back.

The words Horstberg then cried out turned heads on the other side of the square and rang in Gaston's ears for days afterwards. 'We will hunt them down, Derome. Do you hear me? We will find them!'

He knew then that their stilted yet polite evenings of wine-tasting had come to an abrupt end.

Gaston waited for an hour or two, behaving normally in case he was being watched, and this gave him valuable thinking time. There were two groups of hidden men, Taisne had said. The larger group, the young hot-heads who had tried to blow up the railway, must be found and found soon, and somehow brought north to join the others. The greater the numbers, Gaston reasoned, the less opportunity the Germans would have to treat them as spies and to shoot them against the nearest wall, something that had already happened at Valenciennes.

Gaston sent off sensible Thérèse, his elder daughter, with a note for Madame Léocadie Sohier, which asked if she would care to share a load of young oak with him this autumn, and if so, perhaps they could discuss his suggestion at her earliest convenience.

Madame Sohier came to the back door the following day, a calm, middle-aged, sensible widow he had always liked. Her basket carried two fine cauliflowers from her potager, a match for his own at Rue des Juifs, which would provide them all with a meal that night. He sat down with her, beside Léonie to whom he had already confided all. Léonie sent Thérèse out into the garden to weed their own fledgling potager and keep an eye on Alphonse, Léon and little Marie-Félicie, who was just seven.

'Well,' Léocadie Sohier began with a smile. 'What were we to do with les Anglais, leave them to starve in the woods like abandoned dogs?'

She then informed the Mayor of Bavay with no little pride that her tiny, isolated forest community of Obies had fed and watered a group of seven Englishmen since that terrible time in August when the English had retreated. 'We did not wish to hide all this from you, Monsieur le Maire,' she explained, 'but we understand your position and did not wish to involve you unnecessarily. It seemed sensible to limit the knowledge to the smallest number of people when there were so few men to be hidden, *n'est-ce-pas?*' Gaston praised her caution and wondered how many of her cauliflowers and other vegetables had kept hidden Englishmen alive, instead of feeding her own family.

She continued, 'But now all our own Anglais are under threat because of these young *imbéciles* down at Englefontaine! As we are ourselves. If they had not done this stupid thing, we might have kept them safe for a little longer. As it is…' she shrugged. 'Their leader is young and foolish. This lieutenant believes himself to be *Robin des Bois*. Those who have helped them have grown fond of these boys, Monsieur le Maire, and we are worried sick at what will happen now they are to be hunted down.'

Léonie leaned forward in her chair. 'The Germans will not be looking for them in Obies, will they? They will concentrate on the south of the Forêt, surely, near the railway line they attacked. They may already have been taken. But if not and we could bring them here, would it be safer?'

Gaston shook his head. 'I don't think they have been captured, as Horstberg would have come to brag about it. And I agree that bringing them here would be the best idea, but I do not see how it is possible. The Forêt will be swarming with German patrols, and there will be even more roadblocks and checkpoints than there were already. Are they still in uniform?'

'*Non*,' said Léocadie. 'We told them to take them off and keep them safely in a bundle with their guns and put on old clothes we gave them. That way if they are caught, they can show the Germans their uniforms and surrender their weapons as real soldiers, not spies.'

Gaston did not share her confidence as he had seen the expression on Horstberg's face earlier in the day, but he kept his concerns to himself. 'Yes,' he said, 'we must bring them here. We need to have them all in one group to be more manageable. But how?'

They talked at length about disguising the men as French workers but soon accepted they could not provide civilian boots for over twenty men. It was their boots, not to mention their accents if challenged, which would instantly give them away. Concealment in a cartload of hay would also have been a possibility had the Germans not already been bayoneting these at checkpoints. They had almost given up when Léonie said, hesitantly, 'We need a guide, by night. Should we... could we perhaps use the children?'

At that moment, Marie-Félicie and Léon roared past the window, the weeding forgotten in a tumultuous game of hide-and-seek. His children! Gaston almost refused outright, but then found himself considering the idea. The children of the forest, his own included, knew it better than anyone else, just as he had done in his own childhood. They could cross it by night avoiding the roads without hesitation. Their country too had been invaded. This *was* something a child could do so why not Thérèse, or Alphonse? He looked at Léonie.

Léocadie Sohier saw this and rose to her feet, smoothing down her skirts. 'Not one of your own, Monsieur le Maire. You will have taken enough risks for us all by the time this war is at an end, I suspect.' She nodded firmly and smiled. 'I know just the child,' she said. 'But it is better if you do not, my friends.'

Over the next few days, the plan was carefully set out. The sun shone, the forest was rich with the golds and faded greens of autumn. Suddenly there seemed to be children on every path. It was the season for wild mushrooms and berries and the schools had a little holiday to profit from this. German patrols soon got used to encountering happy groups of young ones carrying broad wicker baskets laden with good things. The children had been told to be especially nice to every German they met and to offer them berries, and the soldiers, many of whom were themselves very young, enjoyed these little gifts without suspicion.

One particular child carried her basket a little further into the forest than the others. This little girl sat down to wait at the foot of a very large beech tree, her back to its warm trunk, in a tranquil glade not far from a little stream. As the moon rose, she would have liked a snooze, as she knew the night would be a long one, but instead remained awake and watchful as instructed. As dusk fell, she stood up and hooted as a tawny owl, three times in succession. Her heart was beating very fast indeed.

Minutes later, Lieutenant Bushell and his men emerged cautiously from the bramble thicket, which had concealed them for the last four days. They had been told to meet their guide here when they heard the owl, and that they would be taken to an isolated house, not far from an *estaminet* – which sounded good, Bushell thought, licking parched lips. A place called Cheval Blanc, which meant nothing to him. He was expecting another *garde-chasse* like Taisne, although he was now subject to a strict curfew, as were all the foresters and gamekeepers, and had to report his whereabouts to the Germans.

The men were in subdued spirits and a filthy state. They had wisely rubbed some pungent animal dung – possibly that of a wild boar – into their hands and faces and clothing to avoid detection by the dogs. The lieutenant stared down in disbelief at the small, solemn girl, and one of his men let out a laugh, but was sharply silenced by the others. The child did not smile or even look up at them at first. Instead she crouched down to examine their boots, pair by pair. One of the brighter soldiers realised what she was doing and knelt to show her an English label inside his uniform tunic. Her face lit up and she pulled back the cloth in her basket to reveal twenty-three tiny *petits-pains*. The men fell on these ravenously, as they had eaten virtually nothing but wild berries and woodland mushrooms for days. Even that quantity of bread in one little basket had been a risk, but Léonie had convinced Gaston that hungry men are less alert than fed men.

The soldiers followed their diminutive guide – one of them carrying her now-empty basket – as she trotted off through the glade. It became clear that she knew the woods exceptionally well. Sometimes the men had difficulty in keeping pace as she wove her way through the forest's thickets and clearings, easily dodging the brambles and nettles that scratched and stung them.

On the outskirts of the little village of Locquignol she made them clamber down into a deep and very smelly drainage ditch. They waited there, barely daring to breathe, until they had heard a patrol pass them along one of the busier forest roads that ran parallel. Then they half-walked, half-waded, for a full half hour along the ditch, often hearing the barking of dogs close by; but perhaps the men stank too badly or perhaps the wind was in the wrong direction, as the dogs did not come.

Crossing the road was the worst part. It was long and straight and the patrol could still clearly be seen walking away from them in the far distance. What if they should turn?

The English soldiers did not know this, but their little guide had considered every eventuality and even had a story ready for this. Over the past few days, she had foraged nearby, using the time to get to know the soldiers on patrol along this road and feasting them with juicy berries. If the patrol did turn at the wrong moment, she planned to wave vigorously to distract the men, while les Anglais took cover as best they could. With luck, *les Allemands* would see only one familiar small girl in need of help. Suzanne planned to cry and say she had been lost and afraid in the dark forest and had fallen and hurt her knee. They would then, she supposed, escort her home. The English soldiers meanwhile could slip across the road under cover of the diversion to be recovered by others later.

This risky strategy had been agreed with her Maman. Papa knew nothing of her adventure.

The patrol did not turn.

At dawn, the little girl led 'her' soldiers as she now thought of them towards the tumbledown house in a clearing near Obies. The men stumbled, exhausted, reeking, through the back door to English exclamations of surprise and delight and: 'Oh I *say*, have you been rolling in a pigsty?'

Once Lieutenant Bushell had assured himself that his twenty-two men were all present and that the injury sustained to his foot was no more than a sprained ankle, he returned to the garden to return the basket and thank the little guide to whom he and his men owed their lives. But ten-year-old Suzanne Matha was already fast asleep on the broad, warm back of her mother's pony, as it carried her safely home.

# 12

# Regimental Manoeuvres
# in the Dark

THÉROUANNE, FRANCE
MARCH 1915

It is fair to say that the first night march of the newly-formed Mhow Brigade was not an unqualified success.

Tom had only been in Thérouanne for a week, but it felt like many months. It was a tiny place, once much grander, an ancient walled town with a cathedral razed to the ground by King Charles V. Or so said one of the interpreters, Nougier, who knew everything (and, Tom was to discover shortly, could also obtain anything). It was Nougier who found Tom a billet, a little thatched place on the outskirts of Thérouanne, better by far than sleeping under canvas. The elderly *paysan* couple it belonged to said little but managed to feed Tom and the youngster who also billeted there well enough from their fine garden.

There were over two thousand cavalrymen assembled at Thérouanne, most of them under canvas, and at night the temperature would often plummet close to freezing. Their tents stretched as far as the eye could see across the undulating landscape, like a haphazardly pantiled roof. Plumes of smoke twisted upwards from the fires the sowars lit to try (and invariably fail) to keep warm.

They had had an extraordinary journey and were glad of rest. Leaving India to sail across the Kala Pani; the steamer (many had never been to sea before and had been very seasick); the arrival in France at Marseilles; the long journey north to Rouen across an alien landscape by train and then on to Thérouanne.

The river Lys meandered lazily through lush water-meadows where now countless horses were grazing in demarcated sections: chargers and hacks for riding; horses for pulling gun carriages and carts; and the lowest order of the three, the beasts of burden. The Indian Army regiments had brought very few horses with them from Bombay: most of these, like Daisy and Rod, were privately-owned officers' mounts.

It was here in Thérouanne that those soldiers within the assembled regiments who were to remain as cavalry troops chose their new horses. Others were adjusting to the disturbing news that they were not to fight as horsemen but as infantrymen in the trenches, undertaking roles they were little accustomed to, such as digging and construction. Most of the men took this phlegmatically. They were there to fight for their king-emperor whatever their role. They had come to serve and serve they would.

Tom noted their deep appreciation of the gifts that young Princess Mary had bestowed on every man that Christmas – Tom had arrived just too late to receive them himself but was given a spare set. One was a rectangular brass tin embossed with her portrait, strong enough to stop a bullet, which had held cigarettes. Tom had given the contents away but kept the tin as a treasured container for his letters. The second gift was a cholera belt. The men enjoyed the contents of the tins, which they believed to be personal gifts from Her Majesty Queen Mary herself, but spurned the belt, which Tom thought would be of dubious efficacy against cholera in any case. Sometimes he would pass a grizzled old *dafadar* with his cholera belt tied around his turban out of respect for such regal generosity.

Uniform had been a constant issue since their arrival in Marseilles. Although some attempt had been made to provide appropriate clothing on arrival, most of the men had stepped ashore to a European December in thin cotton tunics with sandals on their feet rather than boots. As the pride of the Indian Army marched and rode through their city, the people of Marseilles warmly cheered the novel and ferocious appearance of their defenders and threw them a motley array of warm winter garments.

An early inspection by old 'Iron Ration', as their General Mike Rimington was nicknamed, not altogether kindly, led to his insisting that all British officers should wear their *loonghi* uniform, complete with turban, whatever the weather. Tom supposed that this ridiculous order (one of many to come that would have no practical benefit) was merely to cut a dash when on parade alongside more mundane British troops. It was not until Rimington himself developed a nasty boil on his head, which prevented his wearing his own loonghi, that the whole uniform, designed for warmer, drier climes, was abandoned in favour of something more practical for France.

Here in Thérouanne, Tom was surrounded by the men of the 38th King George's Own Central India Horse, his own regiment, and the 2nd Lancers (Gardner's Horse). He could not help thinking of the latter as the great Bengal Lancers, a title belonging to more swashbuckling times. How he had worshipped them in childhood, when he had played with lead horsemen painted with their colourful uniforms, imagining future feats of horsemanship that would see him numbered among them.

Many of these men were career soldiers who had joined the Army through a long martial caste tradition. In the past people had bought their way in with horses. Now they paid, providing one hundred guineas to become a *risaldar* and just thirty to become a *jamadar*. For a monthly fee of two paltry guineas men were still expected to provide all their own equipment – saddle, sword, lance and so forth – plus a quarter-share of a tent and a half-share in a mule. Not forgetting the paid syce to forage for the horses, of course.

His father's own syce had explained all this to Tom when he was very small. Tom had puzzled for days afterwards over how half a mule could survive at all, let alone walk, and what good a quarter of a tent would be if it should chance to rain.

Tom inevitably recognised one or two of the other officers at Thérouanne, notably good-humoured Hutchison ('Hutch'), whom he knew from the old Club days in Calcutta and, to his delight, Risaldar Major Amar Singh, whom he had encountered more than once during inter-regimental horsemanship contests back in Calcutta. This senior Sikh officer was a towering presence among the troops, both in stature and in leadership. A tall, calm and dignified man, wearing the traditional thick beard and pristine turban, he was both priest and leader to his Sikh men, while respected by Indian Army troops of every religion. Tom felt immeasurably reassured by his presence in Thérouanne.

Tom had wondered initially if either man might mention Mary.

To his relief it seemed not to occur to them. All their pasts seemed very distant now. No-one in Thérouanne talked about anything but practicalities: their immediate surroundings, their current circumstances and what lay ahead. Tom felt his spirits lift as he threw himself into training and preparation.

His only cause of distress was frustration at his diminished rank. He had been a competent and respected major with the Calcutta Light Horse and was used to the burdens and privileges of command. The captain's commission, which he had accepted as an escape route from India, had seemed sensible enough at the time. He had assumed it would be a short-term formality and that once he had joined his unit, he would be rapidly reinstated to major. It soon became apparent that it would not be so simple. His commanding officer, the rotund Lieutenant-Colonel 'Tubby' Bell, had explained to him that as he was a volunteer and therefore something of an unknown quantity in the regular army, his reduction in rank was automatic. He recommended, not unkindly, that Tom be 'as keen as mustard, and work hard and be patient'. Then perhaps something could be done.

Tom tried to forget about it for now, but it still chafed him to be lower in the hierarchy than Major Goodfellow, say. A good fellow indeed, but naive and idealistic. Tom had already caught him waxing lyrical over dinner in the mess tent about how splendid it would be to die for one's country in a cavalry charge. Wide-eyed young lieutenants sitting nearby drank in his every word. Tom himself might be knowingly set on making a useful end of himself; but it was quite a different matter for these young bloods with their whole lives ahead.

It was inevitably Goodfellow who volunteered to lead the ill-fated night march. They were gathered around for the morning *durbar* and had decided that a manoeuvre under cover of darkness might be the very thing to bond together the Lancers and the King George's Own men as one coherent force.

It was to be a march of thirty-five miles or so to Amettes, where they would camp for a few days. When he was offered assistance in mapping the route, Goodfellow declined, saying that he intended to navigate solely by the stars. Surely not, thought Tom, startled, but the man was in earnest. Hutch, who also believed Goodfellow was joking, let out a snort and then had to pretend it was a sudden fit of coughing when Bell looked balefully in his direction. Tom thought that there was also more than a hint of amusement around the sardonic eyes of the second-in-command, Major Gourlie, a Scot whom he remembered meeting once before, up at Simla.

The ripple of approval that spread through the tents as news of the night march was passed on was audible. The men, especially the more experienced soldiers, had been longing to do something other than sit there and shiver in the spring damp while their new mounts grew fat and lazy on water-meadow grass. Soon the camp was a noisy hub of activity, with bits and stirrups polished, guns checked and cleaned and checked again, uniforms freshened up and horses groomed until they shone; each regiment keen to outdo the other, even though very little of their handiwork could be admired by night.

Tom was brushing Daisy's tail to their mutual enjoyment when he heard a cheerful 'Hello there! Westmacott!' behind him. 'Oh. *Captain* Westmacott, I mean!' Reggie Durand jumped out of his saddle, took Tom's hand in both his own and pumped it up and down. 'My dear fellow! I *say*, what luck!' Tom was both pleased and disconcerted to see Reggie again. Durand was clearly still keen on befriending Tom, but given Tom's private aim of self-annihilation, he feared placing the lad at risk.

'That's a fine horse, Durand,' he said in welcome.

'Isn't she just!' answered Reggie, burrowing in his pocket and producing a slightly fusty toffee that he fed to his soft-nosed, doe-eyed bay mare, who sported four white socks and a white nose. 'I know I should have brought a charger, really,' he said to Tom slightly defensively, 'but Phoenix is a fine hack. Uncle said he thought she might be steadier for me at first in the circumstances. And she can go quite fast when she wants to.' Reggie's uncle worked at the War Office and would no doubt have a clearer idea of what they were in for than they did themselves.

Phoenix looked at Reggie, whinnied and fluttered her eyelashes. 'She's a naughty girl, though,' he added fondly, patting her neck, 'Her party trick is to nibble through her rope. Never strays, just doesn't like being tied up.' Yes, how could he have left this adoring creature behind in London? Tom could not help smiling.

Tom reassured Reggie that he should be able to find a decent hunter as a charger within the camp if he needed one. He took the lad to report to Colonel Bell, offering to share a billet and his groom, Private

Moore, with Durand.

Reggie impressed Tom and the other officers by agreeing immediately to participate in the night march. This was even though Bell had told him he could, instead, stay at the camp to settle in, riding on to meet them in Amettes the following morning. Bell had nodded approvingly and Tom overheard his aside to Gourlie, 'Well, only to be expected. He *is* a Durand, after all.'

'Wouldn't miss it for all the world,' said Reggie, mounting Phoenix as dusk fell. 'And this old girl is still quite fresh, aren't you, my lovely?' Phoenix turned her head back towards him and pulled her lips back from her teeth seductively, which made both riders laugh. Daisy looked at Tom reproachfully and he bent in the saddle along her soft mane to tell her once more in Hindi that she was his *rani* among horses, which she always liked very much.

The regiment looked quite magnificent as the night march began. Colonel Bell and Major Gourlie solemnly saluted as the column set off. This time Tom saw clear amusement in the Scotsman's face as he wished a beaming Goodfellow good luck. The two senior officers would be riding hard for Amettes by a different route in order to meet them all there.

Tom and Reggie had been ordered to bring up the rear of the Central India Horse, which had been drawn up in rows of six men as they prepared to march or ride out of their riverside encampment. 'I don't think I have ever seen anything finer, have you, Westmacott?' sighed Reggie as the long file of troops set off.

Tom thought they looked grand; but could even now see the first obstacle ahead. 'What about that field gate?' he pointed out. The whole column came to a shaky halt again and Goodfellow barked an order to reform in ranks of two instead of six, which instantly tripled its length. As the head of the column snaked through the obstacle, Tom and Reggie sat and watched, immobile, until the whole military python rippled into motion again. Looking behind him, Tom saw that the Lancers had formed up in ranks of two from the off and were looking smug.

Initially they made good progress, and curious villagers came out to cheer the soldiers on their way. As darkness fell things became more difficult. Tubby Bell had deliberately chosen a moonless night and the stars overhead were brilliant, but they were the only thing visible in an otherwise black landscape, as sleepy peasants snuffed out their candles.

Gaps started to form in the columns as the horses plodded on. At one crossroads, Tom saw that a large break had formed and he halted the Lancers, then sent Reggie cantering ahead to find which fork the rest had taken and to ask Goodfellow to slow down a little. Durand returned full of enthusiasm. 'By Jove,' he said, 'Goodfellow is navigating by the stars! How clever!' Oh Lord, thought Tom, who had hoped that Goodfellow might have seen sense. That kind of thing is only clever if it works. 'Did he say he would slow down?'

'What? Oh, no. Sorry. I did ask. But not really. He said that we needed to quicken our pace to match the leaders and not shirk.'

Did he now! Tom smothered a grin before it spread too far.

It was about this time that Goodfellow discovered that his stellar navigation skills were somewhat wanting and his omission to bring a precautionary map was something of a strategic blunder. Again and again the straggling serpentine column shuddered to a halt, with the Lancers behind them becoming increasingly irritated as their men could not get into their stride.

This time Tom told Reggie to stay put and spurred up the column himself. At its head, he found Goodfellow gazing up at the stars at a darkened village crossroads, which had five almost identical routes leading away from it. Tom did have a map folded away inside his uniform but there was no light to read it by now anyway. He had tried to memorise it and thought it a simple enough task: they had needed to ride a good few miles down a long, straight, presumably Roman road, then turn left a few miles from Amettes. Goodfellow, over-confident, had brought them off far too soon and was now entangled in a never-ending web of unidentified French hamlets.

Tom thought Amettes should lie to the south-east of their current position but could not be certain. If there had ever been a sign at this dismal crossroads, it had been dismantled to bamboozle the enemy.

'That's Orion,' Goodfellow was saying, slightly wildly. 'And if so, that's Cassiopeia...'. Tom heard Risaldar Major Amar Singh's familiar deep voice from somewhere to his left. 'Major Goodfellow Sahib, should we perhaps ask an inhabitant if your starlight navigation is proving – ahm – unreliable?' Good old Amar Singh, thought Tom. That's exactly what we need to do.

At that moment, an upper window over an estaminet was flung

open by a fearfully ugly woman in a lacy nightcap holding a lantern, all prepared to berate whoever had disturbed her rest. She stared instead, open-mouthed, as her guttering candle illuminated row upon row of gleaming bayonets, turbans, white teeth and glossy black beards. She called to her equally unlovely husband to wake up and share this extraordinary sight. It was like watching the first moments of a Punch and Judy show set up somewhere in the Punjab, thought Tom, highly entertained.

'That's the Pole Star there!' said Goodfellow, feigning more confidence than he possessed. 'Ah, I have it now, I think. We need to turn left – yes, left – just here.'

'Oh, why don't you ask the damned old woman and be done with it!' enquired an anonymous voice from within the ranks, voicing the opinion of all. Amar Singh did not wait for a second prompt, but asked Nougier the interpreter to translate his request as to the precise whereabouts of Amettes. The woman pointed a bony finger down the road to their right and she and her man watched the column coil itself into motion again.

Tom, back in position at the rear, lifted a hand as he passed below their window, but they did not respond; just continued to stare at *les Hindous, oui*, there, in their very village, outside their very own café. *Mais dis donc.*

Goodfellow, chastened, was discovering that what would normally be a simple march of thirty-five miles by day was a very different matter by night. The column was starting to tire and fragment. The stars had been obscured by a patchy mist rolling across from the marshes. Looking behind him, Tom could see the Lancers were in the same predicament, frequently disappearing altogether. The stop-start nature of the night march had taken its toll on both their stamina and enthusiasm.

Tom rode up to Goodfellow again to ask him to slow down and remedy this problem but his request was ignored. He could see that what Goodfellow had lacked in navigational skills, the man now hoped to make up for in speed.

'Well, Durand,' asked Tom as they blundered on at the rear of the straggling column, 'What do you think we should do now?' Starlight navigation might be very well for storybooks but was of no practical benefit here.

Reggie glanced behind him. 'There's nothing for it, is there? We're going to lose our own chaps, or we lose the Lancers. If you ask me, Captain, I think we should stick with the King George's Own.'

Tom agreed. They spurred on to catch up the rear of their column, passing a stray donkey placidly munching a thistle by the side of the road. Balaam's friend promptly decided it might like some nocturnal company and so turned with its mouthful of thistledown and started to trot along behind them, chewing contentedly, unnoticed by either Tom or Reggie.

The first birds were starting to twitter as the regiment straggled over the River Nave bridge into Amettes, where Tubby Bell and Gourlie awaited them. Tom nudged Reggie, who had been asleep in his saddle for the last mile or so, poor lad. He started awake with 'Mother?' on his lips, immediately looking suitably abashed. Phoenix made a sound that was very like laughter, and Daisy, who had decided overnight that the new equine arrival was a good egg, joined in.

By the time Tom and Reggie approached, the other officers were already engaged in a somewhat heated discussion with Bell and Gourlie. 'Westmacott! What have you got to say for yourself? You've gone and lost the Lancers!' snapped the exasperated Tubby Bell. Tom, indignant at being scapegoated, started to explain what had happened, when he caught an appealing and slightly desperate look from Goodfellow. The man had after all done his best. Tom cut his explanation short to a regretful, 'Yes, Sir, we do appear to have lost the Lancers, I'm afraid,' enjoying the look of gratitude in Goodfellow's eyes. He did not relish the lecture that followed from Bell on the utter incompetency of volunteer reserve officers.

The locals had quickly grown accustomed to the presence of hundreds of Indian troops and were busy sewing strange chemical-soaked pads on to the ends of the mens' loonghis. These were supposed to be fastened over the mouth to protect them against gas attacks. Tom suspected this would be a pointless exercise. Reggie sniffed at his with disgust and announced he thought a lungful of the gas would probably be preferable.

Tom's morale improved considerably at eleven o' clock when the sheepish major in command of the Lancers led his weary and embarrassed men into the village square, to be greeted by laughter and comments such as 'Detour via Bombay, Major sahib, né?'

Bell lowered at the last of the 2nd Lancers as they traipsed in. Faced with a furious brigade commander, the major hung his head and admitted that they had accidentally marched in a partial circle to the wrong town – Aire-sur-la-Lys, in fact, some miles away, located only a few miles upriver of Thérouanne.

'Really?' said Gourlie, enjoying himself. He proceeded to press them for more details. The mortified major, sweating with misery even though it was a chilly March morning, was forced to admit that he had mistaken Captain Westmacott's horse for an old donkey and followed that instead. A ghost of a smile appeared on Bell's frosty countenance.

Laughter spread through the men sitting along the roads into the village as the story did and soon they were all roaring and slapping their sides. The major, sensing the change in atmosphere, warmed to his narrative and added that they had finally come to their senses in the town of Aire just as the clock had chimed four on its fine bell-tower. He paused for effect. 'That was where the donkey leant against the town pump and had a good scratch, braying all the while.'

This time even Tubby Bell put his hands on his hips and guffawed.

Well, thought Tom, as he rode companionably between Durand and Gourlie up the Roman road to their camp in the forest nearby, the exercise had in a way been both a complete failure and a huge success. Shared laughter bonded men even more readily than adversity. They would be more of a team hereon in, and Goodfellow would be the better soldier, for their combined experience of the night march to Amettes.

# 13

# Surrender and its Aftermath

Gaston sat at his desk with his head in his hands. He knew that the situation could not continue; but the only way forward was so unpalatable he had difficulty focusing on it.

Autumn had been brought to an end early, on the back of two bitter frosts. The leaves of the forest, which had sheltered les Anglais so well for so long, were falling, swift and treacherous. The men were all now hidden in an area near Obies and had apparently constructed nine little huts there out of interwoven branches, tar-cloth and other bits and pieces the villagers had been able to supply.

The thirty men shivered by day, advised by Gaston only to light fires by night when the smoke would not be seen. They warmed up whatever the villagers had provided to eat on an ancient stove one of them had found in a disused forester's hut. Entertainment consisted of talking in low voices or playing card games with a well-thumbed deck that Bushell's men had been given in Englefontaine. Some tried to trap small animals and birds to boost their meagre diet, with occasional success, but even that was not without danger. It was not so much the extended sightlines within the forest, but the risk of sound travelling through the crisp, still air, which now threatened the thirty men, and they knew it.

Gaston had to face it; there was also less and less food available to share. It had been one thing for the villagers of Obies to feed a handful of men, and quite another for them to feed thirty. Autumn plenty was giving way to winter shortage and they were already forced to hand over much of their hoarded produce to the Germans. He knew that some of those involved were having to go without meals to ensure their children, the enemy and les Anglais were fed. No-one complained, but many went short.

Reluctantly, Gaston had found it necessary to bring more people in on the secret to ensure that the hidden soldiers had enough to eat. *Les ravitailleurs*, as they called themselves now, had steadily increased and now included his brother Alphonse, Léocadie Sohier; and a few trusted others from Bavay, Obies and Valenciennes. Gaston knew how easily a careless word or a neighbour bearing a grudge could bring their whole valiant endeavour crashing down about their ears.

Jules had alerted Louise Thuliez, who operated a covert rescue network out of Saint-Waast-la-Vallée. She had helped him once before when he had needed to evacuate some local prisoners from Bavay who had escaped from the forced-labour camp at Maubeuge. Gaston found her as resourceful and brave as his own late wife, her namesake. Louise Thuliez had offered to explore the logistics of getting the men home, a great relief to Gaston. Scouts went out in all directions to try to find some way of moving the men out towards the coast in groups. In the end, even she had given up in despair. One or two would have perhaps been possible, although fraught with danger, but many simultaneously was out of the question. They did not look or behave like Frenchmen and certainly did not sound it. *Non*, being caught dressed in French clothes was likely to lead to a bullet long before any conversation about prisoner-of-war status could be attempted. It was just too dangerous.

Since the failure to blow up the railway line between Aulnoye and Landrecies, the Germans had not given up on finding the perpetrators. Far from it. As Gaston had predicted, the affront to their self-image as magnanimous conquerors meant that every day some fresh and terrible attempt to extract information from the population was dreamed up. All of the mayors in the vicinity of Valenciennes had been warned that they were to be held personally responsible for any concealment.

Horstberg and his men had followed the trail of les Anglais as far as Locquignol but there they had lost it, possibly thanks to little Suzanne's forced detour via the boggy ditch. And so, every day, they took the old Maire of Locquignol, Monsieur Huvelle, and made him stand facing the wall of his own mairie at gunpoint. They made it plain that if they heard a single shot fired in the forest their response would be a swift bullet to the old man's head. When they allowed him to go back to his bed at night, the poor fellow would say that the worst thing was not seeing the guns behind him. Being a little deaf, he did not know when he might be shot; and he found this most trying. Then out he would be marched again each morning.

Not a soul in Locquignol technically knew anything about les Anglais, but this was a forest community, and there were those who understood things without having been told. Those people might well love old Monsieur Huvelle a good deal more than these unasked-for foreigners. Gaston knew that time was running out.

With a heavy heart, he resolved to ask for a meeting with Lieutenant Bushell soon to discuss the only solution possible.

Even Gaston did not know precisely where their huts were constructed. Instead, the food was dropped off at a range of different points within the forest, the next established on the previous occasion. His team of ravitalleurs had agreed it this way so that if any of the food-carriers were arrested, they could not have the location forced out of them. Usually there was no-one there at the drop-off point but tonight, young Bushell sauntered out of the shadows, his hands in his pockets. He looked for all the world as though he were on an outing to see his sweetheart, thought Gaston, charmed in spite of himself. Bushell spoke passable French and they began to talk in the shadow of a forest oak.

It was as though the English lieutenant had read Gaston's troubled mind. 'I thought it would come to this,' the young man said, nodding, as the Mayor of Bavay explained his community's predicament. 'That's why I came tonight. We have had a damn good run. I reckon when we surrender they'll shoot me as an example and take all the others prisoner. That's only fair, really.'

'No,' Gaston said. 'It won't come to that, I hope. You need to vanish the day the others surrender. A reliable friend thinks she can get you out, providing you are alone. Your French isn't that bad, or at least not to German ears. Then your two sergeants can bring your men with me to Bavay and I will hand them over to Horstberg there myself before witnesses. He will be able to announce to his superiors that he has captured them in person.'

'Then he may shoot you instead!' exclaimed Bushell unhappily. 'I can't agree to that!' Gaston hoped that his reasonableness in the early days of the Occupation would stand him in good stead and said so. He added, 'Now, *jeune homme*, you must listen to me. You are in good health, young, a fine officer. You have been very courageous these last months. If you can now return to England you will be able to do more for your *patrie* and mine than you can by staying here, to be shot by les Boches.'

At length Bushell seemed to agree. Then he shook his head. 'There's a problem,' he said. 'It's been so cold we have been forced to wear our uniforms as an extra layer, I'm afraid. They're in a pretty sorry state, some of them, ripped and muddy and missing buttons.'

Gaston looked at him, dismayed, wondering if Bushell could really be suggesting that he should somehow now arrange the mending and laundering of thirty British army uniforms; but he saw at length that Bushell was right. If les Anglais were to surrender and be taken as prisoners-of-war, they had to look the part, like a military squadron, not a handful of spies.

Later that night he arranged for a pile of ancient horse-blankets and clothing oddments to be left with the food supplies over the next week. Les Anglais would then in turn leave the dirty and damaged uniforms at the food drop-off spots. Bushell was correct – their uniforms stank, and some were little more than rags, the trousers especially. Les ravitailleurs returned from the rendezvous each day for a week with the uniforms, wearing them under their own winter clothing to avoid being seen carrying them. The women then took one garment at a time to launder and stitch from the barn where they were hidden, at the back of Gaston's garden. The uniform was returned the same way.

There were inevitably a few near misses. Rose Pley was on her hands and knees scrubbing one pair of trousers in the *lavoir* when a young German private approached her. She had to resort to some serious flirting to distract him, which Gaston suspected was not altogether a hardship when so many local young men had been taken to work in factories elsewhere. At the end, the boy had even politely offered to carry her wash-basket home for her, but Rose had kept her head and made sure a beguiling red flannel petticoat had covered the wet uniform.

And so it was late one night, as Gaston and Léonie were sitting in their kitchen, Léonie sewing on yet another brown button that was a close match for the coarse English tunic, there came a peremptory knock at the front door and the sound of it being flung open. Alphonse had just returned from the garden and left it unlocked. In strode Horstberg and Kraft from the hall, Gaston's elder son trailing behind them, boiling with indignation.

Gaston sent Alphonse to his room then stood to face them. 'Monsieur le Commandant, Monsieur *l'Interprète*, what can I do for you? It is very late in the day to be calling.'

'*Où sont-ils?*' demanded Horstberg, untranslated. He looked exhausted, Derome noted, as though he had not slept for many nights. This time he felt no sympathy. The man's treatment of old Monsieur Huvelle was despicable.

'I have told you before, Messieurs, I do not know if the men you speak of even exist, let alone their current location,' he half-lied. Léonie, he saw out of the corner of his eye, slowly and calmly completed her work on the last button, bit through the thick thread with her teeth and rolled the tunic up into a more anonymous bundle beside her workbox. Then she too stood. There was no offer or expectation of refreshment as once there would have been. Such niceties were behind them now.

Gaston was also exhausted from lack of sleep and the strain of the events of the last few weeks. He took his spectacles off and polished them.

'We could search the town,' threatened Horstberg.

Derome nodded. 'Certainly you could,' he replied, flatly. 'But you know you will waste your time and find nothing.' Apart from the remaining fifteen or so uniforms in different stages of repair, he thought, unconsciously reaching for Léonie's hand, finding it, and holding it curled in his.

Kraft watched this closely, as he watched everything.

Horstberg said something in German and Kraft translated: 'My kommandant says this is your last chance to tell him what you know. And we are certain you know something, Derome. You are seen in too many places, too far from here. You are doing too much walking!'

Derome fought to keep panic at bay and instead, unexpectedly, felt anger rise in its place. In the circumstances, it was his best defence.

'Well then, yes, I do know something,' he retorted. Horstberg brightened and leant forward in anticipation but Kraft heard the tone of the words and looked more dubious. 'I know that your army may control this region for the moment but I am still the Maire of Bavay until you depose me. Of course I am often seen out walking. I am trying to reassure my people, to make sure the old ones have enough to eat, that the young bloods do nothing to provoke the invader. We did not ask you to come. Do not now expect us to make you feel welcome.'

Léonie squeezed his hand tight, knowing he had expressed the feelings of almost every resident of Bavay in those few words.

Horstberg cursed under his breath in exasperation, turned on his heel and stamped out. Kraft remained a few seconds longer, letting Léonie and Gaston see his eyes linger on her sewing basket and the rolled garment beside it. Then he too left, pulling the door of the kitchen shut behind him. They waited to hear the front door close too. Then Gaston sagged at the knees and sat down, his courage draining. 'We need to act fast,' he said weakly to Léonie. 'Can you get word to all the others? It must be the day after tomorrow.'

And so it was that Tuesday morning at dawn Gaston met the twenty-nine men at the pre-arranged spot. They waited for Gaston beneath another of the great spreading beeches, where the remains of an ancient Roman road crossed the forest floor. Some were standing, some sitting on the piles of dry golden leaves that carpeted the ground. Yes, thought Gaston, blowing into his fists to warm them, it is time. The forest has done well to hide them for as long as it has. Winter is coming.

Louise Thuliez had already spirited away young Lieutenant Bushell. The remaining twenty-nine looked magnificent, in their clean and mended uniforms (one or two still slightly damp). The guns on their shoulders took Gaston aback momentarily; he had entirely forgotten they would be armed. The two sergeants, one Irish, one a Scot, were reassuring the more nervous English youngsters.

Gaston's plan was to walk with the soldiers as far as his old house in Rue des Juifs and there to ask Horstberg to accept their surrender as prisoners-of-war. He wanted as many townsfolk as possible around to witness this peaceful transfer in order to avoid any rash action on Horstberg's part.

He should have known that no unit of soldiers from any army was capable of shuffling along in a group. Les Anglais formed up in nine rows of three, the two sergeants at the front of the first and third columns. With a bold 'Attention! Quick march!' they were off. And Gaston found himself marching in step with them, in front, his feet crunching on beech leaves. The rhythm of their feet was impossible to resist as they followed the old track through the forest, echoing the pace of the Roman legionaries who had created it.

This military arrival was not what he had planned at all. As they passed the few houses along the road, which led from the forest, people looked out, some in astonishment; far more, he noted, with a look of sympathy on their faces, as if to say 'ah, so they have come to the end of the road'.

As they approached the town they had not seen a single German soldier, which was unusual. Madame Hauquier stood defiantly on her doorstep and shouted '*Vive la France! Vive l'Angleterre!*' at which point both sergeants turned eyes left and saluted her, a moment she would never let any living soul in Bavay forget. Others shouted 'Bravo, Monsieur le Maire!' Gaston felt no pride in his actions, only growing trepidation.

As they turned into Rue des Juifs, they met Marthe carrying a basket of vegetables towards their home. She almost dropped it in surprise, then stared in open and frank admiration at the soldiers, who came to a smart halt in the road as Gaston approached her. She was bearing dreadful news. The Germans had gone. She had been on her way to tell him.

Very late last night, she told them, orders had come through that Horstberg was to move his headquarters to Aulnoye with immediate effect. He had appeared distressed and she had wondered if he were being disciplined. There had also been talk of reports (false, obviously, unless there were other poor souls out there) that les Anglais had been sighted in the forest further south. Gaston thought it more probable that Louise Thuliez had been trying to help their last few days by arranging a few decoy sightings.

Gaston was floored. He had imagined arriving at Rue des Juifs and handing the men over to Horstberg himself. Horstberg would surely have recognised the opportunity for personal glory and acted accordingly. What now, he wondered.

Then Maître Corbeau was suddenly there at his elbow. '*Vite.* Into the church,' he said. 'Even les Boches will not violate the right of sanctuary. It will give you time to negotiate their safety.'

Reluctant, but unable to find an alternative, Gaston agreed, ensuring that their weapons were first arranged in a stack against the steps of the statue on her column in the centre of the square. One or two of the men were noticeably unwilling to part with them, and the sergeants had to insist; but most laid them down without hesitation. Gaston set a sensible older boy to watch over the guns and make sure no-one touched them. Then he sent others to stand at the entrance to the town on each road with instructions to run back as soon as there was a sighting of a German vehicle.

Gaston sat down at his desk and lifted the receiver, asking the operator for his colleague the Maire of Aulnoye, in full knowledge that the telephone system was already under German control. His message was simple: tell Commandant Horstberg that twenty-nine English soldiers have just surrendered to Maire Derome at Bavay.

His counterpart gasped, then confirmed he had understood. Gaston replaced the receiver, feeling queasy with fear at the possible consequences of this day's actions.

The Germans would not get there for some time, he knew. This delay was a disaster. The longer Horstberg had to think it through, the more he would realise that many in the town must have been complicit in the survival of these men. Gaston returned to stand uneasily just inside the door of the church he had not entered since childhood, wishing he believed in a God to pray to.

Much to his surprise, he found that Maître Corbeau was addressing the men in broken English, doing his best to reassure and comfort them. One man, a Catholic presumably, asked the priest to hear his confession. Otherwise the soldiers sat in the darkness, murmured to each other in low voices, and waited.

An hour passed. Then the breathless figure of Louis Delavigne appeared, goggle-eyed with excitement and fear. 'Monsieur le Maire! They are coming!' At this point the Scots sergeant stood up and addressed his men. 'Right then, boys,' he said, 'I don't know about you, but I'm none too keen on skulking around in here until the Hun turns up.' There was general agreement. In spite of the protests of both Maître Corbeau and Gaston, the men jostled out of the relative safety of the church. They took up their former positions in three columns, beside the neat pile of weapons beside the Colonne Brunehaut.

Gaston could do nothing more and shouted at the spectating

townspeople, dozens of them now, to go back to their houses, as it could be dangerous for them. He saw children there, including his own, and Léonie. To think that he had wanted them to witness this moment! What a fool he had been. He gestured them all away, to go home, to get to safety while there was still time.

Not one of them budged, Léonie included. He saw her reach for the hand of little Marie-Félicie.

The first of the German lorries rumbled around the corner, where Kommandant Horstberg witnessed a complete unit of soldiers in English uniform standing to attention in the town square, surrounded by most of the population of Bavay. Horstberg, white with rage, stepped out of the passenger seat, Kraft soon beside him. The tension was palpable.

Horstberg remained utterly silent.

Gaston stepped towards him. 'Mon commandant,' he said. 'I must inform you that these Anglais have surrendered their weapons to me this morning. I ask formally that you treat them as prisoners-of-war.' Horstberg stared at him, all trace of humanity lost in his own ordeal of the last weeks. He said something to the two soldiers who had just climbed down from the second lorry. They moved so fast that Kraft had no time to translate and Gaston found himself seized under his arms and thrown against the wall of the mairie. The speed and violence of it winded him and he fell awkwardly. As he staggered to his feet, struggling for breath, he found himself looking down the barrels of six German Mausers. Other Boches had their guns trained on the now-captive soldiers and Horstberg had drawn his own Luger.

There were cries of anger and shock from the onlookers; he heard his beloved Thérèse whimper 'Papa!' and Léonie's voice trying to keep them all calm. He willed them to do nothing stupid. 'Monsieur Kraft!' he called out. 'Will these Englishmen be safe? Are they to be taken as prisoners-of-war, as I have asked?'

'The kommandant will have no choice,' came the terse reply. But which does he mean, thought Gaston. No choice but to let them live? Or no choice but to shoot us all?

Kraft now translated rapid questions into English, addressing the soldiers. Who was their leader? No reply. Who is in charge? Again, no reply. Where had they obtained the explosives? Not a flicker. The soldiers were magnificent, standing still as stone, eyes front. Faced with such contempt, Horstberg's fury overflowed. He pushed his way through his own men whose fingers were on the triggers of their weapons and placed his Luger right against Gaston's temple with an unsteady hand. He spoke in German, which Kraft translated, quite unnecessarily, as the intent was clear to all. 'Talk, or we will kill Maire Derome.'

This is it, then, thought Gaston. He had discussed the various possibilities of surrender from the best-case scenario to this, the worst, with both sergeants when they had stopped earlier for a drink from a well. He had told them that in these circumstances they must say and do nothing.

He closed his eyes, accepting it, thinking of his Louise. There was silence. Then Horstberg spoke rapidly again and Gaston braced himself for the shot. Still nothing.

Slow, measured footsteps echoed across the square.

He opened first one eye, then the other and cautiously turned. Maître Corbeau had walked forward and was standing with his head bowed as he uttered prayers beside the Colonne Brunehaut. This was odd, as the mediaeval queen (Brünhilde as the Germans would have called her, if only they had known) had been far from saintly. She was certainly no object of veneration. Much good would that do them all, the old fool, thought Gaston.

And yet something had changed in the atmosphere. Horstberg, distracted, had turned away from Gaston and lowered his gun. He was now watching the priest in confusion. Could the young officer believe the statue to be that of the Virgin, Gaston wondered, with a sudden flash of insight. If he was in any way devout, it might work.

A longer silence followed, les Anglais standing to attention stock-still, not even deigning to make eye contact with the Germans who guarded them, while the weapons of six others were still trained on Gaston's forehead. *Impasse*, thought Gaston, now feeling slightly light-headed and strangely unafraid. Why did they think they needed six men to shoot one unarmed small-town maire? It was ridiculous. And if they slaughtered him here, what a mess it would make of his beloved mairie, hurriedly painted for the arrival of the b.e.f. so few months before. And in front of his dear sister Léonie! And all the children!

Horstberg barked an order, which Gaston understood. Did Kraft look disappointed or relieved as he told les Anglais to get into the lorries? It was hard to tell. At last the Scots sergeant barked the order to move and obey. The firing squad lowered its weapons and began to load the surrendered guns on to a separate truck.

Then they were speeding away, Horstberg with them. He had not looked in the mayor's direction again, but Gaston knew that while his ordeal might be over for the moment, this would not be the end.

## 14

# By London Omnibus to Tower Bridge

VERMELLES, FRANCE
JULY 1915

Tom felt nothing but relief as he boarded the London omnibus, albeit in slight disbelief. It was just one of forty-five elderly vehicles, hurriedly daubed with camouflage paint, which were being used to ferry the Indian Army trench construction team of four hundred men to the Front.

It was finally their turn. Although it seemed surreal to be travelling there in such a very English form of transportation, the overwhelming atmosphere was one of excitement as the men laughed and chattered like children on a Sunday School charabanc outing. All the windows and doors that would open were flung wide to ease the stifling heat.

The 'buses chugged through undulating woodland, which then opened out into wide, spacious fields. Peasants paused at their labour and stood and stared at the fierce dark-faced saviours through the glass. One little boy shouted '*Vive les Hindous!*' and ran a little way beside the vehicle to the amusement of the men, then returned to his mother's skirts after a brusque rebuke.

Tom glimpsed one old couple with their backs turned, stooping to pick something green from the dry soil of their stony field beside an enormous fresh crater, as though neither it nor the convoy of soldiers existed.

Soon conversation started to fall away as they caught sight of those they were relieving – the weary men of the Queen's and South Staffords – who were plugging along in the dust, all masked with mud. They

looked a hard-bitten lot. In a few months, if it came to the worst and
he survived that long, Tom himself would be marching back along this
narrow road. The Queens were reduced to two companies, he heard
someone say. They were singing 'Tipperary' as they marched, the first
time Tom had heard it in France. As each ancient 'bus chugged by,
they cheered and laughed, or stuck out their arms and shouted 'Bank!
Bank!' as though they were at Piccadilly Circus, requiring transport to
the City. They even passed a sign pointing to Tower Bridge, which he
later learned was a latticed double tower used by the Boche for sniping.

Tom was accompanied on this mission not by Reggie, who was now
with a different squadron, but by his servant and groom Private Moore
and the old Risaldar Harnam Singh. Tom and Moore – Harnam
Singh would sleep among the other Sikhs of course – followed the
billeting officer through streets crowded with men of all nationalities
and from all the corners of the Empire. It was an oddly cheery sight,
this hubbub of often-grimy strangers, all smiling and nodding at each
other in the solidarity brought on by circumstance.

Their billet at Noeux-les-Mines was a great deal better than the
previous one at Enquingatte. They had arrived at the latter late one
night during a howling gale, when Nougier the interpreter was on leave.
Goodfellow and Tom, with only a very slender knowledge of spoken
French, had had to get twelve men and horses and ten mules into billets.
They had managed it by midnight, in darkness and rain. When Tom
finally reached his own quarters that night, the relentlessly optimistic
Private Moore, who had seen to the horses and unpacked his things,
had announced with glee that 'This 'ouse is lousy, Cap'n Westmacott,
Sah. The lidy of the 'ouse scratches 'erself something 'orrid'.

As far as Tom knew, he himself had collected no vermin during the
brief time they resided there, but he was not so sure about Moore: he
had described the lady of the house the morning after their arrival as
'obliging', with a leer. Tom had not been inclined to ask or dwell on
what that might have meant. This new billet nearer Vermelles was in
a house, which belonged to an elderly and respectable doctor's widow,
much to Tom's relief and Moore's disappointment.

The mud had been awful only four months ago at Noeux-les-Mines.
Now it was baked hard as a biscuit in great corrugated ridges. It was
difficult to know what was worse, the seeping misery of mud or these
ossified ruts, which shredded wheels and broke axles.

Their new landlady spoke no English but proved friendly enough and even gave them some wine. She proudly showed them both a long, curved piece of shell, which had smashed through their bedroom window only the previous day. The pane was now secured with little patches of brown-gummed paper.

It was by peering out through an unbroken area that Tom first understood the enormity of the expression 'theatre of war'. He gazed at the vast, distant battleground for several minutes, his map on the windowsill, trying to interpret the broken industrial landscape laid out before him. His third-floor room must look out towards the town called Vermelles. This seemed to be the focus for enemy bombardment. In the far distance rose a ridge, Notre-Dame-de-Lorette perhaps, he thought, tracing the line of it with his finger. This was flowering with balls of dust and debris, paired with the distant muffled thud seconds later as each shell made impact and exploded.

Tom went outside, clambering to the top of a towering pile of coal slag to get a better view. The air reeked of cordite, even at this distance. Overhead there were seven captive war balloons: above and beyond them wheeled tiny silver specks, his first-ever sighting of military aircraft. He pulled out his pocket telescope just in time to see one of the kites spiral downwards. Another piercing *who-o-o!* followed by a dull *whump!* added itself to the fracas. Despite screwing his eye behind the lens, at this distance, he still could not tell whose side could claim a kill.

*Ours but to do or die.* He wondered how long it might take before a random bullet released him to join Mary. He hoped it would count for something when it happened, at least. A pair of stray shells screamed almost directly above him and shell debris clattered on the roof tiles overhead, as he returned indoors to drink a perfectly filthy cup of tepid tea. This was crowned with a floating crust of plaster dust, but his kindly landlady had prepared it for him as a treat and he choked it down for her sake.

The following day was even hotter, and Tom was ordered to take his squadron along the trenches to size up the task ahead. He knew they had to work fast, as German batteries would begin ranging up and down the line as soon as the increased activity in the area was noted. There was no shade and he gave orders to his men to march up in their shirtsleeves.

This northerly trench line took them much closer to Vermelles.

From a distance, it had looked as though most buildings were still relatively intact, but closer inspection revealed a mere skeleton of a place. The French had sapped right up to it and then stormed it with fixed bayonets. The Boche had fought well, and the French had had to fight their way from house to house, effectively destroying their own homes as they went. Madness, thought Tom, staring at the remains of a decent little mining town, about the size of Pershore.

They passed many ordinary country peasants, wheeling barrows of vegetables or carrying covered buckets of milk, or cheese perhaps, on carts. They seemed oblivious to the shells that had put holes in most of their farmhouses or fields. Hutch had told Tom that each farm had a kind of dug-out alongside it and if the Boche start shelling, the farmer and his family just popped inside and sat in it and scratched themselves until the game was over.

At one point on the march, Harnam Singh warned Tom that some of the men were feeling faint and needed water, a case of dehydration rather than of fear. The two officers scanned the baked horizon and could not see a single well, stream or river. Tom opted to stop at the next estaminet they passed and ordered cool glasses of beer for all of them. Harnam Singh handed them round approvingly, but some of his men protested, as many of the Sikhs did not drink alcohol. Their risaldar told them in Hindi not to be such fools, and that this was weak French beer not strong English ale, so it could do them no harm. The metaphor was clearly appreciated and even raised a laugh. They were soon gulping it down gladly, much to Tom's relief.

Towards the end of the march, the Germans started the regular bombardment that would become known to them all as the 'afternoon hate'. The hatred was mutual, of course and they soon heard the throaty roar of their own artillery opening up behind them. Tom and his men were all glad to return to their billets; these were possibly little safer than the trenches they had just visited, but at least gave the illusion of security. Tom noted with surprise that he still felt relatively fresh, even after a ten-mile march.

Up in his room, he decided to set about washing himself and his underclothes and accomplished both stripped bare, standing over a tiny basin on a waterproof sheet. Soon the wet underclothes were festooned out of the window. Only then did he realise that in Moore's absence he had no dry clothes with which to replace them. Not keen to shock his landlady by coming downstairs clad only in his mackintosh, he opted to stretch out naked on the top of the bedclothes and try to get some sleep. A noisy bluebottle he was too tired to chase and despatch prevented this; and he found himself thinking of home.

Tom had already written to Dick in India and to his in-laws the Lawsons to tell them he was safe. Sleep would not come, even though he was exhausted. Tom pulled himself on to a hard chair and took out his pencil to complete a rambling letter he had already begun to Evelyn Winnington-Ingram. What she would make of it was anyone's guess, but Mary's sister Grace had made him promise he would keep in touch with their friend. It was a good thing, he thought, almost chuckling, that her boot-faced cousin Evelyn could not see him as he sat there, scribbling away, wearing not a stitch. She might look even more disapproving than she had done at the wedding. With this thought he slipped into sleep.

The following day Tom woke early. His men were not on duty until the second relief at noon, and so he decided to ask to go and take a closer look at shattered Vermelles, justifying it as a precautionary reconnaissance. Colonel Bell called him several kinds of fool for wanting to do so but agreed, providing he took a native officer with him. Harnam Singh soon materialised at his right elbow, as was his habit. Bell shook his head in amused disbelief and gestured them both away.

Once they walked down into the town, they found to their surprise that the Welsh regiment and some gunners were still billeted in Vermelles, mainly in the cellars. An unshaven private lounging against a wall helped them identify the shells by name: the particularly nasty ones, which kept whining overhead, were called pipsqueaks, and the heavy ones, which exploded in a thick fog of black smoke, were coalboxes. 'You gets used to it,' he said, lighting his pipe, and shrugged. 'The Munsters've lost thirteen men already. Unlucky fer some.'

As Tom and Harnam Singh stood there, shrapnel struck the buildings to their left and the Boche put a shell right through the roof of the church nearby, at which point they both decided they had had enough of such an unhealthy spot. The private nodded in farewell and continued his nonchalant smoke.

There were many dreadful sights as Tom and Harnam Singh followed the road out of the town: babies' cots and other household gear lying broken and abandoned in each direction. An old brass bed, its frame shattered, lay across the track, its mattress and the broken earth beside it bloodied. Tom averted his eyes as he picked his way around it. They stumbled over a couple of usefully-abandoned wooden chairs that they could sit on in the trenches. Old Harnam Singh wanted to carry both but Tom would not let him, and so the risaldar stalked along a few paces behind.

Surrounded by so much evidence of domestic life torn apart, Tom found himself again thinking of England. A brief postcard had arrived that morning from Evelyn in reply to the little note he had sent to inform her family of his safe arrival in France. He had heard from her sister Maud once before, but not from Evelyn herself. It was decent of her to write, he thought with gratitude. The postcard showed the spire of the church at Ross-on-Wye and its content was reassuringly dull. He propped it up on the window ledge.

His escapade with Harnam Singh that day would perhaps make a good story with which to respond to Evelyn, he thought. If she replied, it might help him get to know her a little better. He would not include the more harrowing elements, of course, as they would not be suitable for a woman's eyes.

Later he would take out his pencil and add:

> Dear Evelyn,
> You would have laughed to see a six-foot tall, hairy Sikh carrying a kitchen chair behind a filthy, bespectacled solicitor, similarly equipped, with no collar and in his shirtsleeves...

Mary would have laughed at that, he thought, so perhaps her cousin would too?

After about ten minutes of walking out of Vermelles in single file, making conversation with a man he could not see, Tom put down his chair and asked Harnam Singh what the devil he thought he was playing at.

'Why, I am defending you, Captain Westmacott sahib,' said the great grey-bearded officer, seeming most surprised that he had been asked. 'It is my *farz*, my duty.'

'Well you really don't need to! Please don't be such an ass!' protested Tom.

It was as if he had not spoken.

'It is my honour to defend my officer, Captain Westmacott sahib,' Harnam Singh said with great dignity. To protest further would have offended the man greatly and so Tom held his tongue. And that was the end of the matter.

Just as they were about to continue to the safety of the shelter trench, Harnam Singh's eyes lit on something that made him smile even more broadly than the thought of protecting Tom. 'Look, Captain sahib,' he said in wonder. 'Here are roses! And *such* roses!' And so there were, big crimson blooms just visible over the top of a tumbledown wall. Before Tom could prevent him, Harnam Singh had clambered over this with considerable agility and disappeared into the orchard of a little narrow and tall ruined house, which looked back towards the German lines. Tom peered through a gap in the brickwork to witness Harnam Singh inhaling the sweet scent of one rose after another, lost in an ecstasy of colour and perfume. 'Not as fine as those from my own garden,' he exclaimed, turning around slowly in this unexpected and overgrown paradise, 'But I am sure that Colonel Bell sahib will like these.' And with that he drew his knife and cut a great fragrant armful of budding blooms.

Tom did not like this activity one little bit, either from the point of view of being shot by a hidden sniper – he thought he had seen a movement in the upper window – or the plucking of roses, which might be reported as possible looting. There was however no stopping Harnam Singh once he had put his mind to something. And so Tom waited, looking up at the cloudless sky, enjoying a lark's song overhead in a brief lull in the shelling.

Moments later, the tell-tale whistle through the air instantly extinguished the birdsong. With a great hollow *crump*, the shell exploded a hundred yards or so behind them in a cloud of filthy black smoke, just where the unshaven private had been leaning against the wall. This now wavered, as if turned to jelly, before crumbling outwards. Tom scrambled up from where he had flung himself and took several involuntary steps back towards the dreadful scene, then stopped again, appalled. Men were already emerging from the cellars, like ants from a crack, some supporting others with injuries. A major had appeared from somewhere and was shouting orders. These were not men of Tom's regiment and he could see there was little he could do. One of the private's legs, the foot still moving very slightly, poked out from beneath the heavy masonry. Tom could not tell if it were still attached to the private. The man's pipe was lying on the ground, broken in two, the bowl still smoking.

'Come now, Captain Westmacott sahib,' said Harnam Singh firmly, seeing Tom's white face. The risaldar picked up his chair, now piled high with blooms. 'We cannot help them,' he added, recognising that he needed to distract Tom from the scene before them. 'There is nothing that we can do for them, sahib. And we have these roses to deliver, né?'

They walked back in silence, still clutching their chairs, each digesting what he had seen. Harnam Singh's roses shed an occasional red petal as though, Tom thought, they were drops of blood. Death had seemed to come calling more frequently in India than in England, Tom reminded himself, knowing that he should not be shocked after having seen no small amount of injuries on the streets of Calcutta. But the inexplicable brutality of this attack by a faceless enemy who could not see those they had killed or injured shocked him nonetheless. Who had invented and sanctioned the use of such powerful weaponry?

Harnam Singh was merely thinking that it was all the will of God, but that if he were to die, he wanted to take more of the enemy with him.

Their baptism by fire in France had provided a strange mixture of beauty and horror. On their return Tubby Bell, who was a good sport, appreciated the floral joke; but the roses finally found their vase at Tom's billet, where his landlady was their delighted recipient.

More horrible news came in the following day: the Inniskilling (6th Dragoons) working party had been heavily shelled on its way home. After dark that same night, a private soldier had spotted a lamp signal flashing from a house overlooking the road towards the German line – the very house where Harnam Singh had paused to pick the roses – and they had caught a woman and four men, one in French uniform, with a signal lamp. Harnam Singh had seen them all marched off between men with fixed bayonets, their hands tied behind them. These captives would probably be dead by now. Tom felt queasy to think such traitors could have been watching them the previous day. He could understand someone of German blood wishing to betray the British; but the thought of someone French doing this sickened him. Men of all nationalities were making sacrifices for France, among them the Welsh private who had died.

Surprised by the gift of the roses, and hearing of his visit to Vermelles and the arrests of the four, Tom's landlady told him a shocking tale, anxious to prove that not all Frenchmen were traitors: when les Boches had attacked the town, they had shot the parish priest on the steps of his own church as a spy. '*Un innocent, Monsieur*,' the old lady said, wiping her eyes sadly and shaking her head. '*Un martyre*.' She seemed very shaky, and later confided that she had had next to nothing to eat since their arrival, not daring to ask them for a share of their rations. She had been feeding them the food she should have kept for herself. Tom was horrified, assured her that they were not savages, and that he would see what he could do. She proved an excellent cook with the rations he passed in her direction.

Later Tubby Bell told them that eighty thousand French soldiers and civilians died when the French army took the nearby ridge of Notre-Dame-de-Lorette: a very high price indeed for driving the enemy a few yards from Souchy. Bell ordered Tom and his men to take a break from digging trenches – they had filled and piled up almost a thousand sandbags already – in order to dig graves instead.

Some of the corpses they found were days old and still lay rotting in the sun. The stench caught in his nose and was trapped there weeks later. After a long shift spent on this foul activity, which had even the hardest of his men choking and vomiting, Harnam Singh came to Tom red-eyed with exhaustion and frustration, pointing out that one good funeral pyre would be quicker and healthier, and would in his opinion do these men greater honour.

Privately Tom agreed with him. Stacking bodies in stiff-legged heaps in this heat was a recipe for disaster in terms of disease, but the orders were for burial and that was that. 'Promise me, Captain Westmacott sahib,' Harnam Singh said, looming over Tom at the end of a long, hot day of digging. 'Never the stinking hole in the ground. A clean flame, that I may live again.'

'A clean flame,' agreed Tom, absent-mindedly.

Pear trees, thought Tom that night, as he lay on his bed and stared at the cracked and stained ceiling. He imagined himself biting into a fresh, cold pear, could almost taste the juices as they trickled down his throat. If he survived the war, he would not plant roses. He would plant a pear tree against the wall of his home, wherever that might be – a *Doyenne du Comice* such as his grandfather had planted at Chastleton perhaps. Fat, pale-golden orbs of intense sweetness on which the blackbirds gorged.

Not roses. Never roses.

As he felt himself slide into sleep, he did not notice that this time he had thought, *if I survive*.

## 15

# Through a Cracked Lens

They had come for him at night, just as he thought they would.

It had been weeks since Gaston had slept properly. Once in bed he would lie and listen, tensing whenever he heard voices or movement in the street outside. Léonie had kept a bag of spare clothes and food packed and ready for him for many days now.

When the moment came, they would not let him take his bag, but they did point to his coat on a hook beside the door. Léonie had come downstairs wrapped in her old blue *robe de chambre,* powerless, biting her lip. He tried to smile, to reassure her, as he tied his shoelaces at gunpoint with shaking hands.

Before that, they had come unannounced twice during daylight hours, to question him again. He had stuck doggedly to the same story: he knew nothing, he had never met les Anglais until the day they had surrendered in the town square. It was clear to the Germans that he was lying and equally clear to Gaston that they knew it. They were all becoming weary of the charade. Just as a dripping tap would eventually wear a hole through stone, he knew that the next time they came it would be to take him away.

On this final occasion, Horstberg had come for him without Kraft, accompanied only by two burly soldiers. No one said a thing. When Gaston had tried to reason with Horstberg, the kommandant raised his riding crop as though to strike his face. 'Non!' cried Léonie from the stairs, and he could hear the children stirring above.

For a moment or two, the two men just stood there, framed in the doorway, Horstberg towering over his prisoner. Then the German slowly lowered the crop, turned and beckoned to his soldiers. Mausers were pointed at him and the men bundled Gaston out of the house. It had been raining and the cobbles were slippery. He stumbled as they shoved him towards the open wagon. The coat he had been given no time to put on slipped from his grasp and fell into a puddle. Scrabbling, he managed to recover it, only to realise once upright again that his spectacles were somehow no longer on the end of his nose.

Aghast and half blind, he tried to kneel and feel for them but no, the soldiers forced him onwards, upwards, half-pushing, half-hauling him into the back of the wagon. One of the two grey horses whinnied and pawed, impatient to be moving again. Without his spectacles, the men's faces were just a terrifying pale blur against the sky, its dark clouds fringed with stifled moonlight.

One guard jumped up and sat beside him, the other opposite. The driver took the reins. Horstberg mounted his horse to ride ahead.

Gaston called out to Horstberg to ask where he was being taken, in the hope that Léonie would hear him from the doorway. The German officer sat mute on his great steaming beast and did not even acknowledge the Frenchman. It pained Gaston to recall that he had drunk good wine with this man once. Horstberg dug in his spurs and, in a flurry of mud and hooves, he was gone.

Gaston pulled himself painfully into a seated position. He tried to make out his sister's silhouette in the blurred receding square of the doorway and felt rather than saw the stricken faces of Alphonse, Thérèse, Léon and little Marie-Félicie at the upper windows. Perhaps it was better this way, he thought, as the driver cracked the whip and the horses picked up speed around the corner. He could not see when his house and family were gone.

One guard said nothing for the entire journey, contenting himself with humming tunelessly; the other lit a pipe. Later the first pulled his collar up around his ears and dozed against the side of the wagon, supporting his head on a piece of old sacking. The other remained wakeful, his pipe tobacco smelling sweetly of tar and treacle.

Just as it had begun to rain again, Gaston felt a gentle movement in his lap. To his astonishment and relief, the second guard had stealthily handed Gaston back his spectacles. Pulling them on – one lens was cracked but he could see again so what did it matter – he peered at the man, recognising the young private he had once noticed attempting to woo a local lass. He had smiled at them and they had smiled back. Innocents, he thought. It seemed like a lifetime ago.

Touched by this act of kindness and humanity, Gaston murmured *Danke schön. Bitte sehr*, whispered his captor. Then, leaning closer, the boy muttered something else. It took three goes for Gaston to understand his thick Bavarian accent, and once he did so, he wished he had not. His guard had said 'Saint Quentin', where the main German administration in the area was currently based. The rumours of what occurred within its ancient walls had not been heartening. Exhausted through lack of sleep, and increasingly numbed with cold and shock, Gaston eventually dozed off.

The young guard awoke him by shaking his shoulder. Gaston peered up at the sinister slit-windowed bulk of the *château* in Saint-Quentin. He soon found himself being man-handled in through a small gate within a larger one. Gaston did not resist his captors, what was the point? He knew the place by reputation. Those who were taken there would emerge as broken men – or not emerge at all.

Horstberg, still silent, pushed him up a spiral staircase and then into a dark, stone cell, which, Gaston realised, must be located in one of the twin towers of the grim fortress.

The wind whistled through a narrow slit of a window. A pool of water on the floor nearby – blown in perhaps – was frozen. Gaston walked into the centre of the room and turned to look around his cell. Its walls sloped on three sides, which would force him to stoop. There was a thin, straw mattress and grimy blanket in one corner, a tin bucket in another. A wooden three-legged stool was pushed underneath a small table that had a candle-end melted on to it. Next to this sat a tin plate of black bread and a tin mug of water. Both looked like they had been there some time. It was a room that reeked of hopelessness and the stale stench of urine.

Behind him in the doorway, Horstberg said something at last. Kraft, who had joined him, stepped forward, struck a match and lit the candle, placing some sheets of paper and the stub of a pencil on the desk. 'Write,' commanded the interpreter, bluntly. 'Write all you know about these English: who has been feeding them, where they have been hiding. Do this and my kommandant might possibly spare your wretched French skin. Otherwise, Monsieur le Maire, you can write your *testament.*'

Then they locked the door, leaving him alone with the stink and the pencil-stub and the candle-end.

The temptation to fall to his knees with his head in his hands was great. Instead, he decided to investigate his cell, which was quickly accomplished: four small paces one way, three another. There the roof sloped so far down he could go no further. He could see tally-marks scratched in the corner of the wall, the drawing of a voluptuous woman, with the word *'adieu'* scrawled beside her.

Enough. He had to trust the others now. Being there was almost a relief after the tension of anticipation. Ignoring the paper and the candle, he lay down on the damp mattress, wrapped his coat around his aching body and tried to sleep again. His head throbbed with the events of the day, and the voices of his beloved children echoed in his heart.

What would become of them all if he never returned?

Léonie had ordered Thérèse, Alphonse, Leon and Marie-Félicie back to bed in tones that could not be disobeyed. She then allowed herself a moment of utter misery, weeping with rage in complete silence in case the rest of the household should hear her. Then she wiped her eyes and pulled on her dark wool cloak, slipping out into the chilly early morning mist. She and her brother had worked out precisely what might save him in these circumstances. Monsieur Hiolle, the deputy maire, was now in charge and she needed to see him first.

To find and wake Monsieur Hiolle she had to pass by the village square, crossing over the very same spot where she had thought Gaston was going to be shot only a few days before. As she approached the church, she was surprised to see a light shining within.

She looked in through the door to see Maître Corbeau kneeling in prayer before a gruesome statue of some local martyr. Léonie, although more devout than her brother, had never cared for it much. A candle burned low in front of the effigy of a man up to his knees in mud, his arms raised, his eyes rolling heavenwards. The Abbé Lebrun must have been praying there for hours, she thought, but it could surely not yet be a vigil for Gaston?

The priest heard her step and paused, turning to see who was there. She walked swiftly up the aisle. 'Mon Père, they have taken my brother,' she said, swallowing her sorrow. The priest flinched, then rose.

'Oh, *ma pauvre* Mademoiselle Derome. Do you know where?' he asked her gently, taking her by the hands.

She shook her head. 'He wanted them to say but they would not. They would not let him take the bag I had prepared, just an old coat, not even his warmest.' She added, feeling hysteria rise, 'He could already be dead in some dark corner of the forest for all we know!'

'Non,' said Maître Corbeau, adamantly. 'If your brother were to be shot, why would he need a coat?' This was true, and the thought calmed her. 'He only needs to take a coat,' continued the priest, 'If he is travelling a long way or going somewhere cold, or both. Let us think.'

'Landrecies?'

'I heard the Germans moved out of there entirely last week. They keep relocating their headquarters. They are afraid.' Léonie wondered how he knew this, then remembered that some of the German soldiers were Roman Catholics too. 'Since les Anglais tried to blow up the train they have been nervous.'

Understandably so, thought Léonie. 'God knows where they have taken *mon pauvre frère*,' she sighed.

Maître Corbeau swung back to the statue for a moment, staring, and staggered slightly as though he would fall. '*Justement*,' he said, '*Justement*.'

'Mon Père? Are you quite well?'

'God knows. Indeed, he invariably does.' Léonie stared at him. 'You see the statue, Mademoiselle? I could have prayed before any one of these today,' the priest continued excitedly. 'But this one – this is the one that called me, when I found I could not sleep. You see? The feet are not visible. He is rising to glory from the black depths of the marshland. It is *le bon* Saint Quentin!'

'Gaston may be at Saint Quentin?' Even as she said it, she felt the likelihood of its truth and was daunted by it. Few emerged from the château at Saint Quentin intact, either in soul or in body. Everyone knew that it was where the Germans interrogated their captives.

A simple moon-faced fellow from the next village had been taken there a month ago as a punishment for cutting grass for his old donkey too close to the railway line. The Germans had promptly shot the beast between the eyes and dragged the poor man off to Saint Quentin for a night. He would not speak of what they had done to him there. The bruises on his back and face might have healed, but all he could do now was cringe at the slightest sound, wring his hands and cry at his fireside. And Gaston? If they should beat him like that? Or worse? Her brother had never been as strong as she was.

She shook her head to free herself of the unbidden images that were taking shape in its shadows and said, 'Mon Père, tell me, what shall we do? Should we pray together for the salvation of Gaston?'

'Oh, that too, my child,' said Maître Corbeau. 'But for now, sit down and listen to what I have to say.'

Early the following morning Monsieur Hiolle confirmed via his counterpart in Saint Quentin that Gaston was indeed being held in the castle there. Gaston's deputy had soon contacted every *conseiller municipal* he could reach by telephone or by hand-borne note to alert them to Derome's peril. They planned to converge on the castle at Saint Quentin the following morning to present their petition and to try to reason with its commander.

Later that day the townsfolk heard the church bell tolled vigorously, young Louis Delavigne swinging on the rope with all his might to call them to a special *messe* for the wellbeing of their imprisoned mayor. The congregation outnumbered the pews available and some stood in the aisle. They were all surprised to be greeted by the little *curé* from Locquignol, not Maître Corbeau, who was said to be indisposed. Léonie confirmed that she had seen him only the previous day and he had seemed most unsettled. She omitted to mention why.

Maître Corbeau's congregation was torn between curiosity, outrage and concern, as their severe priest was never ill. A few whispered what many suspected: that there was no love lost between the two men and this was one way the *abbé* could show it, scorning to pray for Monsieur Derome in his hour of need. Others went so far as to suggest that it was Maître Corbeau who had informed on their mayor. Some recalled that he had behaved strangely the day of the surrender, praying to the dead barbarian queen on her column rather than to a proper saint. Most concluded that the strain of occupation must be taking its toll on old Maître Corbeau.

As they filed out of the church, their fears somewhat allayed by the curé's soothing words, they found that Monsieur Hiolle had set up a little table beside the door. There they all either signed or made their mark on a petition to free their mayor, over seventy people in all.

Surely it would help persuade the Germans to release Monsieur Derome?

# 16

# The Contents of a Tin of Jam

Tom rode into Thérouanne with Hutch, late in the afternoon of 2 September. He was returning from a brief period of leave and had met Hutch on the ferry. They found themselves arriving, much to their dismay, just before an inspection by their G.O.C. Perfectly marvellous timing, declared Hutch with his usual droll humour, as they unrolled their great-coats from the backs of their saddles and put them on, then handed two tired and heavily-laden horses over to the syces.

It was important to keep the horses in condition since they were being so little used and the hack back from Saint-Valéry had done them good. The two friends had enjoyed the journey, although it was getting noticeably colder at night.

Hutch and Tom could not now button their coats. They looked twice their normal size, wearing as much warm clothing as they could under their uniforms, one layer over another, in anticipation of winter cold. They were also festooned with all kinds of paraphernalia, a practice that had become known as the 'Christmas Tree'. They had some experience now of what was useful: water bottle, field glasses, revolver on a leather lanyard, map in a waterproof case, iron ration, medical case with iodine and bandage, boot oil, socks, leather gloves, shaving kit, a whisky flask in Hutch's case, a brandy flask in Tom's.

At the top of the list of useless but nonetheless obligatory items came the dratted swords: every officer was required to carry one, even though they were heavy and kept catching on things. Tom was particularly pleased with a knitted woollen hood that Grace had sent him. Her card had suggested that if he kept his head warm the rest of him might feel less cold too and he already knew she was right.

Things had slipped at Thérouanne, it appeared, since the King George's Own had moved up to Authuile during Tom's period of leave. The stables were not as neat and somehow two of the light draught horses had managed to break out of their billets the very night they arrived. Tom had to admonish the bumbling corporal left in charge and send him out to look for them.

In the morning when the brigadier and his staff arrived, neither hunter nor quarry were anywhere to be seen. Tom rather suspected the man of having planned the whole thing to avoid the inspection.

As the G.O.C. and his gilded officers approached, Tom found himself standing to attention in the stable, very conscious of the two empty stalls behind him. He hoped the stables might escape with a cursory glance and at first it looked as though they might get away with it. Then a languid, slender figure disengaged itself from the others, paused, turned back, and stared at him. With a nasty jolt Tom recognised the brash young major who had tried to commandeer Daisy on the crossing to Saint-Valéry. 'Oh, just a moment, sir. Something of interest here,' the officer said, pleasantly.

Of course, the wretched brigadier had joined him then, to demand Tom's name and ask him where the devil the brutes were which belonged in the two empty stalls. Tom had to explain that the horses were presumably galloping across some French peasant's land with the corporal in hot pursuit. Futile of course to point out that these horses had vanished before his own return from leave.

All this was closely observed by the smirking young major, who watched with his head slightly cocked from behind the G.O.C., as the great man expressed his extreme disappointment in the capabilities of Captain Westmacott, whom he had only just met. The major lingered after the brigadier had continued in search of another victim just long enough to say, 'Captain West-ma-cott,' stressing Tom's subordinate rank. Then he turned and sauntered after the Brigadier, without ordering Tom and Hutch 'at ease'. As a result, he and Hutch were still standing to, quite unnecessarily, an hour after the visitation.

Tom slept in his clothes for the second night running before taking the regimental transport 'bus back up to the Front the next morning.

The upper trenches at Authuile were a shoddy affair, originally dug by French troops in a hurry, without any traverses or dugouts. They were barely better than scurrying about in the open, thought Tom with disgust, as a stray bullet glanced off the wall ahead of him.

It had been pouring all week, that heavy, warm, drenching rain that falls and soaks the land as summer yields to autumn. The result was a lethal skimming of mud over the hard-baked ridges, which then became invisible beneath. Tom, struggling along with his precious chair as well as his valise, tripped or slipped and fell twice as he made his way through the shallow communication trench towards the area where he hoped to find Reggie. Once he lost his spectacles in the mud and had to dabble in the mess to find them. He then held the lenses towards the sky to allow the clean rain to wash off the worst of it.

Tom was to relieve Gourlie of B Squadron. He was suffering from an agonising bout of gout, the poor fellow. Young Durand would therefore be Tom's second-in-command and the prospect of seeing how the young lad was faring pleased him greatly. He had not seen much of Reggie since last March, as they had been assigned to different areas.

He took a turning signposted 'Gourock' by some Scots wag. These trench nicknames were of some practical use in navigation and served to bamboozle the enemy (in theory at least) but he had yet to become accustomed to them.

A sowar he did not know called Tom back as he floundered down one shallow trench. 'Not that way, Captain sahib! It is flooded again after last night's rains!' The soldier, also from the King George's Own, listened to Tom's explanation of where he needed to get to, nodded and picked up Tom's chair and valise without another word. They scuttled for a full twenty minutes through a maze of trenches, the sowar commenting usefully on places of danger from snipers as they went. They were fired on once, when the man may have lifted the chair clear of the parapet, but it was a desultory pot-shot or two, nothing serious. Both sides were chronically short of ammunition.

Eventually Tom found himself outside a relatively fresh dugout, cut out of solid chalk, where he thanked and dismissed his good-natured guide.

'Anyone at home, Durand?' he asked brightly as he crouched and entered, his eyes taking a while to adjust to the dim light.

'Westmacott!' Reggie was sitting on an upturned wooden crate in the tiny room, using a second crate as a table. There was no room to stand upright, or even to sit down – Reggie appeared to have folded himself in two to fit between the crate and the wall behind it. When he saw what Tom was carrying, he added enviously, 'Oh I say, you've got a chair, you lucky fellow. I wish I did too.'

'Don't complain! You can borrow it when I'm not here. And look, I come bearing good things.' Tom had been surprised to receive a nice slab of fruit cake from the Winnington-Ingrams, precisely cut to fit in a tin with a picture of the king on it; he had not seen the family on this last leave, although he had hoped to. It was accompanied by a hurried note from Maud W-I on behalf of them all stating that Evelyn had just become a nurse at the local Red Cross hospital and would therefore have little time to write letters. This sounded a note of caution and little wonder, as Evelyn had less reason than any of them to wish to keep in contact with him. Still, he would persevere with an occasional note or postcard. Mary would have wanted him to keep in touch with her, he felt.

'Cake!' said Reggie. 'I should simply love a slice after supper, which will, I warn you, be stew again. It's always stew. Nugget always somehow seems to be able to get real meat to put in it – best not to enquire exactly what it might be, though, I fear. I say, did you hear about Hutch's *vivandière?* Some of us should have been eating like kings with a cook like her wielding the wooden spoon!'

Tom had indeed spent the first night of his leave at the Estaminet de la Mer at Saint-Valéry-sur-Somme being entertained by this story, which Hutch, with his usual laconic delivery, had spun out for as long as he possibly could. In July, the food had been so bad on Hutch's squadron's section of the line (Nougier could only stretch himself so far) that he had hit upon the idea of reviving the mediaeval military tradition of the vivandière. In a village not far from Thérouanne, Hutch had 'happened upon' the perfect recruit: as he described her, 'Not a beauty, perhaps, Westmacott, but a fine widow-woman, obliging and a terrific cook to boot!'

Not for the first time, Tom had shied away from the word 'obliging'.

'Well go on, whatever happened? Did you get her to the line?'

Hutch had taken a long swig of cool beer, savouring his story. 'Well, I asked madame to be ready at dawn and so she was – with an entire wagonful of equipment, which I didn't anticipate. She said she could not possibly do without it if she was to cater for the squadron. So I found a reliable sowar to drive it and told her to lie low in the back. Off we went and all was going swimmingly when not far from Vermelles, on a bumpy section of road, I trotted round a corner and there by sheer misfortune, whom should I encounter but the G.O.C.! And that nasty piece of work Lochdubh at his side, of course. They were fresh from another troop inspection. Well, of course they hallooed me and I had to stop and give an account of myself. I thought I did pretty well, Westmacott, and explained that I had been out foraging for food for the squadron. All the time I could see the wagon rumbling in our direction, with Sowar Pritam Singh at the reins. All would have been well, old Pritam Singh would have been magnificent, yes Brigadier sahib, no Brigadier sahib; and the G.O.C. was already congratulating me on my initiative, but then the wretched wagon goes over a wretched rut, which breaks the wretched axle…'

'… and down did fall baby, ladle and all!' laughed Tom.

'It's exceedingly rude to interrupt another man's story, Westmacott. As I was saying, there she lay, all sprawled in the dust, petticoats round her neck and hairy legs akimbo, surrounded by copper pans and wooden spoons and whatnot. She then picked herself up and brushed herself down, giving vent to some colourful French vocabulary, which even Nugget would blush to translate. It was largely aimed at the G.O.C. whom she somehow considered to be responsible, which in a way he was.' Hutch enjoyed another mouthful of beer, relishing Tom's reaction, then continued, 'Well, I thought I was for it, as you could imagine, and it started out that way with the G.O.C. giving me a fine lecture on conduct and morality. Then that Lochdubh fellow slithered up and had a word in his ear and something changed; they just told me to carry on. I honestly thought I'd got away with it!'

'But you hadn't?'

Hutch shook his head and drained his glass. 'I left Sowar Pritam Singh with the instruction to get the wheel mended as quickly as possible.'

'So what happened?' asked Tom, although he could already guess.

'Well, Pritam Singh turned up at the rear of the trenches with the repaired wagon hours later, but no cook or kit. And informed me that Lochdubh had had her dropped off, pots and all, at G.H.Q. I understand,' he added gloomily, 'that the G.O.C. immediately sacked his old cook, whose *boeuf en croûte* obviously wasn't up to scratch. Since his new vivandière arrived, the G.O.C.'s table is quite sought after.

*coq au vin* every night. And as for Lochdubh, the sun shines out of his…'

'Have another beer, old boy,' Tom had said, beckoning to the waitress.

In the dugout, Reggie had not moved from his stool since Westmacott entered, unusual in such a well-mannered lad. Tom now looked more closely at what the boy had laid out before him as Reggie started to explain. 'I am awfully sorry not to be more hospitable, Westmacott, and I shall be presently, but first I need to attend to this, if you don't mind. It's almost time and I need to concentrate. Look, crawl over there and you can get your bed sorted out in that corner while I finish these off. It's quite dry and there's just about enough space.'

The second crate had a couple of used Ticklers Jam tins on it, one plum and apple, one marmalade. Ticklers Jam was filthy stuff, varying in colour rather than taste or texture. Tom found the marmalade palatable enough but would force down the jam when hungry. One of Reggie's tins had a pudgy clay lid with a piece of fuse sticking out of the top. Beside this lay a few scraps of pale fabric – gun-cotton, thought Tom. Well, well. There were also pieces of fuse, a pile of rusty nails, a big lump of ochre clay, some fiddly things he took to be detonators and several rounds of small arms ammunition.

'Let me just finish off one of these for you, then we'll go,' said Reggie, with a curious glitter in his eyes.

Tom arranged his things as best he could. The chalk floor made it impossible to set out his chicken-wire mattress on pickets as he had hoped, so he gave up and just rolled out his bedding on the floor. Reggie was right: it was pretty dry, as the entrance was raised off the muddy base of the trench.

Tom was already worried about the boy. He had lost weight, he thought, and there was an oddity in his manner, a new kind of brittleness. And for goodness' sake, where had the lad learned to make nail-bomb grenades?

Bright-eyed, pale and intent on his task, Reggie packed the ammo and detonator into the second tin, arranging the nails on top in an artistic circle, placed a fuse into the centre and then packed it all up with clay.

Then he relaxed a little and smiled at Tom. 'There!' he said proudly. 'Two beauties! I make one every night when I can, d'y see? Because they can get damp otherwise and won't go off. But I knew you were likely to turn up today, so I got the wherewithal to make two, just in case. Now, come on old chap! We mustn't be late!'

Tom followed Reggie. They took a traverse to the main trench with the fire-step, closest to the front line. All in complete silence, which was most unusual for Reggie. Then at a corner where the trench dipped and then twisted, the young lieutenant stopped, listening.

'What time ith it now, Wethtmacott?' he whispered, lisping the s's so the sound did not carry. Tom pulled out his pocket watch. 'Ten patht eight?' Reggie then checked his own watch. 'Yeth, I have that too. Exthellent. Now, let'th light the firtht!' Tom watched as Reggie lit the fuse, lifted the grenade in his left hand and then lobbed it for all he was worth beyond the trench towards the Boche. There was a terrific explosion and fevered shouting in German, not very far off. They waited for a few moments, and then a machine-gun roared into action. 'Your turn!' said Reggie, grinning as he handed Tom the second grenade. Tom lit the fuse and again threw it, but it did not go so far as the first and exploded closer to home, splattering them with small stones. It was still unexpectedly exhilarating.

'Never mind,' said Reggie. 'Practith maketh perfect. Now, our own food cometh at about half patht eight so let'th get back, thall we?' He led the way, bobbing along the trench bent double, with the German machine-gun still screaming its response in the background. It did not appear to be firing in their direction, which Tom thought odd. None of this felt real. It had all somehow turned into a game in his absence. What exactly had they just achieved?

When back in the dugout, Tom and Reggie ate a lukewarm savoury stew presented by a private who returned later for the empty tin bowls. Once he had finished eating, Reggie finally began to talk. 'This…this isn't exactly what I expected, you know, Westmacott.'

Tom thought of his own boyhood lead soldiers in their bright uniforms and knew exactly what his young friend meant. No-one spoke much about how awful their situation was, because it was so enormously, unsurpassingly bad, that words could not describe it. It was all around one, all the time. But Reggie was trying now, and Tom was listening.

The boy continued without looking at him, 'This isn't a proper war, I mean, is it? It's a mess. And I do miss Phoenix so.' Tom reassured

Reggie that his beloved horse had seemed well fed and healthy when he had last seen her at Thérouanne on the way through, which perked him up a little. 'I just thought there would be more riding. Not all this sitting around.'

Tom nodded in sympathy. None of them could have imagined an ordeal such as this. At the same time, there was no getting out of it now, for both he and Reggie had volunteered for this work.

Reggie continued, 'Did you hear that Gul Baz Khan is dead?' Tom had not, and was deeply saddened. Gul Baz had been a reliable and tough sowar. The man had once accompanied Tom on a man-eating-tiger hunt at his village and he had proved very useful. 'I had to write to his people,' said Reggie. 'They said it would be good practice for me. So, I wrote that he had fought like a hero and died a warrior's death fighting for his king-emperor. I thought his old father would like that. But it's not true, you know, Westmacott. I made it up.' There was silence for a few moments.

'How did it happen?' asked Tom, softly.

'Oh, good Lord. He drowned, poor fellow. In a corner of our own trench,' replied Reggie, one hand reaching out blindly as though to clear the terrible memory from his mind. 'He'd been sent on some pointless errand by the G.O.C. without anyone's knowledge and he just went missing. They said he must have deserted – the Boche have been encouraging Hindus and Mohammedans to go over to them, did you know? I knew that could not possibly be the case, so I went out looking with a couple of others. We only found him when I…'

He stopped, swallowed. Tom remained silent, listening.

'I stepped on him in the muddy water. We pulled him up…' Reggie stopped again, steadied himself and continued. 'Gul Baz Khan must have slipped, wading through one of the places where the water gathers, maybe hit his head. He hadn't been shot, we would have seen the blood in the water, d'ye see? The thing is, he shouldn't even have been in that section, even though it is the quickest way through, as everyone knows it isn't safe after the amount of rainfall we have had. We only found out later from one of the orderlies who overheard it that he had been ordered to go that way. I think Tabasco Jim or one of his staff told him to, and Gul Baz always was a stickler for orders. He was buried before we knew it. And Gul Baz Khan is not the only one, you know, Westmacott. There was an old Sikh before that, one of the muleteers. He was winged by a sniper but it was the water that finished him. They had him buried quickly as well, just to hush up the whole thing.'

'A Sikh *buried*? No cremation?' asked Tom, aghast. Reggie nodded, miserably. 'I know. Everything was wet through, but we would have managed somehow. No, it was all taken out of our hands by G.H.Q. and that was the end of it. Poor devils. Their friends were outraged of course, and I protested, so did Gourlie and the Colonel, but we were just ignored.'

'And Durand, tell me, who or what is Tabasco Jim?' asked Tom.

'Oh! The G.O.C., of course. Brigadier James. You'll have met him?'

Tom nodded, remembering the unpleasant encounter at the stables.

'He comes down here sometimes as we're not far from G.H.Q., poking about. A nasty fiery unpredictable type, d'ye see? I don't know who started calling him Tabasco Jim. Gourlie perhaps. And Westmacott, his staff aren't much better. You must be very careful of them. In fact, that absolute so-and-so Lochdubh, his aide-de-camp, is even worse than the G.O.C, if you ask me.'

Tom felt a chill run down his back. 'Durand, why was it so important that we fire off those grenades at the Boche tonight at eight o' clock precisely?'

The boy looked straight at Tom with his beautiful grey, mad eyes. 'Oh no, not eight o' clock, Westmacott,' he said. 'Ten *past* eight. And not at the Boche, exactly. Tabasco Jim will have just sat down to dinner when the machine gun starts up. I do it every night when I can. It makes them all bolt for the shelter trench, d'ye see?'

Tom did see; and wished he did not. Reginald Heber Marion Durand, proud scion of a noble military dynasty, was trotting down to the corner nearest to the German trenches every night, lighting a specially-made grenade stuffed with nails and ammunition and lobbing it over the wire. This led the Boche to open fire, not in their own direction, but towards G.H.Q. Young Durand was baiting the Boche in the hope that they might polish off the G.O.C. – Tom supposed it must have happened once by chance and had now become a habit.

'I make the grenades out of jam tins when I can get the other bits and pieces, because we're only allowed to fire off six shells a day and we really need those for the enemy,' Reggie explained, helpfully.

After that Tom made sure they talked of other things, and they ate a thick slice of cake each, which Reggie relished, even picking the crumbs off his uniform and eating those. 'My family doesn't often think to send me nice things to eat,' he sighed, as he curled up under his blanket. 'Just bracing letters telling me to be brave and do my duty and make everyone proud at home. My sister did try her best to knit me some socks and if I am really cold I put one on my head.' He wiggled his boots at Tom, then blew out his candle. 'It's really very good to see you again, Westmacott,' he said, drowsily.

Once Reggie was sound asleep, Tom pulled out his map and pored anxiously over it by the light of his own candle-stub. The current G.H.Q. position at Martinsart could only just be within range of the German guns. The likelihood of Reggie doing anything more serious than greatly annoy their G.O.C. with this pre-prandial game was slim.

In theory, of course, Tom knew he should report the boy for what he was up to; but given the G.O.C.'s reputation that would lead straight to a blindfold and a brick wall. And Gourlie, a sensible officer whom Tom respected, must have known already that Durand was doing this. Perhaps it afforded some relief, as Reggie adapted to the horrors of their situation. And Tom had to admit that there was something rather cheering at the thought of the G.O.C. and Lochdubh and the rest of them being forced to take cover every night, as a thin layer of dust accumulated on their cooling *potage du jour*.

And Reggie just carried on, often aided by Tom, for as long as they remained in those particular trenches, and their supply of ammunition, jam-tins and fuses held out. The two friends referred to their enjoyable pursuit as 'Bolting the Tabasco' (or 'an ancient sport revived' when others were listening).

As Reggie Durand often said, it somehow made him feel that life was still worth living.

# 17

# Interrogation

By Saturday Gaston had been in his cell for three days without being able to shave, wash, clean his teeth or brush his hair. The greasy bucket in the corner was only emptied once a day. The lack of mirror affected him the most. He was usually quite fastidious about how he looked, keeping his hair tidy and his moustache neatly trimmed and waxed and could only imagine how dishevelled he appeared. And he had developed a painful cough from the cold nights huddled under the dirty blanket. His thoughts were more of his family, and of his little town, than of his own perilous situation.

Food and drink was water from the tin cup and the foul German bread they called *pumpernickel* or *swartzbrot*. Gaston considered that the entire invasion of France might have been driven by a desire for better bread. Today the guard had slipped a small, wrinkled apple out of his pocket and set it on his desk, then put a conspiratorial finger to his lips. When he had gone, Gaston had eaten it all, including skin and pips. He remembered slipping into Madame Hauquier's sunny orchard and stealing her sweet, peaceful apples – an age ago now.

Every day different Boches came to him. They did not hurt him. Their approach was more subtle than that, designed to wear him down. They constantly threatened violence and their relentless questioning sapped his energy, weakened as he was by hunger and the cough. Every day he refused to talk, but it became harder and harder to do so. They said things like 'It is decided, then: tomorrow, at dawn,' which was hard to bear. He did everything he could to prepare for his execution: little notes to each of the children, to his brother, his last wishes, were piled on the corner of the table. No envelopes. No privacy even for that.

Yesterday they had tried changing tack. 'Your pretty sister, she wouldn't like it here, would she?' asked Horstberg, through Kraft, from the doorway, the menace apparent in his tone. Horstberg never entered the room. 'Léonie Derome was part of the conspiracy too. Helped you out with your dirty little activities. Spied for you. Didn't she?'

Don't react, don't rise to them, thought Gaston desperately as he lied and lied again, replying politely that no, indeed, she would not, and no, that was not in fact the case. He would do anything to keep Léonie from being brought here, except confess.

The man in the hooded black cloak had walked right up to the great studded gate and demanded to be taken to the kommandant. The guard was nonplussed. People generally begged to be released from the château, not admitted. He asked a colleague to take over and clambered through the postern, almost tripping in his haste. A few minutes later, after merely consulting the duty-sergeant about the eccentric's arrival, he returned to say that the kommandant was a very busy man and that the stranger should be on his way if he did not want any trouble.

At that, the cloaked figure pushed past the guard, entirely ignoring his gun. He wielded the twisted hazel stick he was carrying to pound on the main door – bang, bang, bang, like a call to arms. The guard, thoroughly rattled now, went back through the postern for a lot longer and this time returned to admit him.

Once inside the cloaked man stood in the centre of the courtyard, stretched his arms wide in the sign of the cross, closed his eyes and started to pray, loudly and in German, for the souls of all those within the building. He had a powerful voice. Soon startled faces appeared at most of the inner courtyard windows and the spiral staircases echoed to the sound of feet.

Eventually a tall, distinguished German officer walked towards the figure across the wet stone slabs. He looked surprised and somewhat amused. 'Pray stop for a moment, good Father,' he asked in perfect and exquisitely polite French. 'Who precisely are you?'

'I am the Abbé Lebrun of Bavay,' answered Maître Corbeau in

fair German. 'And who might you be, then?' There were gasps at his audacity.

'Well, Monsieur l'Abbé, since you enquire, I am *oberst* – colonel to you – Schlaghecke. I am the officer in command of this establishment and of security within the region. What brings you to Saint Quentin so soon before Christmas? Should you not be tending to your flock?'

'You have one of my lambs here,' replied Maître Corbeau. 'You are holding our mayor, Monsieur Derome, are you not? He and I are both shepherds, in different ways. He cares for their bodies, I their souls.'

'Oh yes, Mayor Derome is here,' acknowledged Schlaghecke, easily. 'He is under investigation for the attack on the railway line between Aulnoye and Landecies. You will know it was carried out by some Englishmen formerly sheltered within your community, whom we have now captured, yes?'

'He knew nothing of any such attack, Herr Oberst. You have my word on that. And it was more a question of surrender than of capture, was it not? It was Monsieur Derome to whom they handed their weapons, in fact, not your forces.'

Schlaghecke smiled, ignoring the tacit insult. 'Indeed. Now really, Monsieur l'Abbé? You mean to tell me that Mayor Derome knew nothing of these men? Who planned the attack? How the explosive was made, from his factory's fertiliser perhaps?'

Lebrun had not thought of that line of enquiry. *Could* Gaston have provided explosives? Surely not. Gaston Derome was many things he disliked, but he was not a violent man.

The questioning continued, polite but relentless. How had they escaped? Where had they slept? How were they fed?

'It is no sin to feed the hungry!' thundered the priest. 'Christ himself did it in the parable of the loaves and the fishes. But you have my word that Gaston Derome did not damage any railway line.'

Schlaghecke shook his head. 'Not good enough. We have informers who say he may have masterminded the whole thing. He will be very lucky to escape with his life, Monsieur l'Abbé.'

The priest snorted defiance. 'If it must come to that, you will take my own worthless flesh instead, not the life of an innocent widower with four young children,' he said. 'And I have nothing to fear from your judgement, Herr Oberst, only that of my Maker.'

With that Maître Corbeau turned his back on the perplexed colonel, spread wide his arms in a human cross and continued to pray aloud.

~

On the morning of the seventh day they shot someone in the courtyard outside. The piercing sound echoed off the walls and woke Gaston, who sat up, gasping with pain where his back had knotted against the damp wall as he dozed. Was it a scream of agony or anguish? It sounded familiar somehow. A woman? Then, another volley of shots, and silence. Had he recognised the voice? Could it have been his dear sister?

He struggled upright, rubbing his face, and pulled on his spectacles. His moustache had given way to a beard. He felt filthy, foul, hungry and vulnerable. Then the door was open and a guard stood before him. 'Come!' he ordered. Gaston staggered forwards to reach for the letters on his table. The guard shook his head and pulled a length of rope out of his pocket. With complete indifference, he tied Gaston's hands tightly together in front of him.

Gaston followed the guard slowly down the spiral staircase, his legs weakened through lack of use; he stumbled, finding it horribly difficult not to be able to hold the rail. Then he was marched straight across the empty courtyard. Out of the corner of his eye he took note of a broken wooden chair and a dark stain on the flagstones.

Not here then, he thought, relishing the fresh air on his face. Or not yet. And yet someone. Who?

Those Germans who saw him avoided looking him in the eye, whether through guilt or disgust or pity he did not know. Was there some other space beyond, where Horstberg would be waiting, with the firing squad and the blindfold?

The guard stopped halfway down a dank corridor, yawned and knocked on a door. When a voice told him to enter, he opened it and pushed his prisoner inside, then shut it smartly behind him.

Gaston found himself in a large, high-ceilinged room with bookshelves and a cosy fire burning in the grate. Instinctively Gaston walked towards the warmth, then stopped. The tall officer behind the desk was writing. 'You may warm yourself, Monsieur Derome,' the man said in French, without looking up. Gaston could not tell what rank he was, but he looked important. 'Please approach the fire.'

Gaston did so, holding his bound hands out towards the flames and glorying in the heat. The officer came and stood beside him. 'So, Monsieur Derome,' he began, conversationally. 'I am Colonel Schlaghecke, your host, after a fashion. The Commandant of Bavay has told me he thought you should be shot for crimes against Germany. Could you explain to me why he might have come to that conclusion?'

Gaston, not prepared for this blunt approach, hesitated. The officer saw this and continued. 'Let me help you a little,' he said. 'Kommandant Horstberg also wished to shoot the Maire of Locquignol as an example, but he was refused permission, since there was no evidence that the Maire of Locquignol was involved in any wrong-doing. The same cannot be said of yourself.'

Gaston shook his head, fuddled with hunger and fatigue, trying to unravel what he was being told to confess to. He coughed, feeling a pain course through his chest. The officer carried on, as though they were old friends sharing a comfortable fireside chat on a winter's day. 'Well now, Monsieur Derome, this morning I received a deputation of your *conseillers municipaux* saying that you had nothing to do with the attack on the railway line. Is this the truth?'

'Yes,' said Gaston honestly, uncertain where this could be leading.

'Good. We are making excellent progress then. I choose to believe you.' Gaston eyed Schlaghecke warily.

'I also received a petition from many of your good townspeople calling for your immediate release,' continued the colonel. 'They too assure me that you are a paragon of virtue and that it was sheer coincidence that the twenty-nine Englishmen marched into your town to lay down their arms. See, here are all the papers concerned.' He held them out for Gaston to see, row upon row of names he knew and little crosses where people could not write. 'This time I do not believe a word of it. A pack of lies. Yes?'

Beleaguered, Gaston did not know how to respond. 'What value do you think I place on all these documents?' asked the officer. Gaston shook his head.

One by one, the colonel tossed the papers into the flames, watching as each blackened, curled and was gone. Gaston felt a burst of indignation, knowing how much time and effort it had taken his friends to collect all these statements and signatures. If he were going to be shot, for heaven's sake, could they not get it over and done with?

With nothing to lose, he decided to try a question. 'Where is Kommandant Horstberg?'

'I am the one asking the questions, not you, Monsieur Derome,' said the colonel, who had taken his chair again behind the desk and was now sipping a cup of strong coffee. Gaston could smell it and his mouth watered. 'Won't you please now sit?' Gaston reluctantly left the fireside to perch himself on the wooden chair.

The officer continued, 'Since you ask, Horstberg has been – ah – redeployed in another region. He is an engineer and needed for other duties. It is unlikely you will see him again.' This was unexpected news and Gaston's surprise must have showed in his face. The colonel continued calmly, 'Please do not feel that your troubles are over, Monsieur Derome. It is still perfectly possible that you will never leave Saint Quentin alive.'

And now it comes, thought Gaston, feeling his heart pound in his aching chest. I hope I can be brave enough.

Schlagehecke continued. 'Remember, the petition and the protest from the *conseillers* are now so much ash in my hearth. A futile gesture. No, there has to be another good reason for me to spare you. What can you give me, Monsieur Derome?

Gaston shook his head, bewildered. 'Do you wish me to beg for my life then, Monsieur le Colonel? If so, I have come this far already. I will not do it. You must just get on with it and shoot me.'

The officer drained his cup of coffee and looked at Gaston. The man could almost be amused, he thought. But what did it mean?

'You are a courageous fellow, Monsieur Derome. I must tell you however that if we choose to take your life today, no amount of bravado will do you any good.' Schlaghecke paused, his eyes piercing, searching Gaston for the reaction to his next statement. 'And in any case, it would not now be your own life we would take, would it?'

Gaston could only continue to appear mystified. The colonel shook his head with a wry chuckle. 'Why, it *is* true,' he said, half to himself. 'He really has no idea.'

He then walked round to Gaston and untied his hands. Gaston rubbed his wrists and coughed again.

'Now, pick up that pen, Monsieur le Maire,' Schlaghecke said firmly, placing some typed sheets in front of Gaston. 'You need to read and sign all three of these forms.' Gaston lifted the papers with trembling hands and read them through his cracked spectacles. The first paper asked him to confess his guilt in supplying food to the Englishmen. Well, he thought, that was something he could admit to honestly, as it was true. And it mentioned no other names.

'If I sign this, is that the end of it? No-one else will be pursued?' The colonel nodded. Then Gaston read the paper below it. The catch. It was the notice of a fine. A massive fine for the breath-taking amount of 35,000 francs in gold coin. He could pay it, just, given a little time. And dead men could not pay fines, he thought, for the first time daring to hope.

The third paper deposed him as Mayor of Bavay, informing him of the identity of a new mayor of the German's choosing who would be appointed shortly. It stated that he, Gaston Derome, would do all he could to facilitate the transfer of authority. He would then need to adhere to a strict curfew of nine o' clock at night until eight o' clock in the morning for the duration of hostilities. Gaston recognised the name of the man selected as his replacement, who was from a town nearby. His father was German but the collaborator would be a reasonable enough fellow to deal with, he thought.

Gaston swiftly signed all three papers then looked up at Schlaghecke.

'There is one final condition to your release,' said the colonel, calling to the guard outside. The door opened. 'Bring him in!' Schlaghecke said in German.

To Gaston's incredulity, Maître Corbeau was then unceremoniously pushed into the room. Schlaghecke watched their mutual surprise, smiled briefly and nodded.

Gaston's old schoolmaster looked dishevelled and unshaven as though he had not slept for several days, which indeed he had not, as he had been housed in a cell not far from that of Gaston. His own had been unlocked and he had been free to leave at any time, but Maître Corbeau had steadfastly refused to do so.

The colonel ignored him and addressed Gaston instead. 'You need to swear to me now, on the lives of your children, who are numerous, as we have been told repeatedly,' and here he did glance at the priest, who looked at his feet, 'that neither you nor this Abbé of yours will ever – ever! – return here to Saint Quentin. If you do, I will shoot you both myself on sight. Do you understand me?'

Both men nodded, overwhelmed with relief.

Colonel Schlaghecke sighed. He was by no means an evil man. Cultivated and a skilled linguist, he had found his niche in the intelligence service of the German Army. He had been fond of history and literature in the years before the war. He sensed these were both men who, in other times, would have made intelligent and pleasant company around a dinner table. Schlaghecke did what he had to do, and did it well, but did not necessarily enjoy it. As he had only remarked to General von Hutier over a fine dinner the previous evening, this Derome seemed to be a man somewhat out of the ordinary.

'Well, Maire Derome, I would ask you now to "rid me of this turbulent priest".' Schlaghecke savoured the quotation, but neither of his erstwhile prisoners recognised the clever allusion to English history. They just stood there, staring at him, Gaston open-mouthed.

The German sighed. 'So? *Allez-vous-en!*' He was torn between amusement and impatience; and had other less diverting (and less lucrative) interrogations pending that would take him many hours. '*Et Joyeux Noel, messieurs!*' He dismissed them with a flick of the hand.

Only once the great gate of the château had been closed behind them, and they had stumbled well away together, did either man say a word. Maître Corbeau, supporting his mayor with a strong arm around his shoulders, spoke first. 'Now, mon petit Gaston. You cannot return to your dear ones in Bavay looking as you do, *hein*? Mademoiselle Léonie would be scandalised and your children alarmed. And we both need food and drink, do we not? I left the bag your sister gave me at the Café de la Gare. The landlady there will allow us to bathe and shave and change our clothes before our train leaves for Bavay, at four.'

Numb with disbelief, coughing uncontrollably and on the verge of tears, all Gaston could utter in response was a meek, 'Oui, mon Père.'

## 18

# The Griffin and the Saracen's Head

AUTHUILE, FRANCE
SEPTEMBER 1915

Afterwards, although he knew it quite unfair to do so, Tom blamed two people for that night's experience: one was Risaldar Harnam Singh and the other, Evelyn Winnington-Ingram.

It was his dreams. Once or twice he had been shaken awake by an anxious Reggie with the words, 'I say, Westmacott, you were shouting out in your sleep again! Are you quite well, old chap?' Tom could have retorted that if Reggie, who could somehow sleep through the heaviest of bombardments, would only snort and fidget less, both of them might well enjoy better rest. Tom could never retain what it was in his dreams that had frightened him; it slipped away like oil through his fingers as he tried to hold the shape of it.

He both craved and dreaded sleep. He could never sink into dreamless slumber as once he had done; he seemed to skim along its surface, one ear cocked for an order to stand-to. This was nothing new: it dated back to that dreadful night in 1912.

Here in Authuile, however, his dreams took on a newer and darker complexity.

Nine months in to this war, Tom was outwardly a calm, stable and respected officer. Inside he felt only turmoil. His plan had seemed so straightforward when he left India: to make a rapid end to himself on the battlefield in some dignified and purposeful way. He should have joined Mary in the hereafter by now, for without her, there was no point in going on. Or so it had seemed to him at the beginning.

Now he found himself seeking to survive. Doing so felt somehow disloyal to her memory. This change of heart was not for his own sake, but for that of Reggie and Harnam Singh and Amar Singh and all the other Indian troops. These men needed his experience to protect them from some of the imbeciles in command. There could be nothing dignified or worthwhile about dying in the trenches at Authuile under Tabasco Jim.

Just before they had left Authuile, the Brigadier had despatched Lochdubh and a medical officer to examine the best locations for permanent trench latrines on the grounds of hygiene. Even Reggie knew that any fixed latrine made a very popular enemy target. The two gilded officers picked their way through the filth, disdainfully issuing orders about the burying of excreta to Risaldar Major Amar Singh and his bemused Indian troops, who had spent their lives doing so with perfect efficiency. In the end, Amar Singh saw that Tom was close to losing his temper and calmly suggested that Major Lochdubh sahib might care to inspect the perfect location, just down the slope and around the corner. Lochdubh and the M.O. sauntered along to this popular sniping spot and bolted after a well-timed burst of rifle fire, at which point Amar Singh had made himself scarce. The officers, Lochdubh with a malevolent backward glance at Tom, soon headed off for G.H.Q. That was the last any of them had heard about fixed latrines.

Such incidents convinced Tom that he was needed in this terrible place; and yet survival at all, and in particular survival there, was a torment.

A few days earlier he had met Harnam Singh at a briefing to the rear of the trenches. The risaldar, who towered above him, had at first returned his salute with a cheerful greeting and walked past him, but then turned and came back. 'Captain Westmacott sahib?'

'What is it, Risaldar Harnam Singh?' Tom asked, wearily.

'You seem fatigued, Captain sahib?'

Tom choked back an acerbic response. The observation was true enough and he knew he had been snappy around the men in recent days. They were long overdue for relief.

He contented himself with 'And what of it? Surely we all are?'

Harnam Singh shook his head. 'Before I sleep, I pray. I pray as Risaldar Major Amar Singh, our *granthi*, directs us and I study the word of the Guru. I know that my destiny is in control of God and not in the hands of men. I fall asleep quickly to dream of my garden in the Punjab. I awake refreshed. And you, sahib? Do you pray to your God before you sleep?'

Tom opened his mouth to reply, then closed it again. What could he say to Harnam Singh that would not sound either rude, defensive or trite? In the end he decided on the truth, or part of the truth at least. 'Harnam Singh, I thank you for your kindness, but I do not believe I shall ever dream of anything so innocent in this place. When I sleep, my dreams are full of shadows from my past. I do not think that my God would wish to hear the prayers of a man like myself. Not all my actions in life before coming to France were honourable ones.'

Harnam Singh, not in the least perturbed, inclined his head and smiled down at him. 'And yet your Christian God is a merciful one, or so I have heard, Captain sahib,' he replied. 'And as you know, my own religion believes that any righteous conflict can redeem a dishonourable act.' Tom thought of Devesh Bosu at Puanco in Calcutta, exhorting him to purify himself through war. He felt a pang of long separation from the old man and his tinkling tea tray.

Harnam Singh then, to Tom's surprise, started to sing. The complex melody sounded familiar, although he could not at first make out the words. He realised after a while that the Sikh officer was giving a passable rendering of 'Onward Christian Soldiers', albeit with much *raga*-like embellishment. 'You see, Captain sahib,' the risaldar continued, 'On your holy day I have heard the English troops sing of Christian soldiers carrying their cross before them, just as we might bear the *Guru Granth Sahib*. I greatly enjoy this fine song. Are our two beliefs so different, Captain sahib?' Harnam Singh paused, and Tom wondered what was coming next. 'Perhaps Captain Westmacott sahib should seek out the Christian priest and discuss this private burden he carries, that he may set it down at last?'

Tom thanked the officer and watched him pick his way back up the line. He thought Grace might get on rather well with Harnam Singh. They had a deep and unshakeable faith in common, albeit rooted in different religions. Was Harnam Singh right? Tom had never spoken to a soul in any detail about what had happened that terrible night with Mary. Had the time come?

A few days passed and the aching monotony of trench life took over again, but the thought of unburdening himself lingered at the back of his mind. Then he received a note from Evelyn Winnington-Ingram. A step up from the terse little postcard she had sent the first time and the short note that had followed it. She had posted this one from Ross over a week before. *Dear Tom*, he read.

> Thank you for your interesting letter that we received this morning. Four pages! I am afraid I cannot match it. My life here is a great deal duller than yours in France.

Tom knew his letters to Evelyn were increasing in length as well as in frequency. Every day now he found himself hoping for post. Anything sent by his parents-in-law, the Lawsons, was always rather worthy and full of scripture, while his brother's letters burst with naïve but uninitiated excitement at the glamour of war. Tom wanted to write to Dick and say, 'Do not come', but as an officer, how could he?

Post from the W-Is was a different matter. Whether it was Maud or Evelyn who wrote (the other sister was a teacher somewhere and did not correspond) he looked forward to their letters, which always demonstrated a bright intelligence he found appealing. Maud was the better correspondent of the two. Her letters, although brief, were full of parish life, often funny. He thought Mary might have written something similar.

The content of Evelyn's more erratic missives was less predictable. Sometimes he wondered if she were teasing him. He found this simultaneously unnerving and intriguing.

> I noticed a fragment of wax seal still attached to it: this one had been opened by the censor. Your family crest, I presume. What is the insect on it? I can see wings and some stripes. A wasp?

Tom smiled at her sharp-eyed curiosity. He still used a last surviving gold button, once fastened to a waistcoat of his father's, as a seal. It was the 'busy bee', the emblem of the Westmacott family. Now he looked more closely, it did seem rather more elongated, like an annoying wasp. Was her comment in reality a jibe? Could she be so unkind?

> Our own family crest is rather more blood-curdling. Maud says our lot, the de Winnes, came over with the Norman Conquest.

We don't have a seal, but the Griffin and the Saracen's head are stamped into all the family silver. Some nasty violent incident to do with the Crusades, decapitating an inconvenient Infidel to teach him a lesson, no doubt.

Etty and Maud would make fine soldiers, I think, and I would make a tolerable stretcher-bearer, but not Teddy or Arthur.

Why not, wondered Tom, who could not remember either brother from the wedding, if they had attended at all.

I am sorry to hear that you are having difficulty in sleeping. Maud may have told you that I am now working as a v.a.d. nurse in Ross? Many of our patients suffer from fitful sleep or nightmares when they get here. Our quiet surroundings seem to calm down most of them, given time. Some are given morphia for pain, and it makes them sleep deeply, but I would not advise it. One man seemed to want more and more and hunted for it high and low. His mouth turned black with the stuff. We keep it in a locked cupboard now.

Tom had seen opium dens in Bombay and Calcutta and understood both the temptations and the pitfalls of taking any substance to numb the senses. He knew that a few men in other regiments did so, using the morphia provided in case of injury as a means of finding oblivion, but their reactions were so dulled as a result that they did not tend to last long.

I mentioned your difficulties in sleeping to Teddy.

'Blast!' exclaimed Tom, standing up. He did not like that at all. It was hard to account for feeling annoyed that Evelyn, whom he scarcely knew, would reveal his weakness to other members of her family, whom he knew not at all. It was human nature and there was nothing for it but to accept it. Why did it still feel like a betrayal of confidence? He could not fathom this, but it still irked him.

He now has his own parish, did you know?

Oh, yes, thought Tom. That was it. Two rather frail boys, the brothers, both priests. Mary had mentioned it.

It is Father's old parish at Bewdley.

Evelyn's father had not stayed at the wedding reception for long, but his grim presence had made quite enough of an impression. Perhaps Evelyn took after him. Oh dear.

Well, Teddy said immediately that you should go and talk to your chaplain. It might help if you feel you have anything to get off your chest, he said.

'Anything to get off his chest'? That had a wasp-like sting, even if it were intended kindly. He was not even sure of that.

I must go now, as there is much work to be done here with my patients.
Yours sincerely,
Evie W-I

Tom took of his spectacles and rubbed his eyes. Had Evelyn written to him again out of kindness, interest or just a sense of duty? He wished he could recall what she looked like. Neither Maud not Etty were beauties, he remembered that. Try as he might, all he could recall of Evelyn was a fleeting impression of disapproval overshadowed by a vast hat. He had not been sure that day whether she frowned upon their nuptials or on the ludicrous headgear. Possibly both. He had not thought of her overmuch at all until arriving here in France. Letters had become such a treat. If she had been Mary's favourite cousin and her friend, though, surely Evelyn W-I could not be that bad?

Tom wondered if he might ever know her well enough to ask her for a likeness. It was the kind of thing a man wrote to his sweetheart, so seemed unlikely.

He read her letter again and this time his spirits lifted a little. She had signed herself Evie rather than Evelyn. Evie was what Mary had called her, he remembered now. *Look Tom! How capital. A letter from Evie at Ross!* A wan smile gathered at the corners of his mouth: for a moment he was back in his sunny bungalow beside Mary with Mehitabel serving them tiffin.

Evie's letter was at least longer than her first postcard and the next little note and it did ask him a question about the bee. There it was again, too, this perplexing encouragement to see a priest. What was more, Evie had mentioned her family crest included a griffin, and although she could not know it, the regimental chaplain's name was also Griffin. Tom might not believe in a Christian heaven and hell, but he had a healthy respect for destiny and fate. Parvati, his favourite ayah, would often tell him that sometimes that the Gods would send signs as guidance for mortals. Now he thought about it, Parvati would often coax him into obedience by teasing him, too.

He resolved on impulse to arrange to see Griffin that very evening, if only to be able to tell Miss Evelyn Winnington-Ingram that he had done so at her suggestion.

Tom had not had much to do with the regimental chaplain. He occasionally attended Sunday services but more frequently made an excuse not to go. Griffin was a spaniel-eyed, rotund man of about Tom's age with a reputation for over-long sermons. Not for the first time, Tom wished he were a Sikh rather than a rather poor Christian, so that he could have talked with Amar Singh instead.

'Enter!' Griffin summoned him into his sparse quarters. 'Well, well, Captain Westmacott. To what do I owe this rare pleasure? It must be, dear me, almost a month since one of my acts of worship has been graced by your presence?'

Tom found himself wrong-footed and stammered an apology.

Griffin waved a plump hand at a canvas stool. 'Forgive me my little joke, Captain Westmacott. I know you are a busy man, tending to your many noble Sikhs. Now. Sit down and tell me how I can be of service.'

Something about the phrase 'noble Sikhs' on the lips of this man felt uncomfortable.

There was a small wooden table between them on which rested a portable silver cavalry cross and two candlesticks containing two candles, both unlit, one slightly bent. There was also an incongruous pair of tin mugs.

Tom sat and watched as the chaplain pushed the mugs to one side. Was that whisky he could smell?

'Forgive me, Captain Westmacott, I had another visitor just before you, my good friend Major Lochdubh.' Tom stiffened, but Griffin paid it no attention. He had assumed a position of pious and professional contemplation, fingertips touching, head nodding; although Tom had not yet spoken a word.

'Well?' said Griffin, encouragingly. 'Missing your family at home, perhaps?'

'I have no family at home to miss, Chaplain. I have a younger brother, that's all. They haven't bagged him for the Front, or not yet. My parents are dead.' Tom's drunken mother might very well be still alive for all he knew, but he was not inclined to share that information with Griffin.

'And where is home, pray?' enquired the chaplain. Tom pondered for a moment before replying, with caution, 'I do not have a home to speak of, although relatives in England always make me welcome enough. I was brought up in India. I am not sure I will ever return there.'

'So. No wife, no little ones?'

'No.' Tom could no longer even bear to wear his wedding-ring, so great was his guilt.

'I see.' Griffin did not and could not see, of course. His tone was warm, but Tom felt uneasy and found himself holding back from an explanation of Mary's death.

'Dear me. And so you are very much alone here.' Griffin moved a little closer.

Tom decided to bite the bullet, as Kipling might say. 'Chaplain, I came to see you because I am having trouble sleeping. Bad dreams,' he managed. 'Troubling dreams.'

Griffin now leaned forwards, lips parted. 'Dear me, dear me. Are you, now? And dreams of what nature, may I ask?'

'I really cannot remember them in detail,' admitted Tom. 'But sometimes, at night, I cry out, and I wake Lieutenant Durand, who shares my dugout.'

Griffin, eyes glistening, leaned back in his chair. 'I see,' he said again. 'And how long have you been dreaming about young Reggie Durand?' Tom stared at him, open-mouthed with shock. He felt himself flush.

This was not going at all well. Why on earth had he come?

'Goodness, no, Griffin! I can assure you that I don't dream about Durand!' This was not entirely true as Tom did recall one nightmare, in which the boy found himself trapped in No Man's Land; but he knew that was not the kind of dream the chaplain meant.

'How do you know, Westmacott?' continued Griffin, softly. 'You just told me yourself that you could not remember your dreams in detail.'

A chasm of implication started to yawn at Tom's feet and he scrabbled at its crumbling edge for any handhold. 'Maybe not, Chaplain, but surely if I were dreaming about Reggie Durand I would recall it.'

'Perhaps,' said Griffin, gazing at Tom with unsettling directness. 'And perhaps not. Captain Westmacott, you are a long way from home, surrounded by men in a foreign land. This is a brutal place for us all. Some would say we exist in a living Hell. You would not be the first or the last to come to me with tales of... how shall I put it... of affection for a brother officer. Strong affection. Such affection must be carefully concealed, of course, as it is a breach of military discipline.'

Tom stood up. So did Griffin, who stepped quickly around the little table that separated them. Tom could see damp patches in the pits of the man's uniform and smell something faintly sweet combed through the man's hair.

'You must feel able to come to me to share more about these dreams of yours, Captain Westmacott,' Griffin said softly, standing rather too close. 'In the strictest confidence, of course.' Was the fleeting touch of a pudgy hand against Tom's own accidental?

Tom stepped rapidly backwards. 'Well. Thank you, Griffin,' he said, too loudly, almost tripping over the stool he had vacated. 'Very helpful advice. Most kind. I shall bear your offer in mind.' And with that he fled and avoided the man as much as he could thereafter.

He said nothing about the incident to Harnam Singh either.

This odd encounter did have a strange and positive aftermath: Tom's sleep slowly improved. He wrote about this in his reply to Evie, so that she would be pleased he had followed her suggestion, without telling her what had occurred with Griffin, of course.

One night a few days later, he had a dream he found he could remember the following morning. He was standing at the edge of an English meadow, full of summer flowers. He remembered one rather like it where he had strolled with Mary and Grace, not far from the Lawson's rectory at Fladbury. Grace, who was fond of watercolour painting, had earnestly told him the name of each flower: golden hawkweed, fat pink clover, stitchwort, trefoil. He had not thought of it since, but it had left a sunny imprint on his memory.

Crossing the meadow in his dream walked a woman, who had not seen him. She was so engrossed in the botanical beauty at her feet that he could not see her face. When he looked more closely he saw that the bloom she was carrying was not a wild flower at all, but a single golden rose.

He started awake, his heart full to bursting. Any dream of Mary that did not end in her death was a wonder to him.

From beneath a grubby blanket on the other side of the dugout came the sleepy voice of Reggie Durand. 'Morning, Westmacott. You slept well. You were snoring like...'

'... like you usually do!' laughed Tom, feeling much better after a good night's rest. 'My turn, Durand!' He ignored Reggie's voluble protest and made his way outside towards the corner they were using as a latrine.

It was only on the way back that a strange certainty hit him: the woman in his dream had not been Mary.

# 19
# Relief, Somewhat Premature

Tom sat with his back to a great elm and eased off his boots. There had been many such trees at Authuile once. Many of the place-names on maps near the Front ended in 'Wood' but few would now have anything other than jagged stumps left standing. Trees, with the cover they provided, had become a common enemy to both sides.

This elm spread its dry leaves overhead, turning from the dry green of late summer to the rasping lemon-yellow of autumn. Tom drank in the utter peace and quietness of it all, without a gun to break the stillness. He closed his eyes, willing sleep to come.

They were only halfway back to their billets, but safely encamped in the disused park of a château within a little cluster of hamlets named Beaucourt. The sky overhead was tranquil and blue, if chilly. Tom still found himself strangely tense, waiting for the whistle of shells overhead that did not come.

He pulled out his latest half-completed letter to Evie W-I and sharpened his pencil with his pocket-knife. He did not keep a diary, as some of his fellow officers did. Instead, he found himself writing more and more frequently to the Winnington-Ingrams. Their own occasional postcards and notes might be brief but at least the few questions they asked were intelligent ones.

There was now talk of the Indian troops being despatched to fight on a different Front. The next period of home leave might be his last and he wanted to tell them this. He was also short of money and so could not just take off to an unoccupied French town, as many did. Unrelenting Fladbury with his in-laws was not an appealing destination, although dear, dull Grace had done her best to make him feel welcome. He recalled the letter that old Edward W-I had written to him all those years before, saying that he would be most welcome to stay with them. Judging by Maud and Evie's letters the company at Bridstow might be slightly livelier than that at Fladbury.

Maud seemed very busy with parish work so he had decided to persuade Evie to come and meet him instead, next time he returned to England. If that worked, then perhaps he could suggest a stay with the family next time. She could surely miss a day of scrubbing bedpans at that little hospital of hers? He had sent her an invitation to afternoon tea.

It had utterly knocked him for six when Evie turned him down flat, by return of post, with barely a semblance of politeness.

Her defiant 'no thank you, I am rather busy at present' rejection had a powerful and unexpected impact on Tom. He found himself thoroughly rattled, reading and rereading her brief note for any hidden meaning. At the same time, he felt a desire to match her challenging response with one of his own. Whatever one was hunting, whether tiger, fox or rat, one sometimes needed to try several different approaches before successfully flushing it out.

Tom decided to be bold, as he now believed that time was running out. He wrote a stronger reply than anything he had put down before, as though he were right there in her parlour and speaking to her in person.

> Dear Evie,
> I do want to see you – awfully much – but I leave you to do exactly what you think right. I believe we go to Egypt en route for Africa in October and I shall get no more leave after this month. I have still got the song of the shells in me – I feel fairly bad – quite mad – and I think, and say, 'be a darling and come'.
> Yours ever,
> Tom

He sucked his pencil, re-reading the last sentence. It was clumsy, he realised. Was 'be a darling' over-stepping the mark? No, he decided, folding the sheet and placing it in the envelope. It was just an affectionate turn of phrase. Surely Evie would understand?

~

They had been relieved the previous day after just over a fortnight in the trenches. Long enough. Tom struggled to recall how to be, how to exist, anywhere other than there.

He looked across at Reggie, who had already tucked his dark head into the vigilant Phoenix's soft flank and was breathing heavily, his mouth slightly open. From the look in the little mare's eye, Tom thought that, even lying there in the grass, she would probably bite anyone who tried to wake the lad. Phoenix was a guard-horse, he thought, and he wondered if Daisy would do the same.

Dog-tired horses and sowars slept or lay still, gazing skywards. Few men spoke, those who did so only briefly and in tones not loud enough to carry. No-one wanted to fracture the welcome peace.

The conditions near the Front had been so very bad that it had taken a six-mile forced march, sometimes through waist-deep mud, trying to lift their weapons and kit clear of the filth, before they could be reunited with their horses. Reggie had grinned at Tom as they approached the long lines of tethered mounts, prepared for them by the sowars. 'Hear her?' he asked. Sure enough, there was a pig-like squeal ululating from halfway down the ranks. Reggie had flung his arms round his horse's solid neck and held her tightly, his face averted from Tom's, for some moments.

Tom was instead greeted by Daisy with a mild look, the equine equivalent of 'honestly, *what* a fuss.' All the same, she was clearly glad to see him, as he was her. He had saved her a very old sugar-lump in an inside pocket to keep it dry. Now she lay so close to him that he could smell her sweet breath on his face.

He had a sugar-lump for Rod too, but Moore was off riding him on some errand. Even though he had missed his horses, Tom was glad the animals had been kept out of harm's way. In the regiment's last days at the Front he had seen a dray horse, which had been delivering a supply of water-barrels, hit by stray shrapnel. The terrified beast, its torn belly trailing entrails, had careered along a track and into a section of trench before being shot by their own side. The Front was no place for horses; or men, come to that.

Tom's toes and ankles were pallid and swollen. 'My hairy aunt, but I'm footsore,' he sighed to Daisy as much as anyone. She looked back as if to say, 'And you think my hooves aren't?' then nudged his pocket, hoping for more sugar. He flexed his spongey feet and winced. Not one member of the regiment had removed his boots for the past two weeks. Colonel Bell had issued a warning about an incident: a man who had taken off his pair had awoken to rats chewing through the skin of his heels.

Tom remembered the rat in the Puanco lift shaft and shivered. The dank pair of socks he had just peeled off had worn through into holes and stank. He did not think they were salvageable but would see what Moore said about darning. At least his old boots fitted well enough and were watertight. He had no bad blisters and no sign of trench foot.

Tom turned his attention to his hands. A jagged rut was torn through his right palm and one small section near his little finger was still pale and swollen. When he pressed it, yellow pus oozed from the scratch. The area around it tingled; he did not remember it doing so in the trenches. Tom undid his brandy flask and poured a tiny amount into the wound, wincing as it flooded the tender area, sucked at it and spat, sucked again and then applied more brandy still. That would do. He had sustained worse hunting.

He had not felt the barbs shred his hand when he had been ordered out into No Man's Land for the first time. Alone, crawling along the ground to check the wire was intact, he had found the experience strangely exhilarating, as though he had drunk strong wine.

In theory, no-one should have known where he was as his mission had been planned in secret; in practice, as soon as he crawled back to the observation trench, there was old Harnam Singh and a group of his sowars, including Pritam Singh, waiting for him. When he admonished them, Harnam Singh shook his head at him. 'And what if you had been hit, Captain sahib?' he chided. 'Our *izzat* would have been to come to your aid.'

They had ridden another fifteen miles overnight to reach Beaucourt, a real night march, which meant their training jaunt from Thérouanne to Amettes now resembled a Sunday School outing. They had a single precious day to rest there before marching onwards.

Tom needed to sleep but as usual found he could not. Instead, his head and belly churned with memories of his almost-permanently-final patrol. He could barely remember the time when he had hoped for a quick and gallant end to his life. Now he hoped to live, because so many others were dying: if only to protect Reggie Durand from his own misplaced bravado.

Reggie and Tom had alternated the command of patrols from their section of trench. Reggie would use any excuse to sally forth at the head of a few brave men, wielding his revolver. Tom was more circumspect, trying to minimise the risk to all present, and his men saw this and loved him for it. Perhaps pointless heroism had been instilled in Reggie from birth. Equally, it might be the dread of shame or disgrace that kept him so outwardly fearless. And yet Tom, who shared his dugout, knew the boy was very afraid.

As for Tom himself, he went out of duty, not as a choice, and hated most of it.

In spite of Reggie's best efforts, the patrols had been uneventful until that ill-fated last. Tom had put four out that evening, Numbers 1, 2 and 3 at fifty, thirty and fifty yards respectively. Then Tom, Harnam Singh and another sowar went out as No. 4, thirty yards to the right of Number 3. Once there, they all prepared to remain concealed from 9.30pm to 12.30am before moving.

Then the Boche had put up a random star-shell just as his own patrol was moving forward into position – how had they developed such superior armoury? It must have picked the three of them out like silhouettes in a Calcutta shadow-puppet show. They had fairly flattened themselves into the mud, praying to the common gods of war that no-one had seen them and there was no machine-gun in the vicinity.

In vain. It started up only seconds later, about 150 yards distant. Dealing death with every innocuous *pop*. Tom could tell the gunner was firing off irregular and single shots to avoid giving away his position. *Pop. Pop. Pop-pop-pop.*

He had a clearer sense of its traverse now. It would reach him in moments. *Pop. Pop.*

A strange sense of calm swept over him then, a feeling of being caressed, as though he were again lying beside Mary on the morning of their wedding night, all shyness flown with the night-birds at dawn. *Tomulloo.* She had whispered his Hindi name, her voice full of love, one sleepy arm stroking his own.

Had Mary come to find him here, in this terrible place, at this moment? His lips formed her name. He closed his eyes and waited for her touch.

*Pop-pop. Pop.* So very close now. His body pressed itself deeper and deeper into the mud in an instinctive attempt to live. The grass and earth flew up from each bullet, spattering him. He had calculated that the bullets would penetrate his shoulder first, then his head, because of his position. He might survive the first, not the second. *Pop-pop-pop-pop.* A clod of earth hit his ear. The machine-gunner pumped more bullets in his direction and he heard their own trench machine guns opening up in response, trying to defend them, but it was too late.

*Pop. Pop.* Receding. He lay just – if only just – beyond the arc of its traverse. He was safe.

So was Risaldar Harnam Singh, prostrated just to his left; his calm face, as always, turned towards Tom. To their right, Sowar Pritam Singh had been hit in the side and lay moaning. He fell silent after a few minutes, one arm held oddly, his hand reaching out towards them. Tom watched his index finger twitch.

Living and dead remained there motionless, until the guns had long since ceased firing and darkness fell around them like a pall. Then Harnam Singh, like some mud-caked creature of nightmares, crawled over to Tom on his hands and knees. The two men hauled each other upright and between them lifted the limp body of Pritam Singh. There was none of the glorious thrill of the wire sortie this time; only the sickly feeling of cold sweat trickling down his back and bitter awareness of the futility of any patrol against an enemy tenfold better armed.

Anxious voices whispered to show them the way, figures emerged to meet them, Reggie Durand and Amar Singh amongst them.

Tom recognised that the fortnight spent in the trenches at Authuile had changed attitudes towards him among his fellow officers. He had always been well liked by the men because he spoke Hindi, Urdu and Bengali. They all knew that he was India-born, but this had been tempered with misgivings about his amateur military status. Now this had been replaced by something subtly different, a sense of true ease and trust, a feeling of being one of them. If he had had the energy to think about it for long, he would also have recognised a change in himself: a new sense of belonging. It was happiness, of a kind.

They marched on to Piquigny under cover of darkness.

There they were lodged in a spacious new billet, a mediaeval brewery in the grounds of an old château this time. Nougier the interpreter (who was so much more) had excelled himself.

Tom and Reggie were at last able to bathe. Good old Nugget had somehow arranged for a whole row of vast beer barrels sawed in half to be filled with hot water. He had even distributed creamy chunks of *savon de Marseilles* procured from goodness-knows-where. When he announced the news that the Lancers were instead lodged in an austere convent *lycée* nearby, he raised the first weary smiles Tom had seen in weeks. Nugget was rapidly acquiring magical status in the eyes of the men.

This savon was strong soap, intended for washing clothes rather than skin, but achieved exactly the smarting, raw cleanliness they all needed. The prospect of a bath helped the men find their tongues again and they began to laugh and chatter as they queued to plunge into a steaming barrel. The shared water rapidly became the colour and consistency of soup.

Tom enjoyed the rare sight of the Sikhs quite literally letting their hair down, allowing their long black tresses loose from the confines of their turbans. Harnam Singh plunged right under the water to emerge and shake his head like a wet spaniel, sending his greying locks flying in a rainbow arc, which soaked Nugget, who as always took it in good part. He stood with his hands on his hips, dripping and grinning, supervising as those who had already bathed took turns with endless buckets of clean hot water to keep the barrels topped up.

In this fashion, the men at last scoured their bodies clean of the trenches.

Without decent mirrors to hand, those who wished to do so shaved each other, the Sikhs cheerfully ribbing Tom and Reggie about the alternative desirability of improving on their fortnight-long beards. Moore took away both their uniforms for a thorough brush, sponge and fumigation. He condemned Tom's foul socks and provided a clean pair along with a change of shirt and underwear. The trousers he merely brushed, but it was better than nothing.

Tom was anticipating a few hours in a bed somewhere close by with a clean blanket or two, possibly even a pair of sheets, when he heard his name being called. Gourlie, now recovered from his gout, was standing in the doorway. 'Sorry, Westmacott. I know all you'll want to do is get your head down, but we've had some unexpected news. The colonel needs to talk to you right away. Durand, you'd better come, too. Look sharp.'

The two men finished dressing. Tom's mind raced. Surely it could not be bad news from home? Had Mary's mother Laura died, perhaps? She had been frail for some time. Reggie, always the optimist, was more bullish. A medal, perhaps, he thought. After all they had endured at Authuile.

Tubby Bell had established a temporary headquarters in the small mairie on the main street. He and Gourlie were adapting to being part of the 1st Division. He looked up from behind a desk at Tom and Reggie as they saluted. 'At ease, gentlemen. Westmacott, you'd better read this. You're not going to like it much, I fear.'

Tom scrutinised the sheet of paper he had been handed. He started to shake his head in disbelief. 'No. No! They surely can't mean it?' He handed it to Reggie.

'I'm afraid they do,' said Gourlie with a bitter smile. 'We may just have traded Brigadier James for General Barrow, but this order remains effective retrospectively. You're one of our best hands with the men by far and now we're going to lose you. It's too bad.' Tom heard his praise, but the disastrous news had blotted out any pleasure in it. A hard lump formed in his throat.

Bell continued. 'We first learned of this while we were still up at the Front, Westmacott. I did not want to tell you at all if we had managed to talk them out of the idea. Here's the correspondence, see?' He held out another sheaf of papers. Leafing through them, Tom could see how hard they had tried to save him and felt choked with conflicting emotions.

'We have already protested in the strongest terms, Westmacott, but they are adamant that you are the man they want,' Bell continued. 'You've got a legal background, haven't you?' Tom nodded miserably. 'Well, there you are. Someone has found out and thinks that makes you perfect for the role. Rotten luck, old fellow. We will miss you.'

Gourlie added, 'We have insisted that you billet with us whenever possible to keep some benefit from your presence within the ranks. For your benefit, as much as our own. They have at least agreed to that. I hope that's some small compensation, Westmacott. Now come on, do cheer up, young Durand!'

Tom looked at Reggie's stricken face. The blow had hit him equally hard. Gourlie continued, 'We have just put in for you to be promoted to captain to replace Westmacott. It'll doubtless take a bit of time to come through, but that'll please the family, won't it, eh? Just work on your Hindi whenever you can, there's a good chap.'

The two friends walked back to their brewery billet. Neither spoke. Their minds and hearts were too full. Reggie knew he was not yet ready to replace Tom, however proud it might make his mother. As for Tom, he was thinking of old Harnam Singh, who had sworn to protect him. For Tom was soon to assume the most hated army role possible. He would be forced to discipline and punish men like Harnam Singh; the very men he had fought alongside and who had grown to respect him.

Tom was quite certain he knew who had put him forward for this new and terrible role as an assistant provost marshal.

## 20

# Sorcerer's Apprentice

It was the last day of the first full year of war.

The drums were being beaten on either side of the entrance as Tom walked up the steps and then bent to remove his boots. He lined them up with the hundreds of others outside the door into the spacious assembly room of the mairie they had been offered for the occasion. Beside the mud-caked footwear lay a much smaller row of tin helmets, these belonging to the English officers alone. While Mohammedan cavalrymen very often perched their helmets on their turbans, only a fool would have expected a Sikh sowar under his command to wear one, as it was against his religion. Tom thought privately that the tightly-coiled cloth of a turban would be just as likely to stop a bullet as a tin hat in any case.

For once the generals had seen sense and not compelled the Sikhs to comply.

Tom had grown up among Mohammedans, Hindus and Sikhs and his ayah Parvati had taught him equal respect for all religions. He considered them his brethren and admired their courage and intelligence and honour. The good-humoured and independent spirit of the Division's many Sikhs was often misunderstood by less experienced officers, who considered their attitude, incorrectly, as insubordinate.

Tom looked around him at the assembly room transformed for the occasion into the gurdwara, essential to the reception and protection of the Sikh holy book, the Guru Granth Sahib. He knew what was to come and the prospect meant more to him than any number of lugubrious Christian services delivered by Griffin the chaplain.

Risaldar Major Amar Singh had issued no fewer than three separate invitations to attend the ceremony. Tom had worked hard to persuade some of his fellow-officers to participate, as he knew how significant this would be for the men under their command. Griffin unintentionally made things easier by taking leave. Without his disapproving influence, Tom was delighted to see almost every British officer present.

To one side of the door, at the very back, sat Bell, Gourlie, Hutch and Reggie among others. They all looked rather comical in their socks, especially Hutch who was sporting a rather jaunty pair of non-regulation knitted red ones. Otherwise, the room was full of Sikhs, drawn from both Indian cavalry regiments of what was now the 1st Division; the 38th King George's Own Central India Horse and the 2nd Lancers, Gardner's Horse. The room smelled pleasantly of freshly laundered cotton and, more faintly, beeswax.

Tom had lived among Sikhs for most of his life and had fought alongside them in France for a year. He too had once unthinkingly considered them a 'martial race', which most of the misguided few leading this war still did. Now he knew better. Many were gentle souls, farmers, often second sons entering the army from rural hamlets because of a long tradition of family service.

Tom's men showed deep respect for any farming families on whom they were billeted (the horses always needed fodder so smallholdings and farms were better suited to cavalrymen than urban billets). Most would help with chores unasked, a boon to women whose husbands and sons were away fighting. There were few complaints on either part after the initial shock of a smiling six-foot Sikh appearing on the doorstep – all white teeth and turban and honey-coloured skin – was overcome.

The British officers were seated on chairs and the Indian officers on benches, the men beside them or on the floor, cross-legged, in rows. There was a sense of calm anticipation. The door at the front of the hall opened and through it came the canopied procession of the Guru Granth Sahib, accorded the same respect as a real guru of flesh and blood. The great book had been carried with them across the *Kala Pani* to France, lovingly tended by its designated *granthi* within the regiments, including Amar Singh. It was tenderly put to bed at night and awoken by them in the morning. Now it was carried in all state on its silk cushion to the *manji* platform at the top of the room, which might in another more peaceful time have been the mayor's desk.

The men stood then and queued to bow before the Guru Granth Sahib, kneeling in rows and touching their heads to the floor before it in obeisance, then making a small offering – a few coins, or just a word or two murmured – before backing away. Tom joined them. He had attended a gurdwara occasionally in his youth and understood the significance of this moment. To his comrades-in-arms, the Guru Granth Sahib was not an idol; it was the words within its pages that were venerated. Parvati had once explained that it was as though the Christian guru Jesus himself were present wherever and whenever a Bible was read.

Tom wondered what Evie W-I might make of it and thought she would probably approve of any heartfelt worship. He could tell her all about it in his next letter.

Tubby Bell, as the most senior officer present, thought it better to continue to sit, somewhat awkwardly, on his chair, as did Goodfellow. Gourlie and eventually Reggie and all the other younger officers followed Tom's lead. Approval radiated from the men at this simple act of respect and solidarity. Tom dropped a shilling into the bowl. The donations would be used to fund the distribution of sweetmeats from the Indian Soldiers Fund, which old Lord Roberts had established at the beginning of the war. They had been specially made, packaged and despatched from England for the ceremony, most thoughtful.

They sat again and watched as Risaldar Major Amar Singh opened the beloved book and gently started to fan the *chaur* over its pages to cool them as he read. 'Gentlemen,' he began, softly, but in a voice that penetrated to the back of the hall and deep into every heart, '*Waheguru ji ka Khalsa, Siri Waheguru ji ki Fateh*. All of you know whose anniversary it is today, what the task is before us and what is the real function of holding such a gathering as this. I am sure every one of you can easily answer these questions...'

Tom allowed Amar Singh's deep voice and powerful words to flow into him, an automatic response rooted in awestruck childhood visits to mandirs and gurdwaras. He soon noted with annoyance that Reggie had started to fiddle with his Sam Browne belt, tapping one foot (clad in a sock that needed darning) against the chair-leg. The boy had spent some of his life in India but had obviously had little encouragement to develop a respect for native culture, or any religion other than the Church of England. Perhaps he had never had an ayah such as Parvati.

Reggie could only just have scraped through the examinations required for service in the Indian Army. If he had remained, Tom would have made sure the lad knuckled down to his studies. As it was, he could only hope others would do so.

Amar Singh then spoke movingly of the birth anniversary of Guru Gobind Singh who had saved the Sikhs from, as he put it, 'the claws of tyranny'. He wisely drew parallels between the struggles of the Sikhs in times past and their current situation. 'There is a maxim,' he continued, 'that people with no past have no hope for the future. We who have such a grand past must take care that our future will be equally grand.' He then quoted inspirational words from the Sikh scriptures: 'Rulers were the butchers with murder as their instrument for cutting. Religion had flown away from the world. Falsehood reigned like Darkness; and Truth, like the moonlight, was rare.'

Tom's concentration wandered as he began to reflect on the unexpected fork in the road that lay ahead of him. He had only just begun to believe he had somehow been intended to join the regiment and survive, to serve alongside these good men. They had grown to trust and to respect each other. Now he was to become their judge and jury and, quite possibly, their executioner.

In future, he risked being perceived as at one step removed from the real war and as having saved his own neck by this sideways move – or push, rather. Tom would now be watching these men, not watching over them. The thought sickened him.

Amar Singh was still addressing the assembled men, who sat in complete silence, absorbed in his message:

'Our great Guru Gobind Singh ji was born. He modelled the sect into an independent military nation and gave it the name of the Khalsa – the 'pure'. By this time, the tyranny of the rulers had reached its highest degree and nothing but a strong military power could resist the same. It was this nation that was entrusted with that task. Just as we are now entrusted to save the small and peaceful nationalities of Europe.'

Yes, thought Tom with a jolt, that's it. I suppose that if I came to France to do anything other than perish, I came here to help us win, not to punish our own side. What will they say, how will they react, when they find out?

Amar Singh was reaching the climax of his address:

'By giving his Sikhs the nectar of immortality stirred with the sword, the Guru filled them with a spirit of heroism and bravery and emphasised the importance of doing one's duty. Brethren, we must not let anything come in our way of doing our duty to our king. We have avowed before our Gurus that we shall never hesitate to sacrifice our lives in a just cause. This is the only way in which we can all be called true Sikhs.

'In the end, just as our forefathers destroyed similar tendencies of our rulers in India, let us pray that we may all be of some help in destroying the tyrannical ambitions of the German Kaiser.'

As he reached the end, Amar Singh laid great emphasis on the word 'all' and looked straight at Tom as he did so. Other heads turned to follow his gaze. He knows, thought Tom, with a mixture of trepidation and relief. He knows already. They all do.

The solemn canopied procession left the hall, freeing them all to move once more. He looked around him, incredulous, as kindly nods of sympathy and smiles were directed towards him. Tom had to swallow hard and stare fiercely at the floor.

Two days later, Tom took up his new role as Assistant Provost Marshal of the 1st Indian Cavalry Division, which was still commanded by grim old 'Iron Ration', General Mike Rimington. Tom was ordered to work alongside Captain Coates, A.P.M. of the 15th Hussars, to get an understanding of what the job entailed.

He shared a billet with Coates, a pleasant enough fellow with no chin and even less imagination. 'No more dugouts for you, all being well, Westmacott,' he said, meaning it kindly. Tom could not explain how oddly bereft these words made him feel.

He hoped Reggie would do nothing idiotic now the boy was due for promotion and left to his own devices. Harnam Singh had promised to keep an eye on him and to improve the boy's understanding of Hindi and customs among the Sikhs and Mohammedans of his squadron.

Coates began Tom's training by having him attend a two-hour-long civilian complaints hearing. The interpreter this time was an intelligent and good-humoured local priest named Luneau. The complaints seemed frequently to arise from disagreement over grazing and fodder, as horses require feeding even when not in use as transportation.

One plaintiff amused them all no end. A young and somewhat fragrant French peasant, very much in the family way, waddled in and refused the proffered chair. Luneau translated her words completely deadpan but with a twinkle in his eye. It appeared that one day some months ago, this innocent young maiden had been out in the fields hoeing turnips. Suddenly a private had appeared and offered to play his mouth organ to her. She had enjoyed that and then he had said 'oh look, there's an aeroplane'. She had looked up and the next minute, there she was on the ground with her knickers around her ankles and her legs in the air. Luneau then turned and informed them in English, in identical tones, that this young lady was a bad lot and it was a pack of lies. He knew for a fact that the father of the child was a man from the next village.

Tom wondered about the truth of it all for a fleeting second, as the woman seemed genuine enough to him. Coates just offered, wearily, to 'look into the matter' and sent her away. Then he clapped a hand to his forehead. 'Oh, good Lord, I've forgotten Binns,' he said. 'Sorry Luneau, but it's been over the two hours. You'll have to tell the others to come back tomorrow.'

Coates led Tom out of the Mairie round to a small area of parkland nearby, graced by a stone Saint Anthony holding aloft the lost infant Christ. This statue made a strange contrast to the dismal figure pinioned beside it.

Coates had brought Tom along to watch and learn as he released the miserable Private Binns from Field Punishment No 1. Tom had heard of this practice but had never seen it. He knew it was nicknamed crucifixion by the men. Was the man slumped astride the pole dead? He was certainly motionless.

Coates ignored the prisoner at first. He walked Tom all the way round the wooden structure, pointing out how the picketing pegs needed to be hammered in at a slight angle to avoid the offender pulling them out again by flexing his ankles. The whole thing reminded Tom of a pillow-fight game at one of the few birthday parties his father Vesey had bothered to attend. Then it had been fun, a pair of boys straddling the slippery pole, set over a huge canvas bucket full of water. Tom had been hopeless, of course, as he could not wear his spectacles, but the others had enjoyed it. Even his father had had a go, deliberately toppling over and landing in the bucket with a huge splosh to howls of amusement.

This was instead a horror. The private, not much younger than Reggie, sagged astride a pole lifted about four feet off the ground between two wooden posts. Both his legs were lashed straight, his ankles tied to pickcting pegs driven into the ground on both sides. His hands were handcuffed behind his back and Tom could see a dribble of blood from the skin of one of his wrists. The prisoner had been positioned there in full view of anyone passing since nine that morning. Those who did walk by tended to avert their eyes rather than mock. 'There but for the grace of God', he thought, remembering how he and Reggie had relished 'Bolting the Tabasco' at Authuile only months before.

Coates turned the key in the handcuffs and passed them to Tom. The private moved at last. He tried to bring both hands round in front of him and down to his crotch, which had been spliced across the pole without support, crying out in pain. Once his feet were untied he rolled off the pole on to the muddy ground below and lay there whimpering. 'Oh, for heaven's sake, pull yourself together, Binns,' Coates said, not unsympathetically. 'I've warned you about your drinking habits often enough. Let this be a lesson to you. Dismissed.'

One of the youngster's friends came to help him away. 'Yes sah, Jamesie'll be on water for the rest of the war, sah, won't you Jamesie?' he said as he helped Private Binns, as yet incapable of speech, to stumble away.

'Hopeless,' said Coates, shaking his head, as he gathered up the picketing pegs and rope. 'The fellow can't cope without the stuff and if his own bottle is empty he steals from the others. They tolerate it up to a point, but when he is blind drunk, he is a liability to the whole squadron. An example must be made. Oh, and by the way, Westmacott, none of us ever leaves rope like this lying about. Too easy for them to get ideas about hanging themselves. Not that there are many trees left, fortunately.' Tom noted the new division between 'them' and 'us' with a pang.

That night, Tom felt ashamed of how much he enjoyed the meal, the best he had eaten in months. Coates told him that as an A.P.M. he intercepted plenty of contraband heading for the men and as a result some nice food and drink came his way. Perhaps there would be some small compensations for the ghastly situation in which he had found himself.

After dinner, Coates entertained them with some clever magic tricks using sleight-of-hand, which he sometimes performed for the troops. He told them that most of the sowars were deeply in awe of him because of this, which was convenient, since they would confess their crimes willingly rather than be submitted to any kind of supernatural investigation on his part.

Once the meal was over, Coates handed him a handful of pamphlets with the words, 'A little bedtime reading, Westmacott,' and a dry laugh.

Discipline was not usually a great problem, Coates explained, so severe punishment was very much the exception, not the rule. The reason for that, Tom could see, lay in these illustrations. Punishment was designed to be standardised right across the army: it was public, painful and humiliating. The images shown were only considered guidelines – many Divisions had their own variations, like old Rimington with his crucifixion pole. Less imaginative A.P.M.s, Coates said with scorn, just tied their men to a gate for two hours, as in the official instructions.

That night, stretched out on his bed – which had sheets, a blanket and even a mattress – Tom read through these instructions in more detail. The leaflets Coates had provided detailed military offences under martial law. Punishments ranged from fines and solitary confinement to death. Tom wondered if the torturers of the Middle Ages were given something similar for the Iron Maiden or the thumbscrews.

It was not in Tom's nature to wish to cause harm to others. Now it had become his working life. Amar Singh and his men had travelled for a thousand miles and more over the Kala Pani, leaving behind their wives, families, homes and land and everything that was familiar. They had come to a strange land where the cold was as much the enemy as the Boche, bound together by a fervent belief in both their military duty and their Sikh religion. And all to fight for a country that had taken their own by force.

As for the thought of needing to execute any of these soldiers, it was too terrible to contemplate. Perhaps he was still under the spell of

Amar Singh's words, for he found himself praying silently that night to any God or Guru who might be lending an ear that he be spared. He could not help but see the need to execute a man as some kind of vindictive divine punishment for his own role in Mary's death.

## 21

# Funeral at Frévent

Lochdubh finished off the thin Frenchwoman with a final heave and a grunt. She had been silent for most of it, hands twisted tight around the white sheets of his bed. A whore would have pretended to enjoy it, but this was no *pute*. It made a nice change. She had been no virgin either of course, but at least she was somewhat afraid of him, and that was something he rather enjoyed. All fair in love and war, eh?

Lochdubh was now the acting town major of the dull but strategically-placed little town of Frévent, standing in for his old chum Jock Gillanders. To arrange the favour, Lochdubh had asked the general he now served, who had been happy enough for him to go for the month.

Getting married, Jock had told Lochdubh. Jock had shown him a photograph of his pretty little filly of a fiancée, half his age and clearly as innocent as morning dew. The same could not be said of Jock himself, as Lochdubh remembered some enjoyable tussles at Eton. Practice runs for matrimony. He felt his loins stir again as he thought of Gillanders giving his new bride a taste of things to come on their wedding night.

Frévent was an impoverished sort of place, a little town clinging to one side of the river Canche – rich water-meadows always meant plenty of grazing for the horses. It was built around a double crossroads of winding streets lined by unremarkable brick and timber houses, some of them still thatched.

Gillanders had wisely commandeered a fine billet for himself within the horseshoe-shaped gatehouse of the massive old Château de

Cercamp. This was on the outskirts of the town with fields between, as though it disdained the lowly community at its noble feet. It was less public and more comfortable than the usual pokey town-centre mairie. Ideal.

The woman had arrived at his door before seven o' clock. She had been shaking with fear and looking behind her down the road from the town when Matheson had opened it. Trap had showed her into the kitchen and made her a strong cup of tea that she did not drink, although she did eat the hard army biscuit he placed on the saucer. She had demanded to see the town major and Matheson had spent some time trying to talk her out of it. Matheson knew what might happen. It had already happened too often elsewhere.

The woman was quite desperate. She refused to leave. Trap gave up and went upstairs to wake his master. Displeased at the early hour, the major's mood improved considerably when he learned of the gender and probable plight of the caller.

Matheson, still anxious, suggested he should perhaps fetch the interpreter Luneau. After a few words with the woman, Lochdubh told Trap firmly that she spoke quite enough English for him to manage the situation himself. The interpreters tended to be either chefs or priests; the disapproving Père Luneau was of the less understanding sort.

Lochdubh got rid of Trap on an errand to G.H.Q. nearby, ordering his groom to saddle up Satan, who needed the exercise, for the purpose. The pretext for this was to assure the general, to whom Lochdubh temporarily reported, that the town had amassed the target amount of timber required for trench repairs. Do a good job in this interim role, Gillanders had told him, and he might well end up as a town major elsewhere on a permanent basis. Lochdubh had therefore had the troops and local inhabitants hard at work on the stockpiling since his arrival in Frévent the previous week.

He and the redhead were now alone. About time. Splendid.

The woman unfolded her small tale of woe from a chair beside her untouched cup of tea. As she did so, Lochdubh made a useful assessment of her physical qualities. Startlingly red hair, pale skin, a bit skinny and flat-chested – but most Frenchwomen were these days. He compared what he could see of her nether regions within her thin black dress with those of the last whore he had bedded, at Saint-Valéry, on his way back from leave.

The woman's name, she volunteered, was Claudette. Lochdubh nodded and smiled to encourage her and then instantly forgot it. She was from Brittany originally, but had moved to Frévent to be with her husband. That had been seven years ago. She and Antoine had not been blessed with a child. She lived at present by taking photographs, she said, shyly drawing from her pocket a photograph of her husband to show Lochdubh. Many soldiers wanted a keepsake to give to their loved ones. Her eyes filled with tears as she told him she had had to leave all her photographic equipment behind in her little darkroom.

She appeared to think *le bon* major would be interested in all this dreary detail for some reason, so Lochdubh cocked his head charmingly as usual and smiled again.

The woman hesitated, then stood up and began to pace the kitchen. Her voice took on a pleading tone. Her husband, it appeared, had been mobilised at the start of the war and reported missing after the battle of Charleroi. 'Then yesterday, monsieur, someone sent the commissioner of police an unsigned letter advising him to search the house. They found my husband in the cellar I use as my darkroom.'

Well, well, thought Lochdubh. Alive and kicking. All was now becoming clear. 'Pray tell me how this miracle came to be, madame?'

'Oh, no miracle, monsieur. My Antoine was wounded at Charleroi and came back with a lot of refugees. He slipped into the house in the dark and half frightened me to death, monsieur, for I thought at first that he was a phantom. When I told Antoine that he had been reported dead, he jumped at the chance of hiding. What else was I to do?'

Her husband was not strong, she said, wringing her hands. The army had been too hard for him.

'I fed him, monsieur. What else was I to do? I fed him on my own rations for almost six months so that no-one would suspect. We half-starved together.'

Ah, that explained the bony arse, thought Lochdubh.

'Antoine only dared come up into the house after dark. We… we slept together at night. The soldiers burst in and found us like that. And now I have lost him, and lost… everything.'

She did not know who had informed on them. They had dragged her husband away. And today they planned to cut her hair and beat her through the streets, perhaps worse. Her own neighbours, people she had known for many years. One woman had said to her, 'Why should you be pitied for keeping back your man when all the women of France have given theirs?'

She lowered her auburn head in grief. Rather pretty hair, thought Lochdubh, who was becoming bored and wanted to get on with it. Had she finished? Oh, not quite.

'Such women, monsieur. Faces like flints and not a spark of pity among them.' She faltered into silence.

Lochdubh liked to read Dickens and wondered if the women would not have been like that during the French Revolution, tigresses out for blood, latter-day Mesdames Defarges. Her story really was rather dramatic. All the same, he could hardly blame her neighbours after what she had done.

'And then, monsieur, this morning I climbed out of my bedroom window to escape them. But they will come for me, I am certain, for they set a man to watch me and follow where I went. Can you do something, anything, to help me?'

Lochdubh had considered her then, wearing the same deceptively-alert expression he adopted in dull military briefings. Not a beauty, certainly, but not unattractive. He reached out suddenly to cup her chin in one hand. She was taken aback, but she forced herself to meet his gaze and smile. Her teeth were good.

It was clear to Lochdubh from her behaviour that she understood a physical transaction was about to take place. He could make no promises; and she had said 'me' not 'us', so must surely realise that her husband was probably already dead or a prisoner for life. If there was little point on the man's account, he might just be able to save her own scrawny skin.

He took her hand and led her into the entrance hall.

She looked around her nonplussed, perhaps in fear of being sent out into the arms of the mob. He pushed her ahead of him upstairs to give her the right idea. Once there he hustled her into his room and against the bed, swiftly pulled up her petticoats, hauled down her drawers and bent her over. As he began, she stifled a sob.

It had not been awfully satisfying, as it turned out, but better than nothing. The woman lay silent on the bed now, one hand between her legs, her face turned away from him. He eyed her, wondering about a second go. It had been a bit more fun than his first night with his wife, that much was certain.

Dash it. Not that. The unwanted recollection of Vera Forbes-Fraser flooded in to cool his ardour.

Vera had caught his eye across the floor of the Northern Meeting Ball. A distant relative on Aunt Gertrude's side. Vera had asked him, cheekily, if he remembered the games they had played around the great Wellingtonia that grew near the door of her home at Dunain House, not far from Inverness. He vaguely recalled hanging the stems of the hard little cones on his Fair Isle pullover and ruining it. He had certainly once bombarded another child with these natural grenades. They had both been very young, five or six perhaps.

He had believed then that the urchin he played with was another little boy. There was still a kind of dark-haired gamine appeal. Vera had sparkled on the dance floor and seemed amused by his wit. She laughed readily and seemed a good sport. He had liked her immensely and there was no-one to say no, after all.

The engagement and wedding happened in a blur. And the staff of the Big House and the islanders of Meall Mòr had lined the harbour walls to welcome them home. He had thought it a fine moment.

A languid honeymoon in Paris and Venice might have made a difference to how things went on. Instead he found himself bringing his new bride straight home to Meall Mòr.

He had wanted to show her the stables and his beloved horses. Vera had had had other ideas, claiming she was tired from the journey. His parents' room had been all set out for them. She had dragged him off to the big bed, giggling. This was presumably where he himself had been conceived, which was an unappealing association. Vera was at him before he had even had a chance to take a dram for Dutch courage, surprising him with her sweet, moist eagerness. She was also rather more experienced than he had anticipated, quite unafraid.

As a result, his performance that day had been a disappointment to them both. And Vera had laughed then too, meaning to lighten the moment. He was beginning to realise how often she did so. It was a cross between a bray and a cackle.

Oh, they had managed it later that night of course, but for James, the damage had been done.

The staff and islanders all adored Vera from the start. She was the perfect laird's wife, but he felt she somehow diminished him for that very reason. She visited the sick, tramped the hills, arranged the ceilidhs, remembered the names of unprepossessing offspring and contentedly shot things. The right things. And laughed.

Then, oh so quickly, she was expecting their child. Ghastly. He had expected years of jolly romping before that happened.

As Vera swelled, and ate, and laughed, and endeared herself to the entire island, the approaching war came to his rescue. As Old Lochdubh had predicted, an army commission was easy enough to come by through his Aunt Gertrude's husband. Vera said he looked rather splendid in his uniform. In 1911, dry-eyed, she waved him off in it.

Every bit the dashing young Highland laird, Lieutenant James Macbane of Lochdubh impressed his regiment with his quick wits and good looks and nerve. He embraced his new world wholeheartedly. After a few strokes of good fortune, he found himself was speedily promoted.

Thereafter Lochdubh returned to Meall Mòr as little as he could, preferring to spend his leave at their little-used London house, which was close to several fine theatres. Vera wrote to him to tell him she had had a baby daughter who looked perhaps a little more like her than she did Lochdubh. 'And she is already laughing,' she had added, happily. She called the child Margaret, after their mutual forebear.

He had sent Vera a fine pearl necklace. He thought that would do.

The hammering on the door below startled both Lochdubh and the Frenchwoman. She gasped and gathered the sheets up to her neck, gabbling something in French he did not bother to try to understand. He stood and buttoned his trousers and stamped down the stairs. Could he protect her from them? Perhaps. She had not been that good, all things considered, but she was also quite convenient and probably somewhat cleaner than a local whore. And he had found that whores were generally harder to come by in these little rural towns, where everyone seemed to watch everyone else, than in the cities or even the countryside.

The hammering continued. 'Very well! I'm coming!' shouted Lochdubh with irritation as he fastened his uniform tunic. He prepared himself to do battle with the irate citizens of Frévent and flung open the door.

Outside instead stood that frightful prig Westmacott and a good thirty of his precious Sikhs. Their fine horses were tethered to the gates. Both men were wrong-footed, but it was Westmacott, dash it, who recovered first. 'I was told to report to Major Gillanders for assistance. Sir.'

Westmacott always somehow managed to sound both proper and insolent simultaneously, thought Lochdubh. Once he had believed it would be to his advantage to uproot the man from his Indian Army chums and get him transferred as an A.P.M. Now he was not so sure of his ground. In terms of military law, Westmacott had virtually become his equal.

'Well, he's not here, Westmacott. He's on marriage leave. What do you want? I'm busy.'

Westmacott turned and gestured to the silent, turbaned men behind him, who kept a disdainful distance. 'We have a funeral to arrange, Major Lochdubh. Risaldar Harnam Singh died of his wounds last night. It needs to take place as soon as possible, for religious reasons. We were told that Major Gillanders would provide us with some timber and a bit of fuel for the pyre?'

Lochdubh saw now that four of the native troops, all some sort of Hindus he supposed, were holding a stretcher on which lay a shrouded form. 'Oh, can't you just bury the fellow?' he asked impatiently, thinking of the redhead upstairs.

Several of the men muttered or gestured in horror but Amar Singh raised a wise hand to quiet them. 'My men would no more bury Harnam Singh than you would burn your own father on a funeral pyre, Major Lochdubh sahib,' he said, unwittingly touching a nerve.

Westmacott continued, 'You will know of course, Major, that the G.O.C. has just instructed all A.P.M.s to encourage the tactful support of all different religions within the Indian Army, too. Or perhaps you didn't see that order?'

This was a trump card and Lochdubh knew it. 'Just a moment,' he said, reluctantly. 'I need to pull on my boots.' Matheson, who was nowhere to be seen but whom Lochdubh sensed was listening somewhere nearby, had placed them beside the door in gleaming readiness.

There was a stiff breeze when Lochdubh finally emerged. He suppressed a shiver. Westmacott promptly surprised and delighted him by excusing himself with an apology, saying that he had a disciplinary hearing to attend elsewhere.

Well, this was a bonus, thought Lochdubh, as Westmacott cantered off, on his fine charger this time, rather than the nice little mare he still coveted. He turned to the native officer in the turban and said brusquely, 'Very well then. This way.' The man beckoned to the funeral party to follow him.

Lochdubh led the Sikhs about half a mile down the road to an open area just out of sight of the little town. Here beside a broken shed he had already amassed a large depot of timbers and beams intended for trench repairs, together with a smaller pyramid of sealed metal drums. These contained fuel for all the army lorries in the area.

Tactful, the G.O.C. had said. Very well. Lochdubh shouted at the private on guard as he emerged from the shed, where presumably he had been dozing. The man snapped to attention. 'Oh, go and have your lunch early or something,' Lochdubh ordered. The guard did not take a second telling and vanished.

'There,' Lochdubh said, beckoning to the native officer, and speaking to Amar Singh in a deliberately loud and slow voice as though he were slow-witted. 'See? Timbers. Fuel. Take what you need. I must get back now. To my duties. Understand?' With that, he turned his back and left them to it.

Amar Singh nodded and gave an immaculate salute, but Lochdubh was already walking away.

Amar Singh's Sikhs stood silently and alert, watching Lochdubh go until he was out of sight. They remembered what he did not: that Harnam Singh had died of wounds sustained in an action the major himself had played a part in ordering. Amar Singh had endured the durbar, where he had been discouraged from speaking. Lochdubh's only contribution had been the recommendation that men on guard in the trenches should throw grenades towards a target they could not hope to reach. This, he had reasoned, would demonstrate high morale amongst the Allied troops. Amar Singh had protested that in fact it would serve only to help the enemy locate their position, but in vain.

Harnam Singh and Reggie Durand had thrown their futile grenades as ordered. There was instant and vicious retaliation from the enemy. This piece of sheer military theatre had very nearly done for Reggie Durand too. It was only the intervention of Harnam Singh that had prevented the young officer's death or capture.

When Tom Westmacott had asked Harnam Singh to transfer his izzat duty to Lieutenant Durand, he could not have known the tragic outcome of his request. In saving Reggie's hide, the risaldar had caught a machine-gun round across the ear instead. A tough old soul, he had lingered bravely in a hospital ward for a good few days, refusing morphia. Amar Singh had sat with him as he died and read aloud from Guru Gobind Singh's epic epistle to a Mughal emperor, *Zafarnama*. The old soldier's last words had been of the roses in his beloved garden.

There was no further discussion about what happened next. All of them saw the opportunity and looked eagerly at Amar Singh for his consent. He nodded again, almost imperceptibly.

The six men who carried the stretcher on which lay the mortal remains of their brother started to pick their way up the entire vast stack of wooden props. At the top, some twenty feet in the air, they tenderly laid out the body, wrapped in white linen. Captain Westmacott sahib had found some early wild roses from somewhere, a tribute they all appreciated: many of the men remembered Harnam Singh's floral prank at Vermelles, although it now seemed a lifetime ago. One sowar carefully framed the body with the fragrant white blooms.

Then they heaved up two enormous barrels of fuel that others had rolled over to the foot of the pile. They poured the entire contents over the corpse and the upper timbers. The warm and gusty air swam with fumes. The men clambered down again and retreated to a safe distance, leaving Amar Singh standing alone before the pyre.

He prayed silently for a moment, then spoke to his men in Punjabi: 'Our brother Harnam Singh sleeps for but a moment before his rebirth. Perhaps this was even his final journey before attaining *moksha*. We will remember a steadfast friend, and a fine warrior. The moment is come for him to travel onward.'

With that, he began to sing the *Anand Sahib*, the great Sikh 'Psalm of Bliss': *Anand bhaiaa meree maai satguru mai paaiaa...*

His torch dipped and touched the longest trickle of fuel seeping from the bottom of the pyre. Amar Singh stepped smartly back.

Flame licked uncertainly along to the base and then there was an almighty *whoosh* as the whole lot caught. Great sheets of flame blew horizontally in the direction of the town, fanned by the wind, which carried the sparks over every rooftop.

The funeral party stood intent and immobile as Harnam Singh's body became ash.

Trap Matheson, trotting back on Satan along the rutted track from G.H.Q., smelled the smoke just as he turned a corner and saw the flames engulfing the town. He kicked the stallion into a willing gallop and they rode for the château like black thunder before a storm.

Meanwhile Lochdubh had returned to his quarters to find the Frenchwoman hesitating at the top of the stairs. 'Where do you think you're going?' he asked, blocking her exit as he returned, step by step. She shrank back against the landing wall as he approached. He jerked his head. 'Just get back on the bed,' he said, and she ducked her head in fearful acknowledgement. He had just reached for her again when he heard the door downstairs flung open and Matheson's shout of 'Lochdubh! Come quickly, laddie, the whole town's alight!'

It had been an exceptionally dry month. In the time it took Lochdubh to ride there, the whole of the town centre was ablaze, from the thatched roofs on the older houses to the wooden tiles on the Canche watermill, which ignited and pinged off like firebirds when the nails heated up. Even the lead on the church roof was now partly molten and flowing down into the streets. The rest of the fuel nearby had gone up in a couple of almighty explosions. Lochdubh choked on the clear prospect of a court-martial ahead as much as the thick black smoke.

To give him his due, Lochdubh kept his head. He organised human chains of local civilians and troops with buckets, all the way from the Canche up into the town centre. It took him six hours in all to bring the situation under control and by sheer luck there were no fatalities.

He returned to his temporary quarters exhausted, filthy and furious, demanding that Matheson draw him a bath. He could not face his c.o. like this.

Several miles downstream from Frévent, Amar Singh poured the ashes of Harnam Singh from their tin box into the sluggish waters of the Canche. The hot silver dust hissed, swirled and became one with the river. Then he and his men rode cheerfully for home, their duty done.

When next Captain Westmacott sahib came over to his old regiment, he sought out Amar Singh to ask if all had gone satisfactorily. The risaldar major thanked him politely and assured him that it had indeed. Harnam Singh had been a good man, the captain told him, and he would miss his courage and loyalty. He deserved a fine end. He had saved many lives, including Captain Westmacott's own.

If Tom or Amar Singh had set out to count all those the old soldier had saved from disaster, they would always have omitted one unknown to them. In the fracas surrounding the fire, a slim, flame-haired figure slipped from the door of Lochdubh's quarters. Pausing only to fork both fingers at the doorstep, Claudette turned her back on the smoke and chaos of what little remained of the town of Frévent.

# 22

# Martial Law

The boy tied to the broken chair tried to bolt. He looked faintly ridiculous, like a snared rabbit, his futile struggles only tightening the wire.

Then they shot him in the chest. The prisoner collapsed back into his seat, upright, letting out a ghastly keen. Everyone just stood there frozen, including the wretched A.P.M. Someone else in the firing squad mercifully took pity on the victim and shot him again, through the head this time. The soldier's gun should not have contained more than a single cartridge, but he still managed to fire twice. Perhaps he had not pulled his trigger the first time. The red-faced A.P.M., whom Tom did not know, bawled at the unauthorised marksman, who had turned his face away in revulsion.

Tom was just grateful that someone had acted quickly to put an end to it. The boy had fallen to one side, blood pouring from his shattered forehead, fragments of brain and bone spattering the oak-tree behind him. Dear God, thought Tom, staring. It was a shambles, in its most literal sense. Sheer pointless slaughter.

The A.P.M. cut the body loose and it was dragged off by two of the firing party. The grass was streaked with gore from the chair all the way to the lip of the shallow grave into which the corpse was rolled, falling face downwards, limbs akimbo. Only then was the unfortunate firing-squad ordered to about-turn and march off.

Tom was no stranger to death. He had first ridden to hunt with his father, aged about ten and had killed his first tiger when still a young man. In India, death was rationalised through the Sikh and Hindu religions he knew so well; a cycle of birth and rebirth and a whole series of interconnected lives. Mary's own death seemed more distant now but no less real and his guilt was undiminished; just set aside, somehow. On the Front, a bullet or shell meant that any moment could end in the oblivion he had once sought.

But this execution? This was beyond words.

Tom had watched the boy being brought in. He reeked of drink and was babbling to deaf ears about how this could not be, no, no, he had to get home, his old mother needed him on the family farm – why could they not see that? He was forced down into the chair, one sergeant-at-arms holding each arm while they tied him. The firing-squad had stumbled up noisily as someone still fumbled away with the blindfold. The prisoner saw this and began to pant with terror, words failing him. Tom noticed that one of the firing squad appeared to be sobbing.

And now they had shot the boy as he had tried to run, chair and all. Now it was fixed there forever in each of their heads. The inhumanity of it. And he, Tom, was one of the executioners.

These terrible days of extreme military justice were interspersed with duller and more frequent duties. Tom had a natural aptitude for languages and he found that his French improved quickly as he interviewed local civilians to assess complaints or stood on the doorstep of a reluctant farmer whose barn was required as a billet. He became very friendly indeed with the three interpreters: 'Nugget' Nougier, who had been a chef in London, and Luneau and Bourgeat, both priests. He preferred their company to that of his fellow A.P.M.s, most of whom were a rum lot.

The second execution he had to witness was better organised, but still no less distressing than the first. Tom, still in training, was billeted with Bowring, A.P.M. of the 51st Division, and a relative newcomer like himself. Bowring, an unsmiling sort, told him that he had been a London detective constable in civilian life and so the A.P.M. role was 'more of the same'.

They had both received orders to attend a second execution, that of a deserter in the Cheshire Regiment. The man had disappeared when his battalion was in the trenches and had been caught in Paris.

Sentenced to death, but then remitted because of his good character, he was sent back to his battalion. He did so well in the trenches that he was allowed leave in England. Once there, he deserted again. No-one bothered to ask why. There was little point. After being arrested a second time he was sent back to his battalion in France. On arrival, they sentenced him to death.

Bowring and Tom got up at 3.30am to be driven to the H.Q. of the 5th Division, but the car broke down on the way. Tom regretted not taking Daisy or Rod, but Bowring was not a cavalry officer and hated horses.

This execution was being organised by Coates of the 15th Hussars who had told them he intended to show them how these things should be done. Coates had also witnessed the botched execution Tom had attended and had deplored the poor organisation, if not the inhumanity *per se*.

By the time Tom and Bowring got to D.H.Q., they found Coates had gone on ahead with the firing party. They finally caught up with them under a damp railway embankment, earning a glare from Coates, a stickler for timekeeping. He even had out his pocket-watch.

A company of the Cheshires was drawn up opposite the chair, for these executions were used as an example to others in the same regiment. Before the condemned man arrived, the firing party about-turned after grounding arms, and Coates and Harrison, the officer-in-charge of the firing party, mixed up the rifles. Some were unloaded, so that those administering the fatal shots would be chosen at random.

The condemned man had spent the night half an hour away. He was led from there blindfolded, with the doctor, the parson and an escort. He walked quite steadily to the parade, sat down in the chair, and told them cheerfully enough not to tie him too tight. Harrison's hands shook as he pinned the small white disc over the man's heart.

The calmest man on the ground was the prisoner himself. The firing party was only fifteen paces distant, stock-still, twelve strong with six kneeling and six standing. This time, Tom noted approvingly, Harrison, with his eye on Coates, did everything by signal. Then Harrison called the firing party to attention and it was only at that moment that the brave victim flinched. This should have been done before, thought Tom. On the word 'Fire!' shots rang out and his head fell back.

The doctor examined the prisoner, shook his head at Coates and said the man was still alive. Harrison brought out his revolver, hand shaking again. He could be no more than twenty or so himself, thought Tom. Fortunately, the doctor stepped in again to check the prisoner's pulse and confirmed the man was dead, having felt nothing, or so Tom hoped. The company was then marched off.

This time the body was at least wrapped in a blanket. Coates oversaw its burial in the grave that had already been dug close by, unmarked and unconsecrated. Tom thought he saw the priest's hand move in a swift and casual benediction, but other than that, nothing.

That night the three A.P.M.s shared a subdued meal together. Bowring said he thought there were already moves afoot to change this rule of burial in an unmarked grave. Perhaps even those they had seen rolled into a shallow grave would one day be buried with their fellows. Today's prisoner had been no coward and, they all agreed, had deserved better.

James Macbane of Lochdubh found the heat of the trenches in the summer of 1916 somewhat trying. He had been transferred permanently only a few weeks before to active service within the Indian Cavalry Division. It was hard not to see this move as somehow connected with the regrettable incident at Frévent. He had only just escaped a court-martial after the fire – somehow his actions were seen to have saved the town from annihilation. In fact, the decent old maire, who had never learned of the original cause of the conflagration, had sent a kind note to the general thanking Lochdubh for his efforts. In some quarters, there was even talk of a medal for him.

Then, out of the blue, the transfer papers had come through.

The truth was that there were fewer and fewer surviving Indian service officers and Lochdubh knew it. They were desperate for someone – anyone – to fill each dead man's shoes. It was his turn.

The sowars appeared to regard their original officers as father-figures; Indian-born most of them, until now. If Lochdubh had been remotely interested, he would have learned they even had a word for such a worthy leader: *bahadur*. The troops expected the same kind of devotion and support from newcomers like Lochdubh, but it was hopeless. He did not speak any native languages and had no interest in learning them. Not that there was time anyway. He knew little or nothing of their culture and they all looked the same to him, thought Lochdubh despondently, surrounded by an unfamiliar sea of sullen brown faces. He despaired of ever being able to identify the group of men who had set Frévent alight. One of them might have been Risaldar Major Amar Singh, he thought, but as Amar Singh turned out to be a high-ranking native officer whom the others respected, Lochdubh said nothing. If there might be a medal in it for him, best not to muddy the waters.

Lochdubh had not seen Westmacott himself since the fire. When he did, Westmacott would be certain to catch it.

The regiment was currently billeted near the H.Q. of the Lucknow Brigade, awaiting orders, in a little village well behind the lines. Lochdubh had just met with General Morton Gage, like himself a newcomer to Indian Army action. They were standing on the steps of the mairie discussing the fine weather when the volley of shots rang out. Both assumed it was someone practising his aim and ignored it. Then the screaming began. Closer and closer it came, while startled sowars appeared from all over the village, converging on the square.

Lochdubh and the general watched the man come. He had no rifle – he had thrown it away – and he was almost naked. He ran, staggered, almost fell, stood again, zig-zagging towards them past the fountain they now used to water the horses. His clothes littered the street behind him. There was blood on his hands and legs but he did not appear to be injured.

He ran straight at the general, throwing himself to the ground at his feet. Half-weeping, half-howling, he confessed his crime and begged for mercy in Hindi.

'You can jabber away all you like, we can't understand a word of it, my good man,' said Lochdubh in frustration, as the general scanned the group that had formed around them for anyone who might shed some light on this perplexing behaviour.

To their relief Amar Singh, who had only just left their morning durbar, rode back around the corner, grim-faced. He dismounted and saluted. 'General Gage sahib, Major Lochdubh sahib, you must place this man under arrest and send for the A.P.M. He is Yadram Singh, a Hindu *Jat* of the 29th Lancers. I am afraid he has just shot and killed his *woordi-major*.'

The impact of this news on the crowd of young soldiers was interesting. There were audible gasps and whispers as the words were translated for those with less English. Several younger boys began to embrace each other. One older *jamadar* stood with his hands raised and his eyes turned skywards. Not that General Gage or Major Lochdubh paid this strange behaviour any heed.

'You and you,' said Lochdubh, pointing at two of his driver corporals nearby. 'Take this murderer away and lock him up.' Yadram, all force spent, was pulled to his feet and hustled off.

Amar Singh followed them on foot, leading his fine horse. He called over one of the reliable men he knew. 'Go now and go quickly,' he said. 'Find Captain Westmacott sahib before they do.'

# 23

# The Nature of Injury

BRIDSTOW, ENGLAND
APRIL 1916

It was Evie's day off. She awoke with a guilty start and stared in disbelief at the bright daylight picking out motes of dust through the gaps in her curtains. The clock on the wall said half past eleven. A Sunday morning and she had not gone to church.

With a jolt she remembered Armitage. His hand had groped for a glass of water and she had recoiled. It was not just the blistered sockets under the bandages; there were the more visible burns around his nostrils and the bilious tautness of his skin. Although Evie tried hard not to show it, she found poor John Armitage repugnant.

Evie had not yet acquired the knack of taking off her working day like an old coat and hanging it up by the front door. Would she ever be able to do so? Consie and Bertha seemed to manage it.

And – oh no! – she had missed Arthur's special sermon. She felt tears fill her eyes. Arthur had finally been ordained and was to become the vicar of Kimbolton where he had been a curate. The whole of Ross and Bridstow had been eager to hear him preach when he came home to visit before taking up his charge. He had been most secretive about his topic of choice.

Why had they not woken her? A little voice inside her head replied: because it is rude to snore in church, ninny, especially if your brother is giving the sermon.

She yawned, still fatigued from the previous week's nursing, stretched her aching arms and rolled out of bed. She poured a little water to wash with from the ewer into the basin, giving thanks for the miraculous convenience of taps at work.

The house was silent. Even the servants would be in church. She relished the unusual feeling of not having to rush. Her whole new life consisted of doing as many things as possible, simultaneously and as fast as she possibly could, although not always as well as she would like to do them.

Last year Miss Fox had been offered two locations in or near Ross as potential Red Cross hospitals. One was at Caradoc Villas, a pair of adjoining brick houses on the outskirts of Caradoc Court, the local stately home. Old Colonel Heywood was happy enough to allow convalescing men to wander in his fine grounds providing they did not peer through his windows and they were escorted, in his words, 'by pretty little nurses'.

The other was a smaller, altogether cosier house at Westfield, rather closer to Ross, which had only six bedrooms. It had been lived in by an elderly lady who had now gone to stay with her sister in Wales for the duration of hostilities. Its modest walled garden sheltered an orchard of plum, cherry and apple-trees. It also had the advantage of two spacious bedrooms on the ground floor.

Miss Fox, being Miss Fox, had accepted both premises.

As Maud had suspected, Miss Fox was not in the business of taking on critically injured men straight from the Front. Those were despatched from the Clearing Stations to hospitals in London or the south-east that offered urgent and short-term specialist surgical treatments. Commandant Fox, as she was now known, instead worked closely with two old friends from their suffragette days, both now qualified doctors. They sent men on to Ross whom they now considered simply in need of convalescence, fresh air and peace rather than further medical treatment. Not that their patients were without severe injuries. It just meant that there was little more that could be done for them elsewhere.

Doctors Louisa Garrett Anderson and Flora Murray had struggled to establish their all-female-staff hospital in the face of both disguised and open hostility and vicious bigotry from the Royal Army Medical Corps. It seemed that many R.A.M.C. men were sceptical of the ability of women – suffragettes at that – to run a military hospital. No-one had ever dared to try such a thing before. One beastly colonel had been so outraged at the prospect that he had proclaimed the endeavour would fail and the hospital close within six months. On the contrary, Evie could see that Doctors Garrett Anderson and Murray were gaining a reputation for kind and compassionate care through their tireless work. She had read one or two articles they had already published on the treatment of afflictions of the mind, a mixture of pioneering science and sound intuition.

On Evie's first day at work Miss Fox had handed her a bucket of whitewash and a broad brush, rather than the smart uniform she hankered after. Evie had returned home triumphant and speckled with lime after they had both spent the day painting the inside of the garden wall at Westfield. It might have been a bit blotchy, but its brighter colour certainly cheered up the place. They had been expecting the very first intake of patients on the following Wednesday. As Maud had hoped, Evie was there for the very beginning of something important. The sisters had celebrated her new adventure, as Maud described it, with hot buttered crumpets.

That had been April. It was now September, and Evie had the smart uniform – three of them in fact, since one was constantly kept clean in readiness for a change, while one was away being washed. She also had aching joints from the heavy lifting and turning, plus blistered feet from being on the move all day. Barefoot this morning, she enjoyed the cool flags of the kitchen floor under her soles.

Evie had seen sights she could never have imagined a year ago. She was doing something useful. She was surrounded by horrors but happier than she had ever been in her life. She had learned to love and trust her new friends and fellow v.a.d. nurses. Consie Allen was a small, kind brunette, while Bertha Jefferson was tall, fair, docile and sweet-natured. They were called respectively Nurses Ingram, Wood and Jeff, to make it easier for the patients.

Consie and Bertha 'lived in' at Caradoc Villas and Evie knew they struggled to do their own washing: she would sometimes sneak theirs into the vicarage laundry too if Kate, now their maid-of-all-work, was willing.

In general, patients who had a physical injury were sent to Caradoc Villas, while those whose afflictions were of the mind, the blind and visually impaired occupied Westfield; the walled garden was easier for the men to find their way around than the great sweeping lawns at Caradoc Court. It was further away than Westfield, so Evie worked mainly in the smaller of the two hospitals.

The commandant was pragmatic – she did not see the same merit in an exclusively female establishment on the same lines as her friends in London did. Her nurses were all women but her three orderlies, either too old or too infirm to fight, were male. There was also a cook who prepared meals at both hospitals. Lunchtimes were staggered: the good lady could be seen trotting, red-faced with exertion, between the two houses on a small, fat donkey.

Medical care was supplied by the local doctor, Philip Eley, who, fortunately for them, had flat feet and had not been accepted for military service. There was also old Arthur Flint, a handyman and gardener loaned to Miss Fox by Colonel Heywood. Miss Fox could charm the birds from the trees when it suited her purpose.

Evie tended to many of the gas patients. They had passed through the worst stage in the army hospitals but those who had survived to come to Ross still struggled, the night wards full of the sounds of coughing and choking as the men tried to sleep. They dozed propped upright on many pillows, and their snoring would shake the foundations of the house.

Today, Evie was trying not to think of Emett who had lost a leg and had yet to find his balance with a wooden one, nor blind Armitage, who used to have such a sweet shy smile when he worked at the Post Office in Ross. No, today she was trying to work out what to do about Tom Westmacott.

She had taken the battered old cake tin where she stored his letters down to the kitchen with her. The contents were now spread out over the table in date order. There were seven letters in all, ranging from one to six – six! – pages long. Evie had sent him just one postcard (a cautiously dull one of the church in Ross) and three short notes of no more than a single sheet of Father's best notepaper. She felt faintly guilty about this but reminded herself of how busy she was, and that she was only writing to Tom on sufferance because of Mary. He would keep writing, and now he had started to ask Evie to meet him when his leave came along.

Kate had come in with a basket of ironing and asked her if the letters were from her beau. She had send the poor girl away with a flea in her ear. A few days before, Consie and Bertha had caught her reading the latest missive from Tom while snatching a bowl of soup. They had also started to rag her about her 'sweetheart'. Evie did not feel inclined to say anything beyond 'He's not my sweetheart' but this just made their giggling curiosity worse. In the end she told them the bare truth: that Tom was the husband of a very dear friend who had died a few years ago in India. That shut them up.

And it was true, wasn't it? Tom meant nothing more to her than that?

Evie looked at the variety of stamps, postmarks and one – just one – showing a mark that suggested it had been passed by the censor. Tom was a captain and it appeared that the powers-that-be considered it unlikely that any officer could be a spy. Evie had her doubts about that, given some of Tom's descriptions and criticisms of the war. She unfolded an early one, written before he had been so reluctantly appointed an A.P.M. She read it again, even though she had done so many times before, and even though each time she had done so it upset her.

> Dear Evie,
> In your last note, you asked me about where we sleep and what we eat when we are at the Front. Well, we are back in our billets now well behind the lines so I have time to write again. I am so enjoying taking the horses out! Moore my servant makes a good enough fist of looking after them but they both seemed glad to see me back again.
> I shall try to paint you a picture so you can imagine me back in the trenches now, though that will happen soon enough.
> The dug-out is exactly like a family vault, always damp and cold. I sleep like a top whenever I get the chance. We have tea and bacon & eggs (doubtful ones) at 5am. Coffee and a stew of ration beef & potatoes at noon; if we get tinned milk we are lucky. Tea at 4 and coffee and what was left of the stew and jam at 7 or 8 p.m. It was not exactly luxury but Grace has twice sent me a cake and some vegetables.

Evie wondered if that were a slight reproach but decided to ignore it. She did not want to encourage him with gifts.

> One has to stand up to the men sometimes if they are not quite happy. For instance, the Boche always puts in a bit of heavy machine gun and rifle work between 3 and 5 a.m. All

our casualties happened then. One day I found a recruit firing his rifle from the bottom of the trench and I d---d his eyes and got up and emptied the magazine from the parapet. That is the sort of thing I mean. One doesn't like it, but it has to be done. Reggie Durand of course is entirely fearless & likes walking up and down under heavy fire.

She smiled at that. Tom's descriptions of the ingenuous Reggie Durand were something she did enjoy.

Taking them all round the men behave very well – one must have some cowards in every Regiment – and one realised the feet of clay in one or two idols.
Now I will tell you a little thing, Evie, which has pleased me.

Ever since she had forgotten herself and signed her note Evie rather than Evelyn, Tom used it whenever the opportunity arose.
 She turned the page.

The Regiment have been awfully nice to me ever since I came back from the wire incident in the trenches which I told you of. They have always been nice but I somehow always felt that they looked on me as an amateur. They are quite different now. One of the senior officers said to me the other day 'Well, Westmacott, we have made a real soldier of you.'
I will write again soon.

Oh dear, thought Evie.

Yours ever,
Tom

Not for the first time, she crumpled this sheet in her fist. There it was again, in spidery ink on paper. How could he. How *dare* he! Did Mary mean nothing to him anymore? How could Tom sign himself 'Yours ever'? He *had* been and always *would* be Mary's. To Evie he was merely an unsettling almost-stranger whom she had met only once, at his wedding to her beloved friend; a friend who had then died, in most dubious and unexplained circumstances, with only Tom present to witness it.

Later, when she felt calmer, Evie uncrumpled the page, also not for the first time. She then gritted her teeth and re-read all Tom's letters in their entirety, not because she wanted to revisit the contents but because she wanted to try to work out to her satisfaction why his most recent correspondence should trouble her so greatly.

She did envy Tom the immediacy of his war. Not that the bedpans she scrubbed and the hands she held, the brows she mopped and the comfort she gave were not any less real. It was just they were a reality one step removed from its cause.

It also seemed to Evie that there was almost a gloating quality in his most recent correspondence. Although at first it had seemed to her that some of the A.P.M. work had disturbed him, Tom now wrote that Captain Thomas Horatio Westmacott had gained such a reputation for correcting drunkenness through harsh discipline that the generals of other Divisions had begun to send him their men. That dreadful troop newspaper *John Bull* had got hold of it and declared that 'the A.P.M. of the 1st Division must be a Hun'.

She could not tell if Tom were genuinely proud of this, or whether he was simply trying to make light of the situation, thinking it would amuse her. If the latter, he could not be more wrong.

Her three replies to this deluge of correspondence had all begun with a crisp 'Dear Tom'. She hoped she had kept the tone brisk and pleasant rather than warm or encouraging. Each successive letter from Tom was longer than the previous one, and his tone softened more every time. She reopened the last received and reread the opening line, 'Oh Evie, you would like it here…'. He wrote as though he knew her well. He wrote, she realised with a flash of insight, as though he were writing to Mary.

No. It all seemed too fast, too intimate, a betrayal of her dear friend's memory.

The door of the kitchen swung open and to her delight and surprise in limped her younger brother. 'I missed you in church, sister dear. Is there any of the lamb left from last night?' He hooked his walking-stick over the back of the chair and came to embrace her.

'Arthur!' Evie pushed her letters into a pile and got up to hug him back. She then went to root about in the larder, knowing that Arthur was always hungry, in spite of his frailty. 'Oh dear! Not much in here I'm afraid. What about a bit of brown loaf and cheese and some of Cook's pickle?'

'A veritable feast!' said her younger brother, rubbing his hands as he sat down opposite her. 'Just what my fancy painted. Remember Mother saying that?' Evie nodded, smiling as she busied herself with a knife and plate each for them. She sliced the cheddar and popped a thin silver spoon still marked with generations of baby teeth, including Arthur's, into the jar of walnut chutney. 'Where are the others?' she asked, as she poured them a glass of milk each.

Arthur made a face. 'Oh, goodness. They're all attending Miss Bunce's war effort soup luncheon. How could you forget? I made an excuse to come home and keep you company instead. Miss B. has four other family victims in her clutches, so she did not need me there too.'

Evie doubted that. As the day's preacher, newly-ordained at that, Arthur would have been the prize. For once Miss Bunce's social aspirations had been thwarted. Arthur had chosen his youngest sister's company instead, and Evie was glad of it. They ate in companionable silence for a few minutes.

'Father seemed a little distracted,' Arthur said. 'He lost his way twice during communion.'

'Did he? That's unlike him. What did you preach on, in the end?'

'Aha! A masterstroke. Not scripture directly. Or not exactly. I had it all planned, Evie, you would have been proud of me. I chose good old Piggy Pokey!' Evie grinned at their childhood name for Bunyan's great allegory, *The Pilgrim's Progress*, a family favourite. 'You should have seen Maud and Etty beaming away in the front pew,' Arthur continued, 'Even Father looked pleased. Then we sang 'He who would Valiant Be', of course. I missed your fine voice in the descant though.'

He started to load cheese and chutney on to another thick slice of brown bread and eyed the scatter of envelopes on the table. 'I say. Do I recognise that old tin?'

Evie stroked its slightly rusted floral sides. 'Yes. Do you remember? We ate most of the fruit-cake in it that day, too. Maud let me keep the tin once all the cake had gone, even though Etty wanted it for her very own too.'

There was still the faintest scent of distant spices, Evie thought, sniffing the lid.

'Lady de Vere's best,' recalled Arthur, smacking his lips.

'Lady de Vere's cook's best, rather. Dear Mother. I can't ever part with it.'

'So,' enquired Arthur firmly, 'Are those letters all from Mary's Tom?'

'It's rude to talk with your mouth full,' said Evie automatically, hurriedly replacing the letters. She closed the lid and changed the subject. 'Now I think of it, Father probably was a little distracted today. He had to go and visit the Armitages first thing this morning. John is their only son. They're taking his blindness very hard, and his face is so dreadfully scarred it is difficult to look at him. Were they in church?'

'I don't think so,' said Arthur. He sighed. 'They'll realise soon enough just how lucky they are to have him out of the war early, even if he is disfigured, you know. Remember how everyone said it would be over by Christmas? Such nonsense. Now that everyone is hunkered down in those frightful trenches, it could drag on for years. Have you had many gas patients through yet?'

Evie nodded. 'The first few from Endell Street, earlier this month. Guns are one thing, but gas? How can one fight that? Or any of it for that matter? John Armitage just isn't John Armitage now, because of a shell burst. No girl will ever look at him again without shuddering, I fear. Poor boy.'

'I wouldn't be so sure about that,' said Arthur. 'A woman was advertising in *The Times* a few days ago for any blind soldier to marry because she had lost her fiancé. By the end of this war there may be so few men left that even those who are maimed will have women fighting over them.' Taken aback by his bluntness, Evie could only stare at her younger brother, who seemed suddenly older than his years.

'As for the gas, the Germans may have started it, but we're making it now too, you know,' Arthur continued, colour rising to his cheeks. 'It's the war itself that is savage, not especially either side. All 'eye for an eye, tooth for a tooth'. Not much cheek-turning going on in France, is there? All weaponry is harmless until a man picks it up and uses it. And who makes the guns, and who sells them and who profits by it all? *Cui bono*, as ever.'

He noticed Evie's pale face and hastened to lighten his tone. 'Now I am an upright English clergyman and a pillar of my community, I would be careful where I spoke of such things openly, of course.

Mmm, good chutney. I must take a jar of it with me, if Cook can spare some.'

Evie watched her little brother chew and swallow a large mouthful of bread and cheese. He added, more soberly this time, 'In spite of everything I have been told about the Front, and how I feel about this beastly war, I would give a king's ransom to be there in the trenches, to be part of it. I really would. Most of my parishioners understand my infirmity, but all the same. I still wish I were in Tom's shoes. I think Teddy may yet join up, you know.'

'Oh no, don't say that! He mustn't!' exclaimed Evie. 'I do see such awful things at work.'

'I am sure you do. And you are working very hard indeed, I know. Now, enough 'dismal stories'. We were talking about Tom Westmacott, I believe? Before you so neatly derailed me? Rather a lot of letters from that quarter, I understand.'

'Arthur!'

'Oh, don't blame me!' He held up both hands to protest at her glare. 'Etty mentioned it!'

'Oh, Etty would.' Evie swallowed a mouthful of her tea, stumbling over her thoughts as much as her words. 'The thing is, Arthur, it is just as you said. He is Mary's Tom. Mary's, not mine. I must have signed one of my letters Evie, rather than Evelyn. So stupid. He has taken to addressing me as 'Dear Evie' rather than 'dear Evelyn'. I am just bracing myself for 'Evie dearest' next. He says he wants to meet me when he is next on leave. He even wrote 'be a darling and come' at the bottom of his last letter.'

'And will you, Evie?'

'Will I what?'

'Be a darling and go.'

'Of course not!'

There was a silence as they both drank their tea. Arthur, changing the subject, said, 'I say, I thought the Indian troops were being sent to Africa or somewhere?'

Evie shook her head. 'Tom thought he would have to go for a while and so did we. The infantry have left, but the cavalry was reprieved.' She faltered. 'Oh, Arthur. I really don't like it at all. He isn't my dear or darling Tom. He signs himself 'yours ever'. I am not sure I should write to him again, let alone go to see him. It only seems to encourage him.'

Arthur reopened his dwindling sandwich and added yet more of Cook's pickle. 'Well,' he said. 'It's Mary to whom Tom should be writing of course, but he can't, can he, poor fellow? Isn't it logical for Tom to want to write to Mary's best friend instead? In a way, you are all he has left of her.'

'Well, that's not true.' Evie felt defensive without understanding why. 'There's his brother Dick, isn't there? We met him at the wedding too. And dear Grace and Ruth, and Uncle Fred and Aunt Laura.'

'That's not the same as writing to you, Evie, and you know perfectly well why, without me having to spell it out. I don't remember much about his brother, but he may still be in India for all I know. Uncle Fred is a dry old stick, Aunt Laura is ill, poor soul, Grace is godlier than I am, and Ruth is already a nun.'

All at once he became more serious and took Evie by the hand. She remembered his smaller fingers from childhood, equally sticky with chutney, wrapped tightly in her own. Now the roles were reversed.

It hit her then. Arthur's main purpose in coming back early and alone had been to talk to her about Tom. She flushed, unaccustomed to receiving advice from her younger sibling.

'Look, Evie old thing,' Arthur continued, oblivious to her discomfort, 'Maud and Father have the parish here, Teddy and I have our own churches now and Etty has her studying and teaching. Not to mention all those peculiar lady-friends like that rather odd Miss Nalder. What do you have, Evie?'

She opened her mouth to remonstrate but the fledgling priest was in full flow.

'I know you are up to your neck in your nursing and that's all very worthy and splendid, but it's only one half of life, isn't it? 'Let fancies flee away', Evie. Could you not be a bit more decent to Tom, even if just for Mary's sake? He seems fond of you to write so frequently. There is a war on, and he is away fighting it for us all. You could be kinder.'

Evie knew this to be true but still shrank from it. She turned away, fighting her dismay at this pressure from such an unexpected quarter. 'I really don't know, Arthur. I don't want to encourage him with false hope. I am simply not interested in Tom, or not in that way, at least.'

'Surely you are interested in the war, though? And he's right there, in the thick of it. Have you asked him how he survives in the trenches?

What the food is like? How well he sleeps? It only takes a few questions to make a decent letter. That's hardly a declaration of undying love.'

'I have been doing that already to a degree. I just don't want to give anyone the wrong idea, least of all Tom himself,' replied Evie, still feeling she was losing ground. How could Arthur ignore what they all knew about Mary's death? And yet she could not bring herself to speak of it.

Arthur was now becoming a little impatient. 'Oh, for goodness sake, Evie. 'I'll fear not what men say!' Remember? Just think about Tom, all alone over there surrounded by mud and death and shells falling like apples in September, will you, instead of yourself for once?

That stung. Could he be right?

They were silent again for a few moments. Then Arthur, with a twinkle in his gentle eyes, started to paraphrase Bunyan's great hymn of courage in his funny broken tenor: 'No li-on can her fright, She'll wi-ith a giant fight, She wi- ill ha-ave the right…'

'…to be a pilgrim,' Evie sang back to him softly. 'I am frequently afraid and no giant-killer. Dear Arthur. I didn't miss the sermon after all, did I?'

Arthur laughed, and Evie had to stop herself from joining in. 'Very well,' she said, as stiffly as she could manage. 'I will continue to write to Tom, if you think I should.'

'Yes, I jolly well do,' retorted Arthur. 'And there's just one more thing,' he added a little more hesitantly. 'I wanted to tell you in person. I plan soon to become engaged.'

'Arthur! That's wonderful!'

'Yes, it is. And she is quite lovely. It will be some time before we can marry, of course. I will need to get a Cathedral post first. But you see, Evie dear, although her name is Joan, Joan Lyne in fact, everyone calls her by her middle name: Mary.'

~

The following day Evie arrived punctually at Westfield as usual to be greeted at the threshold by a shaken Commandant Fox with a red-eyed Nurse Jeff at her side. 'Nurse Ingram, I am afraid that John Armitage took his own life last night. He used Emett's razor. Poor Bates found him, so we will be without an orderly today.'

Bertha was sobbing but Evie found she could not speak. She stood there, digesting the news. Death could come as a friend as well as an enemy. Which had it been for John Armitage?

'I have just been with his family,' the commandant continued. 'Understandably they are beside themselves with grief, as is Emett, who blames himself. The Armitage family felt they had lost John once already, now this. I will be reviewing all our patient safety procedures as a result. Now if you need to, ladies, you may both take a turn around the garden before you start on the beds.'

The two nurses dutifully circled the little plot where Evie and Miss Fox had once so happily painted the orchard walls. Bertha talked and talked about how dreadful it was, but Evie did not even hear her. She knew she should be sad or shocked just like her friend, but she was neither.

If she felt anything, it was a flood of gratitude for the boy's desperate action. His daunted spirit had flown. With a rush of shame and guilt, Evie silently acknowledged her relief that she no longer had to look upon his ruined face.

# 24

# Coup de Grâce

Tom leaned forward in his saddle and patted Daisy on the neck. The ruined cathedral of Albert loomed above them. It was little more than a tottering shell. From its spire, a golden statue of the Virgin and Child protruded at an ungainly angle, otherwise untouched. Luneau, the priest-interpreter, crossed himself when he saw them hanging there.

'Caught between heaven and hell,' Tom heard him whisper. Luneau then told Tom that a legend was gaining ground, which linked the eventual fall of the Albert Madonna to the end of the war. 'It is human nature, is it not? To look for signs and portents?'

'Perhaps someone will have to shoot her down for that to happen, poor thing,' Tom replied, nudging Daisy into a trot. Luneau rode easily alongside him. An aristocrat, he had a good seat and when Tom had offered him Golden Rod rather than his own hack he had accepted the compliment with delight. The two horses were relishing a rare joint outing, frequently touching noses as they plodded along, ignoring the catastrophic landscape around them.

Tom and Luneau talked of the sad affair of Yadram Singh, whose court-martial was the following day. 'He won't talk,' said Tom in frustration. 'He won't say why he did it. And yet there are sowars who say that he confessed all to Morton Gage and Lochdubh at the time. Not that either of them could understand a word, of course. Oh, the others heard what Yadram was screaming, all right, but they won't tell me either. Not even Amar Singh. It's like standing outside a castle, hammering on the gate. They can hear me, but they won't let me in.'

'What manner of man was he, the victim?' Luneau asked. Tom frowned.

'I only spoke to him once or twice,' he said. 'Hooked nose, the sort of fellow who never seems to smile or blink, as I recall. Towered over me. High-born, I would think. And an absolute rotter by all accounts, but no-one will say precisely how.'

'This man was a Hindu, was he not? Has he now been cremated?'

Tom nodded. 'Yes. That was another very strange thing, Luneau. I remember at least thirty men turning out for the cremation of Harnam Singh at Frévent. In India, hundreds may attend a Sikh or Hindu funeral ceremony. For this one, only Amar Singh and a handful of his fellow-soldiers were present. Considering the man had been most foully murdered, it makes me wonder why.'

Tom had seen the body being washed ready for the pyre. Yadram had shot the man at close range, between the legs. The image had already joined his private gallery of horrors; this was not a detail he felt able to share, even with Luneau.

Luneau thought for a moment. 'So. You think perhaps they may be glad he is dead? And what of the murderer himself?'

'Yadram is a Jat from Delhi, a city boy. Some kind of policeman, a sulky sort of fellow they say,' said Tom. 'Other than that, I know nothing about him. He has certainly not been in trouble before to my knowledge.' He paused. 'He could also be considered good-looking in a rather soft kind of way; dark flashing eyes, that sort of thing.'

There was another, longer, pause. Tom thought of Chaplain Griffin and shivered.

Luneau looked at him with compassion. 'You know, Capitaine, my family library at home contained many books in many languages and from many cultures,' he said. 'Among them two colourful tomes from India containing sketches of carvings from a temple they call *Khajuraho*.'

'Goodness me', said Tom, a little shocked at this admission by the priest. 'How did you come by those? All that sort of thing was once considered sacred within the Hindu religion, you know, but it is pretty strong stuff nowadays.'

All at once he was transported back to India and a temple visit with Mary. The place had rung with her laughter as she examined the carvings of writhing human forms. Their guide had become very annoyed with them both and they had been asked to leave, giggling helplessly like naughty schoolchildren.

'Oh, I would think my grandfather brought them back from a visit to India as a young man, doubtless for motives other than the improvement of his understanding of sacred Indian culture,' Luneau laughed. 'In the years before I was called to the priesthood I would often leaf though their beautiful pages. When I did so, I too could feel their power. Who would not? They are *érotique*, non?'

Tom nodded in agreement.

Luneau continued, delicately, 'I also wondered that human beings could contort themselves into such absurd poses in the name of love.'

They rode onwards in silence for a few hundred yards.

The interpreter spoke again first. 'Not all the couples or groups shown within these books were male and female, of course, Capitaine Westmacott. Some were solely male.'

'Yes. I can quite see what you are suggesting,' said Tom. 'If I may speak candidly?' The Frenchman inclined his head. 'A few days ago, I walked in on two young sowars in a dugout engaged in something of this kind. They sprang apart, quite horrified, of course. I pretended to have seen nothing. It seemed best.'

'It is never spoken of, but it is everywhere,' sighed Luneau, with a shrug. 'Some of these boys are so very young to be in the mouth of hell, are they not? They are often merely seeking comfort in a terrible situation. None of the native troops are granted home leave, so they have not seen their sweethearts and wives for almost two years. It is too long. A few of the Christians come to me for confession and absolution. I hear them out and I give it. But war is war, Capitaine, and discipline must be maintained.'

Tom was suddenly a small boy again, listening to one of the endless lectures about discipline and impure thoughts delivered by his old Head Master at Rugby, Bishop John Percival. He may have done much to improve morality at the school but he was very dry while he was about it. 'Sir Percival of the Knees' had maintained a militant stance on modesty, notably through encouraging the boys to don knee-length, elasticated shorts. Tom wondered what poor old Sir Percy might have made of some of the moral consequences of trench warfare.

'It is one thing for two men to seek each other out for... for mutual comfort,' Tom said. 'But it is quite another thing for a senior officer to take a man by force. I think that is what may have happened between the woordi-major and Yadram. It would certainly explain why the others are so unwilling to speak of it. I am going to have to say something to the presiding officer before tomorrow.'

Luneau agreed.

It did no good of course.

Only three of the nine members of the court were able to assemble that night. Griffin the chaplain came along unasked and sat there, to one side of the others, pressing his fingertips together and pursing his lips with piety as usual. Tom disliked the man more every time they met. The presiding officer was a Colonel Russell he did not know well. Beside him sat a major called Ainsley who had not been within the Division for long. And next to Ainsley, inevitably, sat Major James Macbane of Lochdubh.

Tom had not seen the major since a very odd exchange between them a few weeks after the death of Harnam Singh. Lochdubh had rounded on him in a little town house where they had both found themselves billeted. Tom had listened with incredulity as Lochdubh had accused him of involvement in a fire that had mysteriously spread from Harnam Singh's funeral pyre outside Frévent into the town itself. Tom pointed out that he had been nowhere near Frévent by the time the fire was lit and not been back there since. Lochdubh had stared at him, in his usual blood-chilling fashion, before he stalked off.

Tom had not yet had the opportunity to ask Amar Singh, the wily old fox, what on earth had taken place, but he could guess.

The colonel opened the discussion with a terse, 'This is dashed irregular, Westmacott. Get on with it.'

Westmacott outlined his suspicions: that Yadram had been forced to endure an unsolicited sexual act by the woordi-major and had therefore been goaded into murder through desperation. A moment of utter silence was broken by Lochdubh.

'And?' he asked.

'And, Major Lochdubh?'

'And, what difference do you think this makes to this particular case?' asked the second major, stifling a yawn. Tom struggled to respond. Surely it was perfectly clear? 'Well, if this man Yadram was...

was somehow coerced, then surely that might make his actions due to temporary insanity?'

'Oh really, Westmacott. 'Temporary insanity'. Next you will be telling us he had a troubled childhood.' Lochdubh glanced at the others and saw they were all nodding like puppets. He smiled at Tom, revealing his perfect white teeth. 'Your precious Yadram is nothing but a common murderer who has brought shame on his fine regiment,' he continued. The others continued to nod. 'He is a Jat and as Major Ainsley here told me only yesterday, the Jats are apparently a bad lot. We cannot consider them one of the true martial races.'

Tom opened his mouth to protest, saw there was little point, and closed it again, looking down at the floor. What did Ainsley know about it? He had never set foot in India, any more than the other three had.

'The General and I both witnessed the aftermath, of course,' continued Lochdubh, 'Or are you poo-pooing the evidence of two superior officers?'

'Not at all, sir. I just…'

'Do you deny that the man threw away his rifle then fell at our feet babbling, virtually stark naked? Or that he made his confession to having murdered the man in writing?' continued Lochdubh.

Yes, but Yadram can barely read and write English, thought Tom; all he did was sign the paper that was put in front of him. He bit his tongue. Lochdubh was enjoying himself too much for Tom to fan the flames.

'What more do you want, Westmacott? There were witnesses a-plenty. So what if the woordi-major *was* a nasty piece of work and buggering Yadram senseless? *That's* not the crime. The point is that your precious Jat then shot him dead.'

'Dear me!' exclaimed Griffin, making a brave attempt to look pale at the very thought of buggery. Hypocrite, thought Tom, who had good reason to suspect the man of similar inclinations himself.

'I have to agree with Lochdubh on this occasion,' said the Colonel, already rising. 'We cannot have discussion of this appalling kind of degrading behaviour brought under open scrutiny. Bad for morale. Can you imagine what the German propaganda machine would make of it? That will be all, Captain Westmacott. Thank you for bringing your concerns to our attention. Now, if there is nothing further, gentlemen, shall we dine?'

Yadram's end was not be the swift and merciful one Tom hoped for. The Division was soon ordered to move again from Albert to Doullens in readiness for another battle along the valley of the Somme and so Yadram was moved with it. Rumours that a British cavalry regiment had been in action there gave Tom hope that the Indian cavalry too might soon be called upon. He and Hutch took a staff car to go and assess the situation for themselves.

At one cross-roads they stopped a cavalry subaltern who told them how his squadron had run into some German machine guns concealed in high corn. His men had divided into sections to avoid the fire as much as possible and beat them out. 'Hah! Just like pig-sticking,' he said. 'We killed thirty of them outright with the lance and took sixty more as prisoners.'

He also told Tom and Hutch that when his squadron's machine gun officer was ordered to make an attack *on* a hill, the man had misunderstood a single word of his orders and thought he was to open fire *from* a hill. He advanced at the gallop and lost all his pack horses at once to machine-gun fire. The officer in question made a gallant effort to recover his own weapons from the packs but was shot dead in the attempt.

And all this carnage was described in a voice that might have been discussing the weather, or the time of day, or a game of cards, thought Tom, as they bade the boy farewell.

Tom and Hutch began to see evidence of the longed-for military breakthrough. Wounded men, including some German captives, began to stream past them. The car could only crawl along this section of road. Tom as always felt trapped inside the vehicle and longed instead for Rod or Daisy but neither had been to hand.

Once they reached the original Boche front line, the way was blocked with freshly-killed horses, and he thought again. He and Hutch gave up on the car and continued on foot, leaving their remarkably cool driver to enjoy a smoke, as coalboxes howled overhead.

The German trenches were impressive: deep, with dug-outs accessible down long flights of neat wooden stairs. It was quite easy to trace the ebb and flow of the fight. The British heavy bombardment must have been terrific. They looked over the lip of a six-foot deep trench blotted out in one place by a shell hole as big as a ballroom. A pool of crimson water filled it.

The German machine-guns had been manned by veterans of the guard who had died at their guns after decimating the attacking troops. Behind a parapet of sandbags lay a wrecked machine-gun rest, bits of German clothing and cartridge clips. Tom picked up a British steel helmet with a bullet-hole clean through it. Had it also passed through the head that had worn it?

Every foot of every trench was ploughed by shells and everywhere lay the litter of the great fight: unexploded shells; grenades, both British and German; clothes; cartridges; trench mortar bombs; entrenching tools; spoiled food; German beer bottles by the thousand; telephone wires; and over everything the sickening stench.

'I've seen enough,' said Hutch, gagging. 'Don't be too long, Westmacott, old fellow.'

British guns were firing hard over their heads to cover the infantry. The shriek of the field gun shells above was all mixed up with the lumbering din of their heavy artillery. White puffs showed where the shrapnel burst. Darker, denser clouds rose more slowly where the artillery was hitting home.

The Germans were making very little reply. The daily strafe in the trenches last September had been very much heavier than this, Tom thought as he picked his way back to the car. Could this be the end, or at least the beginning of it?

They managed to drive on a little further to a crossroads crowded with troops. Many men were eating something from little twists of brown paper with obvious enjoyment. Tom and Hutch joined the queue and bought an excellent lunch made by an enterprising young Frenchwoman. She appeared to be camping there in a corner of a bombed-out house. She had set up an iron griddle over an open fire made from broken pieces of roof-beam and was doing a roaring trade selling freshly-made *crêpes*. She dipped a wooden ladle into her pot of foamy batter and spread it around the iron griddle with a piece of broken window-frame. Tom bought a steaming hot crêpe and smiled at her as he bit into it, admiring both her resilience and her good looks. Her hair was caught back in a blue scarf but a few red strands had escaped and stuck across her forehead.

Tom was hungry, in spite of his surroundings. The first pancake was savoury and good, filled with local cheese. He ordered another, this time spread with a sweet purée made from cherries; and thanked his unlikely culinary angel as she handed it over. He closed his eyes as he ate it to shut out everything but its flavour, marvelling at the ingenuity of the young woman in keeping any kind of normality somewhere like Vermand. It had simply ceased to be.

Here the Germans had fought off the British with the bayonet. A heap of broken rifles lay nearby and showed where the infantry had used the butts as clubs once all their ammunition was gone. A long shallow trench had been loosely mounded and a rough wooden cross had been stuck in it. On it was written 'A German soldier lies here 7/7/16'.

The Frenchwoman had her copper batter-pot balanced on top of this makeshift grave, next to the bowl of cherry purée. Some of its scarlet contents was trickling down one side. The woman saw this and caught it up with a deft finger that she then sucked clean with a shy smile in Tom's direction. As she leaned back and mopped her brow, he saw that she was expecting a child.

Well done her, he thought. She was courageous to remain in such a place, but must be making a small fortune with her little enterprise.

Tom walked with the others into what was left of a wood he remembered from the previous year. It was full of dog-tired infantry bivouacking and looked as though it had been swept by a tempest. The same horrible smell brooded over the whole place.

A British officer of a native cavalry regiment rode past and greeted them both cheerily, in spite of a bloodied sleeve where a bullet had passed through his right arm. 'I shan't go sick!' he declared, with the madness of recent close conflict glittering in his eyes. I bet he doesn't, thought Tom. He felt proud to be an Englishman.

Hutch obviously felt the same. 'If only our disgusting politicians will let us,' he said, 'We shall beat Fritz into a cocked hat.'

Wherever D.H.Q. transferred to, there the prisoner Yadram was escorted too, riding between two of Tom's hefty sergeants. Tom had decided the Jat posed little risk of absconding or injuring anyone else and had allowed him to be untied and to ride his own mount, which saved a lot of trouble in transporting him bound. He noted with approval that the man cared for his bony little beast very decently.

At length, Yadram began to believe he might somehow avoid his fate. He spoke shyly to Tom when he was riding alongside him one day, to say that he was quite certain that Captain Westmacott sahib would not now shoot Yadram, as Captain Westmacott sahib had kept him safe from harm for so long.

This made Tom feel quite wretched. What could he say?

It was not until they had completed a ride of about twenty-eight miles up to Villers-Châtel that orders finally came through confirming Yadram's execution. Tom could do nothing other than promise the man he would make sure his horse went to a kind new master: his servant Private Moore needed a new mount, as his own had gone lame.

On 20 July, Tom rode over to the Lucknow Brigade H.Q. and on to the 29th Lancers from whom the firing-party would be assembled. He had used the delay to plan the execution in minute detail. Small changes would make it a little more merciful, he hoped, and he was able to arrange everything accordingly, including the location. Yadram was then sent on to the regiment under escort to have his sentence promulgated; a formality.

Griffin proved a great nuisance that night, as he somehow obtained leave from Lochdubh to visit Yadram without telling anyone else, including Tom. As Yadram was not Christian, Tom and all those born in India considered this a great piece of impertinence. In any case, Griffin told him indignantly that Yadram had just stared at the wall and refused any comfort. The Chaplain was clearly offended that the man had not provided him with a satisfying death's door conversion.

Moore woke Tom with a mug of tea at 2:45am, an hour before dawn. He took Rod and cantered over to the 29th Lancers with Gordon, the aide-de-camp representing the general and Winckworth his assistant.

The regiment was waiting, drawn up as ordered, dismounted in a hollow square. Tom took command of the firing party and saw the chair placed at the front. The open grave, dug the previous night, lay only a few steps away. His firing party consisted of twenty men, five from each squadron. Tom had them all ground their arms, face about and take three paces to the rear. He mixed up their rifles and unloaded some of them.

The men turned, marched back and picked up their arms.

Well, they seemed quite steady, Tom thought. Steadier than he felt himself. He pulled Mary's handkerchief out of his pocket and unfolded it, ready.

Only then, when everyone was assembled and everything prepared, did Tom give the signal for the prisoner to be brought up under blindfold. The white disc was already pinned over his heart. All present were utterly silent, just as Tom had ordered, but Yadram knew that men of his own regiment would be present. He had saved what he wanted to say for this moment.

As Sergeant Walsh was tying his arms to the chair Yadram suddenly shook him off, rose and shouted out in Hindi, '*Salaam*, oh all sahibs! And salaam, all Hindus and Mohammedans of this regiment! There is no justice. I did this deed because I was abused. Those of you who have been abused as I was, go and do the same, but eat your own bullet. Do not be shot as I shall be!'

Before he could say more, Tom nodded to the officer in charge of the firing party, which then moved soundlessly to present arms. Tom dropped his handkerchief and they fired off the volley. The regiment and the firing party then instantly faced about and marched away, having seen as little as possible of the man's death. That was for Tom alone.

Three steps brought him to Yadram's side. Five bullets had gone through the disc. The men had done well for a moving target.

And yet he still breathed, his eyelids flickering open and shut with blood bubbling from his nose and lips. Tom drew his revolver, placed it against the man's heart and pulled the trigger.

The act was done and would never be done.

In the utter silence that followed his shot, Tom picked up his precious handkerchief and examined it. Eyes shut, he breathed in its faint perfume for a moment, then folded it and put it back in his pocket.

Yadram's body was shrouded in white and then lowered gently straight into the grave. Orders following any execution were for burial, whatever the dead man's faith. A fatigue party from the 29th Lancers filled in and levelled the grave. Gordon and Winckworth came up to Tom after it was all over to congratulate him on a model execution. He nodded in acknowledgement, incapable of speech.

Tom did not return to D.H.Q. that night. He went in search of Reggie and Hutch and found them in an estaminet in a small town a few miles away. Hutch draped a long arm around Tom's shoulders and Reggie said, 'Well done, old chap. Someone had to do it. A horrid business.'

Kind Hutch then changed the subject and reminded Tom of a funny episode from the early days of the war, when they had believed they were flushing out a wild pig from some woodland and then found they were instead pursuing an over-enthusiastic gamekeeper. Tom managed to make a sound that was very like laughter. Reggie gave him a last precious sliver of fruit cake Nugget had obtained from somewhere.

Then they shared tall tales: of bagging tigers in India and hounding foxes in England. And they drank French beer and whatever they had in their hip-flasks, down to the last drop.

The others went to their billet soon after, but Tom sat up until dawn in an old broken chair in the corner of the estaminet, his blotter on his lap, writing it all down by candlelight in a letter to Evie. How could he describe the events of this terrible day to naive Dick (whose own arrival on the Front would come all too soon) or sweet, innocent Grace? Evie's letters might be shorter than he would have liked and sometimes downright abrupt; but it was clear that she had herself experienced death during the conflict, albeit of a different kind. Surely for that reason alone she would understand his need to unburden himself?

He paused, nibbling the end of his pencil-stub. He had not been able to prevent what had happened earlier. So why did it matter to him so much to record the last words of the murderer Yadram, verbatim?

Tom found no answer and his eyelids drooped. His letter to Evie still unfinished, sleep swept him away.

# 25

# Reprisal

'By all the saints, what is this dreadful stuff?' The young man in the queue ahead of Gaston held his chipped terracotta bowl before him at arm's length. The stench of the *bouillie* was overpowering. Gaston watched a meagre portion from the same iron ladle splatter into his own cracked vessel.

He was handed a spoon and fork to eat with, like a child. As he took them, Gaston watched the guards watching them. This food might be poor, but it was warm, and it was all there was. Their guards probably ate little better. He knew what it was to be hungry and that he must somehow tell his companions in adversity to eat slowly, to take time to stretch their cramped limbs and warm their fingers.

The young fellow was still protesting, and some of those already seated had pushed the bowls away untouched. Fools. It could be some time before they were fed again. He was about to warn the boy to hold his tongue when *La Doyenne* intervened, laying a bony hand on the young man's arm. She caught his eye and stared at him in her usual baleful fashion. After a moment he wilted, saying with a sulky shrug, 'Very well, then, Madame. I will force this muck down, but only for the honour of France.'

'*Mademoiselle*, young man,' said La Doyenne, her tone as icy as the weather outside. Oh well done, thought Gaston.

This small incident triggered a few nervous smiles but no laughter. How could anyone laugh there – penned at gunpoint in the buffet at Herbesthal Station, on a journey into the unknown interior of the country of their enemy?

The article in the German propaganda magazine *Gazette des Ardennes* had warned them a week before that a large number of hostages of note were likely to be seized. It came as no surprise to Gaston. When the Allies took hundreds of prisoners from among the German population of Alsace, he knew it would only be a matter of time before the next move in this infernal game of chess.

The usual stories of atrocities among existing captives, including executions and rape, made anticipation of capture worse.

Gaston suspected that his previous notoriety would place him high on any list of hostages. As a former mayor, and as the owner of a large local business, he would be an obvious choice. Two days earlier he had received a message from an old student friend in Lille who had learned he was to be taken. Maurice Wallaert was a factory-owner, like Gaston, and a man of considerable charm and influence. The date set was 1 November. For those city-dwellers like Wallaert, who had received a few days' warning by letter, this triggered an endless stream of well-wishers to contend with. They brought with them absurd and extravagant gifts it would be impossible to carry away and Wallaert wrote of the waste of precious time that could have been spent with loved-ones.

As soon as Gaston received the letter from Wallaert, he spoke to Léonie. His sister set her face in stone once more and packed him a large bag of clothes to keep at the front door. Three of everything, just in case of a longer stay, some writing paper and pencils, even a little money sewn into the lining. She made sure that his best and warmest coat hung from the peg this time, his most solid leather boots awaiting his feet below.

When no letter had come for Gaston by 31 October, they had dared to hope.

The car pulled up outside very early on the morning of 1 November, long before dawn. None of the children were yet awake. Léonie stared at Gaston, waiting, hoping the knock would not come. Gaston said nothing and finished his mouthful of bread, looking down at the grain of the scrubbed wooden table as if to commit it to memory. He lifted his blue coffee-bowl and drained it, savouring even the gritty dregs. It might only be coffee made from oats, but his sister roasted them with the ground roots of chicory and it made a good substitute.

Someone pounded on the door. Léonie flinched as Gaston rose to obey the summons. Outside was a young German lieutenant he recognised, but whose name he did not know.

'Monsieur Derome? You must come with me.'

Gaston looked beyond the uniformed boy not much older than Alphonse to where an older and armed driver waited beside an army vehicle, smoking.

'I need to say goodbye to my family,' said Gaston, firmly.

'Very well, I will give you fifteen minutes to say your farewells and pack your bag.' He hesitated, then added, 'I think... no, I know... you will do nothing foolish, Monsieur?' It was more plea than order.

Of course he would do nothing, thought Gaston as he trudged up the stairs to the children's rooms. He could hear Léonie below as she flew about the kitchen, packing what little food she still had into the remaining side-pockets of the bag. How could Gaston attempt anything remotely heroic with the lives of his sister and of his own children at stake?

Both girls were still asleep. He stood for a moment, listening to them breathe, then bent and patted Thérèse on the shoulder. She was awake in seconds. 'Papa? What is it?' His eldest was no longer a child and should hear the truth.

'I have to go away with some soldiers, *ma biche*, probably into Germany this time. I do not know how long they will have me stay there.' His daughter held his gaze, allowing the unspoken to float between them. Then she nodded, trying hard to smile as she bit her lip.

'I will look after Marie-Félicie and the boys, Papa, you must not worry. And I shall help Matata Léonie all I can, even when she is cross.'

'*Especially* when she is cross, Thérèse. I know I can rely on you.'

The bedroom door opened behind him and his sons appeared in the doorway. Alphonse, almost as tall as Gaston himself, looked wary; Léon tearful, rubbing his eyes. Gaston explained what had happened. He saw Leon's soft little fingers coil into tight fists. 'I hate them, Papa,' he said. 'If they hurt you I think... I think... I could *kill* one.' Alphonse put an arm around his brother's shoulder, whether in concern or solidarity Gaston did not know. Both his sons had hardened and grown fierce during the two years of Occupation.

He got down on his knees in front of Léon to take him by the shoulders but addressed his three elder children as he did so. 'Listen to me. What is happening is wrong and terrible, but war is a time of terrible and wrong things. Adding to the horror of it by killing someone yourself will achieve nothing. It will blacken your heart and soul forever. I will come back, but while I am away, I need you all to be brave and to protect yourselves by putting up with the enemy, for as long as you must, for my sake and for your own. Look at your sister.' Little Marie-Félicie slept on, curled up under her blanket like a winter dormouse. 'She and all of you will know life after this war ends,' Gaston continued. 'You must continue to believe in peace, whatever happens. War is not normal. It makes savages of decent men, French and German alike. You must do nothing that prevents you from being able to enjoy the peace when it comes. Nothing! Promise me?'

'Oui, Papa.' Alphonse tried to look like the man he was not; Léon remained sullen and angry; Thérèse ready to weep but holding herself in check, if only just.

There was another sharp rap at the door below. Marie-Félicie began to stir, muttering something indistinct from her warm nest. Gaston bent again quickly to kiss her dark, downy head, pulled his three elder children to him in a desperate embrace, and then left them. Downstairs he pulled on his hat, coat and boots, wondering what on earth was crammed inside the now-leaden bag his sister had handed him. Léonie was determined not to let the enemy soldiers see her distress. 'Take care, brother,' was all she said as he kissed her farewell.

As the door closed behind him, he heard Marie-Félicie begin to howl.

The car thundered straight past the Abbé Lebrun's house and the church. Good, thought Gaston, relieved. His unlikely personal saviour was nowhere to be seen this time, so had clearly been spared. Old Maître Corbeau might not have withstood another period of captivity so well, nor found the enemy so amenable to his wiles.

Then, on the very outskirts of the town, they suddenly lurched around a corner and up the laurel-lined drive that Gaston knew well. What was this? Surely not! Gaston twisted in his seat to see a tall and imperious figure clad all in black awaiting them on the doorstep.

Another German soldier stood guard beside her. Mademoiselle Brasseur of Bavay's famous brewery wore her round fur hat like a crown. She glared at her guard, who promptly picked up a leather valise as though he were her footman. The young man also offered her his arm, which she ignored, taking each step in her own time before marching to the car, back ramrod straight and head held high.

'Monsieur le Maire,' she said through the open door, without surprise. Most Bavaisiens still used his former title.

'Mademoiselle Brasseur?' he began, as the young soldier beckoned the driver over to help him with a small trunk on the doorstep. 'What on earth…' She silenced him with an imperceptible shake of the head. The soldier handed the valise to the lieutenant who placed it at his feet. Then Mademoiselle Brasseur climbed in beside him and settled herself on the hard seat.

A cry came from the house and an elderly servant rushed down the steps after them. 'Wait, please! You need your *parapluie*, Mademoiselle Marguerite!' She thrust a furled black ebony-handled umbrella into Gaston's outstretched hand. The unnerved guard finally clambered in to sit beside the lieutenant and the driver slammed the door. Mademoiselle Brasseur took the umbrella and inclined her head graciously towards Gaston.

The lieutenant began to stammer something about sticks not being permitted as they might be used as a weapon. Its owner snorted. 'And if I do not bring my umbrella to lean on, young man, I may fall down,' she said. 'Do you and your little friend here then propose to carry me into captivity over your shoulders?' The officer fell silent, abashed, and no more was said. Mademoiselle Brasseur then raised her umbrella and brought its brass tip down twice on the floor of the car. 'I am ready now,' she announced. 'Drive on.' As if she were seated in her own carriage, thought Gaston admiringly. Her fine grey mares had been a regular sight in Bavay until the enemy had taken them for the war.

The two Germans looked at her open-mouthed.

The car moved off as though doing her bidding. Gaston glimpsed a flurry of distraught handkerchiefs being waved from the front door step. He raised a hand to respond. Mademoiselle Brasseur did not. The rest of the journey to the station was made in complete silence, the old lady's white knuckles clenched bravely over the head of her panther's head umbrella-handle. Gaston knew better than to ask questions, but his mind was in turmoil. If they had taken a woman – and such a woman – who else would they find at the station?

Mademoiselle Brasseur was an astute but cruel choice of hostage. As her surname suggested, she came from a grand old Belgian beer dynasty that stretched back into medieval times. She had run one famous family brewery just over the border from Bavay for years. When her sister had suddenly lost her brewer husband, Mademoiselle Brasseur had left a nephew to manage her Belgian establishment and came to live and work in Bavay instead. The arrival of the good lady at the Brewery galvanised the remaining workers and family members into renewed commitment and activity. She inspired both loyalty and fear in equal measure. That had been over ten years before and the two sisters were still very much involved. Bavay beer had been brewed in the town for over three hundred years. The Germans now drank most it, of course, so did not wish to stop production. Taking its matriarch hostage would ensure the co-operation of townsfolk and employees alike.

Gaston had no idea of her age. Her sister was in her early sixties, and he knew Mademoiselle Brasseur to be the elder of the two. La Doyenne, as the brewery workers had dubbed her, liked to say that she was married to the hop and the hop alone; Gaston suspected that even afloat on her fortune of beer, no man would have taken her. La Doyenne had a view on everything and everyone, including Gaston, and was never one to keep it to herself. She always wore black; why, he did not know. He had also never once known her smile.

Gaston had a better idea than most of what they might be facing and hoped Mademoiselle Brasseur would manage to bridle her sardonic tongue. If she failed to do so, he feared for her and for them all during the time of trial ahead.

A sea of other anxious faces awaited them at the station in Valenciennes, where cars and trucks bearing hostages now converged. The train stood before them, darkened compartment doors gaping, ready to swallow them whole. To Gaston's distress he saw that La Doyenne was far from being the only woman: about a third of the throng on the platform were female. They parted before Mademoiselle Brasseur and the tap, tap, tap of her umbrella like the Red Sea. Gaston, who followed in her wake carrying her bag as well as his own, knew most of those present, at least by sight. The Germans had clearly skimmed off the rich cream of the north. All around him stood men of importance: bankers and lawyers, a few other industrialists such as himself, but also shopkeepers, brewers, bakers and pastry-chefs, even a doctor and a curé or two to see to their spiritual and physical needs. The women were all wives, genteel ladies of independent means, or businesswomen, like La Doyenne.

A German major stood up on a bench and announced in excellent French that they need have no fear, that they would be honoured guests of Germany and treated as if they were German officers. This seemed to reassure some of those present, especially the women, but Gaston looked at the battered old train and thought that the words might only be intended to ensure an orderly boarding.

He heard his name called and saw an old friend elbowing his way towards him through the crowd. Vital Chamberlain, the Maire of Houdain-lez-Bavay, embraced him warmly. Gaston felt torn between relief and distress to find him in the same predicament.

'Derome! My poor fellow, I wondered if they would take you again. What bad luck, but at least you have done this before?'

No, thought Gaston. This time it was different. There was still fear, but it was suppressed. People talked in hushed voices.

'There are so many of us!' Chamberlain continued. 'They will treat us honourably, I would think. Surely they must, with all these women present. What do you say, Derome?'

Gaston thought that one sweep of a machine-gun would kill them all within seconds but did not share his doubts. Instead he lifted his shoulders in resignation. 'You have seen that even La Doyenne is here?'

Chamberlain turned to gaze at the great lady as she stopped to talk to the two wealthy Dupont brothers, brewers from Valenciennes. He shook his head. 'The Germans must be mad,' he said, sadly. Far from that, thought Gaston.

There was luggage everywhere and some of the ladies were seated on the trunks. La Doyenne went to join them, but soon the guards were gesturing them onwards and into the waiting train. The women were handed up into their second class carriages, the men packed into third. The doors were locked.

The train stopped first in Brussels, where much shouting and jolting told them that several other carriages, the section from Lille that would include Gaston's friend Wallaert, were being added. No-one was permitted to leave the train, however desperate the need. A smell of urine soon began to permeate the carriages where the very young or very old had not been able to hold it. After that they halted only at Herbesthal and then again at Paderborn, where they forced down watery sauerkraut without bread and could have coffee only if they paid for it. Very few had had time to acquire any German marks so most drank water. Then the train rumbled onwards into Westphalia.

It was raining hard as they disembarked at Holzminden station. The women and children and older men were quickly taken off in army cars. Gaston noticed with anger that one old gentleman he knew well was weeping with shame at having soiled himself. A German officer in charge ordered the rest of the prisoners to stand in groups of four for a head-count and this was repeated at dreary intervals all the way to the camp. Gaston never feared a walk in the open air and relished the feeling of the clean, cold rain on his face after the grimy railway carriage, but others had come less well-prepared for the elements.

Off they were marched into the darkness.

After a mile or so of trudging up a track rutted with cartwheel and tyre tracks the camp appeared on a slope ahead of them. Row upon row of symmetrical lights gleamed dully through the murk. They picked their way along the track in silence, punctuated by an occasional oath when someone slipped and fell into the mud. When this happened, a guard would come and urge the man onwards at gunpoint. Soon the rickety gates of the wire enclosure opened to engulf them all.

They were herded into a large reception area. Many of the men had slept little on the train and were now swaying with exhaustion. Each was given two coarse blankets that stank of disinfectant, a bar of chocolate, a tin of paté and a tin of jam.

When they lined up in front of a desk to give their name, their age and so on, Gaston was pleased to find the clerk noting the names was French, not German. The man was harassed. 'We were not expecting so many of you,' he exclaimed when it was Gaston's turn. 'God knows where you will all sleep tonight!'

The hut that he and some others were allocated at random was in complete disarray. Metal bed-bases were strewn pell-mell about the room, and few had mattresses. These were a disappointment in any case, damp and stuffed only with shredded paper. Too tired to care, Gaston pulled a rusty base into a corner, laid one blanket on the bare metal, covered himself with the other and was asleep in seconds.

## 26

# Blighty is the Place for Me

Commandant Fox had learned her lesson after the terrible incident with John Armitage. Neither of her Red Cross hospitals now permitted dressing-gowns with cords. No trousers had belts. The men were encouraged to grow beards: if they required a shave, then the old one-legged town barber came in. The men looked forward to Alfred's regular visits as a source of entertainment and news, so most were clean-shaven. The commandant had banned all newspapers and advised visitors against any detailed discussion of the war. Old Alf had a standing agreement with her only to pass on the more positive stories from the Front, without too many specifics, and never a word of casualties. The patients were of course unaware that the news he provided was selective.

It was laundry day and Westfield smelled strongly of Wright's Traditional Soap. These days of hard labour alternated between Caradoc Villas and smaller Westfield House. Mondays and Tuesdays were the worst of all, as there was Sunday's backlog of washing too. On the Caradoc days one of the Westfield nurses would go up and help at the Villas and vice versa. Although the male orderlies usually hung out the heavier laundry like the blankets, the commandant insisted that her nurses did most of the washing. This, she reasoned, would ensure that its hygiene remained top-notch.

Sheets and blankets, pyjamas and dressing-gowns plus clothing for ambulant patients all went through the deep laundry sinks. On sunny days the washing was pegged out in the walled drying-green behind the Villas; or at Westfield on the sagging ropes, which Evie had once climbed the gnarled orchard trees to secure. When it rained, there was a drying-room near the boiler inside the Villas: at Westfield, there was no such luxury; sheets and blankets had to be festooned around the house in any available corner.

The other nurses complained about washing duty, but for Evie there was something soothingly mechanical in its routine. She liked to see the grimy evidence of suffering drift away into nothingness in the soapy water. She only wished she had as easy a solution for the men's scarred minds. Endell Street and a few of the other London hospitals were sending them more and more patients who were not casualties in the usual sense: men outwardly unscathed but inwardly so damaged by what they had seen and done that they could barely function as human beings. Some tried to hide whenever there was the slightest sudden noise. Others sought out and crawled into cramped, damp, dark places. Evie got a terrific fright one day when she found a patient curled up fast asleep under the sink in the kitchen. The same young man could not stop wetting the bed and slept on a rubber sheet like a child. He could not even begin to describe the nightmares from which he suffered. She did not think he could ever recover fully.

Perhaps it was the smaller premises, or more the birdsong, green fields and the distant blue hills of Ross, which lead to a higher success rate with such traumatised cases. This meant, of course, that these men were often healed only to be sent back to the very place that had damaged them. That, of course, was something that Evie found it wiser not to dwell on.

Today, for once, she was not thinking about the patients or the sheet she was scrubbing. She was instead mentally reviewing the latest long and exasperating letter from Tom Westmacott. Whenever an envelope arrived for her (delivered to the vicarage by the postmistress with an irritatingly knowing smile), she felt a mix of pleasure and dread. There was an unsettling tenderness about Tom's many letters that, if she was honest, she did not find altogether unappealing. It was simply that there were far too many of them.

In this one, Tom attempted to explain the difference between ordinary soldiering and his work as an A.P.M. A previous foray into No Man's Land that had involved tanks and machine-guns and all kinds of excitement he described as 'utterly glorious'. Was he hoping to impress her with this kind of absurd talk? And yet further on he told her he had felt 'very near the valley of the shadow' and how he had turned to prayer of a kind on the battlefield. Was he being sincere, or had he thought that a clergyman's daughter would be impressed by a timely expression of piety? It was so very hard to tell with men in general, and with this man in particular.

In a previous letter, which began with his description of the terrible execution of a poor Hindu prisoner who had clearly lost his mind, Tom's language had subsequently become almost childish as he pleaded with her to meet him next time he was on leave. It made her wonder about his own mental state.

She had not yet been able to bring herself to reply to that one, although she had received it some time ago, and then yet another letter arrived.

Tom had seen fit to chide her in his latest missive, piqued by her lack of response perhaps, writing that she really must *put your pride or whatever your dream is in your pocket and see me.'* This particularly awkward phrase stuck in her mind like a burr as she worked away, rubbing a stained sheet against the side of the washboard. Her pianist hopes might have been swept aside by war, but she now found she loved her nursing and excelled at it. Perhaps she too could run her own hospital one day, just like Miss Fox. There were advantages to a single state in life as Maud and Etty's relative independence had showed her.

Then, after ticking her off, he appeared to think that she might like fragments of brass shell and shrapnel as a souvenir of the horrors he related! Reading about them was quite bad enough. As if she did not see enough at work of the damage these beastly weapons could cause. It reminded her of the jackdaw couple that had nested on the roof at Westfield. The male would prance about with shiny twigs or tufts of moss in its beak to try to tempt its mate into renewed domestic union.

Worst of all, Tom had begun to confide in her about his personal life. Evie could scarcely believe it, but he had had his fortune told by a man from Port Saïd with whom he had shared a cabin on the steamer from India. Tom had allowed this total stranger, a commercial traveller of all things, to peer at the lines on his hand: such superstitious twaddle! The man had told Tom many details about his past life and his war-to-be, it appeared; that he had lost a great love; that he would be injured; and would find solace in an 'unexpected quarter'. Evie strongly suspected that Tom would like her to become this unexpected quarter.

Financially, Tom also appeared to be in a complete tangle. He had left India too fast and now a wretched man named Pugh appeared to be swindling him: both over the business, even though Tom had been a partner for over twenty years, and in withholding funds from the disposal of a bungalow on the outskirts of Calcutta where he had lived with Mary. Tom had told Evie he was owed £2,000 (although what business it was of hers, she failed to see) but thought he would be lucky to get back £20.

One day, she thought, passing a clean sheet through the wooden mangle, he would probably have to go back to India to sort it all out. And that would be that. Why risk becoming entangled with a fellow with such limited prospects? It was perhaps for a regular pay-cheque that Tom was considering the army as a potential career beyond the end of the war, if an end ever came. This Evie found utterly inexplicable. Why would any sane man choose a military life once peace had come again? She tried and failed to imagine life as a soldier's wife. No. It was surely out of the question.

And then there was Mary. Any interest in Tom could only feel disloyal.

In his most recent letter he confirmed one detail she did find of interest and which she and the other nurses already knew all too well. The troops sometimes held one hand above the parapet to secure a swift passage to a comfortable hospital and then back to India, which had become referred to as a 'Blighty'. Tom wrote that his friend Reggie Durand had heard a rumpus in the trenches one day and gone to investigate. Lying there was an Indian sowar with only a bit of his right hand left, pumping out blood, with his sergeant-major beating him for all he was worth, calling him a disgrace to the regiment.

Evie reread this part of Tom's letter several times, shaking her head as she did so. Did it not occur to him that that she herself experienced the aftermath of war every day? Tom did not seem to realise that her capacity for compassion was now very limited. It was the faces of her patients she saw in her dreams, their trembling hands and twitching limbs – not the gory scenes that Tom Westmacott forced on her through his endless correspondence.

The patients at the two Red Cross hospitals now fell into four overlapping categories: the mad, the blinded, the maimed and the gassed. At present their haul at Westfield comprised the one incontinent madman who had to be watched most of the time as he was convinced there were enemy soldiers in the orchard; and one local sergeant blinded in his right eye who would keep singing about the advantages of this comparatively mild injury: 'tiddly eye-te eyeeee-tee, hurry me y'ome to Bliiiiiiiighty, Blighty is the place for meeeee...' His voice was tuneless and abrasive and little enhanced by a gluey cough. The next time he tried it, Evie was ready to knock him senseless with a well-aimed bedpan.

She had more sympathy for the young boy from Ross whose left arm ended in a mangled stump at the wrist. Sam Wyeford had been transferred from Caradoc Villas where all the other patients had sent him to Coventry, turning their backs on the lad whenever he entered the room. They believed the injury to be self-inflicted. Sam swore blind to Evie and anyone else who would listen that it was genuine, sustained during an enemy raid on his trench. 'You do believe me, Nurse Ingra-ham, don't you?' He would ask plaintively and repeatedly, and she always nodded and smiled and replied that of course she did. Whatever the truth, Sam would not be going back to the Front and for that she was glad.

Later that night she wrote Tom another polite but stilted little note saying how very interesting she had found his accounts of life on the Front, and she hoped he would write to her again while enjoying a well-earned period of Christmas leave with Grace and the Lawsons at Fladbury.

She hesitated, tapping her pen on the side of the inkwell, before adding that due to her work at the hospital she was very much afraid she would not have time to meet him during his leave. Then she added another two words: 'this time'.

# 27

# The Unifying Properties
# of Snow

Gaston Derome lay face down in the snow, motionless. A trickle of red seeped into the drift that pillowed his head. Heedless of the risk, the others ran towards him, shouting his name.

One of the guards on the watchtower above pointed and barked with laughter, the sound echoing across the frozen camp.

Once they had recovered from the ordeal of the journey Gaston and his fellow hostages settled into Holzminden with relative ease. After a few days of quarantine, they emerged to find themselves living in what was effectively a little French town operating within a high chain-link and barbed-wire boundary. There were shops where they could buy food and essentials with coupons, a laundry, a bakery, a library, even a medical centre, where the women were relieved to be allowed to use the showers.

These poor souls had fared even worse than the men as their hut had not been disinfected after the last occupants, a group of Polish prisoners, had left. Indeed, it seemed to Gaston that many different nationalities were held in Holzminden Camp. Famished blood-sucking insects emerged from the wooden bedframes and all the women awoke striped with painful and itchy bites. Killing these *punaises* became a nightly occupation for the duration of their stay. Mademoiselle Brasseur, who ran her hut as though she were the colonel of an army regiment, recorded who killed the most (the best trick was to capture them on the end of a piece of wet soap, scrape them off then crush them beneath something hard). She allocated a little tin of jam or paté to the lady with the highest weekly total when she could obtain one – the Germans took the nicest things for themselves.

As a nod to the number of married couples in their ranks, the women were permitted to visit their husbands or friends for a few hours each week. Otherwise they were strictly segregated; a source of much hardship. Sometimes even those visits were suppressed as a punishment for some misdemeanour or another.

When such encounters were permitted, Mademoiselle Brasseur would sometimes take a cup of what passed for coffee with Gaston. She explained quite matter-of-factly that in fact a letter had had come for her sister, not for herself, but that she had replaced her without informing her captors until she arrived at Holzminden, blaming her sister's bad nerves. They had told no-one outside the family to avoid distressing the brewery staff. She told him a little of her life, one of adversity, hard work and devotion to her family trade in equal measure. When the time came to depart she would rise and thank him politely for his company, but never with so much as a hint of a smile.

After the quarantine period was over, Gaston found himself sharing a different hut with twenty-six others of his choosing. They included fellow Mayors Vital Chamberlain, Ernest Plet and Alexis Pillion; the appropriately-named factory owner Aimable Bosquet; Henri Dechy, a jovial doctor who sported a magnificent beard and whiskers, and a number of others from small communities that neighboured Bavay. The curé Joseph Vallez from Bellignies was no Maître Corbeau: a placid, cheerful man, he passed most of his time reading from his prayer book, seldom straying too far from the rickety stove on which they warmed up their supplies of tinned food.

The biggest problem for Gaston was the unexpected boredom of captivity. He was an active man both physically and mentally and had been anticipating some form of forced labour during his internment. Instead the days stretched endlessly without much useful activity. He was unused to a life without purpose. It felt wrong to be so indolent when he knew his family and townsfolk would be struggling with day-to-day life under the army of Occupation.

Gaston like most of the hostages lived for news of the outside world and it soon began to trickle in, before turning into a deluge of food parcels. He read letters from Léonie and Thérèse over and over again, trying to read between the lines what could not be expressed for the eyes of the German censors. He pinned up drawings from the younger children to decorate the walls beside his bed, treasuring a fine scarecrow painted by Marie-Félicie. Léon and Alphonse corresponded least, and he worried about them the most. He could only hope they would keep their mouths in check.

There was a relentless determination among the French hostages to keep up everyone's spirits. Those who could sing organised a choir, those who played an instrument, a little orchestra. Sometimes concerts were unfairly cancelled at short notice as a reprisal of some kind, but this did not affect Gaston as he was tone deaf. The more intellectual in their midst improvised lectures in a small hall, which they dubbed the 'University'. Gaston was once invited to participate and spent an anxious week preparing his talk on the different properties of natural and synthetic fertilisers. To his chagrin, only five people came, and all of them were friends from his hut.

They all dreaded the head counts. These could happen at any time of the day or night and could sometimes lead to the men standing in lines for hours on end in bitter cold. It was on one such occasion, after some misguided youngsters attempted to escape, that Gaston looked across at the Command Building and saw him.

He looked thinner and older than he had been in Bavay, but there was no mistaking the blonde hair and thin mouth. He was talking to the camp commander to one side of the muster ground, a roll of paper in one hand, pointing at the fence.

Gaston took an involuntary step backwards. 'Derome, what are you doing? We haven't had the order to dismiss yet. Keep still,' hissed Chamberlain to his left.

'He... he knows me, that German,' Gaston whispered back. 'If he sees me here...'

Henri Dechy had overheard the exchange and had himself recognised Horstberg. 'Dear God! Derome, is that not the man who...'

Gaston nodded, feeling sick.

'Take off your spectacles, Derome,' urged the quick-thinking curé Joseph Vallez. 'Now, before he looks this way again.' Gaston slipped them, one lens still cracked after his last encounter with the German officer, into his coat pocket. He stared at the ground, painfully aware that he was praying.

Horstberg's pale gaze travelled over the shivering hostages, paused for a moment on the short little man with the guileless round face, then moved on without curiosity or recognition.

For the second time in his life, a priest, and quite possibly the Almighty himself, had come to Gaston's aid in his hour of need and he would never forget it.

Over the next few days, Dechy, Chamberlain and the others hid Gaston as much as they could, pretending that he was unwell and bringing him his rations. They found out that Horstberg was there to work on a camp extension and some improvements to its boundary security rather than for any more sinister purpose. He was not expected to stay for long.

The moment that Gaston had been dreading came a few days later, a bright and sunny Sunday, visiting day for the ladies. Gaston longed to be outside with the others but was instead sitting inside the cabin writing to his sister. He stood up, stretched and came to the window to look out at daylight only to see Horstberg walking purposefully towards him. Dear God, someone must have told him. An informer? There were some in the camp, everyone knew. What should he do? What *could* he do?

Gaston stayed motionless – surely a sudden movement would draw more attention to himself than attempted flight. His glasses were perched on the end of his nose; there was no help for it. He would be instantly recognisable.

Horstberg paused to salute and exchange a few words with two young Frenchwomen as they crossed his path: they giggled, bobbed a disdainful curtsey and walked away. On came Horstberg, until his face was only inches from the glass, staring straight in at Gaston. Or so it seemed. Gaston felt tension give way to disbelief as the German officer then took off his cap, removed a small tortoiseshell comb from his pocket and drew it through his fair hair. Then he licked a finger and smoothed both eyelashes and, pulling a small tin from his pocket, he then proceeded to wax his moustache. Thus beautified in his makeshift mirror, he turned to follow the women.

Invisible behind the reflection, Gaston finally exhaled, weak with relief.

Soon after this the camp extension work was completed and Horstberg was gone again. Henri Dechy, who spoke good German, heard from a friendly guard that the man had in fact been sent back to the Front. Good riddance, Gaston thought.

Then he forgot him.

The winter dragged on. Gaston, increasingly miserable with inactivity, was poor company. He took to walking the perimeter of the camp ten times every day, scuffing his boots on frozen soil in which he could not even plant anything to improve their dreary diet.

Then the snows came and changed everything.

It did sometimes snow in Bavay, of course, but it never lay on the ground for long. One Sunday morning Gaston awoke early at Holzminden with cold feet and hands. There was a strange glittering brightness in the air. Outside was a marvel of white where snowfall had softened the brutal symmetry of the camp. He looked at the little village and the mountains beyond as if for the first time. Once for a childhood birthday his mother had prepared him a very special cake that had had a soft, crisp, white top, slightly golden where she had held a hot iron over the sugar. Swiss meringue, she had called it. These mountains reminded him of that now, touched with the gold of dawn. Like all the hostages, Gaston often thought and talked about food. It was rather more difficult for him to express his love of nature openly, but here the two collided into one glorious wonder that made him gasp and call to his cabin companions 'Get up, my friends! You have to see this!'

Soon the few children in the camp were building snowmen (one or two constructed scowling 'snow-Boches' instead and had to be castigated). Within the first hour, they and many of the younger men had started to slide down the main 'boulevard' on anything they could lay their hands to: raincoats, wooden planks, tin trays. One lad sent a snowball flying that accidentally caught a patrolling guard on the back of his head. The man turned, stony-faced, and everyone held their breath. Then he stooped, rolled a ball himself, flung it back over their heads, grinned and marched on. The snow had brought with it a holiday mood.

Gaston went back to the hut to warm his hands and found Aimable

Bosquet, Ernest Plet, Alexis Pillion and Henri Dechy hunched over a pile of planks on a table, a boy of about Léon's age beside them. Bosquet was holding a hammer he had borrowed from somewhere. Pillion had a small tin of nails and Plet had drawn a picture on a fragment of paper.

'Derome, help us,' said Dechy, rolling his eyes in mock despair. 'None of us can remember how to make one.'

'How to make what?'

'Oh, a toboggan, monsieur,' said the little boy, his eyes bright with appeal. 'There is to be a sledging competition this afternoon when Maman and the other ladies come for their visit. Everyone is talking about it.'

There was something so ridiculous about a group of serious mayors and industrialists all clustered around such a childish project that it lifted Gaston's spirits.

'And you want to win,' he exclaimed, smiling at the boy. 'Well, I think we have enough timber there, but you will need iron runners for the bottom.'

He walked to his bed, threw off the damp covers and turned the base upside down. 'Look. I am short and light. If we unbolt the slats just at the head and foot, that will give us two broad metal strips. Heated in the fire of the stove then hammered on to the base, they should fuse everything together.'

For a few hours he was utterly engrossed in his creation, Dechy, Bosquet and the others rushing off in search of additional items as they were needed. By the early afternoon, a substantial toboggan both tacked and tied together with strips of blanket was lying upside down on the bench. Gaston was dribbling hot candlewax on to the runners. 'The final touch,' he said. 'There!'

They all agreed it was quite magnificent and the four of them walked up to the top of the boulevard. Others had beaten them to it and the track of compacted snow was already polishing down to a gleaming sheet of green-black ice. They watched as one enterprising fellow took off down it with barrel-staves lashed to each foot, but he did not get very far, much to the mirth of the onlookers, including the women who had just arrived from their own quarters.

The 'Hut 99' toboggan, as he and his fellows had called their handiwork, drew many admiring comments, but Gaston began to feel some concern. The lad was so excited. What if the toboggan was not strong enough to support his weight? What if he injured himself in front of his mother?

In a moment of reckless folly, Gaston took off his precious spectacles and handed them to Dechy. 'Hold those for me,' he said.

'Derome, wait a moment. You can't mean to...'

Too late – Gaston was already sitting on his creation, dragging himself forward with his heels to the brow of the hill. The toboggan found its own momentum in a second or two and picked up speed, faster and faster, the crystalline landscape becoming a glittering blur. He was a boy again, playing with his fellows, laughing with the sheer exhilarating fun of it. Applause and cheers from the onlookers lining the track made a blur of sound as he flashed past, laughing in triumph, invincible.

Then he was flying through the sparkling air, landing with a tremendous thump, face down in a deep snowdrift. Ow, that hurt! He must have hit the top of a hidden boulder. He had skinned his cheek a bit on landing too.

As he lay there motionless, winded, Gaston heard laughter from up above him somewhere. He struggled to sit up, spluttering and spitting out snow, and saw a young guard on the watch-tower pointing at him, helpless with mirth. Goodness! He must have made it the whole way down the run! Gaston rolled over and joined in the hilarity, looking up at the peerless blue sky, as did the hundreds of people now lining the track – partly with relief, he suspected. Heedless of the risk, Bosquet and Dechy and a few of his other friends ran down the steep slope to help him up.

'Oh well done, well done, Derome!'

The war was forgotten by all nationalities present in that moment of child-like glee and excitement. Gaston could not believe he had done it, but he had.

As he clambered shakily to his feet, he noted with pleasure that the sturdy toboggan was still in one piece. He picked it up and examined it. It was certainly solid enough. Good. The lad for whom he had made it soon vanished back up the slope tugging it behind him with a joyful cry of 'My turn!'

Gaston made a little bow to the spectators above, who renewed their cheers. One was laughing and applauding him louder than all the others put together. He had clearly amused no less than Mademoiselle Brasseur, La Doyenne.

Well, well.

# 28

# Booty is in the Eye of the Beholder

Tom found himself with a new Sikh servant and syce, Dafadar Arjan Singh. Private Moore had been injured by a kick from a horse: not from gentle Daisy or Golden Rod, but inevitably Lochdubh's monstrous brute, Satan. Every other officer and syce hoped that this vile animal would meet with a shell but its namesake appeared to be looking after his own.

Lochdubh's own man, Trap Matheson, had been on leave and so Moore had been lending a hand. Tom had found him doubled up with pain on the stable floor while Satan foamed and gloated, poised to hurt Tom too. He could see the monstrous horse contemplating how best to crush, bite or kick him. A bullet would be too good for the beast. As for Moore, his only words through gritted teeth as they stretchered him away were 'Well, sah, at least I'll be seeing me ole ma again soon enough, won't I, eh?'

Young Arjan Singh, a fervent young N.C.O. who had taken the order to fight dismounted particularly hard, had apparently witnessed Tom's prowess at polo in the old days at Midnapore. He mentioned it with embarrassing regularity. Where Moore had merely grown fond of the horses, Arjan Singh worshipped those in his care; his four-legged charges understood this devotion and responded accordingly. He was even quick and intuitive enough to judge Satan's moods and keep one step ahead of the vicious hooves and gnashing teeth.

Arjan Singh was a true Indian cavalry sowar and therefore keen to accompany Tom to the Front with the horses on every possible occasion. One morning they rode up together, stopping just half a mile short of the line, Tom on Rod and Arjan Singh on Daisy. Once it was in sight and the occasional shell whistled overhead, Tom had ordered him to take the horses back so that he could continue alone and on foot. Moore would have done so immediately – in fact Moore probably would not have volunteered to come at all, leaving Tom to take army transport – but Arjan Singh looked most unhappy and insisted that he be allowed to keep the horses nearby. 'What if Captain Westmacott sahib should have need of me?' he asked, plaintively. Tom had noted that he had said 'of me' rather than 'of them', which was the main reason he agreed; he knew from his time in the trenches that Arjan Singh could fight as well as ride.

The horses were already browsing the thin forest grass as Tom looked back over his shoulder and raised a hand. He turned up his collar and plodded on towards the line, chilled in spite of the summer heat. Arjan Singh was probably right, he thought; if there was going to be a show, he was sure to wish he had the horses – and yes, Arjan Singh too – nearby.

Soon Verey lights started to flare in the darkening sky and he could hear a machine-gun yammering away somewhere to his left: the everyday noises of modern warfare.

Tom's orders today were to await the completion of a raid. After that, all being well, he was to collect his first batch of prisoners from the Front – or 'hot from the grid' as the intelligence officers put it. Even Lochdubh was working in intelligence now – they were short-handed and he had gained a reputation for adaptability (entirely unmerited in Tom's view) so had been moved in to substitute for an officer on compassionate leave. Tom pitied any enemy who ended up in the unpredictable clutches of Major Macbane of Lochdubh.

This was not a King George's Own action but one due to be carried out by the Lancers. They were attacking the unnamed farm the Boche had been using as a base for some very unpleasant activity in recent weeks. Tom collected a nervy young escort from a checkpoint on the way into the trenches but lost him as soon as he could, among the sandbags behind a quarry where the lad would come to no harm. It was all top secret, of course, but as usual, everyone knew something was in the offing.

The soon-to-be raiders were lying about resting when Tom arrived. There was a sense of calm expectation, very little talking. Lieutenant Lewis was at the field telephone. Tom went and yarned to him for a bit and then they both sat and waited. About midnight the verbal order to advance came through – no whistles, which all too often gave the game away. The plan was for Lewis and the men to form two separate parties and attack from both sides. Tom watched them fall in in and march off almost silently, one party slithering over the top on their bellies, the other creeping northwards along the trench. Tom felt forlorn as he watched them all go, missing the hard-won front-line camaraderie of Vermelles and Authuile.

Everything was quiet for a while except for the usual trench noises; pack animals passing by with rations and so forth. Then at 1am sharp the night sky gaped wide its dark mouth to vomit blazing shells. As the enemy-occupied farm was a comparatively small target, the concentrated power and pandemonium of this assault filled Tom's entire body with an intense vibration that went beyond sound alone. He watched this precision shooting from the fire-step through his field glasses, breath held, as the shells burst in one straight line of gold. The roof collapsed with a dull whump and he could hear the voices of the injured Germans inside crying out, some squealing in pain. Good, thought Tom. Good.

Save for some desultory return gunfire, there was no significant response. The enemy signalling apparatus must have been destroyed as no reinforcements appeared either. They did not even send a rocket flare up for help. Good thing too, thought Tom, as his current exposed location offered few places in which to hide; the nearest was the quarry a mile or so to the rear.

The Boche did keep plugging away with a spot of rifle and machine gunfire; this caused quite enough near misses for Tom, and others who had remained behind, to realise that the response was no mere firework display. After a while, the raiding party signalled that their job was finished and the watchers, Tom among them, exhaled. Minutes later he heard the covering-fire barrage lengthen out to protect their retirement. The entire well-planned and worthwhile endeavour had been accomplished in just forty-five minutes.

The first lot of bloodied prisoners came across with their hands up over their heads only minutes later. They were escorted by some very delighted Lancers, including Bhur Singh, one of Tom's tallest Sikh orderlies. Two Prussian N.C.O.s marched between them like brave men, but the rest of the prisoners were youngsters, clearly terrified. One or two were sobbing bitterly and Tom wished he could reassure them. Bourgeat, the interpreter, whose German was as fluent as his English, soon arrived to translate.

The priest listened to their jabbering then turned to Tom to explain, incredulous. 'They are afraid, mon Capitaine, for good reason. Their officers have been telling them that the Indian troops always mutilate or eat their prisoners.'

Bhur Singh happened to overhear this. A mild-mannered but grim-looking chap with his big bushy beard, he loomed over his prisoners and grinned wickedly, baring his teeth and licking his lips. The young soldiers blanched and clutched each other. Even their stolid N.C.O.s went rather pale.

Although these two officers soon recovered themselves, Tom did not like the way they stared about them, taking everything in. He thought it unlikely that they spoke any English so felt secure enough in saying, 'I say. Let's not tell them the truth about our gentle Sikhs until we get them back to the holding pens for interrogation, shall we?' Bhur Singh and Bourgeat roared with laughter and again, the younger prisoners quailed.

It was a tremendous result for the Lancers that day. Tom thought the bag must have been an exceptionally heavy one. They were, after all, hunter and hunted in the trenches. The German soldiers only seemed to regain their individual humanity, for Tom at least, once they were captured.

Today the regiment was paying its raiders fifteen francs for each Boche, dead or alive. A coat was the accepted visible sign of a dead one, so some of the Lancers were coming in like walking clothes-shops. Each happy fellow would assure Tom that he had killed at least two Germans.

It was strange how this successful raid affected the men in different ways. One or two were subdued and ashen while others staggered about, drunk on adrenaline. One unlucky chap stumbled up to Tom holding his own guts and collapsed in a heap at his feet: the worst casualty of an otherwise successful day. Tom sent him off to the Dressing Station and hoped he would pull through.

Before the raid, many of the troops had been boasting of the brutal treatment they planned to mete out to any enemy they captured. When at last all the prisoners had been dispatched to the holding-pen where the intelligence agents waited to examine them, Tom decided he had better check that his orderlies were behaving themselves. As he approached the pen, he saw that several Lancers, Bhur Singh among them, were handing out tin mugs of tea and hot soup to the painfully thin arms reaching out through the wire fence. He knew quite well that he should have stopped this, as many other officers – Lochdubh for example – would have called it aiding the enemy. Instead Tom turned on his heel and left them to it.

Arjan Singh had been quite right: he was glad of the ride home on Daisy's familiar back as he was able to nod in the saddle. Tom got into bed at 7am and, after a short and fitful sleep, was disgusted to be called again at 11am – another batch of prisoners was being brought in, or so he was told. Tom dragged his weary bones out of bed, managed a quick cup of tea, and then repeated the same ride to the Front. Arjan Singh, freshness personified after just four hours' sleep, bounced back into the saddle with all the enthusiasm and energy of youth. Tom patted Daisy and swung himself back on to her back.

This time they brought the horses as far as the quarry and left them both at the new checkpoint with the frightened young private. From there they continued on foot.

It turned out that some of the Lancers had been ordered out to collect any regimental dead and check for non-ambulant casualties earlier that morning. It was then that their patrol came across a small party of Germans huddled in a damaged building on the edge of No Man's Land. They had surrendered at once. These men were found wearing civilian clothing, which Tom could not understand, and he suspected them of being enemy agents.

They were a poor, thin lot and as they were without uniforms, there was no determining their rank. Tom ordered them to be thoroughly searched.

'Look at this, Captain Westmacott sahib! Money! Much French money!' Bhur Singh held up handfuls of francs in his great fists. The prisoners looked at the ground and shifted uneasily.

Tom again sent for Bourgeat who listened to the men, nodding, and with an increasingly broad smile. 'Now I understand!' he exclaimed.

'They said they have given... no, sold... their watches to their escort, mon Capitaine.'

'Did they now? Tell that Pathan N.C.O. who brought them in that I want to see him right now, would you, Bhur Singh?'

The Pathan, a tall bandit with red hair, soon stalked into the tent. He grimaced all over his scarred face and said when questioned, 'Ah, Captain sahib, these prisoners begged us to take their possessions, but we said we would rather pay for them.' He placed a pile of watches on the table before him, waggled his head and smiled, revealing several sharp gold teeth. The younger prisoners looked petrified again and little wonder.

Tom just stared the man down, without a word, a useful technique learned from Lochdubh. Eventually the N.C.O. lowered his eyes and made at least some attempt to look abashed.

Tom examined the pile of watches. One or two were very good ones – surely the property of officers rather than of ordinary soldiers? Who were these men?

One of the braver Germans, a tall, fair fellow, asked Bourgeat if, given the circumstances, they could have their watches back. Tom had already heard other tales of the dubious habits of the Pathan in question and therefore had considerable doubts about the *bona fides* of the sale.

'Very well. Disgorge!' he said to the N.C.O.

'Captain sahib?'

'Give *all* their watches back. Now! And take back *only* what you paid for them. Not a franc more, do you understand?'

Bourgeat nodded approvingly as he watched this reverse transaction. 'I passed this Pathan escort on the road about an hour ago, mon Capitaine. The prisoners were all sitting down in the dust, as children do playing pat-a-cake. I could not imagine what they were up to. When I came along, in fact, it was the prisoners who seemed more eager to get on than their guards.'

Tom smiled. 'The point of a bayonet and these fine watches will have been at the heart of that, I suspect.'

The interrogation began. The men assured Bourgeat that they were ordinary soldiers. They would not tell him their regiment. Their uniforms had been damaged, they said. They had found some peasants' clothing in a farm building and put that on instead. They had lost themselves attempting to cross No Man's Land back to their own side.

Tom thought this was a pack of lies and said so, then had them marched off to a pen. Bourgeat agreed.

'I think you are right, and they could be escaped prisoners-of-war,' he said to Tom, 'but there's no way of proving it, is there?'

Tom agreed. Conditions in the French camps especially he knew to be very bad; one recaptured prisoner had told him a grim tale of meagre rations, punishment beatings and thefts. Conditions in the English camps might be a good deal better; but his country was not the one that had been invaded by these men. The Germans had even taken hostages among ordinary French civilians, even women, an act he thought unpardonable.

Still curious about the oddly-clad group of Boche, and with time on his hands, Tom asked one of the Lancers patrol where they had captured their prisoners. The sowar pointed out a small cluster of outlying farm buildings, separate from the main farm that had been almost annihilated, and right on the edge of No Man's Land. A plume of smoke rose from them where a shell had hit.

'Oh, let's go over there and see for ourselves, shall we, Arjan Singh?' grinned Tom. He and the youngster, also beaming at the thought of adventure, used an observation trench to get as close as they could, crawled beneath the wire then ran, low and fast, towards the roofless building.

Revolver drawn, Tom entered a door into a broken cottage that was built up against the barn wall. The room reeked to high heaven, in spite of the hole in its roof. Men had been using it as a latrine, that much was clear. On a battered wooden table were signs of a meal interrupted by broken *tuiles* and bits of debris. There was a smashed glass jar containing some form of meat paste, now engulfed in a glistening shroud of flies. Once home-made *rillettes* made by a farmer's wife, thought Tom, wrinkling his nose at the stench. She had probably stored her winter food supply here. What a waste, when so many were desperate for sustenance.

Arjan Singh pointed out a pile of fetid blankets and some discarded clothing in the corner. Uniforms. As he lifted one, wrinkling his nose, a piece of paper fluttered to the ground beside them. He picked it up and handed to Tom: a folded letter of some kind, written in German. He tucked the document into his pocket; Bourgeat could translate it later.

An open trapdoor yawned in the floor, the entrance to the cellar where the food had been found, perhaps. They approached it with caution. Tom listened. 'Did you hear something down there, Arjan Singh?'

'Rats, perhaps, Captain Westmacott sahib. Or another German?'

Tom began to wish he had brought Bhur Singh as support, but there was no going back now. He drew his revolver and started down the steps into the gloom, his heart thumping, calling out *Hände hoch!*

He had taken just three steps when he saw the stacks of broken cylinders, breathed in the sour reek. His eyes and throat swam and he tried to stumble up backwards but missed his footing. The gas reached out to comfort him like a woman's caress as he fell into the darkness.

Where was she? Gone.

Tom was on Arjan Singh's broad back being carried across No Man's Land. Where was she? No. No. Gas moved like a heavy snake. It lurked in dark corners where you least expected it. Tom knew this of course. He had also known that the Germans had been releasing gas from the farm nearby. Mary was dead. There was no woman. What a fool he was.

He could hear someone coughing, choking, drowning. Then silence.

Later, only fragments.

Arjan Singh gasping, 'Hold on, sahib. Not far now.' Lungs and nose and throat clogged. Holding someone's hand very tight. Evie?

Bourgeat on the field telephone. A deep and kind voice. Amar Singh? Was he praying? Part of Tom's left arm all twisted, bubbling, blistered. Then the jangling pain was somewhere else altogether and he was watching for the black and gold slither of it in the darkness.

Daisy's immense back. Perplexingly blue sky and birdsong. Another voice. Harnam Singh. How could it be Harnam Singh? The scent of roses.

Where was she? Where was she?

Gone.

Then nothing again.

Much later, in a tent somewhere, 'Dear God. What is this stuff then?' someone asked. 'Look at his skin!'

'Some new horror Fritz must be trying out to keep us on our toes,' came the reply. And before oblivion and morphia took Tom completely: 'Sure it's Fritz's? Might be our own.' And laughter. He was certain they had laughed.

Five days later, Tom found himself once more on the boat from Saint-Valéry-sur-Somme, bound for England.

The doctors supposed the gas to be a new German chemical weapon. They were sending him to a London hospital where, they said, he would initially be kept in isolation. As they did not know yet how the gas had come to burn him, and Tom was one of the first men to experience its effects, they were keen to see whether he would live or die.

Tom loathed journeys by sea and his inability to stand for very long meant he could not even throw up over the side in privacy. Instead he was forced to sit there with his back to the bulkhead, gritting his teeth to avoid vomiting. He was one of many; the deck was full of men huddled together in miserable little groups, with one corner full of stretcher-cases being attended by R.A.M.C. medical staff.

The discomfort and enforced inactivity of the ferry made his mind race with guilt. How could he have been so careless? He had put both himself and, worse still, young Arjan Singh at great risk. The mad desire he had felt to be part of the action again, as he had been with his regiment in 1915, now seemed so foolish. There had also been a kind of exhilaration about the Lancers returning with all those prisoners. He had somehow caught their mood, as one might catch a cold.

Tom sighed and shifted position. Even the feeblest of coughs made his chest feel as though it were being ripped open from inside; the pain it triggered had a shape to it, coiling and coursing through his whole body like some infernal serpent. He could not lie down fully to sleep – one lung was sluggish to inflate, causing him to choke. Instead, he was forced to doze, fitfully, his back against the throbbing bulkhead, with a worn blanket pulled up over his legs like an old man.

The new uniform felt stiff and unfamiliar; his own, they told him, had been cut off him and burnt because of the mysterious substance that had contaminated it. His right hand kept returning to the inside pocket where Mary's handkerchief and Evie's creased postcard should have been. Both lost forever. A stabbing pain darted through his left hand into the lower arm whenever he moved.

As he looked around him Tom could see he was more lightly injured than many of the casualties nearby. Three men were blinded, with bandaged eyes, although he did not know whether this was temporary or permanent; two others with limbs missing; and one poor lad without legs lay on a stretcher, going home to die, calling out repeatedly to someone named Annie from his morphine-induced stupor.

The five men with injuries to the hand or a hand missing kept somewhat apart from the others, smoking. Tom needed no explanation.

Worst of all was the little trio of young boys, none of whom could yet have reached twenty years of age. Apparently unscathed, they wept or sat silently and rocked to and fro and started up at any sound. It was frightful to see their intent, staring faces. They were constantly watched by an R.A.M.C. fellow in case they tried to find oblivion in the sea. What on earth could be done for them now? Tom, with a good idea of what they might have locked away in their minds, wondered if they should just be allowed to jump overboard. It almost seemed kinder.

Tom remembered very little of his evacuation from the front line but presumed he had been stretchered out by the Field Ambulance crew. He vaguely recalled the R.A.M.C. people talking to Arjan Singh at the Dressing Station, which he thought was inside a dark tent or shed of some kind. They must have then filled him with morphia again as there was a great void after that.

He asked where he was being taken and was told by the tired R.A.M.C. escort that he need not worry, that all had been arranged. First the London hospital for assessment, then 'all being well' he would be moved on somewhere else to convalesce. He understood that 'all being well' meant 'if you live'.

This had been explained more than once, he was told, but it was normal not to remember.

Evie, he thought. When he had recovered sufficiently, he would ask to go to the Red Cross hospital where Evie was, at Ross-on-Wye. Perhaps he had already asked?

Once he had decided on this and was able to fix it in his mind so it would stay there, he remembered the horses. It was fortunate that they were his own mounts and not army requisition, otherwise anyone could have been riding them by now. Arjan Singh would do his best for them, that Tom knew, but he would still have to obey orders.

He tried hard not to think of Lochdubh astride Daisy or Golden Rod.

# 29

# Turn of the Wheel

Lochdubh received the news that Tom had been gassed with complete equanimity. Arjan Singh, Westmacott's servant, had doubtless saved the man's life, but with luck his irritating master would now disappear for the rest of the war.

At this precise moment, Lochdubh was a good deal more interested in the letter that Westmacott had picked up shortly before he was injured. At the Dressing Station, where Westmacott's uniform had been sliced off to treat his wounds, Arjan Singh had remembered the letter and thought to take it back to Major Gourlie. Gourlie had passed it on to him.

Lochdubh examined it attentively: an official-issue prisoner-of-war letter, folded to form its own envelope. The page was filled with cramped writing and it showed an address somewhere in Germany. He asked for Bourgeat, who appeared minutes later, unfathomably distressed at the news about Westmacott. Lochdubh told him to pull himself together and get on with translating it and then to read it aloud.

Bourgeat did as ordered, with increasing curiosity:

> Dear parents and brothers,
> It is writing day again. I live in very good conditions. Thank God! Your image of a prisoner-of-war camp, at least an English one, is completely wrong. I used to think the same. You will be so surprised when Lars will tell you later about his life during his imprisonment.

You believe that we do not have enough to eat, that we are not warm enough, that we have to work very hard etc. Nonsense! Every day I meet English people, can communicate well with them and learn a lot – which, of course, is a big advantage for me. You won't believe if I tell you how very pleasant the English are.

You will say that you can well believe that Lars, the old officer, is fine, but what about little Hans? Only this morning I spoke to a comrade who used to be in Hanschen's company and is now a member of mine. Trust me, Hans wants for nothing: he has accommodation, kitchen, washing and baking facilities, sports club, canteen, etc.

We hope for peace and am looking forward to seeing all of you at home soon.

With best regards

Yours Lars

PS I will write again/more in 8 days…

'This is definitely a letter written by a German prisoner-of-war, *Monsieur le Major*, as Capitaine Westmacott suspected.' said Bourgeat. 'See, the name of the man's family is here on the back. He obviously has a brother in captivity named Hans somewhere too.'

'Indeed,' said Lochdubh. 'And the Brothers Grimm seem to have had a splendid time in our care, do they not? One wonders why this one bothered to escape at all.'

'Either that, sir, or the letter is a decoy of some kind, designed to make his captors think he would not try to run?' suggested Bourgeat. 'It could even be a pre-arranged code, so 'I will write again in 8 days' means 'I will escape in 8 days'? Lochdubh snorted. 'Preposterous,' he said, dismissing the idea. 'What makes you think the average Boche would be cunning enough for that?'

There was a pause as Bourgeat digested the latest of many insults.

Then he turned to Lochdubh to ask, 'And what would their fate be, Monsieur le Major, if they are indeed escaped prisoners-of-war, caught trying to reach the German trenches?'

Lochdubh eyed him balefully. 'Let me see, Bourgeat. Captured lurking in a farm on No-Man's-Land in civilian clothing? What do you think we'll do to them, tuck them up and read them a bedtime story?'

'Of course not, Monsieur le Major, but we do not know that this letter belongs to any of these fellows,' Bourgeat reminded him.

Lochdubh nodded. 'Not yet. Send them back in.'

In filed the group of scrawny-looking men, five in all. Lochdubh remained seated and did his staring-at-them-in-silence thing for several minutes while the men looked at the floor or eyed their bearded, turbaned guards. Then he barked, 'Lars Horstberg!'

It worked. The fair older man – striking in a haughty sort of way – started. And the other four had also glanced at him, albeit fleetingly, before they realized the trick. This was quite enough for Lochdubh. He sent them back to the pen again, all except the officer, Horstberg. Bourgeat, sensing Lochdubh's mood, readied himself for a challenging round of translation.

Lochdubh leant back in his chair affably enough. 'Only yesterday, you claimed that you and your men were humble privates who had lost your uniforms. You have been lying to us, have you not, Horstberg?'

The officer flinched at the second unexpected use of his name but retorted, boldly enough, 'So? If the circumstances were reversed, and you had escaped from a German prison camp, would you not have done the same?'

Lochdubh glared at him in silence for a few seconds more. The German met his gaze. The major continued, softly and dangerously, 'Ah, but circumstances are not reversed, are they, Horstberg? You are my prisoner and I your captor. Tell me now how you came to be sheltering within the farm buildings on the edge of No Man's Land and I may yet be lenient.'

Bourgeat, standing in the corner, shifted uncomfortably as he translated.

'I will not tell you that!' snarled Horstberg. 'Yes, I was in a camp. A French camp. We were badly treated and we escaped.' Here he looked pointedly at Bourgeat, who avoided eye contact. 'That is all I am prepared to divulge.'

'And yet that is not at all what you say in your letter here,' Lochdubh pointed out, unfolding the letter again and waving it languidly at Horstberg. 'How do you explain this. My "old officer" friend?'

There was silence as the thoroughly-rattled German officer contemplated his best course of action. At length he admitted, 'There were perhaps two camps.'

'Ah, I see. Perhaps there were. Now we are getting closer to the truth. So, you escaped from not one but two prisoner-of-war camps, is this correct?' Horstberg nodded. 'First an English camp, then a French one?' The prisoner nodded again. Lochdubh leaned back in his chair, genuinely perplexed this time. 'So why in Heaven's name did you escape from the first camp if you were so well-treated there?'

Horstberg unwisely decided to try flattery. He smiled at Lochdubh and spoke now in reasonable English. 'Yes, Herr Major. Your English camp was very good! I say so in my letter, do not I? It was nothing but the truth. I am an officer, however, and I had a duty to escape when the opportunity arose. Surely you understand? I encouraged the others to do so too. We were captured again. The French camp was different. A terrible place, Herr Major. We were starved there, beaten. They stole all our possessions. You English, you are gentlemen. Your camps were not like that.'

Lochdubh again said nothing for some moments. The German continued, with an edge of desperation, 'Only send us back to your fine English camp and I swear to you on my honour that we will not try to escape again.'

'Ah. On your honour,' repeated Lochdubh. Bourgeat winced.

Lochdubh stood and walked around the desk until his face was only inches from that of the German officer, who gallantly stood his ground. 'Tell me, have you ever heard of a small island off the West Coast of Scotland called Meall Mòr, Lars Horstberg?' asked Lochdubh, smiling now, his tone almost affable. The German looked nonplussed and Bourgeat, equally surprised at this change in tactic, waited for the interrogator to continue.

'Meall Mòr is where I hail from,' the major continued, conversationally, watching with satisfaction as his prisoner appeared to relax a little. 'It is a beautiful little island, purple with heather in summer and the *Bodach* capped with snow in the winter. You are in error, you see, Lars Horstberg. I am a Scotsman, not English. I live in the Big House on Meall Mòr, a *schloss*, as you might say.'

Horstberg had brightened visibly. 'A castle? Then you are a great Lord, Herr Major? As well as a gentleman?'

Lochdubh smiled. 'Oh indeed, I am both. My island is famed for its slate. Half the houses on the west coast of Scotland have been roofed from the West Quarry at Meall Mòr. The island is surrounded by high slate cliffs, lined with quartz that sparkles in the sun. They call it the Striped Isle sometimes, because of this.' Now he patted the man's arm with a reassuring hand.

Beads of perspiration had broken out on Bourgeat's forehead. He knew Lochdubh was heading somewhere unexpected with this line of discussion and he feared the destination.

Horstberg was looking more confident by the moment as he enjoyed this verbal guided tour of his host's quaint island home. He could almost smell a tang of salt in the air and hear the call of the gulls. Lochdubh, his arm now draped over the man's shoulders, continued, 'A few hundred years ago, my family fell out with another clan on the mainland; a feud, we call it in the Highlands.'

The German now looked slightly uncertain at some of these unfamiliar words and tried to move away, but Lochdubh's grasp prevented this.

'Yes, my friend, there was a great battle. We captured the chief of the clan we fought. We asked him some friendly questions about the whereabouts of our missing cattle and he rashly lied to try to save his skin. Do you know what my family did to that prisoner?'

Bourgeat, dry-mouthed with anxiety, hurriedly translated this, not looking at either man. The German officer, sensing but not comprehending the shift in tone, stiffened but said nothing.

'No? Not even a guess? How very disappointing. Well, we threw him off the highest slate cliff into the sea,' continued Lochdubh, amiably. 'He landed on a jagged rock and lived for almost a day, while the seabirds feasted on his living entrails. Not very gentlemanly of my forebears, was it?'

Horstberg, open-mouthed, began to splutter a protest in his own language. Even as poor Bourgeat tried to translate his words, Lochdubh waved the German away. 'Get him out of my sight,' he said to the sergeant-at-arms.

Once both prisoner and guard had left, Lochdubh poured himself a whisky, pointedly not offering any to the disapproving Frenchman at his side. Then he looked at Bourgeat, head cocked, with the usual half-smile playing on his lips.

'They don't call we Scots the "Ladies from Hell" for nothing, Bourgeat,' he said. 'And why should you care, anyway? The man has invaded your country and probably murdered half your family. He's clearly a liar. Did you miss that fine gold watch about his wrist? How did that come to escape the attention of those thieving French guards, your countrymen, hmm?'

Bourgeat turned away in silent anger. Lochdubh called after him. 'I should perhaps reassure you, my good fellow. My little story was of course invented to strike fear into the heart of our enemy.'

The Frenchman paused but did not turn back. Lochdubh continued, 'It was a faithless wife my ancestor threw from the cliff.' His laughter followed Bourgeat as the priest stumbled out of the as he stumbled out into the clean air outside.

Lochdubh waited for a few minutes then summoned one of his trusted corporals. 'Tonight, I want you to go to those Boche. Say you can set them free if they make it worth your while. Make sure you retrieve that tall officer's wristwatch first. Let him think it's the price he is paying for their liberty.' German craftsmanship was always so very reliable. The corporal nodded.

Lochdubh continued. 'Then take them back to No Man's Land, near that ruined house where Westmacott almost met his maker,' he said. 'Tell them they're all free. Let them walk towards their own lines with their hands on their heads.'

The corporal saluted and about-turned.

Lochdubh completed his orders. 'Wait until they are almost there. Then shoot the bastards.'

# 30
# Over the Top

Swish, flick, parry and thrust. James Macbane of Lochdubh was pacing to and fro across his billet floor, practising fencing moves with his sword. He loved the sound of its blade as it sliced the air. He had had Trap polish and sharpen it far more than was strictly necessary. He liked to hold it to his eye and look down the blade, watching the light glance off its razor edge.

He had been inspired by reading some tale in *John Bull* of how a cornered English officer had slain a multitude of Boche by laying about him with his sword. What would that be like, he wondered. A sword this sharp and fine would barely find resistance in human flesh. Well, perhaps over the coming months he would have the opportunity to find out.

Major Chalmers had returned from his father's funeral the day before, and so Lochdubh had resigned himself to leaving his position in Intelligence, which he had relished, for another dull sojourn as an aide-de-camp to the general. Matheson had instead handed him a dun-coloured envelope with his name on the front. As soon as he saw it, Lochdubh knew that this was it. He was bound for the trenches at last.

Sure enough, the orders within despatched him to replace another officer, gone sick this time, alongside none other than his old friend Rawdon MacNabb who was with the King George's Own, Westmacott's old regiment. The Indian cavalry's officers were being decimated both through casualties but also through illness and transfers, like that of Westmacott as an A.P.M.

Lochdubh already knew that they would be going into action in the trenches at Hargicourt, relieving the Lancers, who had apparently covered themselves in glory.

At last he was free to imagine himself leading a band of savage, turbaned warriors to some improbably glorious victory. With a thrill of anticipation, he realised that he had waited his whole life for such a role. There was just one little detail to sort out first.

He sought out Matheson again, who was already preparing his laird's valise for the journey to the Front. Lochdubh noticed with pleasure that Trap had thought to lay out his fine gold German watch on top of his underclothes. He would wear that for his first sortie; it was sure to bring him luck.

'Trap,' he said, looking a little awkward. 'I'll ride up tomorrow as far as I can and you will accompany me on foot. Then you can ride Satan on the return leg.'

'Aye, fine,' said his taciturn servant, without changing his focus on packing.

'And if anything should happen to me over the next few weeks, I want you to swear that you will get old Satan back to Meall Mòr. I'm not fussed about the other one. Vera will cover the costs. I have already written to her. Is that understood?'

'Aye, sir,' said Matheson, this time looking up in surprise. It was the first occasion that he could recall the laird caring much about the fate of anything other than himself. Maybe there was hope for the laddie yet.

Lochdubh and Rawdon MacNabb enjoyed a pipeful of tobacco on his first night there. They had always got on well at school. NacNabb seemed particularly proud of how few of his men had been listed as casualties to date. He also mentioned that Tom Westmacott had sounded a note of caution before he was gassed over a burgeoning rivalry between two of his young lieutenants.

'They were sharing a billet when Cameron first arrived, but I separated them after that,' said MacNabb. 'Durand may be a brave lad but he's not the sharpest. Chubby little Cameron is different, brighter, more of a risk. They knew each other in India I believe. No love lost between the families. Sensibilities when it comes to past battle honours, or so Cameron told me. Cameron is sharing with me now, by the way. And Durand was in with Captain Walker before he came down with the plague of boils that has heralded your own arrival, so you'll meet him properly tonight.'

'Oh, I'll soon steady young Durand,' Lochdubh reassured him. He would of course have preferred to share with someone of his own rank or more senior; but as MacNabb had reassured him that Durand was well-connected and from a good military family, he decided he would make the best of it.

The major soon grew rather fond of Reggie Durand – in fact it was hard not to – and went out of his way to be pleasant to the boy. Reggie himself, always willing to think the best of anyone, decided that perhaps he had misjudged the major on first acquaintance. Soon they were chuckling and marvelling together over the florid stories in *John Bull* over a guttering candle in the dugout. If only he had given his wife a son instead of a useless daughter, Lochdubh thought fleetingly, perhaps he might have turned out something like this fine young fellow.

Lochdubh considered his new regimental companions an altogether capital bunch of fellows. He particularly liked the two spirited young lieutenants, dashed good-looking but in rather different ways. Durand, with his soulful eyes and melancholy expression, seemed to have gained both a friend and a rival in recent days with Cameron's appearance and clearly had mixed feelings about it. Lochdubh detected both envy and irritation whenever Durand looked in the newcomer's direction. Cameron had only recently come out from India; one of the 'war baby' reinforcements. Lochdubh found him a real charmer at first, but after a while he found there was something trying about his fair curls, permanently broad smile and guileless blue eyes.

The major got on with familiarising himself with the layout of the trenches the regiment now occupied. It was baked dry in the heat and the place hummed with the stench of excrement and clouds of flies. Lochdubh could see that both Durand and Cameron were desperately bored and tempers were starting to fray. Durand was moping over some slight in the dugout one night, which irritated Lochdubh no end, so he decided to take matters in hand. Why not, he suggested, plan a daring raid alongside young Cameron to impress MacNabb? The enemy trenches opposite must be heaving with troops. It could be a useful reconnaissance sortie with the possibility of bringing back a prisoner or two.

It worked. Cameron and Durand were soon eagerly plotting over a sketch map, their differences forgotten, encouraged by Lochdubh. 'Look!' said Dickie, pointing excitedly. 'If we skulk all the way along that sunken lane and into the old communication ditch, we could lurk in one of the big shell holes halfway across No Man's Land until the right moment.'

'Yes,' agreed Reggie, 'Then when the Germans are stuffing their faces with bratwurst and sauerkraut for lunch out we pop and take them by surprise!'

Lochdubh traced the network of old trenches and traverses within No Man's Land with his finger. 'Look, these will give us shelter from which we can lob bombs at the enemy. We can arrange covering fire from a trench-mortar battery too.' Lochdubh was more excited than he had been for months and feeling positively avuncular. 'Then we can just grab our prisoners and haul them back.'

'Just like the Lancers!' exclaimed Cameron.

'Just like Papa,' sighed Durand, lost in a dream of how his parents would praise him when he recounted the exploits of the day.

MacNabb agreed to the lieutenant's eager proposal but unexpectedly dug in his heels on one point. Remembering Westmacott's advice, which Lochdubh was inclined to dismiss as over-cautious, he agreed to the raid only on one condition: that both junior officers were not put at risk simultaneously. They drew straws for it at dawn on 29 May. As a result, it was Cameron who led out Lance-Dafadar Fateh Khan and his merry band of Mohammedan brothers, armed to the teeth with any available and doubtless illicit blade, while MacNabb and a desperately disappointed Durand looked on. Lochdubh, who had also been ordered to observe rather than participate on this occasion, shared Durand's sentiments.

From the very start, the raid did not go according to plan. Cameron, brave but inexperienced, thought that he could hear Germans approaching down the communication trench ahead of them and lost his head. The bomb he tossed fell short and only served to disclose their position to the enemy. Fateh Khan and his men now had to fight their way along the trench as far as the junction rather than sneak up on the enemy unawares as had been planned. MacNabb, watching anxiously through field glasses, quickly ordered up support with a fresh supply of bombs.

A burst of machine-gun fire from entirely the wrong direction sent the raiding party scurrying for cover, bullets whipping up the ground around their feet. 'What the hell is going on now?' demanded MacNabb, 'Whose fire is that?' He sent Captain Woodhouse over the top with his orderly, Ghulam Mahomed Khan, to investigate. They reported back that the shots were coming from an outlying area of trench on their own side: one of the risks of poor communication and non-continuous lines. After much frantic waving of the 'wash-out' signal, the regiment's over-zealous and now highly-embarrassed sowars in the outlying trench ceased firing.

As soon as Cameron's raiding party reached the junction, the pre-arranged trench-mortar barrage opened up with devastating impact on the enemy. Lochdubh watched with amusement as Cameron, the emboldened young devil, went much further than intended, gleefully bombing his way along the fire trench. He had to admire the boy's nerve. The lad had lost his hat and like a fool kept showing himself, his head of fair curls a fine target for any sniper. 'Get down, boy, get down,' MacNabb was muttering under his breath.

Lochdubh had a suspicion that Cameron was only following such a risky course of action to make sure he and Reggie and the others could see just how far his raiding party had managed to reach. In fact he only began to retreat when they had run out of bombs, placing Fateh Khan and all the others in great danger. The Germans had already taken cover in shelter trenches and so no there were no prisoners to take. Instead Cameron ordered his raiding-party to grab what few papers and articles of uniform they could as trophies and then turn for home. Once the Boche realised what was happening, they quickly re-occupied their trenches and opened fire again.

Durand, still smarting from MacNabb's refusal to allow him to take part in the raid he had helped to plan, was also now sticking up his head well above the parapet, firing a pair of rifles as fast as his orderly could load them in the safety of the trench below. He was hallooing at Cameron as though he were watching a college rugby match. 'Get down, Durand, and don't be such a bloody fool,' snapped MacNabb, livid. As the lad was clambering back, a bullet flew in through a loophole where Lance Dafadar Ahmad Yar Khan was giving covering fire with a Hotchkiss gun. The shot shattered Yar Khan's wrist into a ragged stump as it passed and grazed Durand's leg. They were both carried off to the dressing station, Durand protesting that it was just a scratch, that they should let him stay; Yar Khan silent, white with shock.

It amused Lochdubh no end to see how unperturbed Cameron was by the dressing-down he received from MacNabb on his return. Ignoring the tirade, he smiled broadly and spread out on the table a detailed map of the German trenches that he had happened to pick up during the raid.

'You have the luck of the very Devil, Cameron!' exclaimed Lochdubh, and MacNabb could only grin and nod agreement. The map was a splendid piece of intelligence.

MacNabb was mollified to such a degree that he agreed to Cameron going out again the following night. The pretext this time was to ascertain whether the German's 'New Trench' was in fact occupied during the hours of darkness. Accompanied only by his stoic orderly, Lance Dafadar Abdul Hakim Khan, Cameron ended up engaging in hand-to-hand combat with some very surprised Germans. Before the enemy had a chance to respond both men had sprinted for home across No-Man's-Land, uninjured and ecstatic.

Meanwhile, Lieutenant Durand was in a filthy temper and making a complete nuisance of himself at the Dressing Station, where he was being told that he would have to be sent home. Lochdubh went over to support his protests, so they dressed his leg and told the boy to try to keep it clean instead. Lochdubh helped him hobble back to the trenches. He was careful with his wound over the next few weeks and it healed well.

Both Lochdubh and Durand planned the next raid in meticulous detail. They had both grown very weary of young Dickie Cameron's endless bragging about his exploits. 'This time I am not going to miss it for all the world,' Reggie told Lochdubh the night before. Then he tried, haltingly, to explain his need to do something bold and heroic on the battlefield. Lochdubh nodded, but was not interested and did not pay much attention. Instead he was thinking about the raid he would lead, the raid that had been designed to allow him to bring back prisoners, lots of them, and possibly place him in the running for a medal or at the very least another fine piece in *John Bull*.

They spent many a night hunched over Cameron's trench map, memorising its twists and turns. This was to be a much larger and complicated raid than the one Cameron had taken part in earlier. There would be two parties this time, one of ten men under Durand and one of fifteen under Lochdubh, with Lieutenant Wilson in support. Lochdubh would command the raid with the aim of creating a pincer movement that would enable them to trap the Germans in their own trench.

At first all went as predicted. Durand's party crept along the disused communication trench as far as the last traverse to await the signal of a Verey light. They could smell something savoury wafting over from the German side and Reggie's mouth watered, as he had eaten nothing before the raid. Lochdubh, an unfamiliar roaring in his ears and his heart pulsing in his mouth, crawled at the head of his assortment of Sikhs and Hindus by way of dusty shell-holes up to the German wire about fifty yards to the right of the trench junction, leaving Reggie and their party far to his left.

Up went the Verey light, the agreed signal. This was it. Reggie immediately climbed up on to the parapet and bowled a grenade into the distant trench ahead. There was little retaliation at first as the startled Germans dropped their bowls of food and reached for their weapons.

His orderly handed him up another grenade but as Reggie was withdrawing the pin something went wrong. He fumbled it and watched it spin from his hand and drop. It rolled and lay still for a second or two. He was still scrabbling for it to throw it again when it exploded at his feet.

The Germans had now started to open fire and there was so much noise above that his men in the trench below presumed that the sound they heard was merely that of another bomb that had fallen short. Reggie pulled his greatcoat tightly around himself and buttoned it up to the neck. Then he called the rest of his party up out of the trench and led them on to the junction as planned, where he posted men to block all three approaches and stopped to wait for Lochdubh and Wilson.

Lochdubh had leapt down into 'New Trench', closely followed by Wilson, both with revolvers drawn, and between them they had shot three Germans at point blank range. The rest bolted down the trench towards the other party. It felt simply marvellous. Perhaps this is what the Old Man had been trying to instil in him all those years ago? He pounded along the trench, his men streaming behind him, driving the remaining Germans straight into young Durand's path. Just wait until that blasted Cameron boy saw their haul of prisoners! That would soon wipe the smirk from his pretty lips.

Then around the bend the trench level dipped and – no! – his prey was scrambling up the wall to run like stags for their support trenches. Wilson fired and winged one, but not badly enough to bag him. As for the others behind them, the trench walls rose too high to take aim. Lochdubh's sword – he had brought it just in case – got caught on the trench wall and made him too slow to fire. The rest got away.

The two officers and their men joined Durand glum and empty-handed. Lochdubh ordered him to go and try to round up a few more of the enemy down one of the secondary approaches but Durand, now grey-faced and sweating, insisted on an immediate withdrawal. Lochdubh could not think what had got into the boy. Disobeying his direct order in front of the men! He had thought him made of sterner stuff. Turning on his heel, raging, he and Wilson went to retrieve a few injured stragglers.

When they returned, Durand now appeared to be lying on the ground in a dead faint, a cluster of his native troops around him. Really, the boy was a disgrace! One old dafadar came forward saying something that the major made no attempt to understand. He elbowed the man out of the way and loomed over Durand, ready to sneer at his cowardice.

Durand's eyes were closed and a dark red tide of blood was now seeping through his greatcoat. What they saw when they unbuttoned it and eased back the sticky cloth made even Lochdubh turn away and bite his lip.

The men carried Durand back to their fire trench as gently as they could, but they could all see it was no good.

Lochdubh rather hoped the lad would not linger, as it did prolong the inevitable, but he remained conscious and in great pain until late the following day.

'Far better to have died in the battle!' cried a horrified MacNabb when he heard the news. The boy's promotion had just been confirmed, too, along with orders that the regiment was to prepare for a major push at a new location, somewhere called Cambrai. They would be doing so without a valiant young officer. The whole regiment was in a state of shock. Young Cameron, in particular, was inconsolable.

Their time at Hargicourt costly the King George's Own dear. Lochdubh was unhurt, of course, but as well as Durand, Wilson and a total of eighteen other good men had been injured there, six seriously. Some, like Ahmad Yar Khan, would never fight again. Brave Yar Khan was beside himself at the nature of his injury, as many would suppose it self-inflicted. MacNabb gave him a letter that confirmed the contrary before Yar Khan left the Dressing Station for England.

MacNabb also had to write a letter to the Durand family, in which he made sure that his version of events was rather more heroic than the suspected truth.

Lochdubh, most unjustly in his view, was ordered to G.H.Q. where he had to endure an interview with the colonel, Tubby Bell, to explain his actions on the raid. It was terse, brief and unpleasant.

'I don't know what happened,' he told the colonel quite honestly. 'But we did kill at least fifteen or so of the enemy, so surely that makes it worthwhile, doesn't it?' He had of course bumped up the numbers somewhat in order to garner more appreciation for his efforts, which he thought only fair.

'If that is all you have to say, you can get out of my sight, Lochdubh.'

After dismissing the unsavoury major, Bell remained alone for several minutes facing his canvas wall with one hand over his eyes, thinking of the young officer on his horse – almost a pony – who had so impressed him on that night march to Amettes long before. He must get word to Westmacott somehow, wherever he was, as he had been fond of the boy. Then he sighed and set the memory aside. In the flurry of regimental activity in readiness for Cambrai, he would forget his good intentions.

Bell later heard from Risaldar Major Amar Singh, a much more reliable source, that the real enemy casualty figure for the last raid was closer to a paltry five. MacNabb was severely reprimanded for giving the order to proceed in the first place. News of all this trickled out to the men and badly affected regimental morale. All but one agreed that it had been an utterly futile exercise. No-one would regret leaving Hargicourt for Cambrai, whatever lay in store for them there.

Lochdubh alone still considered the raid he had led to have been a great success. Oh, yes, of course it was a pity about Durand and all those injured, but war was war. They had slaughtered a good number of the enemy, which was the whole point, surely? And the look on those unsuspecting Boche faces when he shot them! Like startled hares!

Without Durand snoring away in the corner, he also found he could stretch out his legs a bit more in the dugout.

~

For reasons he could not fathom, and much to his indignation, Lochdubh was soon transferred back to his original role as aide-de camp, this time to General Gough. Tubby Bell saw to it that Major James Macbane of Lochdubh would never again be placed in direct command of men in the trenches.

# 31

# A Question and an Answer

It was Tuesday morning. One of the orderlies who normally helped
with the heaviest work was unwell. As a result, Evie and her new friend
Maud Currey, nicknamed 'Puff' as she was plump and permanently
out of breath when she first arrived, were still pummelling blankets.
They had begun just after breakfast and now it was almost eleven
o'clock.

Blanket day was the grimmest wash-day of all. After finding it
almost impossibly hard at the beginning, all the v.a.d. nurses who
lent a hand had developed muscular arms, strong backs and a variety
of entertaining distractions. Puff was Evie's first true friend since Mary
and had somehow reawakened her long-dormant sense of humour.
Evie's new companion often sang comical music-hall songs to pass the
time and her rather rude version of 'Tipperary', which related to the
emptying of bedpans, made them both fall about laughing.

'Oh, goodness me. This looks just like the breakfast porridge, doesn't
it?' Puff sighed over the grey mass in the sink. She leaned backwards
and stretched her soapy, aching arms above her head.

The commandant believed in the power of oatmeal. Porridge was
cheap and nutritious and it 'kept one regular' as she put it, so the
patients had it rather a lot. Evie laughed, squeezing the steaming
cloth, which smelled of wet horse. 'Just so long as we don't have to eat
it.' She transferred the heavy blanket into the rinsing sink with a deft
heave and twist of her wooden tongs.

'I simply hate blanket days,' said Puff. 'Thank goodness we normally
have a bit more help and it's only every other week. Your turn, Evie.

I can't sing today. My throat is a bit croaky. How about some of your poetry to keep us going?'

'Coleridge? Or Wordsworth?'

'No,' said Puff. 'I'm not in the mood for a mariner, ancient or otherwise, nor any of your prissy prancing daffodils, thank you very much. And that,' she added, pointing, 'Is an epic pile of military laundry. I think we require something a little more warlike and substantial.'

'*Lays of Ancient Rome*, then?' suggested Evie, pleased at any chance to recite her favourite work.

'Oh yes. *Horatius* it is. I like the wet bit.'

'The wet bit?'

'"Oh Tiber, Father Tiber. Plunged headlong in the tide." You know. I have this image of "bold Horatius, the Captain of the Gate" emerging from the water in his shiny harness and wet shirt and all these excited Roman girls in gym-slips clustering around him, squealing "Ooo, Horatius!" in unison. I'll see if I can't remember a bit more of it myself this time. "I don't know how you do it, dear Nurse Ingram", like all the patients say.'

Almost since birth, the five Winnington-Ingram children had learned poetry by heart for pleasure. A precise and rolling metre provided a great way to while away chores or rainy days. Evie had assumed that everyone did this and had been astonished to find that most of her peers could no more recite *Horatius* from memory than fly to the moon on a donkey. From the age of twelve, her *pièce de résistance* was to declaim all seventy verses of Thomas Babington MacAulay's stirring war poem. In Evie's view, the story of how its eponymous hero *kept the bridge in the brave days of old* perfectly matched the times. She had found that reciting it at a patient's bedside could sometimes distract a troubled man and soothe him to sleep.

Evie pulled another blanket spotted with bloodied urine into the grey water and began to rub, but before she could do more than declaim 'Lars Porsena of Clusium, by the Nine Gods he swore…' she was interrupted by Miss Fox.

'Nurse Ingram, may I have a word please?' The hospital commandant stood at the door, frowning. 'Carry on, Nurse Currey, would you?'

Unseen by the commandant, Puff rolled her eyes and winked at Evie, but she plunged her arms into the sink up to the elbows willingly enough. The thought of handsome cavalrymen messengers astride their galloping steeds would help see her through.

The commandant closed the door of her office and told Evie to sit down, then took the chair opposite her.

'Is something wrong, Miss Fox?' Evie asked, wondering about Father, who had been rather unwell when she left home that morning.

'No, Evie. Or not exactly. I have had a telephone call this morning from the 4th London General. A non-local casualty.' Not their usual feeder hospital, then? Casualties generally came through Endell Street, unless they were local to Ross, so this was curious. 'The patient has particularly insisted on being sent here for secondary treatment and convalescence. Someone who knows *you*, to be precise.'

Evie considered this briefly. There was one possibility. Oh no. Surely not. 'I cannot imagine whom you might mean,' she said firmly, meeting the gimlet eye of Miss Fox.

The commandant smiled, a touch wearily. 'I'm afraid that this is to do with poor dear Mary.'

'Goodness. So it *is* Tom!' exclaimed Evie, sitting back in her chair. 'Tom Westmacott wants to come here?'

'Ah. You knew Captain Westmacott had been injured, then?'

'Well, yes, Miss Fox, of course I did. Father read out his name from the Casualty List in *The Times* a few weeks ago, and we were all most concerned, but we did not know what had occurred or even where he was.'

After Father had finished reading out the list entry, Evie had shivered as she remembered the fortune-teller from Port Saïd with whom Tom had briefly shared a cabin. He been told that he had lost a great love; that he would be injured; that he would find solace in an 'unexpected quarter'. She was conscious of her heart beating rather fast but dismissed it as only natural that she should feel some concern. Tom was, after all, virtually a member of the family. 'We were hoping it was just a scratch. You can never tell from the injured list. What has happened to him, Miss Fox?'

'No-one quite seems to know. Some Sikh officer was most gallant and rescued him. There is a new kind of gas being used – it sticks to the skin. They are still trying to find out more and we will need to monitor him with care. He certainly has a nasty chemical burn, as well as the usual difficulties in breathing.'

Evie bit her lip and thought of the gaping mouths of her badly-affected chlorine gas patients. A new kind of sticky gas? As if the normal gas injuries were not bad enough! What evil arsenal would one side or the other invent next? Her memory of Tom was far from clear, but she did recall intelligent, kind eyes as he had gazed at Mary with such devotion on their wedding-day. Would his face now be terribly scarred? She thought of poor John Armitage and felt a flush of guilt. How would she be able to bear it if Tom Westmacott should now resemble him?

She said nothing of her fears, of course.

'I think we will have to take him, since he has asked, but I am not sure whether to send him up to Caradoc Villas or to bring him here.' Miss Fox watched Evie closely. 'I am wondering whether the latter would be quite proper in the circumstances. And I have also already lost one good nurse to matrimony.'

It was true. Pretty, dimpled Bertha had fallen for rather a nice army major who had had the lower part of his right arm amputated. She and her beau had left to be married in May. Bertha had asked Evie to be a bridesmaid, but once was enough: she chose to avoid any echoes of Mary and Tom's wedding (not to mention another appalling hat) by inventing a prior engagement.

Miss Fox continued. 'I need to ask you this directly, Evie: do you have any kind of relationship with this officer?'

'Oh really, Miss Fox. No, I do not!' Evie responded. 'It's not my fault that he has asked to come here, you know. I barely know the man.'

'And have you been corresponding with Captain Westmacott?'

'Yes, but only from time to time. I don't write nearly as often as he does. I just ask him questions about the Front and he replies. That sort of thing. And not any silly lovey-dovey stuff, I assure you. He is related to us through marriage, after all. It is the whole family he is attached to, rather than myself.' That was not wholly true, and she knew it. 'He only wanted to come here because Mary is... was... my cousin.'

Miss Fox looked unconvinced, so Evie persevered with mounting indignation. 'It's understandable, surely, Miss Fox, isn't it? He has few family members of his own left alive, and India is so very far away.'

'Hmm,' said Miss Fox drily. 'We will see. I must say I should be sorry to lose you, Evie, you are by far my most reliable nurse.'

Evie felt a surge of pride. She never considered herself the best at anything within her own family where the competition was so fierce and the intellects formidable. 'Miss Fox, I love working here,' she said, rising to her feet. 'I really don't want to go off and marry a patient like silly Bertha did. I am learning more every day from watching you and Doctor Eley. I love helping the men get better – do you know, Lance-Corporal Holden slept through last night for the first time after I recited some poetry to him at bedtime? Even once the war is over, I don't see why this should not be how I choose to spend my life.'

'Indeed,' said Miss Fox, somewhat mollified. 'Well said. Intelligent women may well remain happier if unmarried.' She stood up. 'Very well, Evie, I have made my decision. I am going to bring Captain Westmacott here to Westfield and we can keep an eye on the situation between us. Now, you had better get back to Nurse Currey and dear old Lars Porsena.'

Tom arrived late the following morning by the regular R.A.M.C. transport, sharing the vehicle with a cheery sapper from Ross named White who had lost an ear and been blinded in one eye by shellfire. 'Durn't matter, do it,' he had said in the car. 'I've got another of each and I bain't never going back.'

It had been a long, trying drive. Tom's arm and hand jarred with every pothole and swerve. His incessant coughing had not left much energy to react to White's garrulous delight at his homecoming.

Evie was upstairs, making up Tom's bed, when she heard the car. She walked to the landing window and saw Tom emerge slowly and stiffly. He stood quite upright and to her relief, she could see two unscathed eyes, a nose and a mouth. She realised now that she had not really looked all that closely at Tom at his wedding. All her focus had been on how her own heart was breaking to see Mary, her best friend, marry and leave for India.

Mary's husband coughed, bending double as he did so. She felt her professional compassion rise. Poor man. He seemed older, frailer than she remembered. It was understandable. She turned to walk downstairs to welcome him, as she knew she must, although she was conscious of a strange reluctance to do so.

The commandant greeted both new patients outside and then

escorted White up the steps and through the front door, a practiced arm tucked under his own. He would not yet be quite used to his blind side and risked falling.

Tom walked slowly, but unaided, up the three steps to the front door, one arm in a sling. He saw Evie coming down and hesitated. She stopped awkwardly on the last turn of the stair and felt herself blush, bother it.

'Evie?' he said hesitantly, advancing with his good hand reaching towards her. 'It is you, isn't it?' They had never exchanged photographs. Letters were one thing; seeing him was quite another. How was she supposed to behave? She forced a smile and nodded.

He must have felt her reticence as his own smile faltered. 'Oh. I'm so sorry, Evie,' he said. 'You're in uniform too, aren't you? Of course. I didn't think.'

'It's not that, honestly.'

Tom now looked so taken aback that she came closer, stopping on the last step so they were equal in height. She took his uninjured hand and shook it gently, which avoided embracing him in any other way. It did seem ridiculously formal but anything more was out of the question, there in the hallway.

'Well, goodness me, Tom,' she said, briskly changing the subject. 'I am so glad you are here.' She was conscious that if he had been one of her brothers she would have flung her arms around him and hugged him. Her cheeks flushed crimson again with the sheer awkwardness of it all. She had not asked him to come.

They contemplated each other for a few moments in silence, taking each other in, eye to eye. He saw a taller, leaner and more mature woman than he remembered, with unusual almond-shaped, almost feline eyes. Her sparkling white uniform carried the usual bright red cross on its little bib apron and a cap covered most of her hair and high forehead. She looked very smart, and less feminine, somehow, than when he had last seen her at the wedding. He mocked himself inwardly at this ridiculous thought. Of course she did. She was a working woman now, in uniform. Times were changing. Without the efforts of women like Evie, Britain's Home Front would be crumbling.

At first, he thought her hair was pinned up inside her cap and then he saw that she had instead cut it rather short. It made her appear somewhat mannish about the jaw. Perhaps it was the fashion, now that women were doing men's work, but oh, how he had loved Mary's long dark tresses.

Evie saw him looking and put one hand to her cap. 'It's just much easier to manage,' she said defensively.

'I'm sorry, Evie, I didn't mean…' he tailed off, noticing her reddened, broad hands, so unlike Mary's delicate little fingers. Kind and capable hands, though, used to hard work. When would the poor girl have time to dress her hair?

He must tread more carefully.

In turn, Evie saw yet another tired face with war etched into its cracked skin. It had a sickly, orange pallor this time, which was unfamiliar and worried her. His over-bright, unhealthy eyes were constantly fixed on her from behind his pair of tortoise-shell-rimmed spectacles. She wished he would not stare so. What did he expect of her? What should she do?

'So, Evie. What should I call you here?' he asked, to fill the silence.

'Oh! Yes. Well, I am Nurse Ingram to the patients. You can call me Evie when we are alone.' She regretted saying that as soon as the words left her lips, as his sombre face cracked into an unaccustomed smile.

'No!' she continued, floundering. 'I only mean it's what I do with Miss Fox. I knew her from before the war too. She's Miss Fox when just the two of us are present and the commandant when I am on duty.' Stop gabbling, Evie.

'The commandant?' said Tom. 'She sounds rather like a Hun officer in a prisoner-of-war camp.'

'Puff – Nurse Currey I mean – might think that was funny but please don't let Miss Fox hear you say so.' Evie found herself responding to the unexpected heat of his smile and gathered herself only seconds before the commandant came back into the hall. For goodness' sake! It was not as if Tom Westmacott needed further encouragement in terms of familiarity, what was she thinking of?

Commandant Fox watched with approval as Nurse Ingram picked up Captain Westmacott's valise, which the driver had placed by the door. 'This way, Captain,' said her best nurse, as she turned to lead their new patient upstairs to his small room.

It hit Tom in a liquid rush as slanting sunlight from the landing window lit up Evie's face as she walked up the stairs with his case. He had longed to meet Evie, had begged her to do so, and she had constantly evaded him. And now his first encounter with Evie since Mary's death was as his nurse. He deeply regretted his situation but at least it had brought them together at last, after a fashion.

This strange exultation triggered a sharp spasm across his chest as he climbed the stairs. After another step to reach the turn for the next flight, Tom bent double again and coughed, straining to breathe. In an instant Evie – or Nurse Ingram as it appeared he must call her – was there, one gentle hand between his shoulder-blades. He could feel the pressure and warmth of her touch.

She reassured him that the moment would pass, that he must relax and try to breathe. Her voice, he thought. She sounds just like Mary, even though she looks nothing like her.

Once in his room Evie, avoiding his gaze, instructed him to undress and get into bed. Just as though he were a little boy, he thought in dismay. As though he were still Tomulloo, the devoted slave of his beloved Parvati. He reached for the bedstead, swaying on his feet with tiredness and great sickening waves of pain.

'Do you need my help, Tom?' she asked, lifting his case on to a chair and opening it for him. It was virtually empty. Tom replied that he did not as he could not bear her to think him weak. She left him then and went downstairs to order him some lunch. As he struggled with his trouser buttons he wished he had said yes, for purely practical reasons. He was so tired, and even the fingers on his good hand felt like overfilled sausages. He managed his pyjamas with a struggle, lay down with his head at the wrong end of the bed and was asleep within minutes.

Tom slept in this position through the rest of the day, missing lunch and waking only at suppertime. He felt so weakened that he had to take some soup in bed. The meal was delivered by an orderly, much to his disappointment. He rose reluctantly only to use the commode in the corner, which he knew – oh, the shame of it! – Evie might have to empty. Then he crawled back between the sheets this time and slept again; the disconcerting silence of the night woke him at intervals.

When he did sleep, Tom dreamed, and wished he had not. He was standing at the window peering out at the war through the wrong end of a giant telescope. The landscape was scattered with little soldier-figures no bigger than insects. He could see them eating, sleeping, planning sorties and being blown to bits. It is always there, just further away, he thought. There is no real escape. He was thinking this even as his new reality of peace, silence, trees and fresh air drifted in from the garden to help him sleep again.

The following morning Nurse Allen appeared. She was friendly and efficient but was not Evie. When he asked where she was he was told it was Evie's day off. He fought back his disappointment that she could possibly choose to be absent when he had only arrived the day before. As the days passed, he often saw serious Nurse Allen or comical Nurse Currey but seldom his dear Nurse Ingram, and then only in the company of the others. When he did, she was always polite but distant.

Once he was well enough to walk to the dining-room, he realised that the patients did not even eat with the nurses. Why had he asked to come there, he thought, miserably. It would have been better to be among strangers than ignored by someone he thought had at least liked him somewhat. Why was she being so distant?

On the third day, after a bad night in which he had again relived his terrible flight across No Man's Land on Arjan Singh's back, Tom's burned arm began to swell and throb again. He sat in a bed-chair in the still orchard, instructed to let the fresh air cool the wound. Nurse Allen pinched her brow when she inspected it there and went to fetch the commandant, who looked equally concerned. She dismissed Nurse Allen and sat down in the chair next to his own. 'Captain Westmacott, I have been told to ask you if you can now recall anything else about the moment you were injured? It might help us treat your injury more appropriately.'

Tom did not care to remember it at all after the nightmare that had left him shaking and sleepless, but knew it was his duty to tell her what he could. He quickly summarised the story of his stupidity in entering the strange farm building without orders to do so and of Arjan Singh's selfless quick thinking.

'And can you remember if it tasted or smelled of anything, this chemical you found in the cellar?'

'It was not like the ordinary gas. That stinks of bleach and just makes you cough a bit and your eyes water,' said Tom. 'If you can only keep your head and get your mask on quickly enough, you can just about get through it. This was different. There was rotting meat on the table, so it is hard to remember a separate smell from that. It was spicy, though, I think; like a hot curry, pungent stuff that made my eyes sting. Like horseradish perhaps. Or mustard.'

The commandant wrote down everything he said. She had a strong suspicion that the enquiries were only being made because the army was hoping to make a similarly lethal weapon itself. This disturbing thought was not one she chose to share with Tom. She closed her little notebook and thanked him, then leaned over to pull back a corner of his dressing, which made him wince, and pursed her lips. 'I do not like the look of your wound today, Captain Westmacott. Let's see if we cannot draw out more of the fluid from those nasty blisters.'

She left him alone with his thoughts in the orchard. Unaccountably, the memory of Parvati, his ayah, came to him then. Was it the feeling of being reduced to infancy by Evie's ministrations on the day he arrived? Or that day with the elephant, his earliest memory, a day he had been so happy, and then had his hopes so badly dashed?

Evie had meanwhile been preparing a linseed poultice. She had made these for many patients with burns and sores, but to this mixture she instinctively added some herbs from the warm garden: rosemary and lavender, chopped finely, then stirred in. This she ground into an oily flour in a marble mortar, then scraped into a tin bowl. She added boiled water from the copper kettle, stirring it with a horn spoon to make a paste. She then covered the bowl with a muslin and stood it on the kitchen windowsill.

When it had cooled enough to apply, Evie carefully carried the poultice mixture outside on a tray and placed it on a little table beside Tom's chair. She greeted him cautiously. He had been dozing, but opened his eyes and started in surprise. He then beamed. 'Evie! Why, I haven't seen you for days!'

She flinched internally while smiling in what she hoped was a strictly professional manner. 'It's been so busy. We do have Caradoc Villas to manage too, remember,' she said, pulling up a wicker chair beside him. 'Now, hold out your arm and keep it still for me, please.' Tom did as she advised. Evie eased off the old dressing and sniffed it to see if there was any putrefaction. She found there was very little so wiped his arm with linseed oil to clean it and could see him biting his lip as she touched the swellings. His skin was red, weeping and angry, exactly like an ordinary burn, but with a stickiness she had not seen before. She spread out the steaming mess on a clean linen cloth, then applied another on top, making a fragrant sandwich of the poultice mixture. It was squidgy and warm and smelled wonderful. He gasped once as she applied it, but did not otherwise cry out. She found his stoicism oddly touching. Then she carefully pinned the poultice in place.

'The best thing you can do now, Tom, is to have a nice nap,' Evie said, rising again, 'I can bring you a rug for your knees. You need to give that poultice time to work.'

Tom did not want a rug or a nap. He found that he badly wanted to take Evie's comforting hand in his and hold it against his cheek. Instead he commented, looking up at the tree above him, 'There will be a fine crop of apples this year, don't you think?' all the while cursing himself for being so utterly British.

Evie agreed about the fruit harvest. Even though her nursing duties were complete, she still lingered a while, also raising her face to the blue sky. As she did so her cap loosened and fell back, revealing her shingled light brown hair. 'Oh no! I shall catch it if Miss Fox sees me!' she exclaimed, grabbing at it and securing the errant headgear with a few jabs of a hairpin. Tom, seeing Mary in the gesture, laughed aloud; the first time she had heard him do so. Evie stared at him in surprise, then surprised herself further by joining in.

She did not wish to leave him. Not quite yet. A few more minutes in the dappled shade would do her good too.

A ripple of birdsong suddenly flowed out from a great white dog-rose bush that was in full bloom in one corner of the orchard. 'Beautiful. Is that a nightingale?' asked Tom.

'Goodness no, only a wren,' replied Evie, astounded that he did not know. Then she recalled that his childhood would have echoed to the sounds of rather more unusual birdlife. Evie loved her birds and was glad to have something to talk about other than herself or Tom. 'They're tiny. They make a little round nest out of moss and lichen and feathers. They're called *troglodytes troglodytes* in Latin – rather a mouthful for such a small bird, isn't it? It means "cave-dweller", because they nest in crevices like the wall behind that rose-bush. The cats at home sometimes bring them in thinking they are mice and look most astonished when they fly up on to the kitchen cabinet to scold them. Their song is really the biggest thing about them.'

The wren emerged from the rose-bush, peered at them both beadily, then hopped along the top of the wall, picking at insects, before flying back among the roses. 'She must be feeding a second brood,' said Evie.

'A love found late, perhaps,' said Tom, without thinking.

She did not know what to say to that, so said nothing. She smiled at him. He smiled back. Then Nurse Allen called her from inside and the moment was broken.

~

Two days later the commandant again summoned Evie to her office and asked her to sit down.

'What is it, Miss Fox?' asked Evie, seeing her expression.

'How do you find Captain Westmacott, Evie? Would you say he is improving?'

Evie thought for a moment. 'His wound is making slow progress, but you know how easily infections can take a turn for the worse, especially in this kind of heat. In terms of his chest, and his mind come to that, I would say that he has good days and bad,' she replied. Although Tom was not aware of it, she often took the night shift and so witnessed his turbulent sleep and frequent nightmares. Once or twice he had cried out for Mary as was only natural. Once for someone called Parvati. Some native girl he had taken up with, perhaps? She did not like to think of it.

'Read this,' said the commandant, bluntly. She pushed an envelope across the desk and Evie took it. As she had suspected, it was addressed to Tom.

The letter, which had already been opened by the army censors, was from Hutchinson, one of Tom's fellow officers. It was only the briefest of scrawls and had clearly been written on the move. It contained dreadful news. Evie handed it back to Miss Fox, absorbing the shock and its implications for Tom.

'Do you have any idea of how friendly Captain Westmacott was with this poor Reggie Durand fellow?' the commandant enquired, as Evie handed the letter back to her.

'He certainly mentioned him a lot in his letters. Tom – Captain Westmacott I mean – was worried about him. I think he was afraid Reggie might do something foolish.'

'And now he has,' responded Miss Fox, rubbing her tired eyes. 'Evie, Captain Westmacott has no other family nearby and has been corresponding with you. Given your knowledge of his mental state and his injuries at present, what would you advise me to do about this? Do I pass on this letter on to him or not?'

'Please don't!' said Evie, concerned about the fragility of Tom's current mental state. 'I mean, not yet, at least. He will have to know at some stage, but only when he is stronger, surely?'

'I agree,' said Miss Fox, taking Hutchinson's letter and putting it in her desk drawer. She would only find it again when clearing it after the war had ended, when she would shrug and burn it with many other papers. 'The news may yet filter through some other way, and that cannot be helped, but I think we should postpone it for as long as we can. In the meantime, not a word to a soul, is that quite clear?

'Absolutely, Miss Fox,' said Evie. 'I promise. Not a word.'

Two days after this, Tom contracted a fever that seemed to consume him from within. The weather was baking hot and breathless. Evie stood a bowl of cold water on the windowsill to try to damp down the air inside. It was so frustrating and happened so frequently. Their patients would show signs of improvement on arrival but then sicken as an infection took hold. Perhaps one day there would be medication that would help them fight back but for now all she could do was wash out a wound in salt water or paint it with iodine and recite *Horatius* to get her patient off to sleep, if she could. Some would recover, others would not. It was too often beyond their influence. Soul-destroying.

She and Puff took it in turns to nurse Tom but it was as though his flesh were candlewax being melted by the heat outside. The infection had spread and his hand and arm were once more a weeping mess of sores.

One day after she had coaxed some broth between his lips he snatched her hand, looked her in the face with fevered, unseeing eyes and croaked, 'Reggie.'

She stayed very still. What if he were to die, she thought, and she had not told him the truth?

'Reggie, don't be a fool. Not worth it. Don't... don't...' his voice slurred away into the nightmare. He had already been given all of the morphia she could give him but she longed to make him drink more to ease his suffering. To make matters worse, she knew the greatest horror was still to come, and she still carried that secret within her.

The fever broke six days later, as did the weather, with an almighty thunderstorm. The infection had burned through Tom like a forest fire. She looked up from mending her uniform where it had become caught on the rosebush outside to see his eyes meet her own and, this time, hold them. 'Rain,' he said, his voice cracking with the effort. Sure enough a deluge was drumming on the roof overhead.

'Yes, Tom!' she said, going to fling the windows wide so he could smell it and hear it. 'What a relief!' Then she returned to his side, reaching for his hand to test his pulse. Instead he fumbled for it and squeezed it tight, then fell into another doze. When she tried to extricate herself, he clung to her fingers, obstinate even in sleep, so she sat there and listened to the rumble of distant thunder, like heavy artillery. Puff looked in and Evie sent her for broth and some tea instead while she dressed his wound again.

Tom dozed and woke and managed a little food and then dozed again for several days, until at last he was strong enough to sit up in bed and eat from a tray. Evie now looked in on him whenever she could. One evening he asked her to sit with him.

'Evie, there is something I need to know. I… I don't know where to start with all this. So I am just going to ask it straight.'

Had he heard about Reggie? Had word leaked out somehow?

'Evie, I just wondered if… if you would be prepared to become my wife?' he blurted, reaching for her hand. As he did so, she jumped up, knocking over his glass of water. 'I'm sorry,' they both said together.

No, thought Tom. Hopeless. He had done it all wrong. It was far too soon. And yet he could not unsay the words.

She would not look at him as she mopped up the pool of water on the floorboards. He pleaded with her nonetheless. 'Please, Evie. Please consider it. have been thinking about it such a lot and it would be for the best, I am sure.'

Yes, but whose best? If she said yes, she would no choice but to tell him about Reggie's death. And that could easily alter his chances of survival. The longer he remained in blissful ignorance, the better.

She thought of Mary. Of the unknown Parvati. Of her own love of nursing. Of her mother. How could she marry Tom, knowing what she knew and keeping it hidden it from him? When he did find out, she was certain he would somehow guess she had known when Miss

Fox gave him the letter. If she stayed, she knew she would weep, so all she could think of was escape. Not trusting herself to speak, she turned her face from Tom, gathered up her tray and walked briskly away.

Tom did not see her again before his own abrupt departure a few days later. Miss Fox had gone up to London but Consie Allen who had been left in charge told Tom that Evie had been transferred to Caradoc Villas as they had had a new intake of patients up there and were short of staff. He did not believe a word of it. Consie also told Evie that Tom had asked to be sent on to his in-laws at Fladbury as he was feeling considerably better and did not want to take up another bed that a more deserving patient might need. Evie did not believe a word of that either.

Each felt just as wretched as the other, but for different reasons.

That evening, Tom was sombrely packing his valise with his few possessions as he prepared to go and convalesce for the next few months at Fladbury with the Lawsons. He picked up a supply of the sheets of Red Cross letter-paper made available in every room and tucked them into his case. Writing-paper was in short supply in the trenches and he hoped to be back there soon. He did not know to whom he would write on it now; but thought he should probably take it anyway.

There was a discreet tap at his door. His heart leapt, but it was Nurse Currey instead. She handed him a letter, turned to leave, then paused.

'For what it's worth, Captain Westmacott,' she said, not smiling for once, 'I think Evie Winnington-Ingram is being a fool. And I have told her so.' And with that, she was gone.

# 32

# Three Letters

He could not sleep. *Dearest Evie,* Tom wrote by guttering candlelight, sat on his hard billet bed in Saint Valéry. The unsavoury fellow on the other mattress had been drinking and was already snoring loudly.

> I shall continue to call you my dearest Evie, because you still are, to me: even if I am not your dearest Tom, nor dear Tom, nor Dear Sir nor even To Whom It May Concern.
> Oh, Evie. I have been carrying your long letter about with me since it arrived at Fladbury. I keep it in the equivalent pocket to the one in which I used to hide an old handkerchief of Mary's. Did I ever tell you about that? I kept it folded around your first postcard from Ross. No-one thought to remove them when my uniform was cut off me and destroyed at the Dressing Station near Hargicourt.
> Now your letter burns against my heart instead.

The sleeper muttered something that sounded like an oath under his breath and set off a cacophony of bedsprings as he turned towards Tom.

> No, of course I told none of the Lawsons about what had happened between us at the hospital. I did not want to distress them. Grace twittered sweetly at first about how nice it must have been to see a familiar face. Then when you did not appear with Etty and Maud on their regular Christmas visit, the twittering abated. Grace and your dear old Aunt Laura were

very kind to me, Evie, but I have had more uplifting readings from scripture and nourishing vegetable broth than a soldier should ever have to stomach in one lifetime.

At first, I admit, your letter upset me too much to write you a reply. Then at Christmas, you did at least send me that nice little card with Maud. It gave me a glimmer of hope that we might at least continue to correspond as friends. I sent you a card of my own straight back again, but not a thing from you since.

You asked me not to mention my proposal ever again but oh, Evie, how can I not?

I know perfectly well that you were Mary's best friend and her cousin too, but foolishly I did not consider for a moment that my offer of marriage might somehow make you feel in some way a second-best replacement for her. You seem to be making her an excuse for not marrying me and I do not understand it. Did that moment we shared in the orchard, with the wren and the rose, mean nothing at all?

Dear Evie (there, I've said it again). Please, please, reconsider. There is no second best, there is only different, and different now.

I realise I am explaining all this very badly.

Tom hesitated, but the metaphorical nettle had to be grasped. With a swig of brandy he gritted his teeth and forced his pencil to move again.

You say in your letter that I have never satisfactorily explained the circumstances of Mary's death. At the time, perhaps, I believed it better unsaid. That is unforgivable of me and again I can only apologise for it.

The basic sorry facts are these: we were out riding, and Mary was making splendid progress in her lessons with me. We had gone far further than was wise, right up into the forested hills. We had been married exactly three hundred and sixty-four days. It was to have been a celebration of our first anniversary. Daisy just bolted. I should have been looking ahead and noticed something was wrong, but instead, as usual, I was gazing at Mary. I just had time to see the deadly krait whip away from under Daisy's hooves and slither into the undergrowth before spurring Golden Rod in pursuit.

I was too late. A low branch caught Mary hard across the throat and swiped her from Daisy's back. She did not – could not – avoid it, since her hat had slipped down over her eyes. I can see her little hand struggling to push it back even now.

More brandy. He left the flask unstoppered on the floor beside him.

I knew instantly that her neck was broken from the way she lay. Her eyes were wide open but looked right through me. She was almost smiling.
I knelt beside her and felt for a pulse. There was nothing. I held Mary's hand in mine until it became cold. I couldn't move, numbed with the shock of it all, I suppose. Golden Rod stood right at my back, his head low. Daisy returned to find me as night fell, sweating badly and I moved then, to check her for a snakebite, but it was only fear. Both horses knew something terrible had taken place.
Mary would, I am quite certain, have survived, but for my own neglect. I had checked Daisy's girth and bridle, but the chinstrap of Mary's solar topi was far too loose. I can never forgive myself for that.
You see, Evie? I did kill your cousin, your best friend, my wife. Mary died in an instant, if that is any consolation. It has never been so to me.
Calcutta was awash with stories about it. Can't you imagine it? A man brings his young wife's body home out of the darkness, draped across his saddle, her dress all tattered and torn? It was far too juicy a bone and the beastly gossips gnawed away at it for months. India is like that, you see, and I NEVER want to go back there if I can help it.

Tom put down his pen to rub his red eyes with the back of his hand and took another long swallow from his flask.

I realise now that I have made a bit of an ass of myself. You said in your letter that you are quite used to patients falling in love with their nurses. I had not even given that possibility a thought.

Enough of that. The Allies were losing the war, it appeared from rumours in the port, and so perhaps she was better off not to be saddled with an officer unlikely to return from the long retreat ahead of them.

> It is time I got back to the Division, where it is all change. I found out from a chap in the Lancers that the remnants of my old regiment are preparing for transport to Marseilles and then onwards to Syria. I know from the Casualty Lists that they suffered badly at Cambrai, poor fellows, so it is probably for the best.
>
> I hope to be in time to see them before they go and wish them well: if not I can only hope that Arjan Singh has left the horses somewhere safe for me and out of the clutches of wretched Lochdubh, who collects mounts as a magpie collects shiny things. I shall find out when my train gets in tomorrow.
>
> I wonder what old Reggie will make of going to Syria! I can just see him galloping off on a camel in robes and a headdress like a Sheik. Perhaps he will stay in France instead (as I believe some of the other officers intend to) and see out the war with me. It will be good to see him again, if only for a farewell. Hutch and the others too.
>
> You were right about one thing. This war has been an absolute godsend to me. I came to France thinking I might make a useful end of myself. Now, in spite of my foolishness of the last few months, I find myself very much wanting to stay alive. Thanks to your ministrations, I am also a great deal more hale than a few months ago, in body at least.

Here, Tom stood up and paced the room, so it was a good thing his malodorous room-mate was soundly asleep. He wondered whether to close the letter there, but felt it was still somehow incomplete. It was clear he could expect little else from Evie now but perhaps, just perhaps, he should simply be honest? He summoned his clearest memory of Mary to bring him the strength he needed to answer her question about his health straight from his heart.

> In mind, Evie, I am not faring quite so well. I asked you to marry me because I love you. Not because I have fallen for my nurse or because I want you to replace Mary. How could you or anyone ever do that? You said you would not marry me for

good reasons, but then you didn't say precisely what they are. Do you call that quite fair? I don't. You also asked what would have happened if you had answered differently and I had come home wounded in a different way. That is another delicate question to answer. The war and particularly my last experience of it has rather changed my outlook on life generally. I feel full of hope that it is making me less selfish than I was.

When I first asked you to marry me I don't think I realised the possibilities, as far as you were concerned, if I got badly damaged and you had grown fond of me. I do realise them now, very keenly. I ought to have said nothing until after the war is over.

Lord, this is such disjointed twaddle, what will she make of it? Tom had now drunk a great deal of brandy and felt somewhat unsteady. He wondered briefly if he should tear the letter into small pieces and start again, but persevered.

Luckily no harm has been done, because you have made it very plain that you don't care about me, while the mere fact of loving you helps me a great deal.

'I love you,' Tom said out loud, as though she could hear him. His slumbering room companion said something unintelligible in reply and turned back to the wall with a cough. Tom stared at his flask owlishly and upended it, but not even a drip emerged.

I think some of your hospital patients are lucky men and I wish – no I won't say that, because you will at once get your tail up.

The man in the bed on the other side of the room swore at him in his sleep.

My partner in this foul billet at the port is a sweep and the less said about him the better.
I wonder if you will go on writing to me for as long as I want you to!

How to sign it, wondered Tom, sucking the end of his pencil, which now, curiously, seemed to taste of French brandy. Nothing seemed appropriate. He decided to add a lame:

> Cheeri Oh!
> Yours ever,
> Tom

He quickly stuffed it into the envelope he had already addressed and sealed it, then tumbled on to his rickety bed without even removing his boots, sound asleep in moments.

Only a week or so later in Ross-on-Wye, Evie was feeling somewhat glum, She had not heard anything from Tom since Christmas when he had sent her a timid card in return for her own. She had no idea whether or not he had now found out about Reggie from some other source. And whose turn was it to write, her own or Tom's? She was increasingly aware of waiting for the sound of the postman – or rather postwoman.

Perhaps Tom would not write again. If he did not, she would not blame him.

Evie had asked at the Post Office for any personal correspondence sent on to Westfield rather than to the Rectory. This avoided family scrutiny and meant she would receive anything that arrived earlier in the day.

'Not one, but two from France, Miss Evie,' Jessie sang out one day as she dropped the rest of the letters and parcels into the commandant's office. 'Lucky old you!'

It was the early afternoon. Most of the patients were dozing and she could allow herself a few minute's respite. Evie went into the garden and sat down on the edge of a bench, white plumes of breath curling in the crisp, still air. It felt more like January today than March. There were two envelopes, both addressed in Tom's cramped and crooked handwriting. How curious that there should be nothing for so long and then for two to arrive on the same day! She examined the postmarks – they were only a day apart.

She decided to open the earlier and fatter of the two first and read Tom's long letter from Saint-Valéry. She did not weep when he described Mary's death but felt her face grow hot, in spite of the chill March air, when she read Tom's declaration of love. She stopped when she came to the part about Reggie Durand and Syria and looked straight ahead, swallowing hard.

She looked down at the second letter, considerably shorter than the first. She had guessed already what it must contain. From the first line she read, one hand flew to her cheek and stayed there. 'No,' she said. 'Oh no. Oh, Tom.'

Puff found her there half an hour later. 'Evie? Bowman's been calling for you for a good ten minutes. Don't worry, I saw to him.' She approached her friend. 'You're the colour of bandage, Evie. What on earth is it?' She put her hand on Evie's and tutted. 'And you're ice-cold. Come on, you need some hot tea.'

Evie picked up the letters in her lap and let herself be led through to the kitchen, which was draped with drying sheets.

Puff sat at the table opposite her friend, leaned forward and took her hand. 'Either you tell me what is in those letters you just slid into your apron pocket, Nurse Ingram, or I shall pull them out and read them myself.' Evie, after a moment's hesitation, pushed them towards her. 'Oh Puff,' she cried. 'What *am* I going to do?' And Evie, feeling her normally stoic façade crumble, laid her head on the table and sobbed.

Puff read both letters and looked across at Evie, appalled. Then a patient called and she had to dash upstairs. By the time she returned, Evie had dried her tears and was sipping her tea. Puff drew up a chair, panting, as she had run back down from the first floor. 'Love and death,' she said, dramatic then and always.

'What?'

'It's life, isn't it? You're born, you either love someone or you don't, and then you die. We have so many frightful ways to die at present because of the war. Don't you think that there could also be more than one way to love?'

'You think Tom really does love me? It's not just some sort of silly crush, just because of Mary?'

Puff chuckled. 'Given what you told me you wrote to Tom, I would say this is a remarkably persistent infatuation. Now you know exactly how Mary died! It wasn't really his fault at all, was it?'

Evie shook her head. 'I have thought for many years that it must have been a tragic accident of some kind. It just seemed strange that Tom had never actually told us so. He is quite right, though. I was just using it as an excuse.'

Puff looked bemused. 'You have some other reason for not marrying this man who clearly loves you to bits? He may have been remarkably insensitive to propose to his nurse with so little warning, but he does at least appear to realise that now.'

'Yes, and that's just it, Puff,' exclaimed Evie, her eyes now puffy and red. 'Miss Fox said I might one day have charge of a hospital of my own, just like this one. What about my nursing?'

'Miss Fox is a dried-up old prune who has probably never had the luxury of a proposal to reject,' responded Puff, drily. 'Look. You're a jolly good nurse, I know. Much better than me. Didn't you once tell me that you wanted to be a concert pianist?'

'Yes,' snuffled Evie. 'Well remembered.' How long ago that childish fantasy seemed to her now.

'And you still play the piano now?'

'Well yes, you know I do. Just not as often.'

'And do you enjoy it when you do?'

Silence. Then, 'Yes,' said Evie thoughtfully. 'Yes, I do.'

'So there you are! You see?' exclaimed Puff. 'Plans change. Life opens up many different paths. We women have a far greater capacity for change than our menfolk do. Supposing – just supposing – you did marry Tom. You could still play the piano, and nurse him when he is ill. Perhaps even nurse your own children.'

'Children!' Evie looked uncertain.

'Yes! You would make a wonderful mother. It's not too late. You were forever looking after Arthur when he was little, weren't you? Not everything else has to stop if you choose to marry Tom.'

Evie could not look her in the eye. 'Oh Puff, I simply can't. There's something else. I knew, you see.'

'Knew what?'

'I knew about his friend being dead. Matron told me.'

'Oh my goodness. I see. And you were sworn to secrecy?

Evie nodded, disconsolate.

'Well,' said Puff thoughtfully, 'Surely that was your professional duty as a nurse? Couldn't you consider it a sort of official secret and marry him anyway?

'How could I? He would be my husband. I would have to tell him! And how would he ever trust me after that?'

There was a silence between the two friends for some time as the words settled between them. Puff poured them each a cup of now-stewed dregs.

'Look, old thing,' she said kindly. 'You have a chance to make a decent man – as well as yourself – very happy. There won't be many of them left, the way the war is going. Won't you even just consider it?'

Evie nodded, blowing her nose inelegantly on her damp handkerchief.

By the time she returned to the Rectory that night, Evie was exhausted. She expected the whole household to be in bed already, but a lamp burned in the kitchen. Etty was seated at the table, peering through her thick, round spectacles at an exercise book she was marking. 'Thank goodness you're back,' she said, closing the red inkwell. 'I have never read such a load of terrible codswallop in my life. 'Essays on Divine Love', my foot – more like 'Essays on Divine Distraction'. Distraction in uniform, to boot. This marking is killing my eyes, too. I need new spectacles, but they will have to wait until the war is over. How are you, dear?'

Evie had stopped in the doorway, then launched herself at Etty and hugged her. 'I say!' said her elder sister. 'Steady on, sister mine! You'll break all my bones!'

'Oh Etty,' Evie sighed. 'You are just the person I need to talk some sense into me.' She sat down at the table, gave Etty both letters and watched her read them.

Her sister removed her spectacles and rubbed her eyes. 'Well,' she said in her usual blunt manner. 'What are you going to do?'

'I was rather hoping you would tell me that, Etty.'

'Now let me see. In professional terms, you spend all day long surrounded by the maimed and half-mad. The last time I met him, Tom Westmacott struck me as neither. Would you agree?'

'Yes, but…'

'And he has written to tell you he loves you, even after you have told him repeatedly that you don't love him back?'

'Yes Etty. The trouble is I knew about his friend Reggie dying and I have kept it from him for months, and…"

Etty waved a dismissive hand. 'Tom has commanded men in war. He knows that part of being a leader is to know what to keep hidden from your subordinates, for their own safety. He will understand, in time. Now, Evelyn Winnington-Ingram, listen to me. You have had an offer of marriage from a kind man who says he loves you. He is even prepared to take you on if you don't love him. That kind of commitment isn't to be sniffed at. I think you should accept.'

Evie was astonished. 'Accept? I thought that you of all people…'

'Why "me of all people"? You know perfectly well that I will never fall for a man, but that doesn't mean to say *you* can't.'

'But what about Mother?' whispered Evie, at last giving voice to her darkest, deepest fear of wedlock.

'Oh, I was very young to lose a mother, Evie. We all were. You, however, are not Mother. You are as strong as an ox. Look at those muscles!' That made Evie wince, although her sister meant it kindly. 'Tom might not even be able to make babies anyway, given what he has been through. Some men can't, you know.' She leaned forward: 'You'd be better placed to know about all that, anyway,' she said, with a wicked grin.

'Etty!'

'Oh, don't be so coy. You bathe them, don't you? Clean them up when they are immobile? You must know what can happen between a man and a woman, which is more than our dear Mother would have done the first time Father took her to bed.' Evie was torn between feeling utterly horrified and choking back appalled laughter.

Etty continued, 'Evie dear, I have fallen in love. Several times in fact. My friend Elizabeth Nalder? Not just a friend. It may not be married love, but I know that whatever form it may take, love is a jolly good thing for all concerned.'

'But what about children?' Evie whispered.

'What about them? Little nieces for me!'

'They might be boys.' Evie found herself smiling.

'Well, it can't be helped if they are. Just do your best. You might even enjoy the physical side of things. It is allowed, you know. Goodnight, sister dear.' And with that, she went upstairs to bed.

Alone in the kitchen, Evie unfolded the second letter and read it again.

Dearest Evie, oh Evie,

Reggie died and I didn't know. Hutch just told me. He said he'd written but the letter must have gone astray. I could not understand how I had not heard. It must have been in the casualty lists just after I was brought home when I was not up to much, and I missed it. Then the regiment got caught up with Cambrai and, well, things just move on without one.

Reggie died at Hargicourt on some futile raid ordered by that imbecile MacNabb – and led by Lochdubh of all people! – damn both their eyes. I feel such a fool, Evie. I have been thinking of Reggie as his own cheery self and all the time he was already as dead as all the others, deep in the stone-cold earth.

I now wish I had not sent you that long and foolish letter yesterday. I shall not write of my proposal again. I have utterly lost hope of that. My fate seems to be to lose those I love, as even the Indian cavalry have all gone. Hutch was one of the last to leave. I did not see any of the others to say goodbye, not Amar Singh, not Arjan Singh, none of them.

Things are not looking very good. There is another big push planned soon. I can't say any more. You will read of it in the papers soon enough. If I live, in spite of the absolute hash I have made of everything, perhaps we can still be friends?

Forgive me Evie.

Yours ever,

Tom

Evie read the letter one last time. The pencil was a scrawl, the paper smudged in places. She took a pen and paper from the kitchen drawer, took a deep, determined breath and wrote *My dear Tom...*

# 33

# The Somme: into the Valley of the Shadow

THE SOMME, FRANCE
MARCH 1918

'Did you understand all that, sergeant-major?'

'Yes, sah. Hestablish an H.Q. here sah and hestablish ay prisoner collecting cage here, sah.'

'And?'

'An' do not move from this position until your return, sah.'

Tom did not like or particularly trust this unknown man who had been foisted on him by Lochdubh. The major had sent him speedily enough to replace Tom's own sergeant-major, the stolid and reliable Walsh, who had been badly injured by shrapnel. Tom knew that Lochdubh was unlikely to send him any soldier whose absence Lochdubh would himself regret.

The Front he had returned to seemed to him alien and wrong without the Indian cavalry. Tubby Bell and a few others had remained in France, and so it was his friend Major James Gourlie who had assumed command. They had marched for Rouen and then entrained for Marseilles only a few days earlier. Tom felt bereft.

It was now 21 March 1918, Thursday morning. Tom peered out from his billet window into the thick fog that enshrouded the anonymous village and the makeshift camp beyond.

Golden Rod had his ears pricked, as though he knew his hour had finally come. Tom's new groom and servant, a rotund Highlander named MacKeddie (formerly a stable hand at some country estate called Rosehaugh that he mentioned at every possible opportunity) had turned out his handsome charger to perfection. Water, rations, map and ammunition were neatly packed away in parcels all around his saddle. MacKeddie pressed a small additional package wrapped in oilcloth into Tom's hand. 'Three wee phials o' morphia, Captain sir. Just in case.' Tom gratefully tucked them away into his saddlebag, above his utterly useless but still obligatory sword.

Rod's nostrils snuffed the air with curiosity. He had enjoyed a warm mash breakfast as a treat, sweetened with some maize MacKeddie had found hidden away on the farm. It would need to be plain old grass until their return, if they did. Rod was better by far than a truck or a car, as he never ran low on fuel at inopportune moments. The roads had become more and more impassable for vehicles and fuel was in short supply, so the cavalry's few remaining grass-fed, sure-footed horses were finally coming into their own.

Tom whispered his ritual Hindi farewell into Daisy's ear. Daisy was in a sulk with both Tom and Rod for being left behind and did not respond, standing with one rear hoof poised for a kick, which they both knew would never come. 'Oh, be like that then,' Tom said, trying not to mind. Rod was an acrobat where smaller Daisy was a clown. She had terrific endurance but not quite the same agility and speed. This time, he suspected they would need to ride fast.

He walked Rod out of the stable, ducking under the low doorway. 'Into the valley of death, then, old chap,' murmured Tom, patting Rod's neck. His charger turned to look at him as if to say, 'Ah, so this is it.' Tom mounted, turned his back on the loitering sergeant-major and kicked Rod into a trot towards the battleground that had once been the tranquil valley of the Somme.

Although full of bounce from too little exercise, Rod moved delicately, sidestepping debris and skirting great shell-holes that would have engulfed a tank and one so huge it might have swallowed up a small hamlet.

Tom's orders were to collect and co-ordinate stragglers during the so-called 'tactical withdrawal', as Lochdubh and his ilk had dubbed it. Straggling was inevitable and frequently wilful, as frightened men took advantage of the chaos to save their own skins. He was to intercept, marshal and redirect these troops so that they could be redeployed as fast as possible. G.H.Q. had moved back to Bouvincourt and had taken a heavy pounding. That was where Walsh, on traffic control at the crossroads, had just sustained his injuries.

Tom needed to inspect the three collecting-posts he had set up at the railway cutting east of Vendelles, a farm at Soyecourt and the bridge at Vermand, the only river crossing for some miles. The front line ran roughly east of Le Verguier to the east of Maissemy. If tales told by recently captured prisoners were to be believed, the Boche were aiming to conduct an almighty assault on its full length. If it turned into a rout the Allies would be finished. Controlling the retreat was all.

He could barely see anything of Soyecourt, where all seemed in order. At intervals, the persistent fog was eerily lit up by enemy fire-shells as their front-line troops searched for the battery. At the second post, Tom was greeted somewhat breathlessly by young Private Rudge of the Middlesex Regiment. As if anticipating a scolding, Rudge stammered that the shelling had been too heavy and so he had decided to withdraw the third post. Tom was uncertain whether this was a case of commendable prudence or plain cold feet. He tethered Rod to a shattered tree-trunk. 'Come on, I need to see for myself,' he said to Rudge, and the boy to his credit instantly picked up his rifle to accompany Tom on foot towards Le Verguier.

The fog was clearing. Almost at once, heavy shellfire erupted overhead, high explosives and twisted pieces of shrapnel shredding the earth about their feet. Men of a digging party from the Northamptonshires were attempting to build a redoubt and several others were injured in the same attack. The survivors ignored the one dead man who lay, headless and twitching, at their feet. They continued to work as the injured hobbled away towards a Dressing Station, one man carried on a stretcher. Their coolness under fire was breath-taking, but Tom suspected their task would ultimately be futile.

Tom and Rudge scuttled back to the post, where Tom praised the boy for his initiative and observation. He ordered Rudge to fall back to Vendelles if the shelling got bad and kicked Rod into a canter along the lane beyond.

Men of the 11th Queen's began to appear – marching in perfect order, not streaming in a panic, Tom noted with relief. When an officer wounded in the arm stopped briefly to drink at a village pump, Tom asked him for news. 'Oh, we've hit them hard,' he said, struggling to speak. 'Very hard. No point in holding on any longer. Both flanks in the air.' Tom was dismayed at this news, which meant the regiments on either side of the Queen's had pulled back fast and in considerable disarray. Tom gave the man one phial of his morphia to help him reach the Dressing Station and watched him stumble off.

Vermand was barely recognisable as the town he had once known. It had almost ceased to exist. A stream of wounded men staggered towards him up the hill. One of them, although clearly injured in the thigh, stopped to pat Golden Rod on the nose as though he were a ploughboy heading home from a day's work. Tom immediately ordered the youngster to stay there with Rod in relative safety. He needed to make sure no-one stole his horse; he knew retreating men could be desperate. The lad was surprised but agreed willingly enough, flopping down on the grass beside the horse with evident relief.

The bridge at the centre of Vermand was packed with battered troops jostling to cross. It appeared that enemy had got right on top of the 1st North Staffords in the fog by sheer bad luck and almost wiped them out. He also heard the first ugly tales of surrender: two companies of the 3rd Rifle Brigade had put up their hands where the enemy had broken through at Maissemy. Germans were now pouring through a breach at Villechoilles, only a mile from the bridge where he stood. Colonel Green of the Middlesex Regiment hailed him then. His party was trying to dig in south of the bridge to defend the crossing. Tom offered to support them from the far side of the bridge, closest to the enemy advance.

A group of young Allied fugitives, several injured and being helped along by the others, blundered towards him in a panic. Tom pointed his revolver at the scared young Gunners, lined them all up along the bank north of the bridge and ordered them to start digging in. They looked at him as if he were mad. It was quite hopeless. The moment he went back to the bridge to intercept more stragglers, a great wave of them bolted again. Human nature – fear was contagious.

A big man, a sergeant, staggering with fatigue, approached him. 'Can I help you here, sir? Bloody cowards.' Atkins was one of very few survivors of the gallant North Staffordshires. He towered over Tom and took up his position, legs apart, defiant. 'Hah!' said Tom, his face cracking into a smile as he quoted, "Now who will stand at my right hand and keep the bridge with me?"'

Atkins looked blank, but his towering and glowering presence soon made itself felt and they did much better than Tom had on his own.

'It was very bad, sir.' Atkins told Tom during a lull in their interceptions. 'They threw over a lot of that new gas and we couldn't see it coming in the fog. Lots of us didn't get on our hoods in time and died covered in the stuff. It burns through to the bone.' No need to tell me that, thought Tom, instinctively rubbing his healed, yet still tender, arm. 'Then they rushed our trenches. We fought back. There were just too many of them. I may be the only one left.'

He was wrong about that. Two other men approached soon afterwards to whom Atkins roared a relieved greeting, striding towards them, arms outstretched with relief. It was Stamer, the adjutant of the North Staffordshires with a dazed subaltern stretcher-bearer. Stamer too bravely offered to help but he was badly wounded in the head and the boy almost too weak to stand. Tom sent them ahead to the Dressing Station with the next party of injured stragglers, while he and Atkins continued to hold the bridge alone.

Four long hours later they had collected enough stray troops to defend the bank, including two police corporals who looked like they might do what they were told. Tom gave them orders to shoot anyone who tried to run. No-one else did.

Chevalier, G.S.O. of the Division, finally came over to say that the line was solid again for now. Colonel Green then thanked Tom and released him from his support of the Middlesex. Tom did the same for Atkins, who raised a huge hand in farewell and plodded onwards. Tom made a mental note to commend him for a medal later, if they both survived. As the flood of stragglers had now ceased, he decided to ride back to G.H.Q. for further instruction. Only then did he think of Golden Rod and the young soldier. It had been almost six hours since he had left them.

Rather to his surprise, the young soldier was still there, lying between Rod and the tree, either in a dead faint or fast asleep. The horse's reins were wound tightly around his wrist. Rod was browsing the thin spring grass and looked at Tom as if to say, 'oh, so there you are – what kept you?' Tom bent to wake the boy and only then realised that his own hand was bleeding. There was a small piece of bright metal sticking out from the joint just above his little finger. A bit of shrapnel from the bridge, presumably. He pulled it out and the wound fairly poured blood, drat it. He had not felt anything when it must have happened, but he certainly did now. He touched it with his other hand and flinched. Something was amiss with the bones, he could feel them crackle.

'Can you walk, private?'

'I think so, sir,' was the unconvincing response. The poor boy did look very green about the gills. Tom, biting back the pain from his hand, half pushed, half-lifted the young private on to Rod's back. He could now see the lad had left a sticky pool of bright blood where he had been lying. Tom took out his brandy flask and gave the boy a brandy-soaked pad to hold against his thigh. Then he soused the wound on his hand and wrapped a bandage around it. They started walking towards the field ambulance station at Poeuilly, Tom clinging to Rod's bridle with his uninjured hand, while shells shrieked above them.

The shrapnel had broken Tom's little finger clean across the joint. The Field Ambulance crew set it and dressed it and gave him an anti-tetanus serum. To his shame Tom fainted at that point and so lost sight of the brave young private, whose name he never learned.

Eager for news from the faltering Front, the Field Ambulance staff invited Tom to share their cold rations, which was decent of them. Afterwards they even found him a quiet corner in which to curl up and doze. He took more of his morphia to dull the pain and fell asleep.

An hour later, Tom was abruptly woken by one of the crew shaking his shoulder. 'Awfully sorry, Captain Westmacott. We were told to report the presence of any injured officers to D.H.Q., so we did. Turns out they want you back straight away.' Tom dragged his tired body up on to Rod's back again, his head still spinning from the morphia. The saddle was still crusted with the boy's blood, which he ignored, kicking Rod on, in the direction of Bouvincourt. He was glad of the icy wind to numb his throbbing hand.

Once at G.H.Q. he found Lochdubh alone in a command room, poring over a map. 'At last, Westmacott. We wondered what was keeping you.'

Tom said nothing.

Lochdubh jabbed at a position on the map. 'The 66th have broken badly here, to our left. Our flank's now in the air. We're pulling back again.'

'Very well. I'll need to withdraw my posts then, sir.'

Lochdubh stared at him with his pale eyes as usual, then said, 'I see you have somehow injured your hand, Westmacott. Not self-inflicted, I would hope? Carry on.' He turned his attention back to the map. Tom set off, relieved that the encounter had not been longer. The jibe, one of many accumulated over the last four years, he now barely felt. Back in the saddle, which one of the grooms had now thoughtfully wiped clean, he turned Rod's willing nose towards his observation posts, pulling them back to Bernes, Flechin and Poeuilly. At Hancourt he wrapped himself in his coat with his head laid on Rod's saddle. Lulled by the sweet smell of horse sweat and warm leather, he slept for a few hours until first light.

The next day, Tom was again summoned by Lochdubh. This time the major appeared seriously rattled and had no time for his customary needling. He told Tom that the 73rd Brigade was to fall back along the Bouvincourt to Tertry Road, the 17th and 72nd Brigades fighting through behind them. Tom and his men must get all transport clear of the crossroads at Estrée at once.

Tom's policemen worked splendidly and all was clear by 4pm. Then he heard that somewhere along the road through Vraignes there had been a bomb attack by a German aeroplane on the 24th Divisional Ammunition Column. Many muleteers had come from India, some of them old men considered otherwise unfit for military service, who had still wanted to accompany the regiment. How did they still come to be there? Tom rode up to see if he could help, just in time to watch one old Mohammedan he knew well breathe his last, his arms around the still-warm neck of his dead mule. In all, eleven mules and muleteers were killed.

Tom saw and heard and smelled it all and felt next to nothing.

Near Vraignes, the cavalry had been dismounted and sent into the line to support the 66th Division, with no thought given to concealing the horses. This attracted several enemy aircraft, which made repeated passes overhead, causing the poor, squealing beasts to stampede as they opened fire. Rod coped well with having to walk through a field of panicked horses but put his ears back and rolled his eyes. Tom knew the anguish in store when the men returned from the front line to find their mounts injured, dying or dead.

To Tom's satisfaction, Lochdubh also looked like he had not slept much either. 'Right, Westmacott. The position is now critical. We need to get all our wheels across the Saint Christ Bridge.'

To Tom's satisfaction, Lochdubh also looked like he had not slept much either. 'Right, Westmacott. The position is now critical. We need to get all our wheels across the St Christ Bridge.'

'How soon, sir?' asked Tom, although he already knew the answer.

'Well now, of course, man! You spent plenty of time in this part of the country with the 4th Cavalry Division, didn't you? Just get on with it.'

Tom got on with it. Ours not to reason why, he repeated, willing himself to believe it. He found the bridge at Brie blocked by a broken-down lorry – how Tom loathed these filthy, noisy, unreliable machines – and a damaged sixty-pounder gun. The A.P.M. of the 19th Corps was making a complete fist of dealing with it, but Tom decided it was best not to interfere. He pushed on to Saint Christ and despatched his new assistant Lieutenant Fenwick, a languid boy who pulled a book from his pocket and read it whenever quiet enough, to divert all other traffic away from the bridge there. By 11am, two brigades of cavalry and three batteries of Royal Horse Artillery had trotted across unscathed, with not a single enemy shell fired in their direction. Fenwick had proved unexpectedly efficient, even while reciting Byron to himself. So far, so good.

Three hundred weary and grimy men of the Middlesex Regiment covered the crossing in readiness for the arrival of the enemy. One of its majors, sweating and desperate, stopped Tom. 'We have no food, no ammunition, nothing. For pity's sake, can you get a message to D.H.Q.? Do they expect us to hold off the Boche with our bare hands?'

Frustrated at this logistical disaster, Tom instead stepped out into the road, revolver drawn. The ammunition lorry rumbling over the bridge juddered to a halt. Deaf to the driver's protests, Tom commandeered forty boxes of small arms ammunition at gunpoint and handed them over to the officer.

After a reconnaissance nearby Fenwick reported that the cavalry's canteen had been left standing when the troops last fell back. There were ample stocks of food and even a couple of unused artillery limbers nearby. Tom and Fenwick loaded these with tins and took them back to the grateful men of the Middlesex.

They might still die, thought Tom, but at least they would die with full bellies and bit of ammo with which to punish the enemy first.

Nothing had been learned from the experience of the B.E.F. in 1914. Not a single tree had been felled across a road to slow down the enemy, not one crossroads ordered to be blown up. Food abandoned in the canteens would feed the hungry enemy for weeks. And it was not as though there had been no time to undertake this vital sabotage. The Allied generals in command of the beleaguered 5th Army seemed incapable of planning for an orderly retreat, as though the very imagining of defeat was unpatriotic. Their lack of foresight was likely to cost them dearly. Tom felt sick at the very thought of the waste of life this would represent.

Another officer from the Middlesex, who had taken two German prisoners, further compounded Tom's suspicions. 'They'll come at us across the Saint Christ bridge, I'm sure of it. And we've left all the huts, ammunition dumps and canteens, and even the railways, in one piece. The Boche will just take them over as they stand.'

Tom agreed. 'Look at the trenches. 6-inch scratches at best – as if dog-tired men could be expected to deepen them!'

'We're in real trouble here. Remember when the Boche retreated in the spring of 1917?'

'Oh, yes. Not a teaspoon left for us to use,' recalled Tom sombrely 'You're right, my friend. This feels more like a rout.'

'I hope to God you're wrong, Westmacott,' replied the officer as he prodded his forlorn young captives onwards.

Before he spent another night with his head on Rod's saddle as a pillow, Tom decided to scrawl another quick note to Evie. She would never agree to marry him, he knew that now; but as it appeared unlikely that many of them would come out of this horror alive, at least someone at home would know he had tried to do his best.

He struggled to know where to begin. She might be a nurse, but how could he write about what he had just experienced? Courage and words failed him. Instead, he told her that his hand wound would mean his name would appear on the injured list again, and that none of them should worry.

The early letters he had sent Evie now made him feel ashamed. They had been so naive, so vainglorious. He had behaved like a pompous ass – little better than wretched Lochdubh. His letter became a sanitized description of the hours he had spent holding the bridge but this time he ended his account with the impulsive truth:

I am an utter coward I'm afraid. There was no cover and I feared for my life the entire time.

## 34

# Chanson de Roland: Toccata and Fugue

BAVAY, FRANCE
MARCH 1918

Gaston Derome had not fared well during the war. Neither had his young family, nor yet his little town. He was glad that his beloved Louise had not lived long enough to share the horrors that he, Léonie and the children had witnessed since 1914.

After Maître Corbeau (try as he might, he could never quite think of him as Monsieur l'Abbé Lebrun) had secured his release from the chateau at Saint Quentin, both Gaston and the priest had been closely watched by the invaders. There had been periods of house arrest for various perceived misdeeds. The episode with les Anglais had made Gaston *un notable*. Even his children were the subject of close scrutiny wherever they went. His youngest, Marie-Félicie, had grown from being a child of seven to the threshold of womanhood at eleven in the shadow of conflict. Her little face was often watchful and unsmiling.

Gaston had been kept as a hostage at Holzminden for exactly six months. Others were not so fortunate and remained in captivity, penned in a row of dreary wooden cabins behind barbed wire, women and children separate from the men, and everyone watched over by guards. The thousands of civilians herded into trains and taken into temporary exile in this way later in the war became an unwilling labour force who had to be cajoled and coerced at every moment. It was a futile exercise. Sometimes these people, even the elderly, were taken away as hostages to ensure good behaviour from communities the occupying army viewed as troublesome. Gaston had seen and experienced acts of cruelty during the war that defied comprehension.

When he had returned from Saint Quentin in 1914, Léonie had kept calm for the sake of the children. The second time he came home, this time from Holzminden, she had fallen on his neck and wept. So brave earlier in the war, but the stresses and deprivations were taking their toll on his sister. She had grown thinner, more strained, with every day that passed.

As the war progressed, the Boche had become increasingly obsessed with hidden agents and partisans. Gaston knew that locally this would in part be due to what had happened at Bavay. Men had been shot and whole villages burned on the merest suspicion. On Gaston's orders, therefore, no-one in Bavay did anything untoward, at least intentionally. The inhabitants tried to comply with every excessive billeting order, every absurd requisition.

The first demand had been for machinery. Half the presses and rollers in the family factory had been dismembered and taken. Production was now at a complete standstill. He had to lay off all but a handful of the few workers who remained, although he knew that they relied on him for their meagre living.

Next came wool. Madame Hauquier tried to hide an old woollen blanket made of bright squares that her mother had knitted for their wedding bed, where it had lain every night since. It was in vain. Even the wool stuffing was taken from people's *couettes*, although it was a bitterly cold spring.

The latest requisition had been for copper and other metals suitable for armaments. Léonie had wept with helplessness and rage as her precious *batterie de cuisine*, inherited from their mother, was taken away. The soldiers tossed it, piece by tuneful piece, into the back of a truck. She was inconsolable and took to boiling up dull stews in a dreary iron pot, whispering her grief to the kitchen range.

The hardest loss for the townsfolk to bear was that of their bells. These had pealed out over the rooftops from the bell-tower of Notre Dame de l'Assomption for over three centuries. The parishioners huddled around Maître Corbeau at a safe distance, muttering to each other in disbelief as the Germans scaled their *clocher*. After today, they knew that there would be only silence to greet each hour.

The Abbé Lebrun stood a little apart in his worn black cloak. He was stiffer and more stooped than he had been in 1914. They all watched as the German soldiers struggled to detach and lower the bells, eventually startling the parishioners who staggered backwards as one of the pair plunged to the pavés. It lay there cracked at the abbé's feet, but the priest did not even flinch.

Gaston tried to comfort old Madame Hauquier as she wept and repeated, 'It is the end! The end of all decency in the world!' The Germans laughed with relief and pointed at the great bell as it lay silenced forever. The second bell soon joined it, shattering the cobbles on which it landed. Using levers, pulleys and brute force, they proceeded to lift and tip Bavay's weighty and ancient timekeepers into the truck, one by one. Their heavy clappers gave a dying clonk of farewell as the truck graunched away. It was as though God the Almighty had had his tongue cut out, thought Gaston, as forlorn as the other parishioners.

He stared across to the corner where his replacement, the collaborator from a town nearby, stood looking on. The man soon felt Gaston's silent rebuke and scuttled off. Neither he nor the townsfolk were in any doubt as to who remained the real Mayor of Bavay. Gaston did not blame the fellow – there was a very fine line between collaboration and cooperation for every mayor. The man had doubtless had little choice.

Nonetheless, Gaston did not trust him in the slightest.

'I am so sorry about the bells, mon père,' he said to the Abbé Lebrun, who shrugged in silence. Then his old schoolmaster wheeled to address the small crowd that had gathered, seeking comfort, around their two champions. 'Listen to me,' said the priest. 'Bells are bells, people are people. We need to render unto Caesar that which is Caesar's and unto God that which is God's. Let these invaders take our metal if it is so precious to them! Even if it is an abomination that our enemy could make bullets and shells to destroy us out of the very bells that have so often called us to prayer. They must know in their deepest souls that they will be forever accursèd because of this act.'

He looked at Madame Hauquier, who was trembling and dabbing her eyes with her handkerchief and approached her to speak more gently. 'We ourselves must be like Job; we must endure. The end will come. It is perhaps not so very far away even now.'

Misplaced optimism, thought Gaston, although no-one could fault the grim courage of the abbé. Everyone knew the Allies were once more in retreat. Many in Bavay were losing all hope of a future without German rule.

'The date of the last day of this conflict is already known unto God,' the grey-headed priest continued firmly. 'We must now take comfort in that.' Lebrun then turned and glared up at the ruined tower. 'Come, they have taken away the voice of Our Lady, but not her soul; let us enter Her shrine to lend her our own as we join together in prayer.' He led the way into Notre Dame de l'Assomption through the shattered fragments of broken stone and mortar as though they did not exist.

Gaston followed him too. He now attended mass on a regular basis, believing it the least he could do to support his unlikely saviour. He found himself sitting at the back of the church beside Mademoiselle Gautier. He admired this pleasant, intelligent woman and her sister greatly. The two ladies had moved in together for the duration of hostilities and their fortitude and ability to forage and survive was an inspiration to the whole town.

It was at Mademoiselle Gautier's door that he had stood only a few days previously when les Boches had brought a batch of new prisoners into the square, marching them at gunpoint towards the old stone storehouse they were using as a gaol.

One boy was very thin, his face hollow with hunger. He wore the clothes of a French peasant and yet carried himself upright. He looked Gaston in the eye as he passed. The prisoners' escort included a brute of a man known for beating up the town's youngsters. On the last occasion, Gaston's sons, Alphonse and Léon, had managed to get away, but the soldier had hurt Louis Delavigne so badly for some innocent tomfoolery that for several days the boy could scarcely walk.

Gaston did not know the name of this persecutor of children. He was now far beyond learning the names of the enemy within the town: he saw only their uniform and their actions; he felt towards them only fear and hatred.

As the prisoners approached, the youngest had called out *'Ayez pitié! Du pain!'* Mademoiselle Gautier had rushed to her kitchen where her sister Madame Wambères had been baking: the kindly fragrance of warm bread issued from the doorway, in sharp contrast to the actions in the street. Mademoiselle Gautier ignored the guard and rushed out to press a tiny *petit-pain* into the prisoner's bound hands. The lad had managed one large bite before the guard struck him. The boy staggered backwards, dropping the rest. The soldier then said something uncouth and looked straight at Mademoiselle Gautier as his heel ground the remains into the mud. The guards hustled the prisoners onwards.

Gaston swallowed hard. He was very hungry. They all were. The bread was doubtless made from certain ground-up wild seeds she had foraged but it had still smelled very good. He would have minded less if the guard had eaten the food himself.

The thin lad looked back over his shoulder and managed a nod of gratitude, then he was pushed around the corner and was gone.

Gaston and Mademoiselle Gautier looked at each other in shock. 'Un Anglais,' she said. Gaston nodded. 'Yes. Yes, I think so.' The young man's old-fashioned accent had been good enough to fool a German – but not a Frenchman.

'*Un soldat*? Perhaps escaped and now recaptured?'

Gaston had shivered then. His memories of the Englishmen in the Forêt de Mormal were still vivid. There were times at night when he jolted awake, believing himself once more to be in the cramped and stinking cell of Saint Quentin. 'If they find out they will shoot him, I fear.'

That had been three days earlier.

Now, in the back pew of the church, Mademoiselle Gautier inclined her head as though in prayer and drew a little closer to Gaston. '*Le prisonnier s'appelle Roland*,' she breathed. 'A French name, but he is an English nobleman, of the Queen's very own regiment. Imagine! The Queen's personal soldier, a prisoner here! They are starving him to try to find out who he is and where he is from. But there is a little window, high up, always open. That is his cell.'

'Mademoiselle Gautier, I must beg you to be cautious,' said Gaston. 'As our enemy pushes forward, he will grow in confidence and his tolerance of any misdeed will be diminished.' He could not help adding curiously, 'But how did you learn all this?'

Her simple response took him aback. 'Why, I heard him sing it,' she said. 'He has a most beautiful voice.'

'He *sings*?' Gaston exclaimed, scarcely believing what he was being told. 'Not English songs, surely?'

'*Mais non!*' she said rather more loudly, causing Lebrun to look fiercely in her direction as he led the various prayers and responses.

'He seems a most intelligent boy. He is singing courtly songs in mediaeval French. And yes, I have been feeding him, for les Boches most certainly are not.' Gaston was intrigued, if very afraid for her. She continued, 'He is a clever boy. He takes parts of the real words away and inserts his own, Monsieur Gaston. He was singing '*Dedans la cour du Roy, la-la-la, je meurs ici de faim...*''

'I see! And do you sing back?'

'Ah, *mais enfin, non!*' This time the Abbé Lebrun was glowering at them and for a few moments they remained respectfully silent. Then when the old priest again turned towards the altar, she dropped her voice again and continued. 'I have a voice like an old wheezy crow, as you know full well from when I try to sing the Marseillaise. No, I heard his plea and made him a little piece of bread and cheese.' Gaston knew it would have been her own meal for the day. 'And I wrapped it in an old paper and threw it up at the window. I missed twice but finally, in it went, pop! Now I can do it almost every time,' she added with pride.

Gaston found himself smiling, in spite of the grave danger. It was good to hear of a small blow struck by the town for kindness and normality. 'And I suppose he sings you a thank you?' he whispered.

'Yes! Yes, he does. After he has eaten he always sings *Merci infiniment, la-la-la, la-la-la-la, merci infiniment, j'ai mangé votre pain.* Gaston smiled. 'Very polite, are they not, these Englishmen? What about the guards?'

'There only seems to be the one at present. He shouts at *le jeune* Roland to stop whenever the boy begins to sing. So it is easy enough for us to hear where the guard is. The little window looks on to the back alleyway. It is too small for a man to escape through and they keep it open for air only.' Then she dropped her voice even lower and her next words filled Gaston with fear. 'This young soldier may not survive much longer, Monsieur le Maire. He will not tell them where he comes from. He thinks they will soon lose patience. You know what it is like. And les Boches are winning this war, it seems.'

Gaston closed his eyes and thought hard. Could it be a trap? Could the Germans have set up the whole incident to try to ensnare him and send him back to prison? It seemed unlikely that they would have gone to such elaborate trouble when they could already have hauled him off on the flimsiest excuse. No. This was a genuine Englishman, just the one; and one who could, this time perhaps, be saved. But how?

It occurred to him then that he was in church and this deep contemplation was, in a way, akin to prayer. This came as a small shock. When he opened his eyes, they lighted on a piece of broken rubble lying in the aisle. It was about the size of his clenched fist, carved at one end and sharply pointed at the other.

'Mademoiselle Gautier, did you say there was only the one guard?' he whispered.

## 35

# The Somme: 'For he is an Englishman'

On 24 March, Tom wrote to Evie once more. He had received nothing from her, of course, and did not really expect to, as even if she did reply, any correspondence would be caught up in their retreat from the Somme. She might throw this letter away too, of course; but he thought that at least she might read it before she did. Writing to Evie had become a great solace and a vent for much of what he saw and felt. In spite of what had occurred between them, Tom found that he could not stop.

He tried now to find words to describe the desperate evacuation of civilians. At Saint Christ, he had had great difficulty in persuading anyone to leave, especially if they were elderly or infirm. Many were left behind, clinging to their ruined houses and battered possessions and he knew they would be swept up in the German advance. All the civilians in Vraignes, a village left undamaged by the Germans in their retreat of 1917, had refused to go, strangely unconcerned about the German advance. Tom recalled the abandoned house with the rose garden at Vermelles, which had once sheltered German agents, and wondered.

It was clear now that they were doomed to retreat again and that the Germans would soon break through.

Tom had spent another exhausting day between Chaulnes and Lihons regulating heavy traffic before being relieved at last in the late afternoon. For the first time in days, he was given a decent billet and looked forward to a full night's sleep. He woke instead in the early evening because of a terrific uproar outside. A battery rattled through at a fast trot, followed by a mob of transport at the gallop and the men of labour units running and yelling that the much-feared Uhlan troops were among them. Could the Germans have come so far already, wondered Tom, as he rubbed his bleary eyes and pulled on his uniform tunic. Was this where it would end? He checked his revolver for ammunition.

Down in the street, a woman cannoned into him screaming that it was a rout. He took by her shoulders and said '*Calmez-vous, madame!*' but she shook him off and ran on. There was no time to saddle up Rod and so Tom commandeered a car and driver and they set off to try to quieten things down. Everywhere he went, he found the same strange story: a small officer with a dark moustache had ridden through on a motorbike shouting that the line was broken and the Uhlans were right behind him. Tom was quite certain this man must have been a German agent, playing on the fearsome reputation of these Polish troops. He remembered that the enemy had played the same shabby trick during the Italian retreat, but also recalled the terror of his German captives when faced with the lip-licking antics of his Sikh men only the previous year. In any case, the motorcyclist achieved the opposite result he had hoped for – people were so ashamed of themselves that they were less likely to stampede when there was more excuse to do so.

How easy it was to play with the minds of frightened people. Another extraordinary yarn had spread through the army that Lille and Lens had been taken. The French 5th Army had apparently driven through a wedge on their right, while the French 3rd Army was coming up behind them in support. This lie was especially cruel, as it had the effect of raising and then dashing everyone's spirits. Morale among civilians and troops alike suffered badly when the tale was found to be all smoke and mirrors. Tom would cheerfully have shot whoever spread it.

By 25 March, the retreat was gathering momentum. Tom stayed put at Rosières since it was a useful position to set up straggler collecting-posts. This time a valiant fellow, Stamp of the machine-gun squadron, lent a hand. Together they gathered two hundred stragglers whom Tom reassured, fed, rested and then re-armed.

That night was touch and go as the enemy flung repeated assaults against the three Brigades, who kept on telephoning for artillery assistance, the calls punctuated by the sound of exploding shells and the tinkle of shrapnel and debris on the caller's tin hat. For about half an hour at midnight, all communications ceased with the 17th Brigade. Tom thought they had been annihilated, but it turned out that the wire had been cut by a shell. There was a very close call at D.H.Q., where a shell fell in its courtyard. Had it exploded, Lochdubh and many of his staff would have been killed. Tom was glad that it hadn't gone off, not least because the horses had been stabled nearby.

The next day, an anxious corporal and sergeant from the Royal Engineers came asking for an A.P.M. and would only tell Tom that they needed his help in dealing with a difficult disciplinary situation. As he approached their section of line, bullets raked their feet and they flung themselves down behind a large boulder.

There were more rifle shots, then an odd cackle. 'Good Lord! I didn't realise the Boche had made it this far already,' Tom hissed to the men in consternation.

One of the men whispered back: 'No, sir, that's not a Boche, sir. That's our commanding officer. He's gone off his head, sir.'

The other one chimed in. 'He's been taken like this before, sir, and got better after a bit. But now he's up that broken tree and he won't come down. He's already injured two of our best men.'

'He's a crack shot, sir,' the first man added.

Tom peered cautiously around the corner of the rock. Sure enough, the officer was sitting on a high branch of one of the few surviving trees with his back turned, legs dangling as though he were fishing with a bent pin off a pier. He appeared to be smoking, every so often raising the rifle to his eye, taking careful aim and firing. There was a yelp of pain somewhere across in the German ranks. He laughed again. Then he crushed his cigarette butt against the tree, threw his head back and started to roar, '"Defer, defer! To the Lord High Ex-e-cu-tion-er! Bow down! Bow down…"'

Good Lord, thought Tom. Am I dreaming? Another bullet whistled past his ear. 'I don't care if he thinks he's the Lord Mayor of London,' he said to the artillerymen. 'Someone has to stop him.'

'Yes, but we can't, sir! He's our commanding officer!' said one of the men. 'We'll be done for if we do,' added the other. Tom could see their point. The men had showed sound judgement in coming to find him. More bullets pinged off the rock that protected them.

'Give me your rifle, corporal,' Tom said. He moved cautiously around the boulder on his elbows, then took careful aim and fired. The officer sagged and then toppled slowly headfirst from his branch. The fall would finish him if the bullet had not.

He handed the weapon back to the open-mouthed soldier. 'My name is Captain Thomas Horatio Westmacott,' he said slowly, allowing them time to take in what he had said. 'I am the Assistant Provost Marshal of the 24th Division. Remember that, please. I will take full responsibility for this matter if need be. Do you understand me?' The men nodded miserably as they clambered to their feet.

'Now, if you have any sense,' Tom continued, brushing earth from his trousers, 'You'll buck up a bit now and think. Go and talk to the others in your squadron over there and come to an agreement about what just happened. I think your unfortunate and gallant captain was just killed by enemy fire while up a tree observing the enemy lines. Don't you?' Fervent nodding.

Tom left them to it and heard no more about the matter.

At daybreak, on 27 March, Tom and several other officers went to inspect the old French trenches that ran from Rosières through Vrely and Warvilliers to Rouvroy. Tom's two hundred stragglers were each handed a spade and marched out to commence repair works there.

At Vrely he met three Brigades falling back on the line selected for them, very tired, but in good order and quite cheery. The best of the lot, once again, were the Middlesex. Colonel Green, their c.o., called him over. He knew Tom well and had arrived in France with the Indian Cavalry Divisions himself. Tom's feat of provisioning on the bridge at Saint Christ had reached Green's ears, and even in the midst of the chaos he had remembered to stop to thank him.

Just behind the line, Tom encountered a battalion clambering out of the convoy of battered London buses. Most of the men were carrying brown paper parcels, probably only just returning from leave. The enemy started putting shrapnel over – low bursts, beautifully timed he thought, dispassionately – and most of these precious packages ended up scattered as the men ran for cover. General Morgan turned to Tom as the only mounted officer present and ordered him to stop them from running too far.

Tom rammed in his spurs and galloped Golden Rod like the blazes to catch them up. In Rouvroy, he managed to head off half the fleeing men into the village but the rest broke past him and headed onwards for Warvilliers in a blind panic. He followed them, revolver drawn, and ferreted them out from the dark corners where they hid. The sight of his red cap and revolver did wonders for their courage.

Tom sent all the horses present back to Beaufort out of harm's way and decided to spend the night in Warvilliers. As the numbers of troops there increased and the enemy shelling ceased for a time, the atmosphere became strangely festive. No-one would have thought that they had been fleeing and fighting for their lives for six days and nights. Some of the men found old clothes in the village and dressed up in them, dancing and singing and laughing. To Tom's astonishment, Major Lochdubh appeared from somewhere to take a turn as Hamlet, all dressed in black and clutching a skull (which Tom hoped was not real but feared otherwise). Lochdubh curtailed the lengthy soliloquy when someone at the back booed. He tossed the skull into the crowd and switched effortlessly into a funny scene from *A Midsummer Night's Dream* where he acted all the Mechanicals and the Fairies himself. That was more like it. Men were clutching their sides with laughter, tears rolling down their dirty faces. Tom was forced to admit that the dratted man had unsuspected talents. All the same, he decided it was time to slip away, without the major having noticed his presence. He retrieved Rod from his field and moved on.

After a relatively peaceful night in a farmhouse billet nearby, Tom woke to the news that Stamp had been killed at Warvilliers. He had only come the previous day to inspect the same farm as possible accommodation for his men. Tom felt the loss of a useful officer but nothing more; there were so many deaths now that it was impossible to mourn them all. He was, at least for now, alive and able to do what he could for the men around him. On the right side of the grass, as old MacKeddie put it. That was the only distinction that now mattered.

He mounted Rod and rode wearily back to Demuin via Le Quesnel. There were enemy war balloons clustered right round them on that side. He could see they were closing in. Was it too late? He met a few French Territorials on the road, but where were the other reinforcements they so desperately needed?

Tom trotted back through the gateway of the chateau that was serving as D.H.Q. to a relieved shout of greeting from MacKeddie. His groom looked so delighted that Tom thought the man might embrace him, but MacKeddie chose instead to stand to attention and salute. Then he shook Tom's hand warmly, calling to the others, 'Come an' see who's back from the dead! And someone fetch thon bluidy sergeant!'

Incredulous, Tom took in the news that his unpopular sergeant-major had made his own way back to D.H.Q a full two days earlier, ignoring Tom's orders. He had then taken it upon himself to report Tom as missing, presumed killed. And Lochdubh had been charging about astride Daisy ever since.

'You are an absolute rotten coward! I'll see you are reduced to the ranks for this!' gritted Tom, his face inches from his sergeant's, which was now the colour of putty. The crestfallen warrant officer was led away between two of Tom's own men who looked extremely pleased with this outcome.

MacKeddie somehow managed to provide Tom with a hot bath, the first since the battle began. He lay in it watching the water become murky as the grime of the battlefield dissolved in it. He stepped out of the bath washed clean of body if not of mind. It still felt very good. He then dashed off three quick notes – to his brother, to the Lawsons and, because he could not help himself, to Evie – in order to reassure them. Thanks to his sergeant-major, his name would have been listed in the papers as missing, drat the fellow.

Next he sought out Lochdubh in order to retrieve Daisy. He had clearly been tipped off – Matheson and MacKeddie were good friends. Tom marched into the centre of the mess-tent, came to attention and saluted. Lochdubh did not look up from his plate. Tom elected to try the silent, baleful stare that Lochdubh had so often practiced on himself. Eventually the major had to raise his head.

'Westmacott.' Lochdubh almost spat his name.

'Yes. Sir.'

Silence again as Lochdubh cut up and ate a small piece of cheese. Many eyes were now fixed on them both.

'Not dead, then?' The words rang out, Lochdubh's regret obvious to all in the room. One or two other officers who overheard shook their heads and looked away.

'No. Sir.'

'You had better find Matheson.' It might not be a fulsome apology, but a good deal better than nothing. The major returned to his food but as Tom saluted and about-turned, he noticed to his satisfaction that Lochdubh had flushed crimson with annoyance.

Matheson, in sharp contrast to his laird, gave him almost as warm a welcome as MacKeddie had. Daisy whinnied with relief to see both Tom and Golden Rod. Once tethered in the stall alongside her, Rod immediately took a mouthful of Daisy's mane and began to nibble it.

'Matheson, there is something I have been meaning to find out,' said Tom as he removed Rod's saddle. 'Do you happen to know what happened to Reggie Durand's horse Phoenix after he was killed? No-one seems to know.'

Matheson nodded. 'A fine wee roan, I mind her well,' he replied. 'The major gave orders to have her taken from Hargicourt along with our own horses. He had half a mind to put her to Satan, even though I told him I didnae think that was a very good idea. I tied her up in a stall at our billet, but when I came down the next morning she'd gone.'

'Stolen?' Theft of horses had become an increasing problem.

Matheson gave a snort of derision. 'Not that one! No, she'd eaten her way through her halter rope, lifted the latch with her nose and was well away, long before dawn, leaving Satan biting his way through his stall to try and get at her. She might have galloped right across No Man's Land for all I know. The laird was in a fine bate about it, I can tell you that.'

So even Reggie's horse had been lost, thought Tom, saddened beyond words.

~

The following day General Gough, who commanded (or at least believed he commanded) the 5th Army arrived at D.H.Q. No-one there was pleased to see him. Tom, like most of the others, felt that the general had lost his grip and held him responsible for much of the chaos and carnage of the last days. Tubby Bell told him later that the old fool had paced up and down and even slapped General Daly on the back, repeating: 'It is all going splendidly. Quite splendidly!' Such rot. As though saying it over and over again would make such bunkum true.

Deluded at best, thought Tom. Even Lochdubh did little in the way of sucking-up to Gough, which was most unlike him. The major was at present taking great pains to stay out of Tom's way, which was just as Tom liked it.

After two more days of rounding up and turning back stragglers, Tom's new orders were to picket the main Demuin to Moreuil road and do the same, but this proved utterly beyond him. Men were now streaming back in whole platoons and companies with their officers. Some carried their weapons as though they had never fired them. Bayonet and brute force were the weapons of choice in the trenches.

Tom tried very hard to stop the flood, but they pushed past him, ignoring his revolver, as though they could not see him. The C.O. of an artillery battery stopped to draw breath, telling him that most of his guns were out of action. 'All the same,' he said, 'We mowed down hundreds, maybe thousands of them over open sights at Chaulnes. Great swathes of them. It was glorious.'

Good thing too, thought Tom. If the enemy managed to slip the cavalry and guns through there, surely nothing could then save them.

Tom realised that there would be a block at Castel Bridge and pulled all his posts back beyond it. From then until midnight he again held the bridge alone. This time there was no panic among the troops, so his hardest task was dealing with wave after wave of terrified and distraught civilians flying before the Germans. They were driving wagons pulled by farm horses and even pushing handcarts or ancient perambulators crammed with their belongings. The little single-way bridge with a steep hill leading up from it was too narrow for the overloaded civilian carts, which kept jamming up the traffic.

A furious artillery officer pushed his way through the crowd of people, carts and livestock to Tom. 'What are you playing at, man? Get these bloody civilians out of the way! We must get the guns across now. The enemy will be on top of us at any moment!'

Tom obeyed and there was uproar. He had to fire repeatedly over their heads to calm the terrified mass of humanity. One woman went on her knees in the mud and begged him: 'Monsieur, for the love of God, please let my wagons cross the bridge!' Tom had to point his revolver at her face and turn her away.

By midnight, about five hundred men had passed him on the bridge, as he held crowds of angry and fearful civilians at bay. The troops were all dead beat, hardly able to walk. Tom shouted out, 'Who goes there? What battalion is this?' An officer who knew him answered out of the darkness, 'What's left of the 17th Brigade, Captain Westmacott.'

By midnight, the remnants of the entire Division had crossed the river and the flood of civilian traffic had resumed. Massey, of the divisional staff, told Tom he had to push on to the next river and get the transport over that too. Just as Tom turned away to retrieve Golden Rod from where he was hidden, something in the mud at his feet caught his eye. A small face gazed serenely up at him.

He bent and lifted an irregular muddy shape, which he rinsed in a nearby puddle. It was a cheap porcelain Virgin and Child statuette, a little chipped about the crown. He peered about him. No trace of any church left standing now. Perhaps a refugee had dropped her in the mud? In any case, someone had once treasured her, and so he would look after her now. He wrapped the Virgin tenderly in a piece of old curtain and buttoned her up inside his uniform, thinking he could give her to Luneau or Bourgeat if he came through.

Tom rode his tired charger into Ailly in the early hours of 29 March. They passed what was left of the 73rd Brigade lying dead beat on their arms in the mud with the rain pouring down. No vestige of shelter. Everything in Tom's path had been reduced to mud and destruction.

He met another British staff officer on the steps of the mairie, where Tom told him that he had orders to get all transport across the bridge. The man stared at him and laughed mirthlessly. 'No need to worry about that now, Captain, the worst is over,' he said, pointing. 'Fritz will soon turn tail and run now he has pushed this far. He'll be out of supplies soon enough. Just you wait and see.' Tom, who did not share his optimism, turned in the saddle and saw battery after battery of French guns and columns of fresh French infantry coming up the road towards the line.

At last, but would it be too little, too late?

The staff officer suggested he get some rest then turned and walked off before Tom could think of anything to say in reply. He stood for a long time as other men intent on their own orders milled about him. He became aware of a terrible pain in his hand. The bandage was grimy and stained.

An empty house on the outskirts of Ailly provided an overgrown garden where Rod could graze in safety. Tom bolted the gate and unsaddled and unbridled his exhausted horse, clicking with his tongue to sooth him, incapable of more and hoping the meagre grass would be enough to sustain him overnight.

The front door stood ajar: its residents had clearly left in a hurry. He entered the hall. It had once been a grand place and a chandelier still hung from the opulent ceiling. Other soldiers appeared to have slept there before him, as the thick Persian carpet in the centre of the hall was criss-crossed by muddy boot-prints. A marquetry staircase swept up to the upper floors where, doubtless, there would be soft feather-beds to sleep in. Tom looked at the immensity of the stairs through glassy eyes and decided he could not climb them. His head was spinning, his hand thumped with pain. He could go no further and do no more. Sat on the lowest step, he cracked open the last phial of morphia and drained it. Then he leaned against the baluster and closed his eyes.

Did he sleep?

It seemed to him that he did not. But then he started and looked up at the unlit chandelier to find himself staring at the back of the head of the mad captain, sitting once more on the only remaining branch of the dead tree, which had somehow grown out of the floor there, blocking his path to the front door.

Beyond the tree he could just see Evie in her nurse's uniform, Evie who did not love him and had said she never could. He opened his mouth to speak but she held up a hand and said 'Hush, now. I know.' Expressionless, uncaring, she turned and moved through the doorway and into the twilight, out of sight.

Tom drew his revolver, confused. He was so utterly certain he had killed the man up the tree. Now somehow there he was above him still, dangling his legs. Was he not dead like everyone else? At least he was silent this time. All the same, the fellow might be able to train his weapon on Evie, all the way up there. She might not care tuppence for him, but he, Tom, must still try to protect her.

As the man swivelled to look down at him, flicking uncaring ash on to the Persian carpet, Tom could see that his head was gory and crushed, either by the fall, or caught perhaps by a stray bullet from the firing squad of Indian sowars that had now assembled, completely silently, on the other side of the hall. Now he looked at them closely, he could see both Yadram Singh and Harnam Singh in their ranks. The officer commanding them had his back turned but slowly, slowly swung round towards him. Tense and unsmiling, Reginald Heber Marion

Durand held his revolver in one hand and a white handkerchief in the other. Blood seeped through his greatcoat and dripped to the ground to become dozens of scarlet rose-petals, until the floor was covered by a great drift of them.

Tom refused to be distracted by all this and kept his eye on the dangerous captain above, whose gaze now met his own. He could see the man's face more clearly and it had somehow become that of Lochdubh. The branch had slowly rotated until he was almost directly overhead. Nothing for it now. Tom would have to shoot him down and face the consequences.

He raised his revolver with a steady hand, higher and higher, until its barrel was directly below his own chin. He closed his eyes so he did not have to see the man fall a second time and gave a little sigh of relief as he pulled the trigger.

Click.

Nothing. No ammunition.

The little cold round mouth of the gun brushed his skin and gave him just enough of a jolt to dispel the phantoms.

Enough.

He lay down on the dirty Persian rug and rolled himself up on it, the useless revolver still in his hand, and slept until 5am.

The following morning, after this seeing the French guns across the river, he galloped on to Cottenchy, the new D.H.Q., where the Division stayed put right through to 4 April, there being no very heavy fighting.

The 24th Division was not relieved by the 58th Division until 5 April. They had been fighting continuously since 21 March. To the relief of the entire army, the French general, Maréchal Foch, then took over the supreme command. Tom felt benumbed when the news came through, too late for so many. His Division had paid a bitter price for Gough's incompetency. To those at home, they might appear to have won great glory by defeating eight German divisions and, many were saying, had possibly turned the tide in the war. But at what cost?

It was the following morning, at the new D.H.Q. in Boves, that Luneau hailed Tom with a cheery, 'Monsieur le Capitaine! See, some post for you.'

There were two letters, one of them from Evie. Tom went white and sat down. He automatically opened the other letter first: a routine rejection of his fourth application to have his rank reinstated to major. This he barely felt. He held the other envelope and looked at it without opening it for some time.

Bourgeat and Luneau exchanged glances; Luneau rushed to fetch three small glasses and Bourgeat his last, cherished, bottle of Cognac.

Fortified by the fiery spirit, Tom drew out his ivory paperknife and broke the seal.

# 36

# Double Vision

The whole family, apart from Evie, had experienced an anguished few days in early April when Tom had first been listed as injured and then as missing, presumed dead. Evie herself steadfastly refused to believe that Tom could have been killed and said so. She explained to Maud that now she had at last agreed to marry Tom, she could not believe that Mary would allow him to die.

A brief note from Tom had then arrived to set their minds at rest, but it held no reference at all to Evie's latest correspondence.

Evie had to wait another three days before she received Tom's next letter, brimming with disbelief and joy. It explained everything. He had only received the news of Evie's change of heart after the retreat of the 5th Army was over; her letter must have become caught up in the chaos and carnage of the Somme.

The Division was not able to spare Tom until the fortnight before the wedding, but at last the tide of war had turned and he was able to take the ferry home on leave to marry her.

Evie, feeling all the weight of her thirty-three years, outraged many of her father's parishioners by not wearing white. Instead she insisted on a nice practical and modern grey suit with a nipped-in waist. With trembling fingers, Father fastened her mother's triple string of seed pearls around her neck before they left for the church. Arthur Flint, the gardener at Caradoc Court, appeared on the doorstep after breakfast with some fragrant white blooms from the glass-houses, lilies and jasmine all tightly bound together with myrtle. It appeared that Maud and Arthur had been plotting this for some time.

Neither of Evie's sisters had chosen to take on the role of bridesmaid. Maud was busy enough running the reception and transport arrangements and keeping all the 'church ladies' in order. Etty had also declined, declaring with a naughty smile that she had no wish to outshine the bride.

Instead it was Evie's Red Cross friends Puff and Consie who looked pretty in the plain blue frocks that she had chosen so they could wear them again. They helped Evie make a rather smaller and prettier posy with some of the flowers and entwined a few sprigs of myrtle into her hair. Evie wanted no hat and no veil, using wartime frugality as her excuse for an altogether simpler wedding than Tom's first.

How she missed Mary.

Evie had hoped there would be only a modest gathering of the closest family members and friends after the service at her family's parish church of Saint Bridget's in Bridstow. Maud however firmly pointed out that with so many funerals at present in Ross, a larger and happier affair would lift the whole town's spirits. Evie felt obliged to agree, yielding to duty and the good of the parish, as ever. Father arranged for the service to take place at his old church of Saint Mary the Virgin instead.

Maud, as usual, was quite correct about the location. Evie found herself standing outside the door of the ancient church holding Arthur's arm, with a large proportion of the townsfolk who had not been able to cram into the pews inside gathered around the door. Against all the odds her youngest brother had turned into a gangling young man, taller even than Teddy. Although he used a walking-stick, he was living a happy and active life as a parish priest, engaged to his own beloved Mary. Father was to conduct the wedding and so both Teddy and Arthur had offered to give Evie away. In the end they had tossed a coin for her, and Arthur won.

How proud Mother would be to see Arthur now, thought Evie, with a pang. Oh, Mother. What am I about to do?

They walked up the aisle to the organist thumping away on the middle C that opens the famous Mendelssohn, and Evie risked a quick glance at Tom, who had turned towards her and was smiling reassuringly. She tried to make herself smile back but the corners of her mouth would not behave, so instead she focused her gaze on the altar straight ahead. Arthur patted her hand with his spare one in time to the music. The organ, she noted, was slightly out of tune. Mr Turner was still at war, just like most of the town's men.

Father, the tremor in his hands and head more noticeable than ever, launched into the familiar words of the *Book of Common Prayer*. Evie tried hard to concentrate on the Word of God but felt herself distracted by the presence of Miss Bunce, sitting in the far corner of the front pew, who was already weeping loudly and ostentatiously into a lace-trimmed pocket-handkerchief.

More unsettling still, beside her she could feel the warm strength of Tom's body. She was close enough to feel an involuntary response in him when her father thundered out, 'I require and charge you both, as ye will answer at the dreadful day of Judgement when the secrets of all hearts shall be disclosed…' She would have liked to take his hand but did not dare do so in front of everyone.

Tom could feel Evie's presence beside him. He had thought she shivered as she arrived at his side, and hoped it was just because of the slight autumn chill. There had been so much to do since he returned from the Front that they had not had a moment alone. Her family seemed omnipresent, especially Maud and Etty. This was as close as they had been to each other since that moment in the orchard at Ross-on-Wye when he had got things so badly wrong.

Lord, but her old father was a holy terror! Tom had felt that the 'just cause and impediment' line was aimed very much at himself. He raised his chin defiantly. The past was the past. Both he and Evie had the right to try to make a future together. What had he been spared for, if not for this?

As hymns were sung and readings read, Evie found her mind straying back to the morning's preparations. When she awoke, all was activity, as if she had been pushed on to a steep icy path in winter, and was slipping downhill faster and faster, grasping hopelessly at the frozen hedgerows until each side became a blur.

She was to marry Tom. Mary's Tom. Today.

Her twin supports through the ordeal of her preparations were Puff and Consie. Their gift to her did not come wrapped in paper and string: instead, both her bridesmaids had achieved the impossible and learned *Horatius* by heart. They acted out the whole thing for her, alternating verses, having borrowed hospital sheets as togas – Evie as Horatius, Puff as Herminius and Consie, Spurius Lartius. They all booed false Sextus with gusto whenever his name was mentioned. It helped keep Evie's dread at bay, and she would be forever grateful.

She snapped back into the service as Father finished his rambling homily with the words from the psalm he had chosen: 'Blessed be the Lord God my strength: who teacheth my hands to war, and my fingers to fight.' She looked across at the shoes of the soldier she was about to marry, burnished to a mirror finish with spit and polish.

As the moment came to take her vows, she still felt a churning sense of anxiety. She was marrying a man she had grown fond of, but had not yet grown to love. Would it come, as he and the rest of her siblings had assured her, as the years passed? Only time would tell. And would she ever be able to tell him that she had known of Reggie's death long before he had himself, and had not shared the terrible news?

Even as her lips moved to utter the fateful 'I will', she still felt deep disquiet about becoming the second Mrs Westmacott.

She was of course further reminded of Mary that day by the presence of her two sisters. Even Sister Ruth was permitted to escape her nunnery for the occasion. Grace and Ruth smiled angelically through the whole service and were marvellous with everyone at the reception. Old Fred and Laura Lawson, their parents, had not been well enough to travel, but Tom and Evie had been driven over to see them by Maud the day before the ceremony. Evie could see what a strain it was on Aunt Laura, but they did manage a quiet word together when Evie had wheeled her chair into the shade of a tree. Mary's mother briefly pressed Evie's hand to her heart and said that her forthcoming union with Tom would make her very happy. Even if it were not quite the truth, Evie appreciated the sentiment and had given her a kiss on the cheek.

As they left the church to Vivaldi's *Gloria*, which the organist managed rather better than she had the Mendelssohn, Evie looked down at the thin gold band on her finger with a sense of disquiet and unreality.

And, Tom thought at the same moment, she has not yet looked at me.

The food was unexpectedly good, in spite of the war. Etty sought out Evie and embraced her. 'I say,' she said cheerily, eating a small fruit tart, 'Well done on the vows! Most impressive.'

When Evie asked what on earth she meant, Etty informed her that her sister had in fact omitted the word 'obey' from the repetition of her vows. 'Father definitely raised an eyebrow. Mary would have been so very proud of you.' Then Etty bustled away in search of her friend Elizabeth Nalder who had accompanied her, leaving Evie in emotional turmoil, but soon another guest approached, then another, and she found herself able to smile and nod and chat as though nothing were wrong.

She and Tom cut the cake, his hand over hers on the knife, pressing down on the cold gold band on a finger unaccustomed to any jewellery. The cake was a simple single-tier sponge at her own request, since sugar was in such short supply. Cook had still made it look splendid with a cluster of little icing rosebuds on the top, surrounding a treble clef. She could not even swallow a bite of it; but Etty, who managed several slices, told her it was delicious.

A long table set to one side of the marquee held a lavish display of their wedding gifts. Evie felt even more dismayed by this. She had never owned much until this moment. Tom had surprised her with the little statue of the Virgin and Child that he had rescued from the mud of the Somme. 'I thought she might remind you of the church where we were married,' he had said with a smile, his eyes sparkling.

Evie now felt very awkward, as she had not thought to find a gift for Tom – no-one had mentioned it might be necessary. She saw in the statue's survival a miracle. Perhaps a sign of Mary's blessing, too, although she felt unable to tell Tom this. In fact, it was so unexpected and so lovely of him that she had been unable to speak when she had unwrapped it, let alone thank him properly.

And now his precious gift was swamped with wine glasses, cups and saucers, some hideous embroidered doilies, a trio of saucepans and a set of solid silver fish knives and forks in a blue velvet case. She did not even know if Tom liked fish. She had even overheard one guest wonder 'who had given her the little chipped statue' in such condescending tones that she wanted to wallop her. It was the best present of all.

Etty and Elizabeth had given her a clear glass dish with a matching lid in a new material called Pyrex. American, they had said proudly, oven-proof. Evie could not believe anything so glass-like would withstand the ferocious kitchen range she was accustomed to and Cook, who sniffed that she had made the wedding cake without the benefit of this 'pie-rex', agreed with her. Evie experienced another sudden moment of panic. Would there now be no cook? Would she be required to prepare Tom's meals? She still had no real idea what their living arrangements were to be.

Evie looked around for him, feeling overwhelmed by it all. Tom was chatting to Maud on the other side of the marquee, probably thanking her for her splendid organisation of the reception. He looked across at his bride and smiled again.

Was this it, wondered Evie. Was this how Mary had felt? Her heart was beating fast, true enough, but surely that was as much trepidation as sentiment? Evie had always been better at thinking than at feeling. And she had just vowed to love, honour and keep this man until one or the other of them was dead. The second and third were within her capabilities, she was certain, but the first?

Her thoughts were interrupted by a pudgy hand on her arm. 'Now, dear Miss Evelyn – or I should say Mrs Westmacott,' said bustling Miss Bunce, 'Do pray open my gift! I did not want to bring it to the vicarage, as I did so wish to see in person what you both made of it!' Evie thanked her politely and took the carefully wrapped box she held out. People began to gather round idly as Evie loosened the wrapping. She knew quite well that Miss Bunce had waited until the maximum number of people were present. She was also aware that the old lady was not well-off and hoped it was nothing too costly. She caught Tom's eye again and beckoned him over.

The paper and string fell away to reveal a cardboard box. Its lid was decorated with a picture of an odd-looking elongated mask set upon a handle. For one horrible moment Evie wondered if it were a gas-mask of some kind. Then Tom eased off the lid and gazed at the strange wooden object, exclaiming as he did so, 'Why, it's a stereoscope! That's capital. I have heard of them, of course, but never yet set eyes on one.'

Miss Bunce, pink with pleasure and self-importance, eagerly drew it from its layers of tissue paper, telling the bride and groom and everyone else within earshot that she had sent for it from Harrods in town. So much for economy, thought Evie, although she too was curious.

'And I have two sets of stereoscopic images, too, one for each of you. See, Evelyn dear, these are for you.' Miss Bunce slotted one of a small pile of dual-image cards into the contraption and held it up against Evie's eyes. 'There. The Grand Canyon of Arizona!' There were gasps of admiration and wonder from the onlookers.

It took Evie a few moments for her eyes to adjust and Miss Bunce moved the card slightly further from her nose. All at once, the fuzzy images sprang into sharpness and the effect was startlingly realistic. A man stood on the edge of a rocky promontory jutting out over the Canyon many thousands of feet below him. Evie found herself putting out a hand as though she could touch him. She even felt she could reach into the image and push him off the ledge.

'Oh, that's quite wonderful, Miss Bunce! Thank you,' she said with genuine enthusiasm. 'Tom, you must try this too, it's astonishing.' She handed him the viewer, but was intercepted by Miss Bunce, who removed the image and replaced it with one from the second set. 'I chose this collection especially for you, Captain Westmacott,' she gushed. 'So realistic. Just like being there!'

Tom removed his spectacles and adjusted the position of the viewer to suit his eyes. He gasped aloud then, took a sharp step backwards, and went terribly still. The onlookers took this as a sign of rapt attention and Miss Bunce watched him in delight. Evie was however accustomed to reading her patients' behaviour and could see something was badly wrong.

'Passchendaele!' Miss Bunce announced proudly to her audience. 'Our gallant stretcher-bearers, carrying out an invalid towards Blighty. And the next one shows our brave lads going over the top at the Somme! See?'

Evie gazed at the foolish woman in disbelief and then looked back at Tom. She could see that all colour had drained from his face. Her arm was around his waist within seconds and she took the stereoscope from him moments before he dropped it, handing it to another guest.

'Thank you so much for such a thoughtful gift, Miss Bunce,' she said through gritted teeth, 'please let someone else try it now. I am afraid I am feeling a little faint. It is rather close in here. Tom, would you mind taking me outside for a breath of air?' Supporting him, Evie made for the garden. She overheard Miss Bunce say something fond about the two lovebirds wanting time to be alone together.

Evie only just got Tom around the corner of the summerhouse before he doubled up and retched, as quietly as he could. Then he put one arm across his eyes and leaned against the shed wall, shaking, silent. Evie said nothing, just stood with a familiar warm hand between his shoulder blades until he had finished. Then she proffered a clean handkerchief. Tom wiped his eyes with it and blew his nose. 'Bless you, Evie,' he said. 'It was so real. And here, not there. I didn't... I wasn't...'

'Hush now,' said Evie. 'I know.'

Tom had thought it best to leave straight after the reception. They were to take a honeymoon of a few weeks in Wales. Tom barely knew England. Evie had only ever been to Wales on holiday, so it seemed sensible, as well as inexpensive, to return to somewhere he knew she liked. Evie's family were very nice, of course, but somewhat all-consuming. Tom wanted to be on his own with his miraculous new wife as soon as he could.

He had been very ashamed of the episode with the stereoscope at their reception but was relieved that Evie had been so kind. He had soon recovered sufficiently to go back and view the Grand Canyon pictures with her. No-one had noticed their absence except eagle-eyed Miss Fox, and Evie was able to whisper a discreet explanation in her ear.

The rather peculiar old lady who had bought them the stereoscope had probably lived on bread and butter for months to afford it, Evie had said, and so he made a point of telling the old girl what a terrific gift it was. She had looked pleased as punch and he had made Evie smile as a result. Tom had decided to try to make Evie smile as much as possible, as it completely changed her face. How could he ever have thought her plain? She was often too solemn, that was all.

They had clambered into their railway carriage a little breathlessly, almost falling inside. He was delighted to see that they alone occupied it as their train puffed and chuffed out of the station. They sat down opposite each other, catching their breath and finally alone. When Tom leaned over, as though to pull a stray rose-petal from her hair, Evie stiffened and moved backwards in her seat. So he had not, as he had at first intended, moved closer to gather her into his arms and kiss her.

Later in the journey, just when they had been talking so nicely about the wedding and the guests and he thought Evie might be unbending a little, Tom did something quite unforgivable. He called her 'Mary'.

The horror of what he had done flooded his heart and he just sat and looked at her, appalled and mute. Evie was very decent about it. She told him that she had thought this might happen. In fact, she said she was glad it had! They must both feel able to remember Mary when they were together, she said. He was not to worry about getting their names muddled up at all.

All the same, Tom vowed he would never do it again.

Later still, when the carriage began to fill up and the train became crowded and noisy, Evie held his hand very tightly until his usual fears had subsided.

Once they arrived at Llanfairfechan, where he had hired a nice little skewbald pony and trap as transport, things improved greatly. The farm cottage was delightful, set beside a rippling stream that they could hear from inside their room.

Evie seemed happy when the farmer's wife offered to cook for them, he noticed. She was not a very domesticated woman, which he did not mind a bit. Like Tom, she preferred to be out-of-doors. She, in turn, accepted he would want to spending hours in the stream fishing. When Tom again surprised her with a little fishing-rod all of her own, her delighted smile lit up his heart. Within a few days she was catching fat brown trout alongside him. The farmer's wife cooked them in butter for their breakfasts.

Otherwise Evie contentedly pottered about the riverbanks while he fished, sometimes pointing out the flash of a brilliant blue kingfisher or a patch of vibrant willow-herb or some other more unusual autumn flower she had found. One day she kicked over a molehill with the toe of her boot and found two wafer-thin flint scrapers and a little arrowhead. 'Look at these, Tom,' she said, marvelling as she held them up to the sun, 'you can see the light right through them!' She had made him a wedding gift of them there and then, which meant more to him than anything purchased at Harrods.

When he had taken her to bed on their first night together, Tom had found Evie strangely fearful. She was wearing a voluminous cotton and lace nightgown, a gift from her sisters, but her hands were cold and clammy to his touch. He could see she was frightened, although being brave and trying hard to appear willing. Tom decided he would wait for her to be ready. When he explained that all he wanted to do that first night was to hold her, nothing more, she looked overwhelmingly relieved. Exhausted from travelling and the events of the day, they fell asleep with hands entwined, like children.

On the second night, Tom had a bad nightmare, crying out and pushing away an unseen foe. Just as she had done countless times with patients at Westfield, Evie was able to soothe him back to sleep, stroking his arm and quietly murmuring poetry. Over breakfast, he found he could joke about it and called her his private nurse. All this helped them both relax a little more. And so it went on, with them feeling a little closer each night.

On the third night, he had tried again and again had felt her flinch. 'Oh Evie, my love, don't,' he said. 'I'll try so hard not to hurt you.'

'It's not that,' she replied, her voice as unsteady as her heartbeat. 'It's just that there is something I must tell you first.'

He drew back a little so he could see her face. 'What is it?'

She was so silent he could hear her breathe. Then she whispered, 'Oh Tom. I knew.'

'Knew what?' he asked gently.

She lifted her face to his. Her eyes were brimming with tears. 'Matron opened the letter from Hutch. I knew about Reggie, about how he died. We thought it best not to tell you when you were so ill. And then afterwards I just couldn't. I knew all the time and I am so, so sorry, Tom.'

He pulled her towards him by the waist and squeezed her tight. 'Do you know, I'm glad you found out so soon,' he said, meaning it. 'At least once of us did.'

When the moment finally came, later that night, it turned out all right. Evie said 'Oh!' and then 'Oh,' again and beamed at him, in a very pleased and pleasing way. Then he had kissed her hard and they had done it again and taken a good deal longer about it, too.

Their honeymoon at an end, they returned to Bridstow, then to Pershore, but they had entered a strange state of limbo and neither place felt like home any more. They needed a home of their own, and Evie decided that she would find it when Tom had left. They were both conscious of awaiting the telegram that would call Tom back to France for the final push. Evie also insisted on remaining with the Red Cross in Ross. 'If not,' she said, 'I shall sit at home imagining all kinds of horrid things are happening to you, and that won't do. I must be useful.' Miss Fox had agreed, but only so long as the new Mrs

Westmacott remained Nurse Ingram to the patients and did not wear her wedding ring at work.

Evie saw Tom off at the railway station in Ross. 'Come back to me, Tom dear, please,' she had said, as the guard cried, 'All aboard!' and the train hissed and steamed beside them, the carriage door open. She gave him a hug and an impulsive, slightly awkward kiss. 'And I want you to send me more letters!'

He packed away the 'to me' and the 'Tom dear' and the little squeeze and the kiss along with his other precious boxes of memories.

'I will,' he said, meaning both.

# 37

# Chanson de Roland:
# Clair de Lune

This time Gaston told Léonie nothing of his plan.

Instead, he alerted Louise Thuliez, Mademoiselle Gautier, the Abbé Lebrun and some of the other surviving ravitailleurs. Louise advised that if they could only get the young English soldier out of the prison, the lad's best hope was concealment locally until les Boches were pushed back from the area. Gaston did not know how long this would take, but could see increasing signs of strain among the invaders. There was now even less food and fuel was in short supply.

They all agreed the plan was risky, but as Mademoiselle Gautier pointed out, what choice did they have? Between them, they worked out the details. The prisoners were only fed once a day. They had to take action before the guard brought the midday meal, if the pitiful black bread and water they provided could be called that. All being well, that would give them several hours before the escape was discovered when the guard was changed.

Gaston had picked up the sharp lump of stone from the church floor, feeling like a caveman of old armed with such a primitive weapon. Lebrun had seen him do this and wondered at it. When Gaston confided in him, Lebrun promptly blessed the stone and gave Gaston his hooded cloak. Madame Wambères wrapped the fragment of masonry in an old petticoat with some biscuit and a note giving the young prisoner instructions on his own part in their audacious plan.

That night, after curfew, Gaston slipped out of his house on a pretext, leaving his suspicious sister at the door. It was bright moonlight, but that could not be helped. Once out of sight, he pulled on the abbé's cloak. If anyone saw Gaston, they would now presume that he was the priest, who had permission to circulate after dark if any parishioner were *in extremis*. The bundle containing the stone was pressed to Gaston's chest as though it were the Holy Sacrament itself. He had insisted that he and he alone should do the deed, which had greatly annoyed Mademoiselle Gautier.

Taking the back streets, he made his way to the narrow alley at the rear of the prison. He could just make out the open window, faintly lit. It was higher and smaller than he had remembered. He listened. Sure enough, someone up there was humming. Gaston himself was no singer, but managed to whistle a line of *Dedans la Cour du Roy*, the signal. The boy in the cell started to sing it back at him straight away. Gaston admired the lad's spirit. He himself had never had the courage to sing when imprisoned within the dismal walls of Saint Quentin.

There were faint sounds of shouting in German from the unappreciative guard somewhere within. '*Je serai fusillé, la-la-la la-la-la-la, je serai fusillé, ce mardi, à l'aube,*' the boy sang, blithely telling them of his imminent execution. Then he sang of his gratitude for the food already provided.

Gaston was relieved that the dangers facing the boy merited the risks they were about to take on his behalf. He hefted the stone in both hands a couple of times. It was heavy and his first throw missed the window by an arm's length. He tried again. The sound of the parcel thudding to the ground once more seemed impossibly loud. Surely someone would hear? Sweat was trickling down his back. A third attempt failed even more dismally than the previous two. Gaston's arm was shaking with the effort and he was beginning to despair of the plan.

Then other hands came from out of the darkness to gather up the bundle. Mademoiselle Gautier tossed the stone in one hand to gauge its weight. Then she took a short run along the alley and hurled the stone up towards the window. It disappeared inside. She smiled at Gaston, put a finger to her lips, turned, and vanished into the shadows again.

The following morning the relief guard found his comrade-in-arms spread-eagled in the corridor of the prison. The man was lying knocked senseless with a bloodied head, his keys missing.

Gaston was relieved that no-one had been killed. It might mean les Boches looked less assiduously for the escapees, for more prisoners than just young Roland had taken advantage of the situation. The young Englishman had thoughtfully used the passkeys to unlock three other cells on his way to freedom and the rendezvous point. All four men had melted away into the night: the Germans still had no idea who had freed them or, fortunately, that one of their number was English. Roland had also had the presence of mind to drag the unconscious guard into the corridor and carry away with him both the note and the stone that Mademoiselle Gautier had tossed through the window. The intelligent lad had recognised the mediaeval scrollwork on his weapon and knew it might be traced back to its source at the church.

The guard himself remembered nothing, or thought it wisest not to.

There was fresh talk in the town of *francs-tireurs*. Louise Thuliez encouraged this and had the Germans jumping at shadows. They quickly recaptured two of the prisoners not far from the building: an unlucky third, two days later at a checkpoint. As none of the three had seen who unlocked their cell, no-one could shed any light on the elusive fourth.

A party of Germans soon came to search Mademoiselle Gautier's house from top to bottom, as her act of kindness with the bread had not gone unremarked. She and Madame Wambères did a magnificent job of looking both outraged and mystified, standing with their hands on their hips as the soldiers rummaged through their empty attic and cellar.

Next, just as he anticipated, Gaston was summoned to the mairie. The dreary black and white eagles of the Reichskriegsflagge scowled down at him from the balcony as he approached. Gaston trudged upstairs to the upper room. Its uneven floorboards were scuffed, its great table unpolished.

A German officer he did not recognise, questioned him wearily while the collaborator-mayor fingered his collar and avoided Gaston's eyes in the corner.

'So, Monsieur Derome, what do you know of the escape of these prisoners?'

'Nothing whatsoever,' stated Gaston, looking him in the eye.

'And do you know the penalty this time if you are found to be involved?'

'I told you, I know nothing of this matter.'

Gaston continued to lie and lie and lie again. This time he had decided to keep the young man safe at all costs. He told them, convincingly and at length, that he had done nothing, seen nothing, heard nothing, knew nothing. In the end he exclaimed, exasperated, 'I do not know what has happened to the boy whom you seek! Where is your evidence that I have anything to do with this?'

At that the other men exchanged glances and reluctantly let him go. He went home to Léonie and the children, exhausted but content that he had done all he could for now to protect the English boy. His sister wept once more when he whispered to her what he had done and berated him for the risk he had taken. Then she hugged him and made him go to lie down, saying she would bring him some *potage*. It was always potage. There was nothing else.

Gradually, to those who could be trusted, it was revealed that there was another secret guest present in Bavay. No-one asked where he was hiding, they all knew better than that. Small offerings of food would appear at the doors of the ravitailleurs when something could be spared. The little town revelled in its secret and took heart.

Within the thick underground walls of his eerie hiding-place, Roland talked with his hosts in his strange old-fashioned French. He told them the story of his escape and recapture and a bold second escape; of his classical and musical studies in England; of his beloved regiment, the 11th Queens. He told them of his hopes and dreams, of his desire to find someone special and settle down with them, perhaps in Brighton. None of his listeners knew where Brighton was, but they nodded kindly. Beside the ocean, the boy said. He told them how he missed the sea, the sound of waves on the shingle.

Roland still had his stone and would not be parted from it, even though the sharpest corner was stained with blood. He stroked it like a talisman, even if he too was glad he had not killed the guard.

His hiding-place was cold and smelled of the grave but he endured it bravely, occasionally surfacing when the weather was overcast or the night dark to gasp in the fresh air before disappearing into the depths again.

Lebrun supplied him with books and he would read for as long as his candle lasted. When his visitors could linger a little, he would sing softly to them with his funny accent, songs in a French belonging to a different age, when a greater France had been the one to invade little England. They would sit and listen to his fine voice with their eyes half-closed, thinking of the fickle nature of history.

Non. This time the town of Bavay would not give up its Englishman.

# 38

# Liberation

The telegram from Divisional H.Q. had said that Tom was needed immediately. He would be met at Saint-Valéry and provided with transport from the port. He had supposed this would mean an uncomfortable, slow journey in an army truck or bus, something he dreaded.

It was instead with delight and astonishment that Tom walked off the ferry to be greeted with a cheery call of '*Par ici*, mon Capitaine!' There was his friend Bourgeat, holding not just Daisy, but Golden Rod too. Daisy sniffed out Tom on the air before she saw him. Her head went up and her ears flicked forward. Rod also let out a neigh of recognition when Tom came a little closer. Both received sugar-lumps; Evie had provided a small bagful for Tom's inner pocket.

The two men shook hands warmly. Bourgeat had learned that few Englishmen were at ease with the traditional French greeting of *la bise* and he had adopted English manners accordingly. 'It is good to see you all,' exclaimed Tom, patting Rod with one hand and caressing Daisy's ears with the other. 'Thank you, Bourgeat, old chap! This is a capital surprise. I rather thought I might be taking the long road alone.'

'You would only have got so far by motor transport from here,' explained Bourgeat. 'In places, the main routes are almost destroyed. Craters everywhere. We will need the horses to reach the Division swiftly. And I knew you would prefer to ride, am I not correct, *mon ami*? These two fat creatures have been stuck in the stables for too long, although I have been riding them as often as I could, if only to keep Major Lochdubh from doing so. MacKeddie has also been – how do you say it? – repelling his advances. But come now, first we need to feed you up. You have been living off dreadful English food for two months and that cannot be good for you.'

Over a plate of crisp *frites* in a little café on the port, Bourgeat told Tom how after the Indian cavalry had left for Syria, the battle of Amiens had laid waste to the remaining regiments of the Division. How he had seen men and horses blistered and suffocated by the terrible stuff they were now calling mustard gas. And how relieved he was that the Indian cavalry had at least been spared that final conflict.

'It is good that they went. There would have been no-one left otherwise,' he said sadly. 'Not one man, not one horse. They fought so bravely for France. I hope they are remembered for it. At least, this way, a few have gone on to fight in Syria.'

Tom thought of Arjan Singh, Amar Singh, Hutch and so many other friends and a lump rose in his throat. It seemed impossible that he might never see them again. And he still could not speak of Reggie Durand.

'How close do you think we are to the end of it all, Bourgeat?' he asked, swallowing hard. The Frenchman shrugged, dipped a hot, salty chip into a little pot of Dijon mustard and chewed it thoughtfully. 'I don't know,' he replied, with a shrug. 'I am no commander, mon Capitaine. I just translate when it is needed and pray for peace to come. I think perhaps weeks, perhaps a month or two.' He swallowed a mouthful of beer and smiled. 'They do say that the Golden Madonna at Albert has been shot down at last, if that is any true indication. I do not doubt that we will overcome, insofar as anyone can ever be said to have won this infernal conflict.'

Tom nodded. It had been soon after he had returned from the dead. He had been able to tell by its weight and size that this time Evie's letter would be a significant one. At first, he had not at first dared to open it. But when he did so, it was as though the last trump had sounded in his ears and he had arisen in heaven.

Tom took a long draught of his own beer, contemplating his reply at length. He flexed his hand. The little finger had set slightly crookedly but was now stiff rather than painful and he was used to the dull ache from the gas burn, which he suspected would be part of his life forever. Bourgeat saw this and for a while the two men ate chips in companionable silence. Then Bourgeat added, 'I will never forget the day you received that letter, mon ami. You turned white, your hands shook as you read it. We asked you if someone had died. Then you told us you were to be wedded. We sat you down and gave you brandy, Luneau and I, did we not? A lot of brandy.'

Tom nodded. It had been soon after he had returned from the dead. Tom had been able to tell by its weight and size that this time Evie's letter would be a significant one. At first, he had not at first dared to open this one; but when he did so, it was as though the last trump had sounded in his ears and he had arisen in heaven.

In Evie's curly script, always difficult to read, she had told him that she had reconsidered his kind proposal and had decided to accept his hand in marriage, if he would still have her.

As if he would not!

Her searingly honest letter had moved him greatly. Evie said that while she did not perhaps feel for him quite as much affection as Tom did for her, she thought she might come to love him in time, given patience and stability. She gave two conditions: no return to India, and his time with the army had to end after the war. She wanted to forget the conflict as much as possible and live in peace, not too far from her beloved sisters.

Best of all, she had signed it 'Your' – His! His! – Evie. Yes, Tom had needed the brandy with which Bourgeat and Luneau had plied him.

And now they were man and wife.

With all this spinning in his heart, he simply replied to Bourgeat that his hand had recovered well, the wedding had been most enjoyable and the new Mrs Westmacott was very well indeed, thank you. It was enough for Tom to know that Evie had become his wife. He would cherish her for as long as he lived; he was sure the rest would follow.

The French priest smiled at Tom's typically restrained British joy. He would continue to pray for this unlikely couple's future happiness each night before he slept, for as long as he lived. None deserved it more.

It was two full days before Tom could find time to write to Evie again. He and Luneau had ridden hard towards the front line and could both hear and smell the war as they approached the Belgian border. His new orders were to do all in his power to assist in the liberation of occupied communities and in particular to help displaced or trapped

French civilians.

Until recently, Tom had viewed everything he witnessed only through a soldier's eyes. Now he was starting to understand the full human cost of invasion. He tried to remember as much as he could for his letters to Evie.

On the morning of 7 November, MacKeddie saddled up Daisy. Mary's horse was now the calmer of the two under fire. Since the retreat in March, Golden Rod, like Tom, had become nervy when there were loud or sudden noises.

They rode through village after village, some smouldering and devastated, others intact but abandoned. Near one place, Wargnies-le-Grand, they were informed that civilians there had been trapped in their cellars for weeks. When they got through, people began to emerge very slowly and in disbelief, with tears in their eyes, clasping Luneau's hands to their hearts and saying in wonder '*Mon Dieu! Un vrai francais!*'

It was here that they narrowly avoided two awkward, though amusing, situations: the first, being obliged to spend the night with a group of elderly ladies in a dismal cellar (Tom used his newly-wedded state as an excuse to escape) and the second, an over-enthusiastic embrace from an unwashed mayor rumoured to be a collaborator. Luneau teased Tom mercilessly about the latter for the rest of their ride to the line and long afterwards.

Both men were touched by how these communities, many of them on the point of collapse from extreme hunger and hardship, still wanted to celebrate their arrival with what food and drink that remained. At Saint-Waast-la-Vallée they were offered coffee made from ground oats and told of two little girls who had almost cost their mother her life when they sang a made-up and uncomplimentary version of the Marseillaise to the Boche.

Many of the villagers they encountered were ill, especially the little children, and Tom suspected cholera might be stalking the cellars there.

As soon as they rode into the next town, both Tom and Luneau sensed a change. This more isolated place was somehow different from the other communities that they had just passed through, only a few thousand yards behind the line. They could hear and feel the shells bursting, smell and taste the stench of conflict in the air.

Bavay was about the size of Ross and held great strategic importance;

Tom could see from his map that six major roads converged there. There seemed to be some kind of curious Roman ruins on the outskirts. Like the other towns it seemed utterly deserted, but only at first. It had not yet been liberated but 'pinched out': which meant that the Guards Division had pushed past on the right while their own 24th Division had cut in on the left. In this way, the Germans were forced to evacuate the town without hand-to-hand fighting, though they were continuing to shell it hard as they fell back. The roof of a small brick building they had just passed disappeared with a *crump* and a cloud of dust and they watched one of the ancient Roman columns blown to pieces. They were upwind and had not heard the shells come so hastily moved onward.

Tom and Luneau were the first mounted officers to ride in; the liberators of Bavay.

In marked contrast to the other villages and towns, once the inhabitants here heard the horses' hooves clip-clopping on the cobbles, cellar hatches were flung wide and the townsfolk rushed out from their open doorways, heedless of the shelling around them.

The hubbub grew, and by teatime, Tom and Luneau had reached the Grande Place surrounded by a seething crowd of people delirious with joy. Tom had brought some chocolate for the children – that had been Evie's idea too – but it did not go very far and he wished he had packed more. Luneau was dragged off his horse beside a pillar topped by some ancient queen or other, laughing and protesting and smothered with many more kisses than was seemly for a priest. Tom was almost pulled off too but somehow managed to stick in the saddle.

The *Bavaisiens* kissed Daisy all over and she stood like a statue with her ears cocked, letting them do whatever they liked. The children kissed Tom's boots and stirrups and hands. Mothers lifted up their babies for him to kiss. They were all laughing and sobbing and shouting '*Vive la France! Vive l'Angleterre!*'.

French flags and even a ragged, defiant Union Jack were soon fished out from nooks and crannies to be hung from windows or waved over balconies. Starved of news for so long, men begged for French newspapers and any details of the war that Tom and Luneau could give them. And all the time the Boche was still trying to shell the place to oblivion, but nobody gave a damn.

Luneau gave a sudden cry of surprise and began to push his way across the throng towards the church. Another priest opened his arms to him in greeting and benediction. It turned out that the Abbé Lebrun had been in an older class at the same seminary for a time.

'*Où est le maire, monsieur?*' Tom called out to one of the happy Frenchmen. '*Parti en courant!*' shouted a young boy and the rest roared in response. A woman cuffed the lad affectionately and said, 'Mais non, mon petit Louis, it is Monsieur Derome that the English Capitaine means, not that filthy collaborator, God rot his soul.'

Monsieur Derome! Find Monsieur Derome! Up went the cry and the citizens of Bavay half-led, half-carried Tom and Luneau around the corner. They were escorted to the Rue des Juifs by the town's priest who led their horses, with the growing crowd calling out for Monsieur Derome to come forth and witness this miracle for himself.

Someone had brought word to Gaston only a few hours earlier that the replacement maire had been seen spurring his horse in the direction of the retreating German troops. Gaston had not wasted a moment and had set off in the direction of his old house, which he had not occupied since 1914, and where in recent months the collaborator had been living in his stead. As he had stepped through its door for the first time in so many years, Gaston fleetingly wondered what had happened to Horstberg, the first invader of Bavay, after their almost-encounter at Holzminden; but found he did not care overmuch.

Gaston had been assessing the damage to his garden when he heard the growing cacophony in the Rue des Juifs and crossed the courtyard to investigate. Just as he walked beneath the arched passage, which led to the great wooden street door, an almighty explosion sent him flying across the cobbles. He cracked both his knees but was soon helped up again by kindly hands.

The air was full of dust and the sulphurous sting of cordite. Gaston's eyes prickled and his ears were ringing. He looked back at the now-roofless and burning stables. Still empty, fortunately. It occurred to him that if he had not moved towards the gate at that precise moment to meet these welcome strangers, he might well have been a dead man. Thank God he had left Léonie and the children joyously packing up what the Germans had left of the other house at Place-Verte.

An English officer and a French interpreter – he recognised the insignia – were standing beside him in equal shock, doubtless equally deafened too. A jagged shard of metal about five inches long now stuck out of the half-open street door, smoking. It had somehow sliced between them without injuring any of the three.

Gaston brushed himself down and then looked curiously at the Englishman, who appeared to be having a kind of fit. *Ah, mon Dieu.* Was the fellow injured? Gaston peered at him through his spectacles with the cracked lens. Non. Could he be? It seemed impossible. All at once Gaston felt his own insides quiver, as he too caught the mad laughter of survival.

The townsfolk crowding Rue des Juifs outside the archway looked on bemused as their mayor, the English capitaine and the French interpreter clutched at their sides and gasped with mirth. The Englishman said something and the interpreter laughed again, then translated it: 'My Ca...my Capitaine says 'won't it be a shame if... if he goes and gets done in now just before the end.' With that all three of them doubled up again. The English capitaine was now laughing so hard he had removed his own spectacles (his pair were intact, Gaston noted) to wipe away tears.

Even Lebrun smiled.

A little later, Gaston Derome invited them into his house. The collaborator had left too quickly to have time for any vindictive damage. In any case, Gaston bore the man no ill will. They had all been required to do what was made necessary by circumstance.

From somewhere Gaston produced a bottle of cold white wine, a fine Chablis. He told them as they sipped it that he had been able to brick off one small, precious corner of his cellar and place a heavy oak wardrobe in front of it before the Germans had taken over his home in 1914. In fact, he admitted, he had done this as a precaution the day before the B.E.F. arrived in 1914, just in case the English were partial to fine wine. This made Luneau laugh, but Tom thought of Lochdubh and decided that Derome had perhaps acted wisely. Les Boches had of course drunk everything in his main cellar when they had first invaded, Gaston explained, but had not found his treasured bottles.

Derome refilled their glasses then sat back in his chair. He told Tom and Luneau the story of how he had saved the Englishmen hidden in the Forêt de Mormal, how the Abbé Lebrun had saved him, and of his two periods as a hostage in enemy labour camps. Tom looked with growing approval and astonishment at this small man with his cracked spectacles and neat moustache who looked so ordinary. This is surely a

French version of myself, Tom thought. Would he have been so heroic if England had been invaded by Germany? He hoped so.

Tom stood up, came to attention, saluted Derome and formally reappointed him as the Mayor of Bavay, not that there was ever much doubt of that. Derome bowed his head in assent and then shook Tom's hand in both of his. Tom and Luneau promised to return to help him set the town to rights the following day. Then they set off once more through the narrow streets, planning to ride on to the Divisional H.Q. nearby.

Not a hope. Again and again they were forced to dismount by the whooping, delighted townsfolk. They were about to ride over the crossroads when an old man ran out of a small auberge waving his arms (named '*Bellevue*', it now surveyed little more than rutted tracks and smoking ruins, but had somehow survived intact). He told them his name was Hauquier and declared, to loud cheers, that he and his good wife had hidden a bottle of champagne all through the war, as he was so certain that the town would be relieved in the end.

There was nothing for it. In they went.

Everyone who could manage it crammed in to the little salon behind Tom and Luneau. Monseur Hauquier filled their glasses and then looked expectantly at Tom. Tom in turn looked at Luneau. '*Vas-y, mon ami*,' said the interpreter, who was fending off the enthusiastic embrace of the lady of the house.

Tom found he could not say very much. He was too overcome by the expressions on their thin, eager faces. He raised his glass and said '*Mes amis, à la France, aux Alliés, à la Victoire!*'. Another great happy and defiant shout went up.

I shall never forget this to my dying day, thought Tom, as the cool champagne soothed his dusty throat. He needed to remember every moment so that he could write it all down for his wife. Oh Evie, he thought. How I wish you could have seen this with me.

Tom and Luneau rode back side-by-side in glowing silence. There was the occasional shell but the range was diminishing as the Boche ran for it. Even though the traffic had tied itself in knots and the two friends had to weave in and out of military transport and farm wagons, they felt too delighted – and too merry – to mind anything.

On the following day, the whole Division moved forward to Bavay. Tom spent most of his day at Gaston Derome's side as they worked together to set up a soup kitchen and identify refugees who had taken shelter in the town. Gaston had again recommended his disused factory on the outskirts as a suitable billet for Tom's men. He was resigned to this but found himself looking forward to the day when Engrais Derome could recommence production of fertiliser. The scarred fields of France needed to heal and grow food again.

It was clear from the state of the factory that the Germans had been using it as a barrack for some time. An unfortunate party of men from the North Staffordshires must have occupied it overnight. Tom found six of their dead, still warm, lying in a heap by the gateway. An enemy shell must have caught them just as they were marching out that morning. One poor chap had crawled into a small room by the gate to die. The corporal was wearing the 1914 ribbon and three wound stripes. He had almost made it to the end.

Tom only bothered to look at their faces at all to check whether the gentle giant Atkins, who had helped him at the Somme in March, might be among them. He was relieved to find that he was not. He detailed a sergeant to find Derome and ask him to dispose of the bodies, then stepped over them and entered the factory building, closely followed by Luneau, who paused to make the sign of the cross in benediction over the dead.

It was inside, a little later, that Derome found them taking off their boots. Tom greeted Derome warmly and then looked with interest at the pale young man at his side. Derome said something to Luneau who translated with a broad grin, 'Monsieur Derome says he has a liberation gift for you, mon Capitaine.'

The young man placed a large stone he was carrying for some reason on the table beside Tom, stood to attention and saluted. 'Lieutenant Roland Lees-Warner at your service, sir! 11th Queens Own!' The boy was not in uniform but soon explained why this was the case. Derome modestly withdrew while Lees-Warner sung his praises to the skies, telling them of his concealment in the crypt of a disused chapel in the woods nearby. The boy's surname seemed familiar to Tom and he realised he had been at Rugby School with his brother. No question as to his *bona fides*, then. At one point he tossed his head and laughed and as he did so Tom was reminded strongly of Reggie. At least some gallant young fellows had come through the war unscathed, physically at least. The boy did not talk about the sharp, stained stone he cradled and Tom decided it was best not to ask.

On 9 November, Tom's Division attacked the enemy hard at Feignies. The men drove back a line of machine-gunners defending the retreating Boche to beyond the main Mons to Maubeuge road. Tom rode up to Feignies on Golden Rod and the maire there told him with delight that the last German had abandoned the place earlier that morning. Other than the damaged railway, there were no signs of battle: again, the speed of the retreat had saved the community from further damage.

The maire said that the Boche infantry were three days march ahead of the Allies with no fight left in them but the machine-gunners and artillery were again covering the retreat. The enemy was on the run at last.

'Surely we must now be near the end?' said Luneau to Tom the next day as they reluctantly moved billets. They had traded the comfortable Derome factory in Bavay for a little place at the bottom of a dank valley called Rametz, which they all agreed was a perfectly filthy hole. There the 20th Division at last began to relieve them.

It was there, on the morning of 11 November, that Tom was shaken awake early by a young private holding yet another signal. He sat up, disorientated, and rubbed his eyes after a poor night's sleep on a damp bed. Then he put on his spectacles and read the message. Once, then twice. He had been expecting the news but still felt fuddled.

This was it. Hostilities would cease at 11am. The German Kaiser and the crown prince were in the Netherlands, the Dutch government considering its best course of action. The war was almost at an end.

He dashed off a few quick copies of the signal so that Derome and other local maires would know what was happening and sent them off via Luneau on Golden Rod.

Meanwhile Tom mounted Daisy and rode around the billets and tents to spread the word among his men. He was unsurprised by the absence of open demonstrations of joy as he felt much the same. It was hard for any of them to realise that the war was soon to be over when they had been waging it for so long.

Verey lights were shot off all morning, but that was all. Then came a deafening barrage of fire shortly before 11am. The divisional artillery was letting the enemy have it with every available gun. Tom had never heard such a row, which appeared to be more about venting spleen and using ammunition than inflicting casualties.

The noise was in great contrast to the even louder peace that followed.

Later that day, Tom and Luneau received word that Gaston Derome of Bavay would like to see them again. They knew there was still work to be done in the town and so were glad to ride back to meet their new ally.

The maire received them this time in his rightful place in the mairie. The bright upstairs room where he greeted them smelled of beeswax polish, its panelling, table and mirrors sparkling. Firstly, he handed Tom an envelope. 'It is a letter thanking you, Capitaine Westmacott, for all you have done for us,' he said. He had one for Luneau too. Tom was touched to see that the punctilious Derome had even had them both typed.

They thanked the maire very much and were about to rise when Tom noticed the expression on Derome's face. An awkwardness. Something was wrong.

Then came a knock at the door and in strode the fiery old priest, Lebrun. Luneau stood and began to converse with Lebrun in such rapid French that Tom could not keep pace. There was much gesticulating. Tom did not need to understand all the words to know that the town's priest was not a happy man.

Both he and Derome took off their spectacles and began to polish them.

When Lebrun's lengthy tirade ended, he turned to Tom and spoke to him angrily in passable English. 'Have we not suffered enough at the hands of les Boches, Capitaine Westmacott?'

'Luneau, will you please tell me what is going on?' Tom asked.

Luneau nodded. 'I will, although I am not sure we can do much to help. It seems that stories have been reaching the good Abbé, mon Capitaine. Stories of looting, I'm afraid.'

Derome looked miserably embarrassed. 'I am so sorry to bring this to your attention, Capitaine Westmacott, after you have been so kind,' he said. 'But all this is very wrong.'

Tom sighed. Of course it was wrong. But it was almost inevitable that there would be celebratory looting as the troops adjusted to the war's end. A case of beer here or a souvenir there was hard to prevent, and he said so.

'Non, Monsieur le Capitaine, forgive me please, but you misunderstand us,' said Derome. 'That as you say, well, that kind of thing is inevitable. Non. This is more than simple looting. And there are tales of... of young girls. Of a man. You understand? And as to what has been taken in terms of property, we have made a list of what we have had reported to us so far. See for yourself.'

He passed another typewritten note to Tom, who read it with growing incredulity. The lengthy list included oil paintings, clocks, various antique tables and chairs and three rolls of sanctuary blue.

Tom passed the list to Luneau to read then looked up at Gaston in bewilderment. What was this madness?

'I am also sorry, Monsieur le Maire,' he said. 'I cannot understand who would do such a thing. And what on earth is sanctuary blue?' The question was swept away without response at that point by Luneau, also outraged. 'They will have needed motor transport to carry away these things!' he exclaimed. 'Some are big, heavy!'

Tom agreed. This was no opportunistic looting of souvenirs. It was carefully calculated theft. Curtains, chairs, an *ossuary* and a cooking-pot, for heaven's sake? How could anyone tarnish the joys of the last two days of liberation with this tawdry business?

Lebrun was not done yet. 'Yes, thieves,' he spat. 'Thieves from your own liberating army. There were witnesses. I have asked questions where these things have been taken from. Not just Bavay, elsewhere. The list continues to grow, but the story remains the same. Two or three men in an English army lorry. And another thing, Capitaine Westmacott,' he continued, pushing his lined face so close that Tom could see a vein throbbing in the old man's temple. 'They said there was an English *milord* in charge of it all. A handsome English milord with the eye for a pretty face. Some of our local girls talk of him with fear in their voices. He has hurt several of them, mon Capitaine. The same Englishman every time, with a smile of ice. On a great big fierce black horse.'

Not English, thought Tom.

# 39

# Sanctuary Blue

Tom stood in front of the desk, bristling with frustration. 'Are you really telling me, Colonel Collins, that we should not cashier this man for what he has done?

Collins eyed Tom with distaste. 'I am not saying that we *should* not, Captain Westmacott. I am simply saying that we *will* not...'

'...but why not, sir?' Tom protested, interrupting him. He knew he was overstepping the mark, but was so furious that he did not care.

'You know perfectly well why not,' snapped the colonel. 'And I have to say, Westmacott, the G.O.C., the Q.M.G and I all think you have behaved with an excess of zeal over this Lochdubh business.'

'Why is that, sir? The rules on rape and looting seem entirely clear to me.'

'That may be so,' said the colonel, reaching for his glass of Châteauneuf-du-Pape. 'But you also know full well that Macbane of Lochdubh is rather a war hero. Didn't he save that little town somewhere from going up in smoke? It was all over *John Bull*. What is more, his brother-in-law is big in the War Office. And the man himself almost certainly owns half of Scotland. Think of the damage to morale if the story came to light.'

Tom placed his fingertips on the edge of the colonel's desk and looked down, gathering strength. How could what had happened at Frévent have played to Lochdubh's advantage? The wretch had the luck of the very Devil.

'I wish to protest about this, sir, in the strongest possible terms,' he said with bitterness. 'It does not seem right that Major Macbane of Lochdubh should get off Scot free where others are so severely punished for the same offences.' The colonel unexpectedly guffawed. 'Scot free! Oh, very good, Westmacott.' Then he saw Tom's pinched, sombre face and cleared his throat. 'Well, you can rest assured that I do not think that at all.'

'Sir?' Tom's confusion showed.

'Thanks to you and your precious interpreters, I now have the French authorities breathing down my neck threatening a *procès-verbale* over this affair. Oh, they won't get anywhere with the women of course. Too hard to prove, no witnesses, their word against his. I did however take your letter and the supporting evidence for the looting charge all the way up the line, you know. And so we do need to be seen to do something. The G.O.C. said that now the French are sticking their noses in, he would have to put Lochdubh under arrest if he took the matter up officially. So, Westmacott, he wants it settled, if possible, by returning the things.'

'Returning them, sir? That would take some doing.'

'Yes. But still by far the best course of action.' He leaned back in his chair. 'Look here, Westmacott. I am not a fool. I know Lochdubh often flies close to the sun. That hushed-up business at Hargicourt was a complete mess, too. So yes, you can give him a fright. It may teach him a lesson. But after the goods are returned, no more is to be said on the matter. It must all just be allowed to die down of its own accord. Is that clear?'

'Perfectly, sir,' said Tom, who was already thinking of a plan. 'Not another word.'

'Good. I will forward you the papers. Dismissed.'

~

Tom began his investigation with a visit to the divisional chaplain, Griffin, who had inadvertently triggered the whole enquiry. A few days earlier Lebrun and some other local priests had been invited to take tea with him. They had accepted only out of ecumenical *politesse*. They had been obliged to endure the strange English tea ritual and a condescending hour's lecture on spiritual matters. Typical Griffin, Tom had thought, to be meddling in the beliefs of others at an insensitive time.

It was while Griffin droned away about the pitfalls of Catholicism as compared with the Anglican Communion that Lebrun's gimlet eye had strayed to a small painting of the Virgin Mary on the man's wall. He had recognised it straight away. It belonged in the niche of an ancient village church on the outskirts of Béthune. He had loved it since boyhood. Lebrun had thought at first that the church had perhaps been destroyed, the painting rescued by this appalling man. But the more he reflected on it, the more he felt that something was wrong.

Lebrun had made relentless enquiries. It was then that the whole sorry tale of Lochdubh's systematic looting, and worse, had begun to unfold.

Tom found Griffin in his office. Sure enough, there was the painting hanging on the wall above his desk, its only bright element the little halo of the Madonna picked out in gold leaf. Griffin saw him observing it. 'Isn't she lovely,' he gushed. 'She is an invaluable aid to my devotions, Captain Westmacott. We are inseparable! I would say from the style of painting that she may be 16th century, perhaps 17th.' He added, curiously, 'I did not know you were an admirer of art, Captain?'

'I'm not, especially,' said Tom, peering at the painting. It was tiny with a broad gilt frame and dark, stained brown from many centuries of candlelight. There was still the faintest smell of incense. 'Where did you get it?'

A slight defensive edge entered Griffin's plump voice. 'Oh! Ah. It was a gift from an admirer,' he said. 'The village containing the church where it had hung had been utterly destroyed. He plucked it to safety from the ruins and gave it to me.'

'Really,' said Tom, letting the word hang there for a little while. He enjoyed seeing Griffin's complexion change from florid to ashen as he continued.

Griffin fell over himself to be helpful. 'Oh! Dear me, Captain Westmacott, surely not. I had no idea,' he responded. 'Well, let me see. I was given this work of art by… by…'

'…by an admirer, as you said,' continued Tom, who was warming to his role as inquisitor general. 'Now, which of your many admirers would that be?'

'Oh, dear me,' said the unhappy Griffin again. 'I must think. It was September, I believe? We were just outside Béthune if memory serves me correctly. A truck pulled up outside and a young lieutenant came in who had been to see me for… ah… spiritual guidance. He was accompanied by his driver, a corporal. They gave me the picture and told me its tragic story. Are you sure there is no mistake, Captain Westmacott? He is such an upright young man.'

'No mistake. I will need to know his names, please, Griffin.'

'Oh, dear me. Very well. I believe it to have been a driver corporal and a young lieutenant, both of the 24th Division. I cannot quite…'

Tom caught the chaplain's eye again and turned to look meaningfully at the hefty sergeant-at-arms he had left by the door.

'Oh! Yes, of course. Dear me. My apologies, Captain Westmacott. Now it all comes back to me.'

'Good,' said Tom. 'Who was it?'

'It was young Lieutenant Evans of the 24th. Such a very charming boy.'

That was a start at least. Tom informed Griffin that his painting was to be confiscated and ordered the sergeant to lift it down from the wall. Tom then made Griffin promise on his Bible not to alert anyone else named in the enquiry so far.

As Tom was leaving the room, he stopped and turned back. The chaplain was sitting at his desk gazing at the empty wall where the stolen painting had hung.

'Oh, Chaplain,' he said. 'I've been meaning to mention it. I believe that "dear me" is said to come from *dea mea*, which means My God in Latin? So technically you are taking the Lord's name in vain every time you say it.' He tut-tutted with false sympathy.

Griffin, now puce, was still saying 'dear me' as Tom closed the door.

Tom soon found Lieutenant Evans, who greeted him cheerily enough. Evans was a likable, good-looking and not-very-bright lad with no real harm in him. Tom decided on a less formal approach and soon the boy was telling him all about it. 'Oh yes. We've been kept very busy, Sir. Taking things into safekeeping.'

'Safekeeping?'

'Yes. We take fine things from places where they might be at risk, sir.'

'At risk?' asked Tom.

'Well yes, sir. At risk from bombardment, or from looters and so forth.'

'I see,' said Tom, scarcely believing the boy's naivety. 'From looters.'
'Yes, sir.'

'And who, precisely is 'we', Lieutenant Evans?' The boy thought for a moment. 'Well, there are the two drivers, Corporals Stevenson and Bird. If we need to move something heavy, we ask Matheson to come with us too.'

'Matheson?' Tom recalled the kindly groom who had helped him with the horses on his first crossing to Saint-Valéry and greeted him so warmly on his return from the dead at the Somme.

'Yes, sir,' said Evans. 'Major Lochdubh's servant. Another Scotsman like the major, sir. From the same place, I believe. Not very talkative but my goodness, Matheson's strong.'

'I have met Matheson before,' said Tom. 'And so where is Major Lochdubh keeping all these items he has taken into safekeeping?' Evans beamed. 'Oh, we have just moved them all into a big barn at his new billet just outside Valenciennes,' he said. 'They are quite safe and sound in there.'

It had all started in September, at Béthune. Lochdubh had again been released from his undemanding aide-de-camp duties to replace an injured town major on a temporary basis. The 'hero of Frévent' had, after all, single-handedly saved a town from destruction by fire and was therefore in great demand.

This convenient myth, which Lochdubh himself almost believed to be the truth, had come about when the story of the fire at Frévent had been picked up by the troop newspaper *John Bull*. The illustrated article appeared some months afterwards and had depicted a handsome kilted Lochdubh saving a nubile French 'Marianne' from a burning building. She had, naturally, been drawn swooning in his arms. The Frévent tale stood Lochdubh in very good stead at this stage in the war. He always kept a copy of the article at hand to show admirers, especially female ones.

Lochdubh reasoned that as he had fought so bravely in the trenches at Hargicourt, this pleasant respite was no more than he deserved. That tale, as he told it to the many young ladies of the town, involved his single-handed capture of twenty fierce Boche at gunpoint. The tragic death in his arms of the brave young lieutenant Reggie Durand after

Lochdubh had carried him to safety never failed to provoke murmurs of female sympathy. He found many Frenchwomen were keen to make his acquaintance, and even those who were not could easily enough be nudged in the right direction.

Neither showed anything of consequence, of course, mainly well-endowed singers and comedies and clowning: music-hall entertainments laid on for the benefit of the troops. Lochdubh attended one or the other of these theatres six times a week. He endured night after night of the dubious delights on stage in order to be lulled in the embrace of the warm velveteen seats. It was a buffer against the realities of war outside.

One of Lochdubh's duties as town major was to ensure that the town streets and those of the surrounding smaller settlements were kept clear of broken-down vehicles, rubble or abandoned possessions. Lochdubh had stumbled over the first opportunity at the smaller of the two theatres, the Jeu de Paume, which had caught fire. A soldier's cigarette, probably. Of the two, it was fortunately the theatre Lochdubh liked least.

As the building smouldered, some of the green velvet seats had been laid out in rows in the street outside. Lochdubh dismounted Satan who immediately tried to bite Corporal Bird as he got out of the truck. Lochdubh and Bird examined the seats. They were not too badly damaged. 'We must take these to a place of safety,' Lochdubh declared loudly, as if convincing himself of the legitimacy of his actions.

The agreeably gullible Lieutenant Evans moved quickly to do his bidding. Lochdubh instructed Evans and Bird to put all the seats into the back of the truck. The beginnings of his very own theatre! What else might he find lying around?

Over the weeks, Lochdubh's collection of scenery and props began to grow. Clocks and cauldrons, water jugs and wagon wheels, curtains and costumes, no potential theatrical accoutrement passed him by. It then took Evans, Stevenson the second driver and Bird three separate journeys to move his collection, as Lochdubh now considered it, from Béthune to ruined Valenciennes, his next posting.

Evans had done well – Lochdubh gave him a dull religious painting he did not really want himself and the boy had seemed genuinely moved.

Lochdubh's duties did not cover the town centre of Valenciennes – a Canadian Town Major was in charge there – but instead the smaller communities scattered around its periphery. Fewer onlookers. 'There were some decent girls to be had, some of them quite young. It was easy enough to persuade them to provide an intimate welcome to their handsome liberator.

One splendid little place he found nearby had a scattering of elegant houses and even some genuine Roman columns that Lochdubh coveted. What a Julius Caesar he could give with those on the stage! If only he could think of a way to remove them from Bavay.

Tom and Luneau approached Lochdubh's billet armed with a list of over one hundred and twenty separate items purloined. They saw a glimmer of candlelight from a window, tethered the horses to the fence and banged on the door with their fists.

To Tom's relief, it was Matheson who answered. He recognised Tom immediately and saluted him. 'Ye'll be looking for Himself, Captain Westmacott,' he said, laying the stress on the last syllable of his surname. 'He'll be back within the hour, I would think.'

Tom took a chance. 'Look, Matheson. We're here about some goods that have gone missing. We are pretty sure Major Macbane has something to do with it.'

Matheson eyed Tom thoughtfully. Lochdubh might be a rogue, but he was also *his* rogue, his laird, born on Meall Mòr, and his own distant kin to boot. He knew exactly what Luneau and Westmacott had come for. He had wondered at no-one noticing before what Lochdubh had been up to. But no, he would not say anything that would help these two.

Nor would he stand in the way of their own deductions.

Matheson invited them into the neat kitchen where he had been cleaning Lochdubh's uniform. Tom told him to carry on. Matheson offered them beer, which they declined, and then said, 'If you are looking at stabling for the horses, there's the big byre oot at the back. Dinnae put them too close to Satan's stall, mind!'

They tethered the horses in two of the stalls as far away as possible from Lochdubh's mad beast, which bared its teeth, pawed and snorted, unsettling both Rod and Daisy. The stable was long and narrow, running the full length of a much larger barn. 'Come on!' said Tom when they had finished with the horses. He led the way to a small door at the far end of the wall.

It opened on to an Aladdin's cave of furniture and other *objets d'art*. They walked in, incredulous.

'*Monsieur a du goût*,' murmured Luneau to Tom, as he examined a large ormolu clock. 'I think this is the one from Bavay.'

Hoofs clattered on the cobbles outside and Tom and Luneau walked out of the barn to meet Lochdubh. He turned on them and masked his surprise with irritation. 'Westmacott! What the devil are you doing here?' he demanded as he dismounted Satan, who showed his teeth at the visitors and stood with a back hoof poised. 'Shouldn't you be off somewhere kissing a collaborator?'

Tom ignored the barb. 'Good evening, Major Macbane. We have been admiring your splendid collection.'

Lochdubh by now thought of the entire contents of the barn as his own property and genuinely considered this as a compliment. He relaxed slightly. 'Marvellous, isn't it,' he said. 'I've rescued every stick of furniture personally.'

He could see it all so clearly in his mind's eye. It would be a small, intimate theatre for exclusive, private performances, set up in the ballroom of the Grosvenor Square house. Then Tom waved his hand back towards the stable. 'I'm sorry, Lochdubh,' he said, fighting the urge to smile. 'You're going to be giving it all back.' The walls of Lochdubh's imaginary theatre crumbled.

To give the man his due, it took Lochdubh only a second to work out what must have happened and settle on an appropriate course of action. He chose bluster.

'Why on earth would I do that, Westmacott? None of this belongs to anyone that we know of! It is all here merely for safekeeping, in case an owner eventually comes forward.'

Luneau advanced on him next, adopting his most priestly and blessed-peacemaker expression. He proffered a sheaf of papers, neatly typed. 'On behalf of the French people, Major Macbane of Lochdubh, I must thank you for the good care you have taken of all this private property. Here you will find lists of all the towns and villages these items were… ah… rescued from, with the original owners' names and addresses in a separate adjacent column.'

Lochdubh took the papers and looked through them in disbelief. Tom felt almost sorry for the wretch but added, firmly, 'It should only take us three days, perhaps four to return it all, I would say.'

Lochdubh glared at Tom, still thinking fast. 'Very well,' he said. 'We will set about returning whatever of this property you can prove has an owner first thing tomorrow morning. I will see you gentlemen then. Shall we say at ten o'clock?'

Tom knew that most of the contents of the barn would have vanished long before dawn if they agreed. 'We'll be billeting with you, major,' he said firmly. 'In that way, we can make an earlier start. Can't we?'

Matheson came forward from the doorway, where he had been listening. 'I have made up two spare rooms ready for ye, Captain Westmacott.' Lochdubh glowered at him.

Once the others were out of earshot, Matheson turned to Lochdubh. 'Come on now, laddie,' he said, affectionately. 'The game's up.'

In the middle of the night, while the others slept, Lochdubh rose and donned his satin dressing-gown. He tiptoed downstairs, pulled on his boots and walked over to his barnful of dreams. Part of him longed to set the whole place on fire, but he knew he could not destroy so much beauty. He walked among it all instead, quoting his favourite pieces of Shakespeare under his breath. He stroked the polished table-tops with his delicate fingertips and gently wound the ormolu clock '"Howl, howl, howl, howl," he whispered into the darkness. '"Oh, you are men made of stones."'

There had to be something he could do.

Then he remembered the horses.

# 40

# The Settling Dust

From the balcony window of the Town Hall of Bavay, Gaston observed a convoy of sleek vehicles sweep into the square below, doubtless carrying the English King, Georges V and his party. No, the *British* King, he corrected himself, remembering the gallant Scots and Irish troops he had helped in 1914.

Gaston had allowed Monsieur Hiolle, his deputy, to announce the arrival of the king in his stead and to stand proudly at his side on the steps of the Colonne Brunehaut, next to a soldier carrying the battered standard of the regiment on parade. Hiolle had also served his town well and as he loved the pomp and circumstance of any military parade he deserved the honour. Gaston would join them a little later for the service at the church. He saw his friend Capitaine Westmacott there too, astride one of his fine horses, and raised a hand in a farewell salute. The capitaine nodded back, sitting straight and proud. They had already said goodbye, as Tom was now to ride on to join his own Division in Belgium once the king had left. Gaston wondered whether he too had misgivings about his monarch's arrival.

Tom and Gaston's thoughts were in fact almost identical at this moment. The portly bearded gentleman who descended from his vehicle was the cousin of the German Kaiser who had largely caused the conflict that had taken such a heavy toll. One could not choose one's family, it was true, but surely this kind of carnage could have been avoided through closer, kinder relationships? Not for the first time, both men wondered what Europe would have been like now if the king's mother, Queen Victoria, the so-called 'Grandmother of

Europe', had still been alive. Perhaps, thought Gaston, she had not been grandmotherly enough.

Many were saying that Germany would become a republic now and punished for her aggression, but for Gaston it all came too late to make any difference. He hoped the retaliation would not be too harsh – he had learned from old Père Duriez many years before that the seeds of future conflict were often contained in previous wars.

Europe was better as one, and at peace.

The king and his entourage must have found the road from the coast slower than anticipated. Tom and the other officers and men had been waiting in the town square for over an hour. Golden Rod stood stoically, shivering in the fine drizzle that was also beginning to permeate Tom's uniform. Tom would rather have been doing something of practical help for the people of Bavay than awaiting the king, but his duty was to sit there, and sit there he did. Even his refugee repatriation desk and the soup kitchen he had erected under canvas, both of which had proved most useful, had had to be dismantled to make way for the visitation of the great man.

When King George V finally clambered from his vehicle, and the troops dutifully huzzahed him, both Gaston and Tom's simultaneous reaction could be summed up in a single phrase from scripture: 'Put not your trust in princes.'

Golden Rod, who had become increasingly chilly and anxious through inactivity, began shifting his weight from one foot to another in a sign that Tom knew all too well. His horse hooked his tail neatly to one side before letting fly, noisily plastering the shoes of the royal party behind them with the aftermath of his breakfast oats.

Ignoring the vocal consternation that ensued, Tom leaned forward a little and discreetly patted Rod on the neck.

Tom and Luneau had kept their word. They had told no-one about the return of Lochdubh's hoard of looted goods and managed to track down almost all its owners. The inhabitants tended to stare and say nothing as they observed a peculiar little party of officers unload their possessions, which they had once believed lost forever, from the back of an army lorry. They then thanked Lochdubh, Tom and Luneau and asked no questions. It was enough to have their treasures returned.

The old curé at Saint-Aubert had swiftly redecorated his miraculously-returned Madonna's niche with the starry sanctuary blue wallpaper. He even invited them all to a special mass in the ruins of his church when the painted icon was re-hung. Luneau told them later that this was for the forgiveness of sins, but this aspect passed Lochdubh by.

By the final day of the four it took to return everything, Lochdubh found he was starting to enjoy himself. He even surprised Tom and Luneau by behaving almost amiably. He now conducted himself as though the whole thing had been his own idea from the outset.

Tom never found out who it was that talked. Certainly not faithful Matheson, nor the drivers Bird and Stevenson, whom Lochdubh paid well enough to hold their tongues. Perhaps Evans blabbed the story in all innocence to someone rather brighter than he was. More probably it was the chaplain Griffin, once he realised that all personal risk of cashiering was past.

The war was over, but Lochdubh found himself stranded in the doldrums of Valenciennes. No-one would tell him why. Invitations were turned down, conversations ended abruptly, and it soon became apparent that although no-one spoke of it, *everyone* knew. His fellow British officers spread the rumours about Lochdubh's looting, the French about his behaviour towards their womenfolk. The two mingled, merged and grew in the telling.

In the end, the British Army did not need to cashier Major James Macbane of Lochdubh. It merely did not seek to retain him.

By late 1919, Lochdubh himself decided that he had had enough. He returned to his London house as a civilian and enjoyed it there, if only at first. As other officers trickled home, the story of his dubious actions spread with them. Doors that had once been wide open were now firmly closed. Even his Aunt Gertrude and her family avoided him. He went to the theatre alone and hated it. He even tried to put on a play or two, but what was drama without an adequate audience?

Then Vera wrote from Meall Mòr telling him that she wished to bring their daughter Margaret to London. The girl had reached the age where she needed a taste of city life to burnish her future marriage prospects. They planned to reside at the house in Grosvenor Square for the summer, possibly longer.

Lochdubh saw this as a sign. He wrote to his wife that he thought this a capital idea, but that he would return to Meall Mòr in her absence so that the islanders still had a presence in the Big House. At least, he reasoned, he could see old Trap Matheson, talk about the war and ride Satan again.

Lochdubh never returned to London.

After the Armistice in 1918, Tom found himself swept on by the advance of the victorious army into Belgium, this time as A.P.M. of the Second Corps. He felt torn between longing to return to Evie and exhilaration at the euphoria of liberation that hit him as he made his way through Valenciennes, its old walls pockmarked with damage from bombardments; and beyond into Belgium. To Tom's delight Luneau, his work almost at an end, announced that he wished to accompany him. 'Well, Capitaine Westmacott, will you lend me that fine horse of yours one last time?' he asked with a smile.

All the roads in Brussels, where they eventually caught up with the Corps, were festooned with flags and garlands. Tom only had to walk down the road in a British uniform to be cheered. There was too much of a press to make much use of Daisy or Golden Rod, so they remained in a stable eating their heads off while Tom and Luneau resigned themselves to using a car instead.

The streets were crammed with people, including ecstatic prisoners of war, newly released and drunk on freedom and fine Belgian beer: British, French, Italian, Portuguese and even Russians, about 1,600 of them. Tom would need to get them sent off by steamer, sooner rather than later, but for now, it was a time of celebration.

The men had exchanged their harsh uniforms for anything they could lay their hands on and were draped in all sorts of unlikely garments. Although they were having the time of their lives, Tom was pleased to see the British troops stand out from the rest and remember their manners. One lad staggered past clutching the hand of another, turned, and planted a smacking kiss on his friend's lips. The first was wearing a long, striped skirt over his trousers. The second wore a bonnet and what appeared to be rouge. When they saw Tom staring, they grinned, leapt unsteadily apart, then came to attention and saluted. Tom smiled in turn, returned the salute and waved them away.

He and Luneau met General Jacob on the steps of the Hotel-de-Ville, a beautifully carved building, only to be told that King Albert of the Belgians and his wife Queen Elisabeth were due at the palace at noon. Tom was ordered to hurry over to keep an eye on their arrival, just in case an over-enthusiastic response led to trouble. 'And enjoy yourself, Westmacott,' added the general, kindly. 'The war is over.'

Yes, thought Tom, looking around him at the crowds, so it is. All the same, peace might not come instantly, or easily.

A massive throng was already collected around the palace gates. Tom, one of very few British officers present, took a deep breath and marched through the gates, Luneau striding along at his side, half expecting to be stopped. Instead, the sentry presented arms as though Tom were a general, or at least a major. Tom smiled to himself.

Inside the palace, a wide windowsill offered them a lovely view over the heads of the crowd. Tom and Luneau climbed on to it. When a flunkey in red plush breeches and white stockings told them to get down and go away, they just smiled affably and said, 'bonjour monsieur' with strong English accents – Luneau included – and he disappeared. A fat Belgian soldier with a gun came next, to hint more forcefully that they were not wanted, but they grinned at him and off he went too.

There was a dense mob below, quite uncontrolled, but very orderly. Tom and Luneau, legs dangling from the windowsill, settled down. Below them, a group of old gentlemen in top-hats carrying an array of richly embroidered banners struggled to form themselves into a line. Luneau said they were from all the different guilds of Brussels.

Little parties of Belgian soldiers kept passing by. Tom thought their march discipline was perfectly laughable and said so, but Luneau shrugged 'Perhaps they have had enough of marching for a lifetime. I feel much the same myself.'

Then the British contingent approached, smart as paint, in perfect order. Tom felt himself ready to burst with pride. A cloud of waving handkerchiefs heralded arrival of the royal family. Up came a troop – or rather a mob – of Belgian cavalry, followed by the king and queen, both on horseback. The brave monarchs made a handsome couple. Queen Elisabeth looked absolutely topping, thought Tom, trying to memorise her smart clothing in case Evie asked him about it later: she was all in bluish-grey with a little round hat. One of the British princes was with them, young Prince Albert, looking very distinguished in a Flying Corps uniform. The Belgian King had fought for the entire war from the tiny part of Belgium not occupied by the enemy. Only the younger of the two Belgian princes seemed to be present. One of the other spectators told them that the crown prince had fought in the trenches alongside the ordinary soldiers as a humble private since he was just fourteen; doubtless he was still with his regiment. He would make a fine king one day. Their sister Marie-José rode beside her little brother and Tom was impressed that she sat her horse like a workwoman, straight as a lance.

Tom and Luneau cheered from their window until they were hoarse. 'Is it not strange,' said Luneau, 'That we should be upstairs in a palace cheering a king and queen down in the street?'

As the long procession of troops trailed past they left the monarchs to review them and joined the huge crowd outside again. Tom thought the cheering was rather more muted than an English crowd in full cry. There was none of the real euphoria of France. Perhaps feelings in Belgium were more ambivalent towards the outcome. All the same, it was homely and nice, and it showed that people were genuinely fond of their king.

'I wouldn't have missed that for a bagful of pennies,' sighed Tom to Luneau over dinner. 'You and I must have just seen the last time that a European monarch will ever ride in triumph into his capital after so long under the heel of an invader. The war to end all wars, eh?'

'I pray you are right, my friend,' said Luneau, clinking his beer glass against Tom's.

A few days later Tom and Luneau found themselves near the famous battlefield at Waterloo. They took a detour to see it. Luneau was relieved to find that the Germans had not touched the great Lion's Mound of Mont Saint Jean and stood at its foot while Tom slogged up the mound all the way to the top. The view was well worth it. The farms of Belle Alliance and Saint Jean were still intact, but he could not quite make out the fateful hollow road where the French cavalry had come to grief. He could see for miles and felt a strange sense of serenity in that place of past bloodshed, as though the wind were blowing away the most bitter layer of dust from the memories of his own war.

Beside him a soldier wearing a kilt was contentedly carving his name into the pedestal of the lion. For once Tom thought it was pardonable vandalism: someday it might be interesting to know that Private Jock MacPherson of the Black Watch had marched across the battlefield of Waterloo in December 1918, following another beaten enemy.

Luneau had found an elderly nun to talk to. They were examining the painted panorama set in a rotunda at the foot of the mound. It showed all the country that Tom had seen from above, each named village and hamlet depicted as they had existed in 1815. Few survived. The French cavalry charged the British guns and squares: the pictures were all swords and cuirasses and flags, the pomp and circumstance of war as it was once waged. The horses were magnificently rendered, with flaring nostrils and tossing manes.

The old nun asked them, 'Tell me, messieurs, is this then what the last war has been like?' Tom explained politely in his best French, 'Non, madame, not quite like that. In this war we dug holes in the mud.' Luneau looked at him, his heart full.

They could tell she did not believe a word of it.

On 13 December, Tom and Luneau rode into Cologne side by side, part of the triumphant entry of the Allied forces. It was from this great city that Tom penned his final letter to Evie as a soldier.

> December 13th 1918
> My dearest wife,
> I have seen a sight today which I shall never forget.
> Our infantry began to cross the Rhine at 9:15am, the 9th Division by the Mulheim bridge, the 29th Division by the Hohen-Zollern bridge and the Canadians by the suspension bridge. They poured across simultaneously in three dense columns, all beautifully orchestrated and quite solemn. The German police had been told to see that no wheeled German traffic was allowed in the streets, and to give them credit in difficult circumstances, they obeyed their orders to the letter. Big crowds of Germans turned out to look at us in spite of the rain. They seemed more curious than anything else. I saw one woman in tears, poor soul, but bar that it might almost have

been an English crowd.

Every ordinary civilian of every nationality is sick of war. As am I.

General Jacob, my Corps Commander, stood under a Union Jack beside a big statue of the Kaiser, at the west end of the Hohenzollern Bridge. There he took the salute of the 29th Division, one of the finest fighting divisions in the British Army, which earned undying glory in the carnage at Gallipoli. The men marched with fixed bayonets, wearing their steel helmets, and carrying their packs. I wish you could have seen them: each man making the most of himself, and full of pride and élan. Then came the guns, turned out as our gunners always turn themselves out. Our Division was fighting hard all through the last battle, and we have been marching steadily through Belgium and Germany for the last 30 days.

Oh, the horses, Evie! They were all as hard as nails, the buckles of their harness were all burnished like silver. Daisy and Golden Rod rose to the occasion, stepping out in unison, soaking it all up. Even the old mules were just as fit and went by waggling their hairy ears as if they crossed the Rhine every day of the week. I heard a German looking on say that the Division must have just come over fresh from England.

It is difficult now for us now to remember what we were like last March and April, during the retreat of the 5th Army. Now we find ourselves here as conquerors in one of the proudest cities of Germany.

Our work here is almost done. When the time comes, and it cannot now be long, my friend Luneau has said he will ride Daisy, who has been getting fat through lack of exercise, back to the port with me and leave us there. I hope he may visit us in England one day so that you can meet him as he is a fine fellow. I should be home for Christmas or failing that in the early New Year. All I long for now, dear Evie, is to turn the noses of Daisy, Golden Rod and myself for home.

With love,

Yours ever,

Tom

Evie, with a little help from Dick, his brother, had found them an inexpensive cottage in Burmington, near Shipston-on-Stour, adjacent to a farm where Tom's two beloved chargers could be stabled. One morning early in 1919, soon after Tom's return, they strolled across the sunny farmyard together to feed them. There in the corner stall, beside a bemused Golden Rod, they found Daisy looking smug. She was licking a small black foal with a crooked white blaze down its nose.

Later the same month, Tom received a crisp white envelope among the day's post. He read through its contents at the breakfast table in silence and shook his head in disbelief. Then he read it aloud to Evie.

The letter officially confirmed his promotion to the rank of 'Acting Major'.

'Oh hurrah! About time too,' exclaimed Evie, filling the silence and watching anxiously for his reaction. She poured her husband a second cup of strong black Indian tea from her mother Bessie's silver teapot. 'Nothing "Acting" about it, either.'

Tom said nothing, looking down at the sheet of paper in his hand. He took off his glasses and rubbed his eyes.

Evie added a lump of sugar from the silver box, under the benevolent eye of the Somme Madonna, who gazed down on them from the top of the corner cupboard in their kitchen.

Tom still said not a word.

Evie stirred his cup with a teaspoon that carried the Griffin and the Saracen's head. Tom looked up at the tinkling sound of silver against porcelain; his fingers brushed hers as he reached for it.

'Well, Major Tom,' said Evie, meeting her husband's slow smile with her own, 'Shall we have another boiled egg to celebrate?'

# Afterword
# Of Love, Death and Horses

At 11am on 11 November 1918, peace was declared. The First World War had ended at last.

Ninety years later, this book began its long, slow journey into print, initially as a simple transcription of Tom's war diary. My nocturnal jottings soon became a compulsion. As I began to read through his letters, photographs and documents, I found I wanted to understand not just what had happened, but how it had felt at the time.

After two years I was forced to give up through pressure of other work, but Tom and Evie kept tapping at my subconscious.

I then happened to re-read *Testament of Youth*, Vera Brittain's unsurpassed account of the impact of the First World War on her own generation. One comment she made changed everything: '*My original idea was that of a long novel, and I started to plan it. To my dismay it turned out a hopeless failure.*' My own experience was the same, but in reverse. Her admission freed me to write *Major Tom's War* as a work of fiction, albeit firmly rooted in real people, events and documents, thereby giving Evie a voice too.

Evie and Tom are of course my grandparents.

Did all the people in *Major Tom's War* exist?

Almost.

Only one or two very minor characters have had to be entirely invented. I have sometimes given others a name where they were anonymous. It has also occasionally been essential to combine several protagonists into a single character. In order to protect the innocent and the not-so-innocent, I have also changed a name here and there: these include Lochdubh, Horstberg and Griffin.

Meall Mòr is fictional, so please avoid confusing Caledonian MacBrayne by trying to book a crossing.

I have slightly adjusted timescales in places, but only a little.

So is the plot of *Major Tom's War* true?

Again, almost entirely. I have sometimes woven together real events and characters more closely than in Tom's own account. A century on, I hope both he and Evie would approve.

All my original family source documents and photographs have now been assembled into a complementary website, www.majortomswar.com, which also includes much Gaston Derome material gathered in Bavay. If you wish to burrow further into the factual details of Tom's story, read a chapter that did not quite make the final work, or plan a tour of Northern France based on the book, you will find everything you need there. You can also add your own comments or ask the family questions online.

If you prefer to leave 'what happened next?' to your imagination, you may wish to close the book now. If not…

Captain Reginald Heber Marion Durand died of his wounds at No 5 Casualty Clearing Station on 29 June 1917. Reggie's six siblings would all survive the conflict. Many families, of course, ended up making such sacrifices during the Great War.

Reggie was buried in the front row of a freshly-opened cemetery at Tincourt, his grave hurriedly dug out of what had once been a sloping field of potatoes on the hillside above the village. He was soon to be joined there by his friend and rival Dickie Cameron and many other Indian Army troops he had fought alongside. His mother, Maud Ellen Heber-Percy, Lady Durand, would contribute a brief inscription for her fifth child on his white Portland marble headstone that reads 'God's Will be Done'.

The Central India Horse fought as valiantly in Syria as they had in France. Most of the troops welcomed the move south. Syria was at least a little closer to home. They returned to India with decimated numbers and as changed men, with a less trusting and more bitter view of the world.

Harnam Singh is one of the most common names in the Indian Army 1914-1918. Many men named Harnam Singh died in France and Risaldar Harnam Singh, Tom's kind protector, is commemorated on the monument at Neuve Chapelle among almost 5,000 other courageous souls who sacrificed their lives so far from home.

Risaldar Major Amar Singh survived and was awarded the Order of British India, Second Class, with the well-merited title of *bahadur*. He was also granted an assignment of land to the value of 400 rupees.

He and all those who returned to India were soon faced with the callous betrayal of Amritsar and the agony of Partition.

~

Old Matheson the Trap remembered the moment he came to tell his laird that Satan had died until the day he did so himself. The auld beast had managed one last feeble kick when he came in with a bucket of steaming morning mash; into which Lochdubh had, as always, added a dram of his single malt from the decanter kept on the hall table.

Satan had collapsed then, with a final snort and curl of the lip, at Matheson's feet.

Lochdubh had said nothing when he heard the news, but he shambled down to the stables through the rain and mud in his stained dressing-gown and carpet slippers.

Trap told the other stable hand to make himself scarce and then left his laird to it but was himself too slow to avoid seeing Lochdubh drop beside his horse's outstretched neck. Trap was the only one to hear the long overdue howl of anguish and loss.

After that there was a dog or two, but never any more horses.

The accident with the gun a few years later came as a surprise to no-one on the island.

~

Six decades later, Matheson the Trap's granddaughter was to lead the pioneering community buy-out of Meall Mòr.

~

When Gaston Derome died at the venerable age of 86, every citizen in Bavay mourned their town's hero as they would grieve for their own grandfather. He had asked them that there should be 'no flowers, wreaths or fine speeches, just heartfelt prayers for the peaceful repose of my soul'.

As time went by, Tom found he had increasing difficulty in sleeping. It made him short-tempered and forgetful. Evie took him back to see old Doctor Eley at Ross-on-Wye, who told Tom that his lungs were still affected by mustard gas. He advised him that he would need to find work in the open air for a year or two before taking up his profession as a solicitor once more.

Evie spoke briefly with the doctor in private. He made it very plain that he thought this outdoor cure was as necessary for Tom's mind as for his body, but she wisely kept that to herself.

Tom wrote at length and repeatedly to the perfidious Pugh in India. He explained the circumstances of his abrupt departure but pointed out that he had fought for the duration. He asked for a cash settlement of his stake in Puanco and for the value of his Calcutta house. As he and Evie feared, only a tiny percentage of what Tom should have received was ever sent, accompanied by an abrupt little note from Pugh making it plain that if Tom wanted more he would need to come and get it.

Tom and Evie decided not to contest the settlement. Neither had the stomach for a passage to India, nor the lengthy legal fight with Pugh.

Tom instead surprised the rest of the family and became a ploughman on the farm next door. It secured an income, got him out into the fresh air and kept him from brooding. Tom pulled the steam-operated contraption across the field towards him and soon learned to plough a straight furrow. Many such devices were being invented to compensate for the absence of all those thousands of men who lay beneath the turf of northern France.

In 1920, Evie gave birth to their first daughter, whom they named Elizabeth Mary. Tom's disappointment was tangible, although he tried to hide it.

It was the men who needed to be replaced. And one in particular.

There were thousands of women who would be unable to find partners; so much so that Maud and Etty invariably warned the young ladies they taught not to expect to marry. Evie's clever sisters sowed the seeds of successive feminist movements by showing their students that there were other ways of fulfilling their promise, through careers in academia or service to good causes. They both lived to a ripe old age.

Evie knew how badly Tom longed for a son and in 1922, at the advanced age of 37, she tried again for him. She had another daughter, Penelope Margaret, my mother. There would be no more children.

Tom and Evie used a small legacy from her father to move their family to a new home at Lawford in Essex, where Tom was able to set up as a solicitor. He drove to and from his office in Manningtree every day in a trap pulled by Daisy's unexpected offspring. She had inherited her mother's sweet nature and they named her May.

A burned-out ruin came on the market and Tom and Evie bought it the very day they saw it. The long reconstruction of Abbot's Manor struck a deep chord within both of them. They planted a *Doyenne du Comice* pear against one wall and, at Evie's insistence, trained a stately golden rose up another. It was a variety named 'Climbing Lady Hillingdon' that had grown at Ribbesford. After a time, Tom found he could inhale 'her Ladyship's' fragrance and remember Harnam Singh and Vermelles without flinching.

There was still never any question of planting a red rose, of course.

Tom did love little Libba and Numpy, especially when they grew up enough to converse intelligently. Both girls attended the village primary school, riding each way on horseback, often sitting backwards in the saddle and doing their homework on their ponies' broad, warm rumps. Libba would later don a pink coat and ride to the hunt with Tom, who had become the local master of foxhounds. Numpy, my mother, was not so brave in the saddle but inherited her parents' courage in every other aspect of her life.

Dick Westmacott, Tom's younger brother, married his first cousin and returned to India. Their neglected children, yet another Richard and strange, beautiful Veronica, found sanctuary with either Tom and Evie or the Lawsons during their boarding-school holidays – but that is another story.

When trains and horses became less practical for a family of four, it was Evie, not Tom, who learned to drive the black Morris to convey the family on their Welsh holidays. On bad days, Tom would travel on its back seat with a blanket over his head and one of the children holding his hand.

Tom fished whenever he could, which helped, and Evie encouraged him to keep bees. Sometimes she would look out of the upstairs window and see him down at the hives in the orchard clad in his gown and veiled hat, deep in conversation. He swore that their hum changed pitch when he talked to them, as though they were replying.

One morning, just after my mother was born, Tom must have received a letter from a Major-General Watson inviting him to contribute to the official history of the Central India Horse. The opportunity would have delighted Tom but worried Evie.

I imagine that it was then he took out the wartime scrapbook album that Evie had assembled from his letters, photographs and other documents. If he noticed the two pages pasted together where she had had second thoughts about revealing his account of 'Bolting the Tabasco' at Authuille, he never did anything about it. They remained firmly gummed as one for years; I noticed the thickness of the pages and steamed them apart in 2014.

Over several weeks, during which he would barely have slept, Tom must have pieced together a careful, long and detailed account of his war years between 1914 and 1919 and sent it off to Watson, keeping a copy within his war diary.

Two years on, he would have eagerly unwrapped the long-awaited brown paper package and spent a day reading Watson's work in his study.

There is no copy of this regimental history within our family bookshelves, highly unusual as we seldom dispose of books! What happened? Did he walk into the kitchen, open the door of the blazing stove and toss it inside, never to be spoken of again? Although it is a readable enough work, there are unfathomable discrepancies within Watson's account that particularly relate to Tom and his rank. Could these be explained by 'Lochdubh' also having been invited to contribute?

We may never know the truth of it.

When the second of the great 'wars to end all wars' came, Tom was first in the queue at the recruitment office. How they sneered at the grey-haired veteran. He was too old, they said, and his eyesight and lungs would not be up to the job. Evie, as she often did, had to absorb Tom's anger and disappointment as he watched younger and less capable men marching off to war.

He became instead the commanding officer of the local Home

Guard, constantly preparing for an invasion by Germany that never came. It helped a little. Tom again stood ready to risk his life to defend his country. His mercilessly-drilled men, whom he referred to as an absolute shower, called him 'Peppery Poona'; usually with affection.

When the Second World War ended, he rushed to tell his bees first.

Evie worked as a land 'girl' when she had time, digging for victory and planting potatoes in local parks. She was asked to drive a monstrous truck on an agricultural meat pie round, providing lunches for farm workers. Although she never ran a hospital, Abbot's Manor became a refuge not just for young family members on leave but also for nursing mothers and mothers with toddlers from the East End of London. Tom found the presence of these tiny evacuees rather trying, especially when one little girl insisted on knocking on the lavatory door when he was occupied inside to ask him in piercing tones if he could 'manage'.

Evie lived an independent life for a married woman of the times and was to survive well into the age of hippies and flower power. She loved to walk, to bird-watch and to garden. She would feed me colourful 'pretty dinners' as a little girl and pressed a precious double daisy I found for her in the front of her *Book of Common Prayer* for me to find, five decades later.

Looking back over her life, she might perhaps have described herself as content rather than happy; but I believe she prized that contentment greatly.

In 1951, six years after the end of the Second World War, and a decade before my own birth, Thomas Horatio Westmacott, Major Tom, the grandfather I am too young to remember, but whom I have grown to love through writing this book, died at seventy-five years of age. Evie and the girls were at his side.

His last words were, 'See to the horses first. Then the men.'

The End

# Illustrations

*Glimpses of Tom and Evie's war diary*

Explore over 400 digitised images and documents from
the original war diary at www.majortomswar.com

Mary Lawson and Tom Westmacott's wedding day, Fladbury, October 1911.
Evie is seated second from the left in the front row. Her father, Edward, is
standing behind her, wearing a top hat.

Mary's family in Fladbury, September 1918. Standing (*from the left*) are Grace,
Sister Ruth, Tom Westmacott and Evie Winnington-Ingram. Seated (*from left*) are
Fred and Laura Lawson, and Vera Westmacott (Dick's wife and first cousin) with
little Veronica on her knee.

The Winnington-Ingram
siblings in 1892 shortly after
the death of their mother:
(*clockwise from top*) Maud,
Teddy, Arthur, Evie, Etty.

A relaxed and happy
Evie, probably in Wales,
September 1918, on
honeymoon with Tom.

v.a.d. Red Cross nurses in Ross-on-Wye, 1917: (*left to right*) Bertha Jefferson, Maud 'Puff' Currey, Evie Winnington-Ingram and Consie Allen.

Tom mounted on Golden Rod
in Saint-Valery-sur-Somme,
Christmas 1916.

Tom sketched by the
famous Valenciennes portraitist,
Lucien Jonas, June 1915.

Captain Tom Westmacott with brother officers in Thérouanne, January 1915: (*from the left*) Lt. Colonel 'Tubby' Bell, Lt. Colonel Browne (c.o.), unnamed, possibly Captain Rawdon McNabb, Major James Gourlie, Captain 'Hutch' Hutchison, Interpreter 'Nugget' Nougier, Major Goodfellow (in *loonghi*), Captain Abbott, Lt. Reggie Durand and Tom.

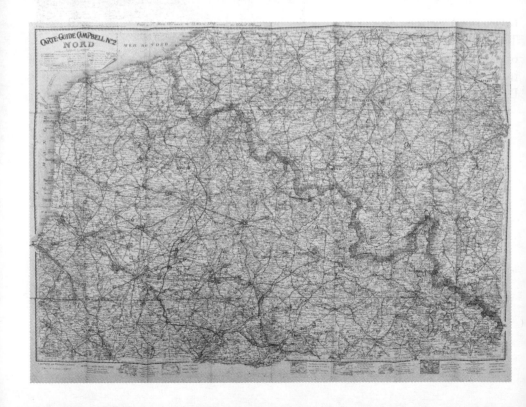

T.H.W.

Indian, French and British military police in Marieux, May 1917. Tom is seated in the second row above his initials 'T.H.W.'

(*Opposite*) A section of Tom's annotated map of his wartime travels through France, ending in Bavay, November 1918.

Tom in *loonghi* with Risaldar Major Amar Singh in Thérouanne, January 1915.

(*Opposite*) Tom and Reggie in the trenches at Authuile, September 1915, with a Sikh *sowar* using a trench periscope.

This cartoon of a Muslim cavalryman in Tom's war diary, one of several drawn by his friend Lt. Colonel Maitland, illustrates the thorny issue of tin hats and turbans. Tom noted how 'Sikhs absolutely refused to wear helmets as it was against their religion'.

The Centre Horse.

(*Opposite*) A French woman darts out to pin a rose on the tunic of an Indian Army cavalry officer on Bastille Day, 14 July 1916. Two rows behind him (with white under-turban showing) is Risaldar Major Amar Singh, a leading Sikh cavalryman on the Western Front.

Tom's groom, Dafadar Arjan Singh, mounted on Daisy in Saint-Valery-sur-Somme, Christmas 1916. He was awarded the Distinguished Conduct Medal.

Tom (*front, nearest to the camera*) at the head of B Squadron of the 38th King George's Own Central India Horse at Amettes, May 1915. The Indian officer directly behind him may be Risaldar Harnam Singh.

(*Overleaf*) One of dozens of letters within the Westmacott Family Archive, this is a rare surviving fragment of a personal letter of unknown date from Tom to Evie following her rejection of his proposal.

of happiness there. One day I found a man firing his rifle from the bottom of the trench & I did his eyes & took his rifle & emptied the magazine from the parapet. That is the sort of thing I mean. One didn't like it, but it had to be done. Reggie Dun and of course is utterly fearless & keeps walking up & down under a heavy fire. I don't, but it has to be done.

Taking them all round the men behaved very well — one must have some cowards in every Regiment — and one noticed the fact of cowardice in one or two idiots. Now I will tell you a little thing, which pleased me awfully. The Byfl have been awfully nice ever since I came back from the trenches. They have always been nice but I wonder if always felt that they looked on me as an amateur. Well they are quite different somehow now & as one of them said to me the other day "Well you are a real soldier now".

We dont expect to go into the trenches again for some time, as we hope to have other fish to fry

I dont know what happened to the wee cat, she disappeared. I heard a French Interpreter was seen carrying her, so I hope she has found a home out of the range of the guns.

I think your hospital patients are perfect swine & I wish — no I wont say that because you will not give your Card up.

My Welsh partner is a sweep & the less said about him the better

I wonder if you will go on writing to me as long as I want you to!

Cheer oh!

yours ever

To—

Tel. Ross 83.

British Red Cross Hospital,
Ross.

Gaston Derome as a young man, Bavay or Lille, circa 1886

Gaston and his motherless children in Bavay, mid-1914: (*clockwise from top*) Alphonse, Léon, Marie-Félicie and Thérèse.

Gaston (*standing on right, reading paper*) with other civilian hostages, Holzminden, circa 1916–17.

République Française

Bavay le 18 Novembre 1918

## VILLE DE BAVAY

Je soussigné, maire de Bavay, suis heureux d'exprimer, en mon nom et au nom de tous mes concitoyens ma bien vive reconnaissance à Monsieur le Capitaine Wesmacotte, A.P.M. XXIVe Division pour les services qu'il nous a rendus depuis la signature de l'armistice jusqu'à ce jour.

Non seulement il voulut surveiller et aider à l'évacuation des réfugiés valides, se tenant sur la Place publique du matin au soir; mais il organisa lui même un service spécial pour les infirmes et il installa pour les émigrés de passage une cantine qui distribua des milliers de tasses de bouillon.

Notre population lui fit un accueil très cordial quand il entra dans notre ville le jour de la délivrance; elle le voit aujourd'hui partir avec regret.

Le Maire de Bavay,

Gilerons

Gaston's formal letter of thanks to Tom, Bavay, November 1918.

Gaston post-war, Bavay, circa 1919.

(*Opposite*) Tom dressed for a post-war regimental dinner wearing his medals, including the Croix de Guerre awarded by France, circa 1919.

Tom and Evie in later life, sharing a joke with their daughter (the author's mother) Numpy, circa 1949.

The author (aged 3) takes her 84-year-old Great Aunt Maud Winnington-Ingram for a brisk walk up Cleeve Hill near Maud and Etty's home in Prestbury, 1964.

# Glossary of Terms

## IN FRANCE

| | |
|---|---|
| *l'abbé* | abbot |
| *adieu* | farewell |
| *ah, mon Dieu* | 'my God': oh, my goodness |
| *les Allemands* | the Germans |
| *allez-vous-en!* | Move! Go away! |
| *mes amis, à la France, aux* | my friends, to France, |
| *Alliés et à la victoire* | to the Allied Forces, to victory |
| *les Anglais* | the English |
| *arrêtez-vous* | stop |
| *l'aube* | dawn |
| *l'auberge* | premises offering basic accommodation, often with food |
| *la baguette* | stick-loaf bread |
| *le bar-salon* | lounge bar |
| *ma biche* | 'my doe': term of endearment for a female |
| *la bicyclette* | bicycle |
| *la bise* | traditional greeting, a kiss on both cheeks |
| *les Boches* | French pejorative term for German forces at the time |
| *chez les Boches* | where the German soldiers live |
| *le boeuf en croûte* | 'Beef Wellington': beef encased in pastry |
| *bon* | good |
| *la bonhomie* | goodwill |
| *le bon Dieu* | God in his goodness |
| *une bonne bouteille* | a fine bottle, usually of wine |
| *la bouillie* | bland, sweet or savoury porridge |
| *calmez-vous* | calm down |
| *la cantine* | the canteen or communal kitchen |
| *mon Capitaine* | my Captain |
| *ce n'est pas logique* | it doesn't make sense |
| *les champignons des bois* | wild mushrooms |
| *les Chiques de Bavay* | hard mint sweet traditional to Bavay area |
| *la châtelaine* | bundle of keys on one ring |
| *le château* | grand house or castle |

| | |
|---|---|
| *au clair de lune* | by moonlight |
| *le clocher* | bell-tower |
| *le collège* | middle school |
| *le commandant* | commander |
| *la commune* | town or village in the sense of its community |
| *le conseiller municipal* | town councillor |
| *les confitures maison* | home-made jam |
| *le coq au vin* | classic dish of chicken in a red wine sauce |
| *la cour* | court or courtyard |
| *la crèpe* | thin sweet or savoury pancake, traditional to Brittany |
| *je crois* | I believe |
| *le curé* | curate or junior priest |
| *dedans la cour du roy* | at the court of the king |
| *dis donc* | 'you say so': goodness me |
| *la Doyenne* | 'the Dowager': a grand old lady |
| *la Doyenne du Comice* | succulent variety of French pear |
| *l'école* | school |
| *enfin* | at last, for goodness' sake |
| *l'engrais* | fertiliser |
| *érotique* | erotic |
| *l'estaminet* | small café selling alcohol |
| *exacte* | quite so, precisely |
| *mon fils* | my son |
| *la forêt* | forest |
| *formidable* | great, marvellous |
| *les fraises des bois* | woodland strawberries |
| *les francs-tireurs* | partisans |
| *le frère* | brother |
| *les frîtes* | thin chips |
| *le froideur* | coolness |
| *la fugue* | interwoven melody or a frantic flight |
| *ils vont me fusiller ce mardi* | they are going to shoot me on Tuesday |
| *les gardes-chasses* | game-keepers |
| *la Gazette des Ardennes* | German propaganda newspaper for occupied France and Belgium |
| *le génerale* | general |
| *les girolles* | chanterelles, wild mushrooms |
| *les Grandes Ecoles* | elite colleges in Paris |
| *la grenouille de bénitier* | old lady, usually widowed, who frequents churches |
| *chez les habitants* | in civilian homes |
| *hé* | ho there |
| *hein* | don't you agree |
| *les Hindous* | Hindus: incorrectly used in France at this time to describe Indian troops of all religions |

| | |
|---|---|
| *l'homme* | the man |
| *des hourras* | cheers |
| *l'imbécile* | idiot, fool |
| *l'impasse* | stalemate |
| *l'innocent* | innocent man |
| *l'interprète* | interpreter |
| *le Jeu de Paume* | 'Game of Palms': royal tennis |
| *jeune* | young |
| *Joyeux Noël* | Happy Christmas |
| *Jules César* | Julius Caesar |
| *justement* | just so |
| *le lavoir* | communal pool for washing clothes |
| *le lycée* | secondary school |
| *le maire* | mayor |
| *la mairie* | town hall |
| *mais enfin* | 'but at last': for goodness' sake |
| *mais non* | but no |
| *le maître* | 'master': schoolmaster |
| *le major* | major (in a military sense) |
| *Maman* | Mum, Mummy |
| *Mamie* | Grandma |
| *la marjolaine* | marjoram |
| *le Maroilles* | pungent cheese made in the Bavay area |
| *La Marseillaise* | French national anthem |
| *le martyre* | martyr |
| *le massif* | block, extensive area |
| *merci infiniment, j'ai mangé* | thank you so much, I have eaten |
| *votre pain* | your bread |
| *la messe* | mass (in a religious sense) |
| *les messieurs* | gentlemen |
| *je meurs ici de faim* | I am dying here of hunger |
| *le Milord* | a general term for an English aristocrat |
| *monsieur* | mister, sir |
| *Monsieur a du goût* | it appears sir has refined tastes |
| *Monsieur le Major* | Major |
| *n'est-ce-pas* | don't you agree? |
| *la noblesse* | nobility |
| *un notable* | 'a person of note': under the eye of the Germans |
| *non* | no |
| *nouvelle et chère* | new and dear |
| *les objets d'art* | fine or decorative art objects |
| *oui* | yes |
| *où est le maire?* | where is the mayor? |
| *où sont-ils?* | where are they? |

| | |
|---|---|
| *du pain à l'ancienne* | traditional bread |
| *la parapluie* | umbrella |
| *par ici* | this way |
| *parti en courant* | ran off in haste |
| *la patrie* | homeland |
| *pauvre* | poor |
| *les pavés* | cobblestones, paving slabs |
| *le paysan* | peasant |
| *mes petits* | my little ones |
| *mon Père* | my Father (in a religious sense) |
| *les petits-pains* | little bread rolls |
| *petit* | small |
| *la pièce de résistance* | the party-piece or key feature |
| *la politesse* | courtesy |
| *le poney-chaise* | pony-cart |
| *le potage du jour* | soup of the day |
| *le potager* | vegetable garden |
| *le prisonnier s'appelle...* | the prisoner is called... |
| *le procès-verbal* | a writ |
| *la punaise* | bed bug |
| *une pute* | pejorative term for a prostitute |
| *les ravitailleurs* | 'the feeders': nickname Gaston Derome gives those who carry supplies to hidden Englishmen |
| *les rillettes* | thick and fibrous meat paste made of pork or duck |
| *les tuiles* | roof tiles made of clay or wood |
| *la robe de chambre* | dressing-gown |
| *Robin des bois* | Robin Hood |
| *la salle d'honneur* | reception room, often in a town hall |
| *le salon* | drawing-room |
| *sale* | dirty |
| *le savon de Marseilles* | coarse soap used for washing clothes as well as skin |
| *s'il vous plaît* | please |
| *le soldat* | soldier |
| *la soûtane* | priest's robe |
| *tant pis* | too bad |
| *la tarte au croque-poux* | gooseberry tart |
| *le testament* | will (in a legal sense) |
| *le théâtre municipal* | municipal theatre |
| *les Uhlans* | Polish, Russian, Prussian and Austrian troops much feared by Allied troops |
| *vas-y, mon ami* | on you go, my friend |
| *le vélo* | bike |
| *le vin d'honneur* | a toast |
| *vîte* | quick, quickly |

| | |
|---|---|
| *la vivandière* | a female regimental cook |
| *Vive l'Angleterre* | Long live England (often used wrongly in France at this time to mean the whole of the UK) |
| *Vive la France* | Long live France |
| *Vive les Hindous* | Long live the Indian troops |
| *les voiles* | muslin curtains |

## IN INDIA

| | |
|---|---|
| *amrit* | Sikh initiation rite |
| *Anand Sahib* | collection of Sikh hymns on happiness |
| *ayah* | nanny, nursemaid |
| *bahadur* | brave, leader, hero |
| *chai* | tea |
| *chauri* | ceremonial fly whisk used to keep the Guru Granth Sahib cool |
| *chota peg* | small whisky and soda |
| *dafadar* | sergeant in the Indian cavalry |
| *durbar* | meeting room, originally of a royal court |
| *farz* | duty |
| *granthi* | a reader of the Guru Granth Sahib |
| *gurdwara* | place where Sikhs come together for worship |
| *Guru Granth Sahib* | Sikh holy book |
| *izzat* | honour |
| *jamadar* | lieutenant |
| *Jat* | agricultural community from northern India and present-day Pakistan who are Hindus, Muslims and Sikhs |
| *Kala Pani* | 'Black Water': term used for crossing the seas to foreign lands |
| *karah kahani akath kayri kit duarai payii* | how can we speak the unspoken speech (of the One): through which door shall we find him? |
| *keema naan* | bread stuffed with meat |
| *Khalsa Panth* | 'Community of the Pure': collective of initiated Sikhs |
| *loonghi* | Indian Army uniform with turban |
| *maharani* | empress, great queen |
| *mahout* | elephant handler |
| *manji* | 'seat': an administrative unit set up by the Sikh Gurus |
| *memsahib* | formal term for an Englishwoman |
| *moksha* | release from the cycle of death and rebirth |
| *nahin maa, aap haathee ko dara rahe hain!* | no mother, you are scaring the elephant! |
| *né* | don't you agree |

| | |
|---|---|
| *nitnem* | Sikh hymns to be recited at various times throughout the day |
| *pagri* | turban |
| *phir* | again |
| *puri* | Indian deep-fried bread |
| *raga* | a musical framework that traditionally has an emotional significance and symbolic associations with seasons, times and moods |
| *rani* | queen |
| *risaldar* | Indian Army captain |
| *risaldar major* | most senior Indian Army captain |
| *sahib* | mister, sir, formal term for an Englishman in India |
| *salaam* | greeting |
| *solar topi* | lightweight but strong helmet worn in hot countries for protection |
| *sowar* | cavalryman |
| *syce* | groom |
| *Waheguru ji ka Khalsa Siri Waheguru ji ki Fateh* | Khalsa belongs to the Wondrous Teacher, Victory belongs to the Wondrous Teacher |
| *woordi-major* | adjutant |
| *Zafarnama* | 'Epistle of Victory': letter of admonishment sent by Guru Gobind Singh to the Mughal emperor, Aurangzeb, in 1705 |

## MILITARY TERMS

| | |
|---|---|
| A.D.C. | Aide-de-camp, an assistant to a senior military officer |
| A.P.M. | Assistant Provost Marshal |
| B.E.F. | British Expeditionary Force |
| C.O. | Commanding Officer |
| C.R.E. | Commander Royal Engineers |
| D.H.Q | Divisional Headquarters |
| G.H.Q. | General Headquarters |
| G.O.C. | General Officer Commanding |
| N.U.W.S.S. | National Union of Women's Suffrage Societies |
| Q.M.G. | Quartermaster General |
| R.A.M.C. | Royal Army Medical Corps |
| V.A.D. | Voluntary Aid Detachment, often women volunteers contributing to the war effort through nursing |
| V.D. | Volunteer Officer's Decoration |

# IN GERMANY

| | |
|---|---|
| *bitte sehen* | you're welcome |
| *danke schön* | thank you |
| *doktor* | doctor |
| *hände hoch* | hands up |
| *Herr* | Mister |
| *die Jagd* | the Hunt |
| *kommandant* | commander |
| *motorrad* | motorbike |
| *pumpernickel* | kind of German black bread |
| *Reichskriegsflagge* | German war flag |
| *swartzbrot* | a German black bread |

# IN SCOTLAND

| | |
|---|---|
| *awfy* | awfully, very |
| *bairn* | child |
| *bodach* | old man |
| *cailleach* | old woman |
| *clan* | extended family of the same name, connected by blood |
| *garron* | mountain pony |
| *haar* | sea-mist |
| *Himself* | oblique reference to someone familiar who is of significant status |
| *Laird* | Lord |
| *thole* | endure |
| *thrawn* | obstinate |

# IN ENGLAND

| | |
|---|---|
| *Boche* | pejorative term for German forces at the time |
| *Hun* | pejorative wartime term for German forces at the time |
| *ossuary* | box or container in which the bones of a saint may be kept |
| *toccata* | 'a fleeting touch': Baroque musical term for an intricate piece |

# LATIN

| | |
|---|---|
| *bona fides* | proof, evidence of identity |
| *cui bono* | who profits |
| *in extremis* | dying or under extreme duress |
| *ipso facto* | the same thing as |
| *mens sana in corpore sana* | a healthy mind requires a healthy body |
| *per se* | of itself |
| *sal volatile* | acrid smelling-salt |
| *troglodytes troglodytes* | wren |

# Acknowledgements

Without my grandfather Tom Westmacott's wartime letters and other ephemera being assembled into one 'diary' by my grandmother Evie Winnington-Ingram, there would be no *Major Tom's War*. In many ways I feel I have co-authored this novel with both my grandparents.

In Bavay, I have been overwhelmed by the support of François Duriez, the town's historian, who also lent me his name for a kind teacher, and the many descendants of its brave mayor Gaston Derome. I am grateful to the latter for allowing me to publish photographs from their collective family archive. The Mirapel family have always made me most welcome at the Auberge de Bellevue. The town is a second home to me now.

Research staff at the Imperial War Museum in London, the Musée de l'Armée in Paris and Herefordshire Archives have also been very kind. It was an honour to receive advice from Rana TS Chhina, head of the United Service Institution of India's Centre for Armed Forces Historical Research, who helped me with one of the most challenging issues thrown up by my research. I am particularly grateful to the team at the National Army Museum in London, especially Jasdeep Singh, for their advice and interest; not to mention the splendid book launch on 20 September 2018, the eve of what would have been Tom and Evie's 100th wedding anniversary.

Bryony Hall at the Society of Authors has been a tower of strength and the Society's support through a grant from its Francis Head Bequest was most timely.

I must particularly thank the veteran novelist and historian Elizabeth Sutherland, who has been my mentor and inspiration since childhood, and my fellow writer Eleanor Bird for her merciless red pen work and moral support. My photographer, Andrew Dowsett, has worked tirelessly on the fine images both within this book and online at www.majortomswar.com.

Steve Apted, Lilah Dowsett, John Hughes-Wilson, Jatinder Kailey and family, Mark Walker, Caroline Wickham-Jones and Maggie Wylie all received early versions of the manuscript for feedback and encouraged me onwards. Bärbel and Holger Barelmann provided German translation, legal advice and a name for a good doctor.

Military historian Andy Robertshaw made useful observations on the manuscript and is working with me to develop a Major Tom's War tour, based on some of the sites in Northern France mentioned in the book.

The team at Fortrose Library have shown an uncanny knack for sourcing hard-to-find reference material and the Women in the Arts Scotland Facebook group provided generous and detailed feedback on the evolution of the cover. The legal team at the McIlhenny Company kindly advised me on Tom's use of the name of a certain trademarked sauce in the trenches at Authuile.

In Paris, Richard and Marina Kausch have been invaluable with their advice and support of the forthcoming French edition of *Major Tom's War*.

John Winnington-Ingram, Evie's nephew, helped me with childhood memories of his Aunt Evelyn and Uncle Tom at Abbot's Manor. Tom's two other surviving grand-children, my cousin Philippa Clegg (owner of the original diary) and my sister Stephanie Whateley, have been most helpful with manuscript feedback and family reminiscences. At home my other half Philip Eley and daughters Matilda and Adelaide have put up with me reading my work aloud to them, sometimes twice daily, with admirable stoicism.

I owe a substantial debt of gratitude to the remarkable Kashi House publishing team: to commissioning editor Parmjit Singh for squeezing my book into an already hectic publishing schedule and to Harbakhsh Singh for his kindness and interest from the very beginning. I am grateful too for the editorial input of Arjan Singh Grewal, the meticulous design work by Paul Smith and original cover artwork by Keerat Kaur. Above all I must thank my endlessly-patient content editor, Dr Bikram Singh Brar, for taking my original story and helping me to burnish it until it shone.

Finally, I could not have written *Major Tom's War* without frequent use of a number of online resources, most notably: The Commonwealth War Graves Commission's Roll of Honour (www.cwgc.org); Long Long Trail, my preferred First World War website for sheer accessibility (www.longlongtrail.co.uk); The National Archives, which hold a wealth of useful information such as regimental war diaries (http://discovery.nationalarchives.gov.uk); The Peerage, which is handy for checking on family history details if your family is listed (www.thepeerage.com); Wikipedia, which is useful on individual regiments; and the late Claudine Wallart's exemplary research at the French Archives du Nord into the taking of civilian hostages from occupied France in 1916 – it was especially invaluable for the first-hand account of Doctor Eugène-Victoire Carlier's imprisonment, which I have drawn on heavily in the chapters covering Gaston Derome's experiences in Holzminden (www.persee.fr).

For a list of further recommended reading and to explore the original images, documents and letters on which *Major Tom's War* is based please see www.majortomswar.com, where you can also post your own comments and queries about the book.

# A Note about the Author

VEE WALKER is an experienced museums and heritage consultant working in the UK and Europe. The discovery of a long-forgotten family tragedy led her to spend almost a decade researching and writing *Major Tom's War*, her debut novel. It is rooted in her grandfather Tom Westmacott's account of the 1914–18 conflict as contained within his war diary scrapbook, lovingly assembled by her grandmother, Evie Winnington-Ingram.

@veewalkerwrites
www.majortomswar.com
www.facebook.com/MajorTomsWar
#MajorTomsWar

# A Note from the Publisher

KASHI HOUSE CIC is a media and publishing social enterprise focused on the rich history and culture of the Sikhs and the Punjab region in both India and Pakistan. We jumped at the opportunity to publish *Major Tom's War*.

Not only does Vee Walker's debut novel serve as a fitting commemoration to the centenary of the Armistice on 11 November 2018, it also recognises the remarkable yet largely forgotten contribution of the Indian Army – and particularly its cavalry – during the First World War. The decimated cavalry remained on the Western Front almost to the end, only departing for Syria in March 1918.

Based on Tom Westmacott's unique and unpublished eyewitness account, the book offers an authentic insight into the strangely cosmopolitan camaraderie of the trenches, set against the harrowing nature of warfare on the Western Front. Notable among the characters encountered are the Sikh cavalry officers Risaldar Major Amar Singh and Risaldar Harnam Singh, who embody military nobility and courage, their names hitherto unknown, their stories untold.

Within these pages the Great War unfolds on a very human scale. At its heart is a poignant yet gritty and pragmatic love story: Tom is not handsome, Evie is no beauty, neither is young. Damaged, intelligent people sheltering behind a tough facade.

The four differing perspective strands of this book are beautifully interwoven around the key events of the War from its opening chapters set in India, England, Scotland and France into the stirring denouement that sweeps Tom onwards.

*Major Tom's War* is a novel to laugh and cry over, to cherish and share – lest we forget. If you enjoy it as much as we think you will, we hope you will recommend it to others.

*Parmjit Singh*

Parmjit Singh
Managing Editor, Kashi House CIC

# Also by Kashi House

THE TARTAN TURBAN: IN SEARCH OF ALEXANDER GARDNER
By John Keay
*'Minutely researched, wittily written and beautifully produced, it is one of John Keay's most memorable achievements'* – William Dalrymple

1984: INDIA'S GUILTY SECRET
By Pav Singh
*'Nowhere else in the world did the year 1984 fulfil its apocalyptic portents as it did in India'* – Amitav Ghosh

IN PURSUIT OF EMPIRE: TREASURES FROM THE TOOR COLLECTION OF SIKH ART
By Davinder Toor
*The remarkable story of the Sikh Empire told through a spectacular selection of over 100 rare and beautiful objects from the world's finest collection of Sikh art*

For further details of our books, authors, prints & events visit:
kashihouse.com
facebook.com/kashihouse
twitter.com/kashihouse
instagram.com/kashihousecic

EDI | FISURE+CULTURE